Angels
of the mud

ISBN 978-1-4452-0646-2

Angels of the mud is a work of fiction.
The story's location is the author's hometown
of Portsmouth, England. Street names, shops, and some buildings
mentioned, do or at one time, did exist.
All characters excluding Barry: the author as a young boy,
are fictitious and any similarities to persons alive or deceased
are purely coincidental.

A Mud larks Prayer

Oh please let the tide be out today
Let us give our audience pleasure
If travellers throw their coins today
let the mud give up its treasure

Oh keep the sea at bay today
Let clouds be a memory
Let the warm sun be our friend today
From chill breezes keep us free

Oh let the mud be kind today
With no Jetsam to mar our feet.
Let the travellers know our hunger.
And decide, today this child will eat.

Acknowledgments.

To my wife Margaret, without
whose encouragement, this book
would not have been finished.
Also a sincere thank you to a dear friend
Gaynor Wells
for her generous help, advice and
proof reading of this book.
Words can not express how much
her efforts have been appreciated.

Prologue

The outside washroom was so very cold. Inside the WC, the sound of her own trickling water was all that interrupted the stillness of early dawn. She was just sixteen and it was only her second week in her present place of employment. Being the youngest and latest employee, her daily chore was to arrive an hour early, open shop and light the workshop stove before the arrival of the women employees. Once lit, she would normally sit by it and wait the seamstresses arrival. This morning she was reluctant to leave its warmth, but nature had called. The trickle stopped, and with numbed fingers she stood and began re-adjusting her clothing when there came the faint sound of the shop's inner bell. She became stressed, her senses alert. It was inconceivable that the bell should ring now. The rest of the employees were not due to arrive for at least another half hour. She suddenly remembered some of the women's idle talk. Could the rumours be true? She became frightened. Surely he wouldn't, not with one so young, one who had never…. Had she bolted the washroom door? She wasn't sure. She stepped quickly out of the cubicle. Her gaze went immediately to the washroom door, as feared it was unbolted. She heard footsteps outside in the yard. She moved quickly toward the door, but before she could slide the bolt across, the door opened.

He stood there smiling and she knew the rumours were true. God! He was handsome. She stepped back as he came toward her. Was this all she could do to resist? Should she not cry out, or even scream, but who would hear? Should she plead with him, threaten to tell his father? How far would he go? There was no harm in a little kiss, but the rumours, how many others had there been? Her back was now hard against the wash basin. He moved toward her and gently lifted her chin. He was searching her eyes looking for some sign of resistance, some indication that he'd misread the signs, that maybe she wasn't attracted to him. He saw no such indication, only a look of adoration, surrender and consent. With his thumb he gently parted her lips before pressing his mouth to hers. It was too late to cry out now and she was glad. She felt her arms slide around his neck as a brazen current of cold air brushed lightly against her, now, naked thighs.

Angels of the mud
By
Barry William Doughty

Part 1

Chapter 1

Nell Masters

"Nell!" Violet Masters called from the warmth of her own bed, "have you lit that fire yet?" Downstairs in the tiny dining room Violet's daughter shivered while cutting a piece of cardboard to fit the inside of her shoe.

"Not yet Mum." Nell slipped the cutting neatly in place then called out again, "I'll have to nip up to Fosters, we're out of firewood."

"I thought I told you to get a bundle yesterday," Violet replied irritably.

"Sorry Mum, I forgot."

"Well hurry up, I've got a cold coming, and I'm not getting up to a freezing cold house. There's some pennies on the mantelpiece."

Five minutes later Nell stepped off a snow-clad pavement and through the little side door of Fosters. Until a few months earlier, Fosters was a working forge with Mr Foster as the local farrier and blacksmith; its double doors, however, had not opened since he died of consumption. Nell missed being able to watch a horse being shod. One of her fondest memories was holding her father's hand while watching Mr Foster shoe a horse. She missed the smell and warmth of the furnace, seeing white-hot steel being pounded to fit a horse's hoof, but Mr Foster was gone now and so was Nell's father. Old mother Foster, as the local urchins called her, continued with her own work to maintain a living. This she did by chopping logs into kindling and selling all things combustible: logs, coal, candles, paraffin and of course, bundles of firewood. Even with snow thick on the ground, as it was that morning, Nell would run an errand to

Fosters without complaint, not that she would dare complain, such was her mother's officious and overbearing nature.

Nell was an only child, a pretty girl of sixteen. At seven and a half stone, her tall frame was understandably thin, but this only added to her gracefulness. Her shoulder length hair was the colour of chestnuts, sometimes fashioned in plaits, the plaits often pinned in loops, enhancing the elegance of her long neck.

The make-do corrugated building of Fosters retained the earthy smell of horses and coal. Nell breathed in deeply, letting the smell conjure up memories of happier days when her father was alive. In so doing, she was content to wait and watch Mrs Foster finish chopping a log before serving her. Nell looked on, fascinated by the skill with which the old lady could turn a log into kindling. She held the log, bringing down the cleaver with the self-assurance of a trapeze artiste. She'd split it in half, and then quarters, right down to the correct size needed to form a penny bundle. It was always that last chop that made Nell hold her breath. She felt sure that one day she'd hear news that the old woman had lost a finger.

"Morning Nell, just the one bundle is it lovey?" The old lady said, while stacking a fresh batch of kindling beside her little bundle-press.

"Yes please Mrs Foster," Nell said, stamping her feet and huffing little grey clouds across numbed fingers.

"Your aunt Annie came in earlier for paraffin. I let her have it on the slate this time, Nell, but I can't keep doing it. She owes more than the limit. If she asks again, Nell, I'll have to refuse. She looked very unhappy; she's worried about her Janie. Sounds like it could be serious, and the poor girl's baby is due soon."

Nell's aunt Annie and cousin, Janie, lived only two streets away from Nell's house.

"Yes I know about the baby, but I didn't know Janie was ill. I'll go see her as soon as I get a chance."

" Oh! Mum's keeping you busy then, is she?"

It always amazed Nell how quickly Mrs Foster could pick up on the most innocent remark and turn it into something gossip-worthy.

Nell just smiled, although she knew it to be true. Her mother did give her an unfair amount of chores and errands. She considered that maybe Aunt Annie had made some remark about it to the old woman, but then dismissed the thought; she liked her aunt and knew Annie was not the kind of person to malign her own sister. No Nell would let on to Mrs Foster that her mother overworked her. She could imagine her mother suddenly confronting her with: *"What's this I've been hearing! Treat you like a slave, do I".* Then would come the silent treatment for at least a week, and that to Nell was worse than a beating.

No, Nell knew better than to give old mother Foster any ammunition. It would not be the first time the old woman's gossip had caused trouble for people in Lyons Terrace.

Shuffling two handfuls of kindling into the little round press, Mrs Foster then pulled its lever in a 180°arc. Ingeniously, two semi-circles of cast iron came together clamping the wood in a tight circle allowing the old woman to nimbly secure it with hairy string.

"Where's your cousin Janie's husband, Nell? Haven't seen him around for ages,"

"No I think he had to go away somewhere, maybe to get work." Nell was being economical with the truth, she knew full well, that Janie's despicable husband had suddenly disappeared when Janie's pregnancy forced the girl to give up work.

"And what's this I hear, about you starting at Boswell's next week?" she said, handing Nell the bundle and taking her penny.

"Yes, I must say I'm a bit nervous."

"Oh you'll be okay lovey. Just don't let that Ivan Boswell get too friendly. I've heard how he likes pretty young girls. He's got a reputation, that one. Oh! And be sure to wear something warm; the skinflint doesn't spend much on heating that old place."

Nell ran the short distance home for no other reason than the snow had penetrated the large hole in her shoe, and the cardboard insert was making an embarrassing loud squelch with each step.

She dropped the string-attached key back through the letter flap of number eleven Lyons Terrace.

"Is that you Nell? Have you lit that fire yet," called Violet, though fully aware that Nell had just returned.

"Won't be long Mum, I've just got back."

Nell quickly raked the ashes from under the fire grate and shovelled them into the empty coalscuttle.

"Don't use all the wood, Nell, it only needs four or five sticks. Do you hear?"

"Yes mum."

"I'll be down in a minute. Put the kettle on when the fire's lit, will you?" Nell carried the coalscuttle out through the back door, emptied it on the growing pile of ashes in the bottom corner of the yard, she then refilled it from the outside coalbunker. By the time her mother came downstairs the fire was already glowing in the grate and Violet's mug of tea was on the table.

Entering the tiny dining room in nightdress and woollen shawl, Violet settled down at the bare wooden table with her mug of tea.

"You're a good girl Nell."

"Aren't you going to get dressed mum? I thought you had an interview at that big house in Percival Street."

"I did but I really don't feel up to it, and I don't want to start a new job and then have to take time off. There'll be other cleaning jobs."

"Yes I suppose so. Pity though! It would've saved coal with us both out to work."

"Yes, anyway, working at Boswell's will mean not having to light the fire any more in the morning."

"Do you think I'll be alright Mum? I mean with the work. They say Boswell's really fussy!"

"Of course you will, just remember what I've taught you, and watch the other women, you might pick up some new sewing methods; it's a while since I did any intricate work. Anyway, just do your best and you'll be fine. Oh! I almost forgot. Go look in the cupboard under the stairs I think you'll like what you find." Primed by her mothers grin and filled with anticipation, Nell hurried into the hallway. On opening the cupboard, she let out a squeal of delight at the sight of a shiny pair of lace up ladies boots.

"Annie brought them round yesterday," called Violet. "She said she bought them in Arundel Street, in a second-hand shop. She bought them for Janie but they were too small." Nell came back in the room and excitedly tried them on. "She kept telling me how much they cost," Violet continued. "I think she wanted me to give her what she paid for them, but she wouldn't ask, so I didn't offer."

"Oh mum! That was mean? You know how Annie's struggled since Janie's husband ran off, she even had to get paraffin on the slate this morning. How much were they? If you lend it to me, I'll take the money round to her. Look! They fit perfect."

"Oh yes! That's right, start borrowing before you've even got your first wage. I can see the kind of future you're headed for, and don't you dare call me mean. I've always been good to Annie, but she's weak; always spending more than she can afford."

"Yes I know, Mum, but never on herself, and you always said I should learn to stand on my own two feet and pay my way!"

"Well you please yourself, if you want to give Annie the money it's two shillings, but I'm not encouraging you to borrow. You can take it round to her when you get paid."

2
Boswells

"Dolly! Come on girl, it's your turn on watch." The order came from Sadie Drew. Sadie was the largest of Boswell's twenty-two women seamstresses. She was in her fifties and considered herself the protagonist among Boswell's staff and unofficial overseer. In fact, the women accepted her as such, being the longest serving and most skilled. But she was easy going and well liked among the women.

Dolly Fields, a younger and, by comparison, smaller woman, lowered the naval officer's cap she was working on and scowled irritably at Sadie and the women around her. Sadie ignored her.

"No good you making that face Dolly," Sadie said. "We all have to take our turn. Freda did it on Saturday and you're next in line. We all agreed, didn't we? Or maybe you'd rather old Bossy and his missus came in and caught us skiving?"

"Yeah, I s'pose you're right," mumbled Dolly. "But I wish he'd get that window fixed; it's enough to give one bleedin' pneumonia, sitting there."

Reluctantly, Dolly picked up her chair near the warmth of the potbelly stove and sweeping her long black skirts across the dusty floorboards, she shuffled to the window. There she sat shivering while gazing down on an awakening Queen Street and tried to ignore the flurries of snow that fluttering through the broken glass to melt against her face. Soulful cries of "Rag-bone" and the rumbling of a street vendor's handcart on cobblestones, these were the sounds that drifted up to the poor and wretched team of workers.

It was a quarter to nine on a Monday morning and so far the coldest November morning of the year.

The women in Ivan Boswell's little clothes factory had started work at 7.30am. Boswell, however, and his wife, Irene, who served in their shop below, had not yet arrived. The two of them travelled each day from their home near the village of Cosham. This they did by pony and trap for a distance of some five miles. Added to their torment on such winter mornings, much of their journey took them over rutted cart tracks. With the ground frozen hard, their journey was extremely uncomfortable. It was usually an hour, at least, after the workers had started that the Boswell's would arrive. This gave the seamstresses ample time to impart any of their previous day's gossip.

In their typical Hampshire accent, the women would call out along the workbench any tittle-tattle they wanted to impart.

"'Ere, Brenda. Did young Alfie Button come round yesterday like he said he might?"

"No, the rotten sod! I waited in all day as well."

"I reckon you're too soft and obligin' with 'im, Bren," joined in Sadie. "You ought to play a bit more 'ard to get, gal!"

"'Ere, what you saying Sadie? I hope you're not suggesting I lets 'im 'ave 'is way with me."

Sadie winked and grinned at the giggling women sitting opposite her.

"No! Course not Bren, wouldn't dream of it, lovey."

"Well I should hope not," said Brenda Scopes, pouting. "I'll have you all know that when we was in the back row of the Globe last week I slapped his hand at least twice before I let him slip it inside my bodice."

The women started to laugh. It was the kind of banter that helped them forget their cold discomfort. "Yeah, but I shall have to keep an eye on that Alfie Button," Brenda continued, "I reckon he's only after one thing."

"Just as well you've only got one then," said Sadie to another burst of laughter."

Sadie, for most of the time, kept the workforce in good spirits. Leaning forward again while weaving a needle skilfully through the fabric in her hands, she called out again,

"Hey Molly! Did the preacher teach you anything new with his sermon yesterday?" Sadie's question caused more giggling, The women knew it would be completely out of character for Molly Gill to even enter a church, let alone pay heed to the teachings of a priest.

"'Fraid not Sadie", Molly answered, "never had time for church this week." Molly winked at her sister Rose sitting next to her. Molly Gill was nineteen, a year older than her sister and strikingly pretty. The pale blue of Molly's eyes were embellished by the darkness of her lashes and eyebrows, suggesting that her hair was probably raven black like her sisters, yet few of the other women had seen her without her ever-present headscarf. Her sister, Rose, would also have been very pretty but for the dental treatment she desperately needed.

The Gill sisters lived in Portsmouth's most deprived area of Old Portsmouth, or Sallyport as some called it. It was here, their large family had acquired a bad reputation, and the name Gill had become a warning to which most locals took heed. However, the banter between Sadie and the Gill girls was a regular occurrence and a source of entertainment to the team of workers.

"Why was that then Moll? How come you couldn't make it to church?" Prompted Sadie,

"Cause I was still practicing what the preacher taught us last week."

"What was that then, gal?"

"Love thy Neighbour. Only thing is, by the time me and the neighbour had finished lovin', we was both too bloody late for church and his old lady was right peeved about it."

The women fell about laughing until Dolly fields leaped from her chair by the window gesturing frantically,

"Shhh they're here!" The laughter died and the sound of horseshoes sliding and stamping against ice-covered cobblestones. could be heard down in the street. Mr and Mrs Boswell, the owners, had arrived.

The workshop was situated over Boswell's Naval Outfitters in Portsmouth's notorious Queen Street: at that time England's busiest street outside of its capital. It was also notorious for its red light reputation and the drunken violence that frequently occurred in its numerous pubs and grog houses. Only the district of Sallyport had a worse reputation. This was not surprising with its nautical surroundings, and no surprise that Boswell's trade in naval attire was such a lucrative business. The Boswell's arrival each morning was routine and the daily sounds of their arrival told the workers of their downstairs movements. The entrance to the establishment had two doors. For the employees to reach their upstairs workshop, they would enter the street door to the right of Boswell's shop window and ascend the single flight of stairs to their right. However, for customers to enter the shop, they would enter a second door, thus ringing an overhanging bell on the inner door.

Dolly Fields quickly moved her chair back to the bench and as the women's chatter died. They heard the street door being opened. Then, above the sound of the inner door being unlocked came the usual booming voice of Ivan Boswell.

"Good morning ladies." He called up from the bottom of the staircase. With that, the bell sounded on the inner door.

"Good morning Mr Boswell. Good morning Mrs Boswell," returned the workers chorus in unison, just as it did every working morning. The women's reply suggested a happy environment, but the workers face pulling that accompanied it told a different story.

The establishment was very old and the upstairs workshop was the most dismal of places. Having just two windows, the light was most inadequate for the intricate work that the women carried out. To add to their hardship high oak rafters and draughty roof made it impossible to keep the place warm in the winter.

Most of the twenty-two women were dressed in long high-necked dresses of the day, while one or two younger unmarried girls braved the icy morning in low cut dresses though usually accompanied by a thick woollen shawl. The workers also wore white cotton-elasticised caps; this was not so much for their fashionable value, but because Boswell demanded it. He believed that the caps helped contain any lice that employees may have, and he did not want his new garments contaminated by them. For Molly Gill, however, he made an exception; allowing only her to wear a headscarf.

Twenty of the women sat on chairs: ten each side of a long workbench, while three worked on treadle machines; this particular morning, however, one chair was vacant.

At one end of the upstairs workroom was a paper strewn desk. Here, Boswell would deal with business matters and oversee his workers. Against one wall, was a long table used for cutting materials. Under this, bales of material were stored. On the opposite wall, a banister surrounded the top of the stairs: this was the exit and entrance to the workroom. To use the only toilet and washroom, the women would have to descend these stairs. They would then go through the shop and into the yard at the rear of the building. Here, a stable doubled as a toilet and washroom. It was, however, an unwritten rule that workers were not to descend the stairs if a customer could be heard in the shop below, and only then with Mr Boswell's permission.

In one corner of the workroom stood a potbelly stove, and although at present its coals glowed brightly, it struggled to keep the large room warm.

Talking among the women was not exactly a dismissible offence, but Boswell constantly preached to them that the more time spent talking meant less concentration, hence more mistakes. If his wife complained that their chatter could be heard downstairs while she was serving a customer, then they were in for a bad day at Boswell's.

Five minutes later Ivan Boswell called out again. "I'll be with you in a few minutes ladies. Any queries, have them ready."

The workers heard the outer door close again, this told them that Boswell had opened the back gate and had gone to stable Blacky, their horse. However, the women were intrigued by the sound of voices downstairs. Mrs Boswell should have been alone, unless a customer had entered the building with them. But it was rather early for customers. The women whispered their speculations about the voices until they heard footsteps ascending the stairs. Then Ivan Boswell's head appeared above the safety banister.

He was a handsome man of average height and slim build. At 48 years old, he looked immaculate and a credit to his own trade, being dressed in a light grey suit, crisply starched shirt and silk tie. His brown wavy hair was made to look darker by the oily brilliantine that he used to groom it each morning. His long greying sideburns were trimmed to perfection, each of them meeting the outer edges of his equally neat moustache.

Behind him followed Nell Masters. She stood beside him shivering and looking pale, frail, and nervous. Her black stockings were holed and wrinkled where they fitted loosely to her thin legs. Her shiny black ankle boots appeared to put the rest of her clothing to shame. Her coat, though warm looking, was badly frayed with it's inside lining hung below the hem. Her chestnut-coloured plaits hung from under a black straw bonnet. This was held in place by a totally inadequate crocheted scarf tied beneath her chin. Being obviously embarrassed by being stared at by twenty-two women and the fact that her nose almost glowed from the cold did not deter from Nell's looks. The women could see she was very pretty.

"Ladies. Your attention please," came Boswell's unnecessary announcement. He then produced a silver snuffbox from a waistcoat pocket and loudly inhaling a pinch of the brown substance into each nostril. He then nudged Nell, prompting her to recite the words with which all new employees were instructed to introduce themselves.

"Good morning everyone," she said. "My name is Nell Masters and I am very pleased to meet you." Nell's enunciation could by no means be regarded as posh or upper class, but Molly and Rose Gill compared the girl's diction to their own and held their noses aloft in a gesture of derision, spitefully slighting the young girls word-perfect recital.

Boswell ignored them and went on. "Nell is sixteen, and has come to join us. Now, it is with unfortunate circumstances that she is here. I am, of course, referring to our recent loss of Mavis Barns, but I want you to make Nell feel welcome." At this point, some of the women turned to glance at the empty chair. One woman started to weep and there followed a moment's silence. Nell was staring at the empty chair when Molly Gill's voice broke the silence.

"Yeah, another two snuffed it round our way last night Mr Boswell. Hope me and Rosy don't catch none of that dipferier [sic] business." There was a pause as Boswell inspected some hand stitching on one of the garments being worked on. He then looked at Molly as if remembering that she'd spoken,

"Oh I shouldn't trouble yourself unduly, Molly." He answered nonchalantly, while walking slowly around the workbench as he did most mornings. He spoke loudly, peering over the women's shoulders to survey their work,

"It is generally accepted among the medical profession," he said pausing behind one very buxom girl. He then leaned over her with the pretence of scrutinising her work, while furtively ogling her cleavage. The women secretly nudged each other and grinned knowingly. Boswell looked up and realised his lecherous habit had been exposed. He gave an embarrassed cough, saying, "Double row of stitching there, Brenda." Recommencing his walk, he continued, "Yes, as I was saying, on the subject of diphtheria. I shouldn't let it trouble you unduly Molly. It is said that the lower classes have a unique resistance to infection that the upper classes do not have; rather like a mongrel dog has a resistance to diseases that a pedigree does not have; that being so, I think it would be extremely unlikely that either you, Molly, or your sister Rose, could even catch a cold."

The room echoed with laughter. It took a few moments for Molly and Rose to realise that they had been insulted. Nell had understood the joke and, influenced by the women's laughter, she laughed with them. Molly, inwardly fuming from the insult, focused on Nell and in that moment Nell had unknowingly made a formidable enemy.

"So moving on, ladies" Boswell's attention was suddenly drawn to a young fair-haired girl whose laughter had turned into excessive coughing.

"Marie!"

"Yes Mr Boswell?" The girl answered, trying desperately to control her cough.

"I have explained to Nell that the youngest employee has the honour of making the midmorning tea, and that she is to arrive an hour early in the winter to light the stove. So, you will be pleased to know that you will soon be relieved of those duties. However, for a few days I want you to take Nell under your wing and help her until she is proficient in those duties. You will also pass the keys on to her and explain the door-locking procedure."

"Yes Mr Boswell." Boswell then addressed the others,

"In fact I want you all to treat Nell with kindness for she also has recently suffered a bereavement with the loss of her father. Her mother informs me that Nell is already quite proficient in the art of needlework, so with your help ladies, in a very short time, I expect her to be producing the quality work that our customers have come to expect. Now there is one…" Boswell's voice trailed off and he started to sniff the air. He moved slowly around the line of women until he stopped at Molly and Rose Gill. Still sniffing he moved closer to them. Suddenly he drew back, with a look of anger on his face he addressed Molly Gill,

"What did I tell you on Saturday, Molly?"

"I know what you said Mr Boswell." Molly's face began to turn red. "But it's not easy, not with my Uncle Tom living at home. He keeps coming in the room when me or Rose's in the tub. Mum's always having a go at him about it, but 'e don't take no notice, see, and it's too cold to bath out back."

Boswell leaned toward Rose and sniffed. "Rose appears to have found a solution to the problem," he said, staring angrily at Molly while waiting for an explanation.

"Yeah, well that's because she don't give a toss who sees her in her birthday suit." The women started to laugh again until Boswell ordered them to be quiet.

"I cannot be held responsible for your toilet arrangements at home Miss Gill. Now, not only is it unfair that my staff should have to put up with body odours; I will not have my products polluted by them. This is the last time that I am going to tell you. I will see you first thing tomorrow and if you are not bathed and smelling considerably sweeter than you do now, you will be dismissed. Now do you understand?" Molly gave an embarrassed nod.

Nell found her first day at Boswell's long and demanding. Her mother had stressed to her how important it was that she earned a wage, and that keeping the very house where they lived depended on it. Nell wondered if she would ever be able to match the output of the other women. They amazed her with their skill. She was surprised when Mr. Boswell had told the women that she had sewing experience, and wondered if her mother, whom had applied for the job on her behalf, had lied to him about this. One consolation, however, was that Boswell's factory was only ten minutes walk from her home in Lyons Terrace.

Circumstances had become so much harder for Nell after her father died. Jack Masters was a sailor in the merchant navy. He was just thirty-eight when, while aboard ship, he stumbled backwards over a mooring rope. His fall into an empty hold was fatal, and his death was almost instant from a broken neck.

The loss of her husband made Violet, very ill. Nell had just finished school and Violet kept her home for over a year. They lived on Jack's small insurance settlement while Nell did practically all the cooking and housework. Violet put more and more work onto Nell. She would make all kinds of excuses like, she couldn't cope, or that she was too ill. Nell felt sorry for her mother and did whatever was asked of her. After some months, Nell came to realize that her mother's alleged illness was just a feeble excuse for her laziness. Her mother had gotten over her husbands death but had come to depend too much on Nell's help at home. The insurance money started to dwindle, prompting Violet to send Nell out to work. She approached Ivan Boswell, her old employer, and Nell was taken on.

With Nell's wages being as meagre as they were, it needed both Nell and her mother working, for them to have any kind of living standard, but each time Violet was offered work she seemed to find a clause as to why she couldn't accept it.

3
Violet Masters

With her first day at work thankfully over, Nell reached home. She let herself in using the key hanging inside the letter flap on a string,

"Nell! Is that you?" The voice held no tenderness as one might expect from a mother welcoming her only daughter home from her first day at work.

"Yes Mum, I'll be up in a minute. I'll just put the kettle on. Are you feeling any better?"

"Yes—a little," came a mournful reply.

Since Jack Masters demise, Violet had become a sad and miserable woman. Having a mildly pious nature, she felt that God had a hand in her husband's death. She told Nell that she believed it to be God's way of punishing her, yet never divulged to Nell what she thought the punishment was for. Nell, who was not convinced that there was a God, could not understand why this dubious God in all his wisdom would take the life of a kind and loving father just to punish his wife.

Violet had spent the last week in bed on the pretext that she had a touch of flu. Nell was aware that no housework had been done that day, ashes were still in the grate.

She entered her mother's bedroom carrying a mug of tea. As Nell stooped to place the mug of tea on the bedside table, her mother shouted angrily, causing Nell to spill hot tea on her own fingers.

"Don't put hot cups on there! How many times must I tell you? It will leave rings in the varnish. Now look, you've scalded yourself. You silly girl, think before you act."

"Sorry mum. Look, I'll put this book under it," said Nell, blowing on her scalded hand.

"No! I'm reading that one. Get an old one from on the dresser."

Violet Masters, could easily be mistaken for Nell's elder sister, and not much older at that, being only eighteen when she gave birth to Nell, but illness seemed to come all too frequently to Violet. It would be a cold, a headache or some such ailment that she deemed serious enough to take to her bed, while leaving Nell to do the cooking and run errands.

It seemed strange to Nell that during these times her mother never really looked ill, but innocently remarking on the fact one day sent her mother into a terrible frenzy, hurling all kinds of abuse at her daughter; Nell had not questioned her mother's complaints since.

Violet, having propped up her pillow, said, "Well! Tell me, how did your first day go?"

"Oh I don't know mum, those women are so clever at what they do. I don't know if I will ever be good enough to…"

"Now don't start that," Violet interrupted. "They had to learn same as I did when I worked there and you'll do the same, given time."

"That's all very well mum but one woman told me that if anyone is too slow at learning, old Boswell soon gets rid of them. Mind you he seems very nice."

"Well don't let him get too friendly, I know what he's like. Just do your best. And it is **Mr** Boswell don't forget. He's your employer, if you get into the habit of calling him old Boswell, one day he'll hear you. If you get the sack, how will we live? Anyway he's only in his forties, you can hardly call that old."

"Alright mum, I'll try to remember."

"I don't suppose any of the women that I worked with are still there." Violet paused, leaving Nell wondering if it was a direct question until she continued, "I expect most of them would have got married and left by now."

"I wouldn't know mum. They know me as Nell Masters but they wouldn't have known you as Masters would they, you weren't married then?"

"No—I suppose not." Violet said thoughtfully. "Now listen, we can't afford for you to lose this job. I had to use all my powers of persuasion to get you in there. We're lucky I had the sense to keep paying your fathers insurance otherwise we'd really be in trouble. Anyway, we still have to feed ourselves. If we can't, the house will be taken from us. Then what will we do?"

"I understand mum, and don't you worry I'll really do my best."

"Just see that you do. Now there's some broth left in the pot from yesterday. Warm us a bowl each, and don't let it burn, Oh and would you empty the ashes in the grate. I think we have enough coal for a little fire tonight. Then I think you ought to go see your cousin, her baby's due any day now. Aunt Annie was here this morning. She seemed very worried about Janie."

"Why? What's wrong with her?"

"I don't know, Annie said she was coughing something awful. Could be flu or something. Anyway, I expect she'd like some company."

That evening Nell walked the short distance to her auntie's house. She knocked and was troubled when her aunt opened the door looking quite ill. She was obviously distressed and upset.

"Oh Nell! I don't know what to do. Janie can't stop coughing. I'm frightened she might lose the baby. Go upstairs love, she's in her room." Nell quickly ran up the stairs. Annie came into the room as Nell reached her cousin's bedside. At first glance, fear gripped Nell as she looked at her cousin. The girl had taken on the appearance of an old woman. Janie's face was grey, her eyes sunken. At first glance, Nell feared the girl was dead. A gas mantle glowed dimly above the bed and Nell moved closer to enable Janie see her, but Janie's stare was fixed with no sign that she recognised Nell. A wet cloth, streaked with blood and thick phlegm, lay under Janie's face while a croup kettle billowed out its camphor-smelling steam from a gas ring in the grate.

"What can I do Nell, it's getting worse?"

"How long since you sent for the doctor, auntie, and shouldn't she have a fire lit up here? It's freezing!"

"I didn't send for him Nell. I haven't got the money, and the coal ran out yesterday. I went round to borrow some money from your mother this morning, but she was in a bad mood and I couldn't ask her."

"Oh! For God's sake, aunty, she's your sister." Nell was surprised at her own anger. "Can't you see Aunty, Janie's dying! She's got to have a doctor." Nell brushed her aunt aside and hurried down the stairs and out of the house.

Forty minutes later, Annie opened the front door to a breathless Nell and a concerned doctor, but Annie's sagging shoulders, and pale and emotionless look on Annie's face said they were too late.

Nell found her new role as breadwinner really demanding. Meagre though the wages were, twelve hours a day was quite normal for the staff at Boswell's and the Gill sister's constant hostility towards Nell made her day seem even longer. Most of the time, however, Nell managed to bite her lip and ignore them. Time passed and with hardly being aware of it, the days became warmer. Spring had arrived.

One consolatory aspect of Nell's working life was the friendship that had grown with Marie. Another came as a complete surprise one morning as Nell and Marie sat discussing the recent flu outbreak, and how many of the women had been off sick. It was almost 10 a.m. and the Boswell's had not yet arrived.

"Here Nell," said Marie. "You don't reckon old Bossy's gone and caught the flu do you?"

Nell had an uncanny ability to imitate any character's speech peculiarities. She immediately put on her best imitation of Boswell's pompous voice: "Oh I would not think a person of his high social standing could catch anything so common. It would have to be a special kind of flu, one that is only caught by royalty…"

Nell's mimicking had everyone around the two girls laughing when suddenly a face suddenly appeared between Marie and Nell and a deep male voice said,

"What are you laughing at?" Startled, the two girls almost left their seats. Marie caught her breath, put her hand over her heart and yelled angrily,

"Alfie Button! If you creep up on me like that once more, I'll kick your arse down them stairs."

The young lad's laughter filled the air and before he'd spoken another sentence, Nell felt her heart go out to him. She guessed his age to be around seventeen or a little older. He wore a cloth cap that had seen better days and Nell wondered how it was possible to wear a hole in the top of it. A silky scarf was knotted around his neck just below a collarless shirt and a jacket that had been patched at the elbows. Leather gaiters enfolded the bottom of his corduroy trousers and overlapped his brown boots. Had his corn coloured hair been short, his head would almost certainly have been a mass of tight curls, but he wore it General Custer style, down to his shoulders and its sheer volume pulled it into shiny golden waves. His facial features were square and strong, and Nell noticed how the spring sunshine had already started tanning his handsome face, giving contrast to his bright blue eyes, eyes that kept laughing after the delightful sound of his laughter had ceased.

He held an open leather holdall from which could be seen the tools of a farrier. If there were anything about him for Nell not to like, it would have been the smell, for he reeked like Boswell's back yard with its horses and dung-laden straw. But no, this only seemed to enhance the strength of him and feelings stirred within her as she stared up at the boy.

"What we got 'ere then," he said in a strong Hampshire accent and his eyes met Nell's. "Old Ivan taking on show girls now, is he?" Nell coloured up and all but buried her head in the Naval Officer's jacket she was sewing.

"Aw get on with you Alfie," said Sadie Drew. "Bout time you dreamed up a new line, and stop making our little Nell blush."

"Yeah," called Molly from the end of the table, "I remember you saying the same thing to me Alfie Button. Trouble with you is, you're just full of what you smell of: horse shit."

This caused as much laughter from Alfie as it did from the women, until Sadie told them to keep the noise down.

"What you doing up here, anyway?" asked Sadie. "You know your uncle Ivan don't like you up here, smelling the place up, and chatting up his workers."

"Oh don't worry I've just seen him in the tobacconist buying his snuff. He knows I'm here. I just came to sort out Blacky. Uncle said he threw a shoe 'smorning on his way here. The missus don't like me going through the shop though, so I thought I'd come up and get Brenda to open the back gate for me. Where is she?"

It was common knowledge that Brenda Scopes considered herself Alfie's girlfriend.

"Brenda's out sick, got that flu that's going about," said Marie.

"Oh – Well maybe one of you lovelies would come down and open the back gate for me."

"I will!" Said Nell, then blushing again as she realized how eager she had sounded."

"Ohoo" came a mocking chorus followed by laughter.

Sadie, seeing Nell's embarrassment, said,

"Go on then love it's time for a break anyway. But don't let young Casanova here take advantage of you." Alfie was still laughing as he started down the stairs. Nell made to follow, but as she did, Sadie grabbed her arm. Pulling Nell to her, she whispered in her ear, "Watch out for Brenda Scopes Nell; she's sweet on Alfie, and she's got a nasty temper."

In the privacy of the back yard, Nell needed an excuse to make conversation, and as Alfie led Blacky out of his stable, she said,

"So you're Mr. Boswell's nephew?"

"In a way, I was an orphan, and it was uncle Ivan's sister and her husband that adopted me when I was a baby so they were like my mum and dad. But Dad's gone now and Mums getting on a bit. Uncle Ivan and his wife, I call them uncle and aunt, have kind of looked after me and always been good to me. I think they would have liked kids of their own. Ivan's always told me that if anything happens to mum, I could live with them." He held out Blacky's rein. "Here, come and hold his rein for me and stroke his nose, he likes that."

Nell obliged without fear while Alfie placed his bag in a convenient place and arranged his tools. There was an awkward silence and Nell decided to change the subject.

"How did you manage to wear a hole in the top of your cap?"

Alfie laughed. "That's easy. If you watch you'll find out."

Watching Alfie work proved no hardship for Nell, she loved watching him. She would have watched him if he just sat and did nothing, but she watched him now as his muscular arms lifted Blackie's front leg between his own, and with fearless ease started pulling nails from the beast's hoof. As he worked they chatted, and slowly without realizing it, Nell's heart was won by this strong and handsome young man.

As Alfie worked, Blackie suddenly turned his head and started to nibble his cap.

"Now you know," said Alfie to the sound of Nell's laughter.

Nell never found Alfie to be the slick-talking rogue that the workers made him out to be. On the contrary, she found him to be quite shy, yet in the time it took Alfie to shoe Boswell's horse he had asked her to meet him at a Victoria Park the following Sunday.

"But what about Brenda?" Nell asked when faced with a decision.

"Brenda Scopes?"

"Yes, isn't she your girlfriend?"

"We've been out a couple of times that's all, last I heard, it don't mean a fella's engaged."

"I know, but I have to work with her and I don't want to…."

"Well I won't tell her if you don't, so what about it?

"Well I don't know. I don't want to upset…."

"Sunday then?"

"Yes—I suppose so—Okay."

Nell's first ever date with any boy was a walk in the park with Alfie Button, but it was enough to produce something more than just friendship between them. It was unfortunate that one of Boswell's employees happened to pass by the young couple just as Nell was gazing lovingly into Alfie's eyes. On the Monday, the woman was quick to tell the woman next to her and the gossip soon reached Molly Gill. A week later Brenda Scopes returned to work where Molly was eagerly waiting to give her the news. Brenda said nothing to Nell and Nell was unaware of the hateful looks that Brenda directed at her, all that day.

It was late Monday evening that Nell left work. She'd been working on an officer's dress shirt and Boswell had asked her to stay and finish it, as it had been promised for collection early Tuesday morning. When she eventually left the works most of Queen Street's shops were closed, and the street was almost deserted. The twilit sky had taken on a reddish hue and carriages had already lit their lamps. Nell reached the point of her short walk home where she always crossed the High St. She stood waiting for an oncoming tram to pass. There were loud clashes of steel against cobblestones as a brace of huge Shire horses trotted effortlessly, while pulling the heavy tram toward her. The noise completely drowned the sound of light footsteps as Brenda Scopes crept up behind Nell. The Shires were almost level with Nell as she felt someone grab her shoulders from behind and thrust her forward into the road. The horse nearest to Nell tried to rear up, frightened by this small human form that had suddenly appeared in its path. Its coupling harness held it down as Nell was suddenly pulled back out of its path by the same hands that had pushed her. The tram driver fought to regain control as the tram sped on. Nell was white with fear as she turned and looked up into the face of the much taller and heavier Brenda Scopes.

"Let that be a lesson you sneaky little cow," said Brenda, her dark eyes glowering at Nell. "The next time I hear you've been seen out with Alfie I won't pull you back. Do you hear me?" Nell was lost for words, but then Brenda's look of anger suddenly turned to one of surprise when Irene Boswell came running up to them.

"Brenda! Are you mad? I saw what you did. You could have killed her."

Brenda tried to recover with an uncomfortable laugh,

"I only did it for a joke Mrs Boswell."

"Well it didn't look like a joke." Irene looked pensively at Nell as if waiting for a denial. Nell knew that to tell Mrs. Boswell the truth would probably cost Brenda her job.

"No its alright Mrs. Boswell," she quickly said. "Brenda meant no harm. It was just a joke."

Irene looked unconvinced as she said,

"Well you two better get on home and don't ever do anything like that again Brenda, joke or not."

Nell slept little that night. When sleep did come, she was haunted by visions of wild horses with hatred in their eyes, hatred she'd witnessed in Brenda's eyes that day. In the early hours, she suddenly sat up, stirred by a vision of her own trampled body. For the rest of the night thoughts of losing Alfie pressed heavily on her mind until she was startled by her mother roughly shaking her to get up.

The following day Nell stayed clear of Brenda Scopes. She made sure they never used the washroom together or in any way came in close contact. Most of all Nell avoided Brenda's stare.

It was mid-morning on the Wednesday, while Ivan Boswell was away on business when Nell was suddenly startled to see Alfie Button's face appear at the top of the stairs. Nell became tense and worried, thinking Alfie was bound to make straight for her. She knew if he started to laugh and joke with her, she would suffer Brenda's wrath.

Alfie reached the top of the stairs and Nell watched him from beneath a deep and worried frown. But Alfie wasn't wearing his usual smile and to Nell's surprise, he ignored her and instead made his way past the women along the workbench. The chatter of women's voices and the clatter of machines died as Alfie stopped behind Brenda Scopes. He touched her shoulder. Brenda spun round and her face beamed as she saw Alfie. However, her smile was short lived as Alfie frowned, pointing a finger close to her face.

"Never try to run my life Brenda, and never threaten any girl that I choose to go out with. Do you understand?"

"But I thought we …"

"You thought that because we've been out twice together, it was as good as being married. Well I'm sorry Brenda, its not, But I'm warning you, if you ever try anything again like you tried on Monday, it could be death do us part." With that Alfie turned and with a scowl, walked back along the line to disappear down the stairs while all eyes were on a very embarrassed and red faced Brenda Scopes: all except Nell's. Both she and Brenda knew that Irene Boswell had talked about the tram incident in Alfie's presence.

Nell neither heard nor saw anything of Alfie Button for some time and she believed, like Brenda Scopes, that Alfie had spurned her. That was until a few weeks later on a Sunday morning when Nell's mother answered a knock at the door. She was surprised to see a handsome, smiling young man in shirtsleeves and shiny gaiters. He stood holding the reins of a beautiful white pony and highly polished trap.

"Good morning. Mrs. Masters?"

"Yes?" Violet said with obvious surprise.

"My name's Alfie Button. I've come to take Nell out for a picnic if it's convenient." With that, Nell came to the door.

"Oh Alfie what a beautiful horse."

"Meet Pegasus," said Alfie grinning. "He's my governor's pride and joy."

"Oh Mum. This is Alfie Button. Is it all right if I go? Please."

Violet seemed lost for words, and though she consented, Nell had the impression that her mother wasn't happy.

The two set off heading north taking the main road out of Portsmouth. Alfie handled the trap like the expert that he was.

"Where are we going?" Nell asked, yet not really caring. To her it was a perfect day and to be driven along in a high-class rig by her golden haired Alfie, was more than any girl deserved.

"Well I got sandwiches and lemonade in that basket there, and I thought you might like to go up Portsdown Hill for a picnic, but if you would rather go somewhere else…."

"No, it sounds lovely I've never been there before," said Nell, soaking up the stares from envious young ladies along the way. Alfie let Nell take the reins for part of the journey. He stood close behind her, his arms about her waist as he guided her use of the reins. She could feel the strength of him, and the warmth of his breath against her neck made her wish the journey would never end. But it ended all too soon. They stopped at a water trough outside the George Inn on the brow of the hill. They then turned west along the chalky South Downs until they found a suitable grassy and secluded spot to spread out their picnic.

Alfie unhitched Pegasus and tethered him to a hawthorn, leaving Nell to spread the blanket and open the picnic hamper. For an hour, they lay among the long summer grass, laughing and chatting under the warmth of the sun.

"I don't think your mother likes me very much." Alfie said as he lay with his head on her lap.

"Don't be silly, she's only just met you."

"I know, but I really felt awkward standing at your door this morning. Do you know what I mean?"

"Yes she made me feel awkward too," said Nell twiddling with one of his long curly locks of hair. "She probably feels that I'm too young to have a boyfriend, what do you think?"

Alfie grinned, "I think you're as old as you feel." Then he quickly sat up and grabbed her waist to tickle her, saying, "How old do you feel." Nell laughed hysterically while kicking and wriggling to escape his grasp. When he stopped, she realized her dress had ridden up high above her knees showing her underwear. She saw Alfie looking at her nakedness, and when their eyes met, she saw the desire she'd aroused in him. His eyes focused on her mouth and when he pressed his lips to hers, Nell wished the moment could last forever. Suddenly Alfie pulled away from her and sat upright.

"Whatever's wrong?" Nell said.

"I'm sorry Nell, but maybe your mothers right. Maybe you *are* too young."

"But I'm nearly seventeen! And I thought you liked me."

"That's just the trouble Nell I think it's more than just, like. That's why I can't take advantage. I don't want to spoil things and if I do anything stupid I'll lose you for sure."

"So are you saying it's not because you don't want me?" Nell said with a knowing smile.

"Nell, a minute ago, I wanted you so bad, I thought I was going to bust my breeches."

Nell laughed, "Alfie, you are funny."

"It's not the first time I've been told that, Nell, but I can be serious. One day I'll have my own forge, I just know I will! That's something I'm serious about. Do you think you could see yourself marrying a blacksmith, Nell?"

Nell grinned. "Well that's got to be the shortest engagement in history," she said.

"Now you're really laughing at me," Alfie said, pouting almost childlike.

"Yes, but only because, you and I are so young, and you are talking so…so, well you know, old. But if you really want me to answer your question," Nell paused to kiss him tenderly on the cheek. "The answer is most certainly yes."

That Sunday on Portsdown Hill was a special day. Nell knew that it would remain in her memory for many years to come, and for the rest of that summer the couple enjoyed many more special weekends. But as all good things end, summer ended and the harshness of another winter at Boswell's was upon the team of seamstresses once again.

Nell and Marie had become the best of friends, their likes and dislikes and especially their sense of humour gave them much in common, and they sat chatting to each other whenever Boswell was out of the room.

"I don't think I'll ever be as fast as you Marie. I really don't know why Mr. Boswell keeps me on. He must have noticed how slow I am."

"Maybe it's the sunshine of your smile," Marie said, quoting the song title and grinning at Nell. "Or maybe the twinkle in your eye. I know! Maybe he's just plain stupid." With that, the two girls burst out laughing until Sadie Drew told them to hush. Nell brought her voice down to a murmur,

"How come Molly's allowed to wear that head scarf while we have to wear these horrible caps?" Marie cupped a hand round Nell's ear, and whispered,

"Mrs. Drew said it's to cover a scar, she said the cap don't come down far enough to cover it, so Mr. Boswell said she could wear a scarf. Actually I reckon there's more between Molly and old Boswell than we know."

"What! After the way he showed her up about her bathing?" Nell whispered, "I wouldn't think so."

"Oh don't be taken in by that, it was just an act. Mind you, I'm sure he likes his women to at least smell nice."

"Women?" queried Nell.

"Yes, from what I hear Molly wouldn't be the first."

Nell jokingly answered, with a giggle "Mmm, do tell,"

"It's true. You watch how many times both Bossy and Molly are both missing whenever his wife goes out to do a bit of shopping."

Just as Marie finished whispering, Nell looked up to see Molly looking at her.

"Who're you looking at?" Molly shouted along the bench to Nell. The workers stopped talking and the room became silent. "Was you two snot's talking about me?" Molly left her chair and walked menacingly towards the two younger girls. Stopping behind Nell she said, "You got something to say ya snotty little cow?"

"I think they was talking about you, Molly," said Brenda Scopes, still seeking revenge on Nell.

Marie, intervened, "Why don't you pick on someone else Molly? Nell's done you no harm."

"Yeah," sneered Brenda. "But maybe that's only because Molly's got no boyfriend for her to sniff around."

"Yeah," continued Molly, "and she thinks she's better than me, with her posh talk. Well she's not. See? And neither are you, so you better not let me see you talking about me again, see."

Marie was about to protest when she started to cough. She pulled a handkerchief from a sleeve in her dress and Nell noticed that it was blood stained. The coughing became more violent and the women stopped working. Some got to their feet but were at a loss what to do. Blood started to appear around Marie's mouth. Nell quickly left her seat and ran down the stairs. She returned with Mr. Boswell to find Marie slumped over the bench.

Ivan Boswell took Marie home leaving Nell worried and wondering how long her friend would be gone or if she would ever see her again.

The aggravation that Nell had to endure from Molly and Rose while Marie was away became worse. For reasons that Nell did not understand, both sisters gave Nell a hard time. They picked arguments with her at every possible opportunity and blamed her for mistakes on clothing that she had not even worked on.

"Who got my bloody scissors?" Rose said on one occasion. She walked around the workbench, searching under material until she eventually found them under a garment lying beside Nell. Nell knew they had been put there intentionally, and was getting used to Rose and Molly's little games. "You again!" Rose said: loud enough for all to hear. "I bet you had them the last time they went missing. My gawd! Gal, you just can't be trusted can you? I'll just have to tie 'em to me."

From then on Rose hung them from a cord around her waist. Nell knew it was done as another way to belittle her, rather than a useful means of finding them.

One snow clad morning Nell unlocked the shop. After lighting the shop's gas lamps, she went straight to the back yard to fill the coalscuttle. It was still dark and the gas light from the shop was little help as she cleared snow from the coal-pile. Filling the oversized scuttle, she struggled with it through the shop to the workshop stairs. She climbed them by pulling the heavy scuttle up one step at a time. Then with the help of an old newspaper and some kindling Nell started lighting the stove. She sat on the floor as she did each morning feeding coal, one lump at a time, into the little cast iron door, while the crackling stove brought the life back to her numbed fingers.

As she waited for the other women to arrive, she heard a faint tinkle of the shop bell. She looked up at the wall clock; it was five minutes past seven. She knew that the women didn't start arriving until at least twenty past seven and even if any had arrived early, they wouldn't enter the shop. They couldn't, she had locked it like she'd been instructed, or had she?

She mentally retraced her actions of filling the coalscuttle and carrying it through the shop. She remembered opening the shop door and hearing the bell ring, but as much as she tried she could not remember putting the scuttle down and relocking the door before ascending the stairs. If she had left it open the wind could have made the bell tinkle but, and more worryingly, had someone entered the shop to steal?

Nell got to her feet and crept to the head of the stairs. She peered down them, to see the beginning of daylight through the glass of the outer door and she could see that the inner door was closed. She held her breath and listened, wondering if her hearing had been playing tricks on her. After some moments, she decided that this was the case and turned back toward the stove. Then she heard another a sound. She feared for her own safety but more than this she feared the thought of her mother's anger if she lost her job through negligence.

She crept quietly down the stairs, while listening for any sound that might warn her of danger. As she feared, the inner shop door was not locked. Slowly she moved nervously through the shop, not really considering what she'd do if she came upon a robber. Suddenly she saw a movement and her heart leapt inside her chest before realizing it was only her own reflection in the full-length dress mirror. Then she heard the sound of running water coming from the washroom in the yard. She tiptoed silently outside. The door to the washroom was slightly ajar. Pushing gently against it, she peered through the gap. Her eyes widened as she saw Molly Gill in a most unrefined pose.

Although Molly stood with her back to the door, it was obvious to Nell what she was doing. Nell found herself transfixed by the sight before her.

Molly stood barefoot on the freezing stone floor, her lace-up boots stood beside her. She faced the washbasin with her long flannel underwear draped over her shoulder. With her legs spread apart and skirts held high about her waist, she bathed herself from the running cold-water tap.

Nell felt only pity for the older girl; she remembered Boswell's harsh and embarrassing threat about the sisters' personal hygiene. She remembered Molly protesting, saying that she couldn't bathe at home. This, Nell deduced, was the result of Molly, fearing for her job. Molly's ever present headscarf hung from an overhead pipe, and it left Nell in awe of the girl's long and beautiful raven hair cascading in front of her as she bent forward. Nell started to retreat, afraid of what Molly would do if she turned and saw her. As she took a slow step backwards, Molly suddenly gave a swish of her head throwing her long hair back over her shoulders to reveal the ugly round scar above her ear. Nell had seen such scars before among the poorer children of her school. Her mother had called it Ringworm.

It may have been a sound, or a movement reflected in the mirror above the washbasin, but something caused Molly to glance behind her. Catching sight of Nell before the youngster could duck out of sight.

Molly screamed at her,

"You spying little bitch!" She rushed threateningly towards Nell.

"I didn't mean to, Molly, I heard a noise, I came…." Nell saw Molly's fist coming but was unable to move out of its path. The punch, surprisingly, didn't hurt as much as Nell would have expected, but she could not remember the transition that took her from a standing position to lying flat on her back. She lay in the wet snow and horse-manure-slush of the open yard with Molly kneeling astride her stomach, making it hard for her to breath. She put a hand up to ease the pain in her nose and felt the wet stickiness of blood. Looking up, she read the hate in Molly's pale blue eyes and knew that her punishment was not yet over.

"Now I s'pose you'll have lots to talk about with the other snooty cow when she comes back, won't you, you nosey little cow? Well let's see you do it with a fat lip."

Nell held up her hands to ward off the blow as she pleaded. "Please Molly I won't tell anyone you were here. This time Nell felt a lot of pain as the punch drove a tooth through her bottom lip.

Molly got up and stood over her as Nell lay on the wet cobbles sobbing through blood soaked fingers.

"You can tell who you bleedin' like, about me being 'ere," said Molly, smirking, as she pulled a hand from down the front of her frock and dangled a key. "You see old Boswell knows I'm 'ere, but you're going' home 'fore anyone gets 'ere, cause I'm not 'avin you bleating to him with a bloody face and getting' me the sack. So, you can sod off home. I'll tell Boswell you felt sick." Then, laughing out loud, Molly added. "After all, I won't be lying, will I?" Nell ran crying from the building.

Three days lapsed before Nell's swollen face had normalized enough for her to return to Boswell's. Even then, she still had traces of a black eye and a swollen lip. She made the same excuse to Boswell for her absence, that she had made to her mother: that she had slipped on the ice. Nell was disappointed to find that Marie was still absent and so expected more abuse and derision from the Gill sisters.

It was now December, the snow was getting deeper and because of the cost of fuel, Nell and her mother would retire to bed early just to keep warm. This, however, was at least one benefit of working at Boswell's; some women could not afford to heat their homes during the day while their husbands were at work.

"Come on gal, taking your time fetching that bleedin' tea ain't ya?" Molly shouted at Nell one morning. "And give that stove a poke while your up, will ya? Me bloody feet's turning blue."

Nell placed the tray of tin mugs on the end of the long workbench; she then started to serve the line of women as they worked. Meanwhile Ivan Boswell was summonsed by his wife to tend some business downstairs in the shop.

"Bet you're lost without your little Maria to hide behind." Molly sneered. Nell said nothing but continued serving mugs of tea to the women.

Because of Nell's tender age, most of the women would have their good-natured fun with her, but Rose and Molly's taunts were filled with malice. As Molly spoke, she cast worried glances at the stairwell. Molly was not in favour with Boswell since his wife had found out that he had given her a key and permitted her to use the washroom in the mornings.

Nell reached the sisters with two mugs of steaming tea. She looked over their shoulders for a space on the bench to place their mugs; the black and rotting teeth of Rose grinned up at her. Then, as Nell reached over to place the mugs, Rose pulled a face. Nell lost concentration and spilled a small drop of hot tea over Rose's hand. Exaggerating her injury, Rose shrieked in pain.

"You bloody little cow. You meant to do that!" Molly shouted,

"I'm sorry it was an accident." Nell said, while retreating out of harms reach. However, seeing Boswell's seat was empty, Molly left her chair and went after her.

"Haven't got your precious Maria to help you now, have you!" Nell took the slap across the face and to Molly's annoyance fought back the tears. Nell carried on about her task. Though the other women felt sorry for Nell, fear of reprisal from the two sisters was such that when Boswell was not about, the Gill sisters could do just as they pleased.

"You best be careful Nell Master's," Molly threatened Nell as she returned to her seat. "I haven't finished with you yet!"

Two weeks elapsed and still Marie had not returned to work, but at least the ill-treatment that Nell had received from the Gill's seemed to diminish somewhat. Nell hoped that maybe Molly was feeling sorry for the ill treatment she'd shown to her, but whatever the reason, Molly started to behave more civilly toward her. What Nell did not know was that Brenda Scopes was about to receive an unexpected home-visit from Molly Gill.

4
Tram ride to Hell

It was a Friday morning while Ian Boswell was out on business when Dolly fields looked up from her stitching.

"Here, young Nell! Brenda, here, was just saying how it's been a long time since young Marie became ill. You *are* her best friend, why don't you go and see her, lovey? Find out how she's getting on, I'm sure we would all like to know. She'd be ever so pleased to see you."

"Oh I'd love to, Dolly. Do you think her mother would mind?" Dolly pursed her lips and shook her head.

"No, course not, I think her mum would be only too pleased, wouldn't you say Bren?" Dolly said, while nudging Brenda Scopes sitting next to her.

Hardly a word had passed between Brenda and Nell since Brenda's embarrassing incident with Alfie Button, and now Brenda looked uneasy.

"Yeah, sure she would," Brenda said, but avoided Nell's enquiring stare.

"But I don't know where she lives," said Nell, "Only that it's somewhere around Sallyport."

"I know where she lives!" said Brenda.

"So do I," called Molly, who had been taking a keen interest in the discussion. "I'll draw you a little map."

Nell could not believe it; had Brenda finally gotten over being spurned by Alfie? Had Molly finally exhausted all of her malice? It would seem that these girls had now gone from just being more agreeable to being downright helpful. Later that day Brenda handed Nell, Molly's little map; showing exactly where in Sallyport, Marie lived.

Sallyport was just a couple of miles from Nell's home and although she had never been there, Nell knew of its reputation. Its name was widespread as a place of filth and depravity. Nell was more than a little nervous of the place, but decided to overcome her fears for the sake of visiting her dear friend. Such was her concern for Maria.

On the following Saturday evening, after preparing her mother's evening meal and tending her needs, Nell decided to brave the cold and pay Maria a visit. She clothed herself in the thickest black woollen stockings and covered her head and shoulders with the warmest of her mother's woollen shawls. Before going out into the icy cold night she made another study of the scrawled map that Molly had given her, checked her little pull-string purse for the fare, and then set off in the darkest of nights to catch the tram to Sallyport.

It was 8 pm and street gas lamps did little to lighten Portsmouth's darkest of streets. Nell was one of only two passengers when, nearing her destination, the horse-drawn tram came to a stop. At a bend in the road where the High Street met Broad Street, the conductor moved along the tram until he stood over Nell.

"This is as far as you go for a penny, Miss!" Glancing once more at the little map in her lap, Nell stepped onto the cobbled street. The tram pulled away, and as Nell watched its oil lamps fade into the darkness, a feeling of dread came over her. She started to walk while pulling the shawl up over her face and nose; this served to filter out the putrid stench of the place, while keeping the biting cold from freezing her cheeks.

From somewhere came the sound of a barrel organ, and as she peered nervously down each narrow alley, she imagined being pounced upon at any moment.

Questionable looking characters and underfed children loitered outside Grog Houses and Pubs. A vile smelling man purposefully stumbled against her as she tried to pass him, his breath stank of spirits and he groped roughly at her tiny breasts. Nell pushed him aside and hurried on hoping to see a street name that she might recognise from the map.

She stopped and stared up at a street name, but a cloud drifted across the almost full moon, cloaking its letters in shadow and making them impossible to read. She looked up to see the clouds moving swiftly and waited for the moon to shed its light again. As she waited, she felt that eyes were watching her. Peering into the shadows of a pawnshop doorway, she saw what looked like a young boy and girl; by their height, Nell guessed their approximate ages to be nine or ten.

"Can you help me?" she said to them. "I'm looking for Bathing Lane."

"For tuppence we'll take you there!" Came the boy's gruff response. Nell moved closer to the doorway, she could see that they were holding hands. The girl was shivering.

"Why don't you take your little sister home, you must both be freezing?" said Nell. The answer was slow coming. "If we go home with no money our father will beat us with his belt," said the boy. Nell felt that although his voice sounded child-like, something about it bothered her.

"Well I'm very sorry but I've only enough for my tram fare home." With that, the boy moved toward Nell, pulling the little girl with him. Then like smoke, the trailing wisps of cloud cleared and the moon shone its light fully on the shackled pair. Nell gasped in fear. The boy was not a boy, but a dwarf with the face of an old man. The girl was ragged and filthy.

"Well give me that then," the dwarf growled, while moving quickly toward her.

Nell stumbled backwards in fear just as the door of a nearby Ale House opened. Three sailors, arms locked around each other's shoulders, came staggering toward them. The shackled pair moved back into the shadows. Nell walked quickly on again with the words of the dwarf fading behind her,

"Come on Jack, just a shilling. She's older than she looks!"

Passing several more Grog houses and Inns, Nell made her way toward the **Point***. She was nervously aware that the amount of sailors on the streets had multiplied along with the rowdiness of the place.

Nell felt at one time she was being followed. Suddenly, raised voices a few yards ahead of her prompted her to tread more carefully. She strained her eyes to make out the jostling shapes of two flat-capped men and a sailor. They were fighting in the street.

*Where broad street ends, by sloping into the harbour.

Nell hurriedly ducked into the shadows of a doorway hoping they had not seen her. She waited, and then she heard a dull thud. She saw the sailor stumble before collapsing in a heap. She quickened her pace. Keeping to the shadows, she peered nervously behind. The two men were dragging the unfortunate sailor into a doorway. No doubt, Nell thought, he would awaken with empty pockets.

Nell hurried on, sorely wishing that she'd stayed home that night. Eventually she recognised a name from the little map, Bathing Lane, a cobbled alley. She entered it, to almost step on something that ran across her path, while the smell of the place brought up bile to her burn her throat.

She found it hard to believe that Marie lived in such a terrible place, but then thought how suddenly poverty had struck her own mother since father's fatal accident. The dreadful thought occurred to her that they might also sink to such an existence. She shuddered and put the thought out of her mind.

As she moved cautiously along the cobbled alley, the cold wind paid no regard for the care she'd taken over dressing. She could not stop shivering. As she passed a window, its glow caused her to turn toward it. What she saw made her quickly look away. The glow came from a large oil lamp, this stood on a pedestal close to the inside of the window. The lamp was there purposely to expose what was obviously a middle-aged prostitute promoting herself. The woman sat facing the window wearing a long silken low-cut dress that exposed her breasts fully, and as she stared out of the window, she sucked on a clay pipe. On seeing Nell, she grabbed the hem of the dress and pulled it up to her waist, exposing her anatomy to the full. Nell quickly looked away and hurried on, but before reaching the end of the alley, she heard a door open behind her, and a woman's voice shouted:

"Av a good eye-full did ya? Ya nosey bitch; go on, piss off and get yer own pitch."

Nell hurriedly turned the corner to find herself in a similar alley. Here, a gas street lamp shone on a wall plaque: Nob Lane. Nell counted the houses hardly believing how small they were. Yes there were five just like Molly had said, and she remembered her saying that Marie lived in the middle one. There was a light in the window but more importantly, the glow of a coal fire. She tapped on the door and waited for what seemed ages. When it opened, Nell understood why it had taken so long. The old woman stood with one shoulder hunched up high from the use of a heavy wooden crutch. She held up an oil lamp and peered long and questioningly at Nell. Shadows thrown by the lamp highlighted the lines and furrows in the old woman's face. Her long whiskers, although sparse, were prominent around her mouth and chin, accentuating the ugliness of the crone. If Nell had believed in witches, she would have made a hasty retreat. Although surprised, Nell assumed her to be Marie's Grandmother.

"Bit of a young'un ain't yer gal?" said the woman, as her eyes followed the lines of Nell's young form. Nell could not fathom the relevance of her statement, and just uttered the words she'd already decided on.

"My name is Nell Masters and I've come to see Marie if its convenient Mrs." The woman seemed to contemplate for a while. Then, craning her neck to look past Nell, as if checking the darkened alley for loiterers, she answered: "Oh aye, s'pose ya better come in then. You look half froze."

Stepping down inside the door, Nell looked about her, hardly believing that anyone could live in such cramped and squalid conditions. To the left of the door was a blank wall, this, Nell guessed, had to be the partition wall to the next house. Directly facing the door, bare wooden stairs ascended into darkness. The old woman ushered Nell to the right. Nell stepped down again into a tiny room, no more than eight or nine foot in both length and width, although it was far from being square. One side of the room was only five to six foot high while the other side was around eight foot and the ceiling sagged badly in the centre. Nell realised she was in one of the Jerrybuilt slums of Old Portsmouth that she'd heard about. A nail had been driven into the side of the stairs just below the ceiling, from this, a tattered blanket stretched to the far wall screening an area below the angle of the stairwell. This, being about six feet long and the width of the stairs, Nell deduced could have contained a single bed. Whatever else it could be hiding, Nell could not guess, but the obnoxious odour in the room was making her feel quite ill.

Along the opposite wall, stood a single bed leaving just enough room for a small dresser. The wall facing the small window held, for Nell, the room's only redeeming feature: a cooking range with coals that glowed with a welcoming warmth. In front of the range was the rooms one and only chair.

"Is it alright if I have a warm Mrs?" Nell said politely.

"Course e can lovey, help yourself." The old woman propped her crutch against the wall inside the door. Nell warmed herself in front of the stove. She was intrigued by the old woman's agility without the crutch. She watched the woman crouch down beside her to shovel coal from a scuttle onto the stove. Deducing Nell's look of surprise the woman said: "Thought I was a cripple did you gal? Well you can't be too careful round here. If I open the door to find a robber, he might take pity on an old cripple woman on a crutch. If not, he gets it over the head," she said cackling loudly.

To the right of the stove was a door that Nell reasoned must be a scullery. Nell could not believe one could be expected to live in a hovel so small.

"I only got the one chair gal, but you can sit on my bed by the stove. I got just the thing to warm you up." The old woman hobbled over to the only cupboard in the room. After fumbling around inside it, she placed on the top, two metal tankards, a stone bottle and something that was hidden by her person. However, Nell paid little attention to the old woman's antics.

"Is she in bed then, I mean is she still ill?" The woman didn't answer but hobbled to her seat and started filling the tankards from the stone bottle.

"I really miss her at work you know," Nell added. "We get on so well."

"I'm sure you do lovey." The woman pulled a red-hot poker from the coals causing Nell to cower back in fear. But the old woman doused it in one of the tankards then replaced it back in the red coals. "Now you drink this and you'll start to really thaw out."

Nell drank, not bothering to smell or even look at the contents lest she be put off and have to shun the old woman's hospitality. Nell disliked the first taste, it burned her throat, but then, like the old woman said, she felt its warming properties radiate within her.

"I've not seen you round here before my lovely, where are you from?" The old woman asked as she took a clay pipe from the shelf above the range and lit it with a paper spill.

"Lyons Terrace." Nell said, then again asking, "Will I be able to see Marie?"

"All in good time lovey. Drink up!"

Prompted earnestly by the old woman Nell finished the drink only to have the tankard quickly refilled by the woman.

"So, is she still in bed then?" Nell said, while still pressing the old woman for an answer.

"Who?"

"Marie!"

"Is that who sent you?"

"Yes, I mean no." Nell was starting to feel tired. "Marie's my friend, she's the one I came to see."

"Oh I see," said the woman, as she clanked the bottle once more against Nell's tankard, filling it to the brim "Are you saying you didn't come here for the usual then."

"I don't know what you mean. Ish Marie here or not?" Nell was finding it harder to deliver a sentence without slurring her words.

"What I mean, my lovely, is when young women knocks my door it's usually for one thing: to make a bit of money. Now who sent you here?"

Nell could not think straight. The room seemed to be spinning. "Brenda and Molly…Molly with the scarf…can't remember her name." Nell was not sure if she was making sense until the old woman said.

"Gill?"

"Yesh that's it, Gill! Molly Gill."

By now, Nell's eyes would not focus because nothing would stay still for them to do so. Then she allowed the weight of her head to slowly pull her down; the room started to spin and Nell could feel her legs being lifted up until she was horizontal. Moments later she heard banging, a cold draught suddenly wisped about her like a door had opened and closed. Then the old woman's voice whispering. "It's going to cost you this time Oli. She's a ripe young thing. Untouched I'll wager, but the Gill's sent this one. They're gonna want a few bob."

Nell heard the clink of money being counted out. She wanted to sit up but had no control over her limbs.

The old woman spoke again sounding nervous. "You going to behave yourself this time, Oli, I don't want no more trouble with the peelers, that gal nearly died last time."

Nell heard a gruff and slurred voice say: "Yeah, but you gets your money though don't you, you old hag. Now mind your own business and get out of my way." Nell felt herself being picked up with ease by strong arms. She felt warm whisky-smelling breath close to her and the feeling that a beard was brushing against her face and finally, before all her senses failed, the sensation of ascending stairs.

Nell opened her eyes to stare at an unfamiliar ceiling. Believing it to be morning, she tried to sit up. This told her that it was her head that was spinning, not the room. She lay back down in an effort to stop the nauseous feeling in her stomach and to stop the infernal spinning, she focused on a gaping hole in the ceiling where plaster and strips of wood hung down. She looked toward the only window where a torn blanket had been stretched across its width and hooked onto nails. She could see through the blanket's holes that it was not fully light yet. Slowly, events of the previous evening came back to her and how she came to be there. She remembered the tram ride, and the freezing walk through frightening dark alleys that led to the old woman with the crutch. She remembered the warm grog that the old woman kept giving her then finally she remembered …

She thrust a hand under the filthy bed cover. Her nakedness confirmed her fear. She started to cry as she thought of eventual consequences that could or would come of the previous night. She leaped from the wooden bed, throwing the filthy cover from her. She found her underwear and dress, it was all torn and she knew it had been ripped from her. Quickly she dressed and grabbed her boots. She dashed to the open doorway. On the tiny landing, she met the old woman coming up the stairs. The clay pipe still hung from the corner of her mouth.

"You did this to me you filthy hag." Nell blurted out through her bitter tears.

"Now don't be like that, lovey, I was just coming to give you your money." The old woman was grinning as she held out what looked like some silver between her bony thumb and index finger.

"Why did you do this to me! You let some filthy beast have his way with me!" Nell shouted, ignoring the old woman's outstretched hand.

"Now I shouldn't go talking about rape if I was you gal," the hag said calmly. "After all, you came knocking at my door remember? And like I said, gals only knock on my door for one reason, I told you that, so if I was you I'd take the money and say no more."

Nell wiped her tears on the sleeve of her torn dress. "I don't believe you—look at me! I'm seventeen, you must have known I didn't come here to sell myself. If you honestly thought I did, why did you drug me?"

The old hag burst into a loud uncontrollable cackle causing her to almost swallow the pipe and fall backwards down the stairs. Eventually gaining control she said,

"Believe me gal, no female has ever gone willingly up these stairs with Oli Matcher, I can tell you. Not when they see the size of him, but he must have liked you, cause it's not often they can walk back down on their own after he's finished with them. Why, you've not even got a shiner!"

Nell had stopped crying and stared blankly for some moments down at the old woman who stood just one step from the top of the stairs. She grinned up at Nell and again thrust out the coins in her wrinkled palm.

Suddenly and violently Nell swung her hand up, knocking the old woman's arm upwards. The coins hit the ceiling and rained down in all directions. With arms flailing the hag started to topple backwards. Nell made a grab for her but in so doing, sealed the old woman's fate. Nell's open palms hit the old woman's chest while clutching her clothing, but the rotting and filthy material tore away in her hands. Nell could do nothing. The old woman's mouth gaped in a gurgling screech, letting the clay pipe drop as she started to topple backwards. She fell, making no effort to move her feet, but tried to twist her body in an attempt to control her fall. Her body hit the stairs sideways. Nell heard a crack and thought it might have been one of the old woman's bones but was not sure. The old woman then slid slowly down the stairs. With her head at the bottom of the staircase, she lay perfectly still.

Nell stood on the landing for some moments staring down at the unsightly thing sprawled out below, hoping it would move—it didn't.

Nell slipped her boots on and trod slowly down the stairs, while stepping carefully round the limbs of the old woman. Finding her coat and scarf Nell quickly put them on and made for the front door. Among the coins lying beside the old woman's head, was a sixpence; Nell remembered her tram fare and picked it up. Gingerly she opened the front door just wide enough to peer outside. A freezing wind nipped at her cheeks but the alley was deserted and the morning had barely reached daylight. She was thankful it was Sunday. She did not have to think about work. She stepped outside, and before closing the door behind her, she looked down at the still figure of the old woman. Silver coins and pieces of broken clay pipe lay scattered around her.

5
Gateway of tears

Monday morning, and as usual, Nell sat feeding coal into the factory stove. Her mind was in turmoil, tortured by the events of the past weekend. She had hardly slept the previous night with so much on her mind. She kept hoping that it was all just a terrible nightmare and that any moment she would awaken. The whole night she'd spent thinking of the coming Monday morning and how she would face the women at the works and how she would hide the guilt that now tormented her.

Could she do it, she wondered? Would she be able to lie convincingly? Could she convince Molly and Brenda into believing that she never visited Sallyport at the weekend? She was sure now that they were behind the despicable trickery that now threatened her very existence. Can they hang a girl as young as her, she asked herself as the first of the workers started to arrive?

By the nature of the women's chatter, it was obvious to Nell that the old woman's death had not yet been discovered. Then a welcome thought occurred to her that seemed to lighten her worries a little. Maybe the old woman's death would simply be seen as an accident. After all, there was nothing that Nell could think of, that could implicate her or even suggest that she'd been to the house.

Nell acknowledged her fellow workers with morning greetings as always. She even gave Molly a bright and friendly greeting with a pleasant "Good morning Molly, where's Rose today?" Nell received a curious and inquisitive stare from the older girl, which served as a warning to Nell not to overdo it.

"She's not well," The answer was blunt and unfriendly.

It was not until Boswell had gone downstairs later that morning that the burning question, the one that Nell was expecting, was eventually asked. Though curiously, it did not come from the source she expected.

"Did you get to see Marie, Nell? You did say you were going didn't you." The question came from Sadie Drew whom Nell was sure had nothing to do with the conspiracy. However, Nell was aware that the question had aroused Brenda and Molly's attention and Nell's answer came loud enough for them both to hear,

"No Sadie, I wanted to, but my mum wasn't very well so I didn't get the chance. Maybe I'll go next week, I've still got the directions that Molly gave me." Nell could feel Molly's eyes burning into her, but Nell was pleased with her little speech and was sure she'd lied convincingly.

"That's right love," said Sadie. "Your old mum comes first. You only get one of them, you know."

The rest of that Monday was fairly uneventful, but the following morning as the women arrived for work Nell noticed an enthusiasm in their chatter, among which one or two words brought the torment of the previous weekend back to her, dispelling all hope that it might have all been a bad dream.

Charlotte Goldridge, another young busty girl that Boswell liked to ogle, came over to where Nell was tending the stove. She crouched down beside Nell rubbing her hands in front of the stove.

"Not so easy to stitch when your pinkies are frozen is it young Nell."

"No, you're right there, Charlotte." Nell liked Charlotte; the girl had always been friendly toward her, especially when Molly and Rose were giving Nell a hard time.

"Ere, bloody glad I don't live anywhere near that place." The girl said.

"What place?" Nell answered.

"Bloody Sallyport! Didn't you hear what Molly was telling the others?"

"No what was that then?" Nell said, thinking if they only knew the truth.

"About that old woman what was murdered?" Nell's heart sank; she now knew that for whatever reason, the police did not believe it to be an accident. "They say they got the bloke what done it though."

"No! Really?" This time Nell's expression of surprise was genuine.

"Yeah, really. Ere Molly what was that blokes name, again?" Charlotte called out.

"Oliver Matcher! Course we all know him as Oli." Molly called back.

Nell shuddered at the name. "He lived only a couple of doors away from us." Molly continued with a proud air of importance. "Rose and me saw the peelers pull him out of his house. It took four of them to get him in the wagon. You should see the size of him, bet he's at least six-foot-four and he's a tough one I don't mind telling you he's always getting into fights."

Midst Nell's fear that her dreadful secret be discovered, there came a sense that maybe justice had been done both to the beast that had raped her and the old woman in league with him.

The next day Ivan Boswell broke the news to them that he'd called on Marie and that she was on the mend and would be back to work the following Monday. This was like a tonic to Nell. By the end of that week, she had become confident that her secret would remain that way.

Life became more bearable for Nell, now that Maria was back at Boswell's. The Gill sisters' antagonism had lost its bite with Maria's return.

The spiteful conspiracy that Nell had endured for so long had now lost its potency. It was as though their malice had run its course and nothing more could surpass the stress or pain they had caused her. Nell's fear had been replaced with a deep loathing for the two sisters. She was convinced that even Brenda's involvement was contrived and orchestrated by the Gill sisters. Fear of losing her job however and the fear of exposure in the Sallyport case, quelled her thirst for retaliation. That is, until one cold and snowy morning a week into the trial of Oliver Matcher.

It happened before Mr and Mrs Boswell had arrived. Nell came face to face with Molly who had followed her down to the works washroom. Molly appeared in the doorway, just as Nell was about to leave. Barring Nell's exit by leaning against the doorframe and with a slight smirk, Molly said,

"That Oli Matcher recons he never done it,"

"Does he?" Nell said, taking a step back inside the washroom doorway.

"Yeah, it was in the paper."

"Really! So, you're telling me what? That you can read?"

Molly's expression was, at first, one of surprise then her eyes blazed and the smirk changed to an angry sneer. "Don't try to be funny. Matcher recon's somebody else was there on the day he was seen coming out of the old gals house. He recons it was a young girl."

"Really! Why are you telling me?"

"Well I recon that was the day you said you was going to see Marie."

"I never went, I told you that! Even if I had, I don't see what my going to Marie's house has got to do with this Matcher business." A hint of a smile played around Nell's mouth that she found hard to control.

Molly stared at her suspiciously through narrowed eyelids. "You're a sly one you are," she said.

"Don't know what you mean," Nell said flippantly.

"I think you do. I think you went to the address that I sent you."

"Where! Marie's house?" Nell was now wearing the smirk and it was starting to prove too much for Molly's temper.

"You bloody well know it was the old woman's knocking-shop that I sent you." The volume of Molly's voice rose with her anger and she spoke through clenched teeth. Nell calmly put a finger to her lips and looked skyward as if in deep thought,

"Knocking-shop! knocking-shop! Now what could that be?"

"You bloody well know what it is, you cocky little cow. It's a bloody brothel." Molly was fast losing control through Nell's cool and nonchalant attitude, and Nell knew that the tables had turned, that she now had command. She also noticed that the heels of Molly's shoes were inside the doorstep.

"Are you saying that you tried to trick me into going to a place where I could have been raped by some filthy beast like this, what's-his-name, Matcher?" Even before Molly had answered, Nell knew her own intentions.

"Yes I did and…"

Before Molly could finish her sentence Nell rushed at her pushing her with all the force she could muster. Her heel hit the doorstep in an attempt to step backwards and Molly went sprawling out into the dung-covered slush where Nell had landed on their first set to.

Molly lay there confused, and feeling the icy cold slush soaking through her clothes. Nell stood calmly looking down at her with a sense of deep satisfaction outweighing any fear of retaliation. She remembered what Marie had said concerning Molly and Boswell, and she prayed that it was true as she quietly but firmly directed her next words at Molly while standing over her.

"If you try to make any more trouble for me, Molly Gill, I promise you, Mrs Boswell will discover your little secret. Know what I mean?"

The next few weeks were uneventful. Christmas came and went and the cold weather persisted. Life for Nell should have been happier now; everything seemed to be taking a turn for the better. Her mother had taken a well-paid cleaning job with a well-to-do family. The Gills were leaving her alone since her rebellion, and because she had become more proficient at her work, all worries of losing her job had diminished.

On top of all this, talk at the factory about The Sallyport Slaying seemed to be fading. But the biggest surprise to Nell, and what had really lifted her spirits, was a report in the paper concerning Matcher's trial. It said that the old woman had been found in her chair and that she'd been stabbed twice through the heart. If the report was true, then it was almost certain that she herself had not killed the old woman, and that this Oli Matcher must have gone back after she herself had left. Yes, she thought, Matcher must have murdered the old woman for her money. All these events should have brought a little happiness back into Nell's life, but something else was troubling Nell, something she could not share, even with Marie, and that something was brought to light early one evening.

Violet Masters came home later than Nell that day and brought home kippers for their evening meal. At the dining table that evening Violet looked attentively at her daughter.

"Are you going to eat that kipper?"

"No I'm not really hungry Mum." Nell said, avoiding her mother's stare.

"That's two days running you've left your dinner, are you not feeling well?" There was harshness in her mother's voice that Nell found disturbing.

"I'm alright, just feeling a bit sick that's all." Nell said, looking down at her plate but feeling her mother's eyes still on her.

"Look at me!" Violet suddenly snapped. Nell looked flushed as she raised her head.

"Can you tell me why the wadding in the toilet cupboard has not been used?" said Violet.

"What do you mean?"

Violet banged the table hard making Nell jump. "Don't start that! You know bloody well know what I mean!"

"I keep some at work mum, I keep it in…."

"Liar! Your a bloody liar." Violet's forearms rested each side of her plate showing white knuckles on clenched fists. "Your lying now and you lied that Sunday morning when you told me you slept at your friend Marie's house."

Nell sat red faced, slowly shaking her head, trying to hold back the tears. "Don't sit there shaking your stupid bloody head. Do you know why I was late home today? I waited outside Boswell's in a shop doorway until you left the factory. Then I stayed for a little chat with your friend Marie." There was a long pause while Violet just stared at the tears running slowly down Nell's cheeks. Eventually she said. "Whose kid is it? It's that bloody Alfie Button's isn't it? I knew it! I bloody well knew he was going to be trouble. He had that look about him"

"No it isn't," with tears clouding her eyes Nell added, "I only wish it were his."

"Tell me who you've been with then! You filthy little cow, is it Boswell's?"

With that Nell broke down completely, crying unmercifully as she repeated, "No I can't. I just can't."

Violet raised herself up, stretched across the table and with gritted teeth swung her fist with all her strength hitting Nell high on the side of her face.

The blow to Nell's head sent the girl and her chair crashing to the floor. For some moments Nell lay there sobbing, Her face buried in her hands.

"Now, maybe you'll tell me," Violet said standing over her.

Nell stopped crying and pulled herself to a sitting position. She stared defiantly up at her mother, her face already turning red and starting to swell.

"You can hit me all you like, but you will never know who the father is. No one will ever know."

Violet read the defiance in her daughter's tone and in her eyes. Grabbing Nell's coat from the coat hook on the door, she threw it at Nell.

"Get out."

Next morning two inches of snow covered the cobblestones of Queen Street and it was still snowing hard. Most of the women had already entered the Boswell works when Marie arrived. She was about to enter the outer door when she heard someone call her name. She hurried along to a pawnbrokers shop doorway two shops away. Nell stood there, hands in pockets, stamping her feet. Her hair covered in snow.

"Nell! What are you doing out here, you'll catch your death. Why aren't you inside? You look frozen. Have you lit the stove yet?" Nell's teeth chattered with the cold so much, she found it difficult to speak.

"No I haven't, I never had my key."

"Who opened up?"

"Sadie, I expect, she has her own key. Look I'm not coming to work Marie But I had to see you about my mother."

"Oh yes, she asked me about the night you slept at my house. It caught me by surprise. I told her I didn't know what she was talking about. Did I say the wrong thing? I hope I didn't make trouble for you. Look at your coat, it's soaked how long have you been out here?"

"No it's alright," Nell said, ignoring Marie's question. "I should not have involved you in a lie. But I want you to make me a promise."

"Ooh you do sound serious. What is it?" Marie said.

"I want you to promise that you will never tell the other women what was said between you and my mother." Marie started to giggle until Nell shook her angrily by the shoulders and shouted, "Promise me! It's important!"

"Alright Nell, I promise. There's no need to hurt me." Nell put her arms around her and hugged her.

"I'm sorry Marie but it is very important. I have to go now and I'm not sure when I'll see you again. But I'll never forget you. Go in now or you'll be late."

"But I saw Alfie and he said to tell you he'd be in to see you today. What shall I tell him?"

"Just tell him I said, sorry."

It seemed to Nell like she'd been walking forever, Her feet and hands had long since turned numb. Had the old man not shaken her awake in the pawnbroker's doorway early that very morning, Nell realised she might have perished.

"You'll die!" She remembered him repeating as he shook her awake. "If you sleep out in this, you'll die. You have to keep moving."

He told her of a place that would help her. She started to follow his vague directions and as she walked, she prayed that the place really did exist. Thoughts of the past few weeks filled her mind, events that had led to her present predicament; how could the innocence of wanting to visit a sick friend, bring such dire misery. It seemed there was no justice and at that moment, certainly no God. Nell couldn't remember how many people she had stopped to ask directions that morning on her journey. Some of them would not even acknowledge her, but brushed her aside thinking her to be a beggar. As she walked, her mind went over that last evening at home. She remembered the rage on her mother's face as she threw her out, telling her never to come back. Then she thought about Sallyport and the old hag's money that the newspaper said she had, according to neighbours. Some said as much as a hundred pounds and that the old woman must have been saving it for years. Matcher must have seen her hiding it. He probably came back to rob her. Nell recalled the old woman's words about using the wooden crutch as a weapon, but how useless it would have been if she knew and trusted her assailant.

Nell's mind then dwelt on her own predicament; if only she had left her little string purse in her coat pocket when she came home that last evening, at least she would have had a few coppers, and the key to Boswell's. At least she would not have gone hungry, and could have slept in the factory.

When she arrived at her destination, her coat was soaked with melted snow. She looked up at the great ten-foot-high walls that the old man had described. Set in cement on the top was broken glass. Nell wondered if this was to keep intruders out or inhabitants in.

She followed the wall until she came to a great arched gate. As she gazed up at the Latin inscription above them, she was startled by a deep booming voice from behind.

"Apparently it's Latin, young lady. Don't know what it say's, but some call's it the gateway of tears."

Turning around Nell found herself looking at the midriff of a huge policeman but as she looked up he smiled, and she considered how long it had been since she'd seen a friendly face. "Mind you, most people just calls it what it is: The Work House, were you planning on going in, missy?"

"Yes, someone told me they give you food and a place to sleep."

"Aye they will, and in weather like this they will most likely keep you alive, but it's not much of a life in there, and they do expect you to work if you're fit enough. Are you sure you want to chance it?"

"I don't have any choice," said Nell. The officer unhooked his truncheon and used it to bang on the gate. As they waited the policeman gently turned Nell's chin to the light,

"I reckon you got a bit of a shiner coming there. How did that happen then?"

"I slipped in the snow." Nell said, wondering how many more times she would use that excuse. After a minute, there came the sound of bolts sliding and the great gates opened just far enough to reveal a wizened little man that appeared to have no teeth. He wore a rather scruffy jacket that was too small and his trousers suffered the same deficiency. In all, his attire did not seem in harmony with his most prominent item of dress, a priests' dog collar.

"Customer for you, St Peter," said the policeman "I recon this one's half froze. Can you fix her up?" To Nell's utter relief the little priest nodded.

Nell stretched up and kissed the policeman. "Thank you." She said. The police officer stood and watched her enter, then waited until the huge gates closed.

Inside, Nell found herself beside a small gatehouse in a large open courtyard. The snow fell heavier now and Nell wondered if she would ever feel dry or warm again. The little man in the dog collar said nothing but motioned with his hand for Nell to follow him. They followed a path toward a tall red brick building; here he produced a great bundle of keys that hung from a rope around his waist. Unlocking a door, he gestured for Nell to enter. Nell found herself in a cold and almost bare room with a stone floor. Apart from one other door opposite the one they'd just entered, the only other item of interest was a wall-to-wall cupboard covering one side of the room.

The little man looked at Nell and while making unintelligible sounds he tugged at her clothes. Nell guessed that he was dumb and that he wanted her to undress. She became afraid and shook her head. He grew agitated, making fierce and erratic hand movements that she did not understand. Nell looked behind her at the door she'd just entered and considered dashing out.

Suddenly the inner door opened and a pretty woman in a white overall coat poked her head around the door. She glanced from Nell to the man and a look of enlightenment crossed her face.

"Up to your tricks again St Peter?" The woman said. The man looked frightened. So the policeman had not said it for a joke, Nell thought. The old man stammered something unintelligible.

The woman ignored his ramblings and crossed the room toward him in a threatening manner. The man flinched as said angrily, "go on, get back to your gatehouse, or I'll report you to the Master and you know what the punishment will be." The old man looked frightened. He turned and shuffled out the door mouthing more unintelligible words as he went, and slamming the door behind him.

"Right young lady, I assume you're in need of help." The look of despair on Nell's face rendered the question unnecessary.

"Right, well my name's Sister Goodman. That's how you will address me." The woman said, roughly unbuttoning Nell's wet coat. "Get it off," she ordered sharply, Nell did so hurriedly. Goodman looked her up and down then opened one of the cupboard doors revealing a pile of linen. "Just as well I came in when I did," said Goodman, as she selected some clothes and a towel. She shoved the pile in Nell's arms.

"But he was a priest wasn't he?" Nell said.

"Who, St Peter? God no! By the way, have you got lice? I hope not I'm not supposed to do this until you've had a bath." The woman's arms were strong and she rubbed Nell's wet head with the towel so roughly Nell felt that heat produced by the friction itself would dry it.

"St Peter, a priest! No, he just likes to think he is, that's why he wears that collar back to front. His only purpose is to look after the front gate. That's why we call him St Peter, you know! After St Peter in the Bible." Nell nodded her understanding.

"What did you mean when you threatened him with the Master."

"The Master is Mr Goodman my husband, he's in charge of the place, I'm second in command and we live in. We have our own rooms. It goes with the job. You will be meeting the Master shortly. he will interview you and decide whether your circumstances meet the criteria needed for you to stay here. At best, you will be given a bed and food. In return, you will be expected to work, the nature of which will be decided by the Master. At worst, you will be given a meal and sent on your way. But in your case I don't think that will apply. The Master is also the man who dishes out punishment if you break the rules. He's not cruel but he won't stand any nonsense."

"So why did St Peter look so frightened?"

"For his punishment he had him locked in the dead room for a night. We had a couple of bodies in there that night. I thought the experience had cured him. That is until today, when he tried to get you undressed. No one knows the old sod's real name. Mind you, maybe he's not as daft as he makes out. You're the third young girl he's tried to get to strip for him I'm not sure what he would do if he ever succeeded. I suppose the collar could be part of his scheme. What's your name?"

"Nell Masters."

"Who did this?" Roughly, she turned Nell's chin to view her bruise. "Was it your father?"

"No! I slipped in the snow."

"Yes, of course you did. When is it due?"

"Pardon?"

"The baby! When is it due?"

"Who, I mean, how did you…"

"Don't be stupid girl, I can see you're not mad, and that's the only other reason young girls of your age end up here. How old are you, fifteen-sixteen?"

"Seventeen."

"Your father put you out did he?"

"Well it was something like that," said Nell, not wanting to argue about it. Her teeth started chattering wildly. She had taken off her wet boots and the stone floor was freezing.

"Look, stand on your coat. I'll be back in a minute." The woman left the way she entered and returned carrying a cardigan and a pair of worn boots. "Here, put these on. You can keep the cardigan but you'll have to keep your own dress on until you've had a bath. You're lucky you turned up today. One of our old residents checked out last night so you can have her bed. Otherwise, you would have been curled up on the floor somewhere. We're always full in the winter."

"People do leave here then?" Nell asked, finding the boots too big but grateful to get her bare feet off the floor.

"Yes, some! Old Bessie certainly did. Those are her boots and woolly you've got there. She died in her sleep last night. The boots look a bit big but never mind we'll get yours dried out. Pick them up and follow me."

Nell stared at the retreating woman; surprised at the callousness she'd shown over the death of someone she'd obviously known. She looked down at the boots, they felt uncomfortable and not just because of their size.

Nell followed, almost running to keep pace with the Sister through what seemed like endless corridors. They passed some of the most wretched individuals Nell had ever seen. In trying to keep up Nell did not have time to peer into the wards, but noticed that many had locks hanging from the doors.

Eventually the Sister slowed and was about to enter a ward when the door suddenly burst opened and a female, looking terribly stressed, came rushing out, almost knocking the Sister over.

"For heaven's sake Beryl what's the matter?" Beryl grabbed Goodman's arm, pulling her and shouting something about a needle; she pulled Goodman toward the door and Nell followed.

Nell couldn't fathom whether Beryl was just a girl or an elderly woman. She had seen people with the same look about them. She remembered her mother called it Mongolism.

Goodman and Nell followed the girl/woman through the door. Inside the ward, five or six wretched looking females of mixed ages were pushing and pulling each other, fighting to get a better view inside another room, one which Nell came to know and dread: the bathroom. A place as cold and unfriendly as any she'd seen with its high ceiling and its tangle of metal pipes. A white enamel bucket stood in the corner of its wet concrete floor, which sloped inward from its four walls to a drain grill in the centre. Finally, there was the uninviting, and enormous copper bath. Sister Goodman pulled roughly at the women until they parted to let her through. As they parted, Nell caught sight of what had caused the commotion and the sight sickened and terrified her.

Sat on the cold floor on the far side of the drain sat a woman dressed in a flannel nightshirt, the bottom of which was covered with blood. The nightshirt had been pulled high above her noticeably pregnant stomach, and she seemed oblivious of her audience now crowding around the doorway. She sat with her legs apart, grinning insanely at the blood that trickled from her down the sloping floor to the drain. In her hand she held what looked like a crochet needle, though the thick blood that covered it, made it difficult to ascertain.

Sister Goodman turned to the now hysterical girl and said calmly, "Beryl. Get two porters. They're in C block, and a nurse if you can find one." Beryl dashed out of the ward. "Viv!" Goodman called out, searching faces among the women. Another pregnant young girl of Nell's age stepped forward. "Go through the wards and find the doctor. Just say the word haemorrhage, and tell him to come to P Ward immediately. Then go to the linen room and bring back half a dozen towels."

Viv ran off while Goodman pushed the women out of the bathroom doorway and closed herself inside with the unfortunate and pitiful patient.

Nell waited outside, still holding her bundle of clothes, not knowing what to do. The rest of the women milled around talking excitedly for a while until they started to wander off down the ward. After a few minutes, Beryl came back breathlessly leading two young men. One carried a stretcher, the other, a blanket. Beryl was almost crying as she tried hurrying them by pulling the youngest one by the arm. The two porters were laughing at Beryl's strange antics, and Nell wondered if they knew the seriousness of the situation, or if they did, whether they cared. They entered the bathroom closing the door behind them. No sooner had the door closed, than Viv arrived with the towels. She knocked at the bathroom door. It opened just enough for an arm to grab the towels and for Goodman to shout, "Where's that bloody Doctor?"

Viv started to make some excuse until Goodman slammed the door on her.

The three girls were left outside. Beryl who was still crying, put her arms around Viv for comfort, and Viv led her down the ward to her bed. Nell counted sixteen beds on the ward and seeing only six women, guessed that others must be at work somewhere.

Some minutes later, Sister Goodman came out carrying the white enamel bucket. She held the door open for the two men. Nell stared at the wretched woman's ghastly white face as the men carried the stretcher passed her. The woman's eyes were still open though the insane grin was gone and her skin had the cold look of greyish marble.

The Sister stood beside Nell, the front of her white overall now red with blood. Nell glanced down, inadvertently looking into the bucket then quickly looked away, fighting the urge to vomit.

"Well, she did what she wanted to do." Goodman said to Nell without emotion "She got rid of it, but if the bleeding doesn't stop soon, she'll not see the night through. Now I've got to get rid of this," she said, indicating the bucket, "See the bed on the left at the end of this ward?" Nell nodded. "Take yourself down there and put your clothes on it. When I come back I'll show you how to run a bath." Nell looked uncertainly toward the bathroom door. "Don't worry it's all cleaned up. Then I'll take you to see Mr Goodman. What about work, special skills; have you worked in a kitchen?"

"No but I learnt to sew fairly well. At Boswell's"

"Boswell's. I've heard that name somewhere. I'm sure we can fit you in," she said, taking Nell's bundle of wet clothes from her. "I'll get these taken down to the boiler room to dry, and we'll talk when I comeback. I've got to find that lazy bloody doctor. Then it'll be time to eat."

After meeting Sister Goodman, her husband came as a surprise to Nell; he was Nigerian and this fact alone was surprising as black people were few and far between in the city of Portsmouth, and Nell just did not imagine Sister Goodman being married to a black African. However, Nell found him to be very pleasant with an exceptionally educated dialect. While Mr Goodman did not pry too deeply into her reasons for being there, he was sympathetic to her plight and wished her a pleasant but for her sake, short stay.

Nell was almost asleep that evening, when the murmuring of a soft-spoken voice disturbed her. She sat up, waiting for her eyes to adjust to the darkness. Gradually she made out a tall figure in a black cloak, standing over the bed of the bathroom victim. In the morning, the bed was stripped bare.

Nell discovered that the empty beds belonged to inmates that were working in various parts of the building and grounds. It was this work that contributed to the upkeep of the Workhouse.

In the months that followed Nell conditioned her mind to accept this degrading downturn in her life, pushing aside thoughts of better, though not always happier times.

It was not long before two more suicides took place in the dreaded bathroom, deepening Nell's fear of the place. On many nights when she first arrived, she had silently cried herself to sleep by reliving warm summer days with Alfie Button, and recollections of laughter with Marie only made her sad and morose. She would find herself analysing the events that had brought about her present predicament, but this only rekindled her hatred of Molly Gill, making her angry and short tempered with some of her fellow inmates. However, one of the inmates she befriended was an old lady who came to occupy a vacant bed beside her own.

The first time Nell met her was when Nell returned from her work place where she helped repair and produce the kind of attire that all the inmates were made to wear. As she entered the ward, she saw a commotion going on close to her own bed. Nell hurried down the ward to survey the situation.

Beryl, who Nell discovered was twenty years old, was shouting at the newcomer occupying the bed next to Nell's. Beryl was trying to pull a slipper from the old woman's hands. Nell had been warned that Beryl had often become involved in fights and arguments with other inmates and usually came out the victor. Beryl was no weakling. The old lady was still in bed but only just, Nell could see that if she didn't let go of the slipper, she would soon be on the floor, and she looked too frail to take any kind of fall. Nell intervened with,

"What's going on Beryl?"

The pulling stopped. "She'ths got my thlipper," Beryl lisped.

The old lady, who Nell judged to be in her seventies, looked pleadingly at Nell and shook her head,

"Can I have a look at it?" Nell asked, while gently tugging it from both women's grasp. "Where's the other one?" Nell said, looking down at Beryl's bare feet and noting them to be much too large to fit the slipper.

"It'ths on my bed."

"So where did this one come from?" Beryl said nothing, but stood like a guilty child with her hands behind her back twisting her body to and fro. The old lady fought for breath as she pointed shakily to the locker beside her bed. "Alright Beryl shall we try something that will decide who the slippers really belong to?" Beryl nodded eagerly like it was a game. "OK then come and sit on the end of the bed." Beryl complied with enthusiasm. "Hell! I feel like the prince in Cinderella." Nell whispered to the old lady. Then, kneeling down in front of Beryl she pushed the slipper onto Beryl's foot as far as she could, she then shook her head soulfully. "It's not going to fit is it love?"

Beryl agreed, shaking her head like Nell. "I think you'd better go and get the other one for the lady, don't you, love." Beryl nodded with a smile, jumped off the bed, and skipped off up the ward. She returned with the slipper, lisped a hasty apology then skipped away again.

"You're a very clever girl," said the old lady when Beryl had gone. "How old are you?"

"Seventeen."

"And what's your name?"

"Nell. What's yours?"

"Clare—well Nell, you're quite a little diplomat, Do you know what that means?"

"I think so. I'd say it was someone who stops old ladies falling out of bed." The old lady let out a howl of laughter that turned into a terrible bout of coughing. Nell sat on her bed and gently rubbed her back until the coughing stopped. Nell took a liking to the old lady. She thought that she somehow didn't belong in that place, She spoke with a well-educated tongue and her night attire looked far too expensive, for someone needing the shelter of a workhouse. Nell imagined her to have been a schoolmistress or a businesswoman that fortune had abandoned.

"Can you read, Nell? I mean, can you read well?"

"Yes, why?"

"If you look in my locker you will find some books. Will you take one out?"

Nell did so and read the title out loud. "Little Women."

"Oh! yes, said the old lady excitedly. Now would you read the first few lines?" Nell did so, smoothly and without hesitation.

"That's lovely my dear. Now if you would be willing to read to me for a while in the evenings I will pay you."

"You don't have to do that, I don't mind reading for you, I like reading, but surely wouldn't you rather read for yourself. I mean you do sound educated."

"Oh I can read, but my eyes are really not up to it, they get tired so quickly especially by candle light, but I do so love books they're my only pleasure."

Evening reading sessions became a regular occurrence and Nell found herself enjoying the old lady's company as well as her choice of books. Even when Nell wasn't reading to Clare, she spent a lot of time tending the old lady's needs. She would help her get to the toilet or bathroom. Even if there was a nurse at hand, Clare preferred Nell's help. The only other person to visit the old lady was Sister Goodman who also spent a lot of time with her. Nell found this a little strange because Sister Goodman never fraternised with any of the other inmates or for that matter even the staff. One day Nell met Sister Goodman in the corridor. Pulling Nell to one side, she said:

"Nell, I want to thank you for reading and looking after the old lady in the bed next to yours."

"Why would you thank me? I like her, and I like doing things for her. Besides, I feel sorry for her. She must have had some real bad luck to end up here. She doesn't seem to fit in here if you know what I mean?"

"Well there's a reason for that which I can't go into, but thanks anyway." Nell found it a rather strange incident, she later mentioned it to Clare but the old lady seemed reluctant to comment.

6
A church does not a prison make

Portsmouth prison stood only yards from the workhouse. Its barbed wire flint walls were twenty feet or more in height, towering above those of the workhouse on the opposite side of St Mary's Rd. The prison's head warden, Henry Clifton, now sat at his desk addressing two of his head guards who sat facing him.

"Well Ryan, you've had ample time to get to know him," he said, banging his pipe out in a stone ashtray, "and Benson here wants to use him. Do you think it's safe?"

"Maybe Sir."

"Maybe, is not much good to me. I have to make a decision here, and if we lose Matcher, I'm the one that's got to answer. Oh, I know he wouldn't get far, we're on an island, but I'm thinking about the possible danger to the public."

"I understand that Sir, and I also understand why Benson, here, wants to use him, but if I say it's safe to take him, and he gets away. I'm the one that fingers will point at."

Clifton sat with his elbows on his desk, fingers interlocked and his forehead in furrows of deep thought. The two officers waited patiently.

"I take your point Ryan," he finally said, "and you're right, but alas, it is my decision so let me ask you this, if he did escape, how dangerous do you think he'd be, physically I mean, to the public or assuming we catch him, to any officers involved in his capture?"

"If I can give an opinion sir," said Benson "I know I haven't spent as much time observing Matcher as Ryan here, but for some reason, Matcher opened up to me when he first arrived. I don't know why he chose me. Could be because of my age, maybe he thought I looked a friendly sort."

Ryan gave Warden Clifton a wry smile, knowing his fellow officer was as hard as any other officer in the prison service. "Anyway," Benson went on. "It seems that Matcher fell for some young woman a couple of years back. He worshiped her, apparently. They got married and he worked his socks off to buy her things and keep her happy, but obviously, it wasn't enough. He discovered that she'd been whoring while he was at work. That's when he took to drinking and reaping revenge from prostitutes. I think much of Matcher's troubles have been caused by drink. At his trial, he swore he never touched the old woman. He insists a young prostitute did it."

"He still does," interrupted Ryan.

"Yes I'm sure he's as innocent as a new born baby," Clifton impatiently intervened. "So is every prisoner in here if you chose to believe their stories, but that's not our concern. Our job is to make sure they do their punishment without being a danger to the public.

"But his reputation of violence around the Portsea pubs did him no favours sir. He told me the prosecution produced no end of character witnesses to finish him: prostitutes that he'd knocked about, men that he'd fought with, but it's like he only ever caused trouble when he drank. I think that's what clinched it at his trial. He admitted to being drunk at the old woman's house. Yet since he's been in here, Ryan will tell you, he's been a kitten." Ryan nodded agreement. "At the trial his employers couldn't speak highly enough of him. Apparently, he was their hardest worker and more importantly, he's an experienced roofer. You keep telling us how you want this job rapped up quick! Well that's what the site manager needs: men with experience. The last bloke we sent up on that church roof froze, and someone had to go up and coax him down. I think with Matchers help we'd get the job done a lot quicker Sir."

Cliffton became deep in thought as he considered Benson's words.

"But if you're really worried about him escaping," added Benson. "Maybe you could spare an extra guard, sir."

"Hell!" Cliffton barked, banging his desk. "Wouldn't you think the church could afford to hire private builders for their blasted work? Then I wouldn't have to make decisions like this, but I suppose a work-tired prisoner is less likely to cause us trouble so maybe its better to let him work. OK we'll chance it. Put him in with the work party tomorrow, but watch him like a hawk and I want those repairs completed within a month."

For the next two weeks, while working with his fellow inmates, Oli Matcher was a model prisoner. Repairs carried out on St Mary's church roof were pleasing the site manager. Unfortunately, and forgetting the old adage of complacency being the mother of all mistakes, the warders became less concerned that Oli Matcher would try to escape.

However, Oli's only thought was to do just that. He had no faith in the judicial system. He doubted that his appeal, even if granted, would have a different outcome, unless new evidence could be found. He believed that even his own solicitor thought him to be guilty. His trial had been an open and shut case. His solicitor based his defence on all the evidence being circumstantial. And though the prosecution had no witnesses to the actual murder, his own barrister's presentation was weak and unconvincing.

Oli's violent reputation and a neighbour's account of seeing him entering the old woman's place the evening before the murder was discovered, gave the prosecution all the ammunition they needed for an easy conviction. The trial had all come about so fast and his mind was not clear. Too many drinks over too many years, he told himself. Since being locked up he'd had time to think. Weeks in his cell without a drink had allowed his senses to recuperate. Each night he lay awake reliving that fateful night, trying to remember something. Anything that would prove he never killed the old woman.

Slowly it started to come back to him. Just bits and pieces at first, just a word here and there that the old woman had spoken, but eventually a whole sentence: *Untouched I'll wager but the Gill's sent this one, and they are going to want a few bob."* Yes, that was the name, he thought. The Gill's, they must know who the girl is.

7
The big house

In some respects, life in St Mary's workhouse for Nell did not prove to be a great deal harder than she was already accustomed to. She was fed and clothed, albeit sparingly, and she didn't have to venture out on freezing cold mornings. But she was missing Marie, and there were also the sleepless nights filled with yearning for Alfie Button to contend with. This instilled in her profound sadness, a sorrow she'd not felt since her father died. She tried each night to put Alfie out of her mind, but for too many nights she fell asleep on a tear-soaked pillow.

Given a choice Nell would have chosen her previous life, but that was gone she told herself. Alfie was gone forever, and this thing, this hateful being that was growing inside her was to blame. Whatever was to become of her Nell had no idea. But she told herself she would have to purge her mind of Alfie. This, she did, at least to the point of not crying herself to sleep each night.

There was a dark side to the workhouse. Much of its tradition was to accommodate mental patients, and at that time, little was known of psychiatric therapy. Patients were often housed there with little knowledge of how to deal with them. Apart from the dangers these patients posed to themselves and other inmates, they were often left prey to unscrupulous staff and Nell found that not all the staff were as friendly or trustworthy as Sister Goodman.

Vivien Price, another inmate who had befriended Nell, was a sprightly, young girl, but Viv's lack of confidence was heightened by her illiteracy. This, Nell was to discover, made the girl somewhat clingy. Viv was a year older than Nell and even slighter in build, to the point of frailty.

Like Nell, Viv's mother had disowned her and for similar reasons. Nell discovered this when she was put to work with her.

Both girls were employed in the clothes factory where they were two of 43 workers. Their task was to help manufacture workhouse clothes, bedding and whatever material products benefited the workhouse. Vivien was full of zest and though she lacked Nell's education, the girls friendship was cemented, not only by the similarity of their predicaments but also, by their sense of humour. Vivien had arrived before Nell, having been rescued from freezing to death on a park bench and brought to the workhouse by the park's keeper.

Vivien saw qualities in Nell that drew her to the younger girl: a strength and intelligence that she lacked herself. She felt safe in Nell's presence and in a way drew confidence from just being in her company.

"You spend a lot of time with that old woman Nell. Did you know her before you came here?" whispered Viv as she searched her section of bench for a lost button. Talking was strictly disallowed during working hours so discretion had to be used; the overseer or supervisor had already warned Vivien once that morning.

"Who, Clare? No, She just likes me to read to her."

"I suppose you're good at it."

"Yes I suppose so. Can't you read then?"

Viv waited for the overseer to walk out of earshot. "No I was never very good at reading and writing and that. My mum's feller, Jim, said girls learning all that stuff was a waste of time cause soon as they was old enough they got married and had babies."

"Not always in that order, by all accounts." said Nell looking down at Viv's bulging stomach. Viv let out a squeal of laughter.

The oversized woman supervisor came up behind Viv and twisted her ear saying:

"Look Price, one more peep out of you and I'll run you up in front of the Master. Do you hear me?" It was some minutes before Viv spoke again and only when the supervisor was well out of earshot.

"Yes my uncle Jim said girls learning was a waste of time. That's why he was always keeping me home from school."

"Yes well we already know why he kept you home don't we," said Nell. "I mean the reason is sitting there, in your lap." Viv looked down at her bulging stomach and was about to giggle again, but remembered the supervisors warning. "Why didn't you tell your old lady what he was up to? Maybe she'd have kicked him out."

"I nearly did at first. But he bought me sweets and stuff. And anyway, I didn't mind all that much."

"Tart," exclaimed Nell

"Yeah, sometimes he bought me tarts as well." Forgetting the supervisor, the two burst out laughing.

"Quiet down there. Masters, Price, I won't tell you a third time," came a stern voice from the end of the works.

"Well, so what?" whispered Viv when she thought it was safe. "It doesn't really hurt anyone does it?"

"Are you saying you don't mind if people call you a prostitute?" Viv did not have to answer. Nell could see by the blank look on Viv's face that she either did not, or that she hadn't an opinion one way or the other. And Nell decided that Viv didn't really care.

A bell sounded the midday break and the workers left their posts to congregate in the dining room. Here, they would queue for the main meal of the day. This was usually some kind of broth with a thick slice of bread and a mug of tea. It was laid out on three long tables with bench seats either side.

Nell sat down and Viv elbowed her way in to sit next to her. As Nell sipped her tea, a grey-haired woman on her left leaned toward her and said quietly:

"Boswell's." Nell looked at her in surprise. "You are Nell, aren't you? Sister Goodman said you worked there, is that right?"

"Yes,"

"How is the old lecher, still touching up the young-uns?"

Nell laughed. "You obviously know him then."

"Yeah, I left there about 1893, not long after his father died and young Ivan took the place over, proper like. You must have been a baby then," said the woman.

"Yes I was." Nell suddenly became aware that Viv was fidgeting like a schoolgirl. "What's the Matter with you Viv, haven't you got enough room?"

"Well you aren't talking to me!" Viv said, pouting like a spoiled child.

"Hell Viv, we talk all bloody day. Now don't be rude." With that, Viv got up and sat at another table. From there, she kept darting evil looks at the old woman next to Nell.

"Sorry love didn't mean to cause trouble," the woman said to Nell.

"Oh don't worry. Viv just gets a bit possessive. So how long were you there at Boswell's?"

"About six years, until I couldn't do the work anymore. That's when the bastard sacked me." The woman looked down at her hands and Nell followed her gaze. They were so gnarled and misshapen with arthritis that Nell had to look away. "I can manage this OK though. Anyone can sew crocheted blankets together." Nell felt sorry for the woman. Then a bell sounded.

"Maybe we can chat again," said the woman. "My name's Betty."

That afternoon Viv found herself another workplace to sit and Nell decided to let her sulk.

Oli Matcher was not a stupid man, at least not when he was sober, and his escape was not a clumsy affair. He had been planning it since his first day's work on the church. Working up on the roof had allowed him to take note of the comings and goings of the church staff and the routine of the warders. He studied the layout of the church's interior from the openings in the roof. Conveniently, he left the last of the roof tiles to be laid, at a location where he could easily climb down through the rafters. Having reached the church floor, he entered the deserted vestry where he found the ideal hiding place: a huge window box, filled with priests' discarded robes. He climbed in, pulling the clothes over him, and here he waited patiently for nightfall.

It wasn't long before he heard loud and excited voices and the sound of doors banging. He knew the hunt for him had begun. At one point he felt that his heart would beat its way through his chest when he heard the vestry door being thrown open and the sound of heavy boots right beside his hiding place. He held his breath as he heard the creak of the box being opened and waited for what he thought was inevitable: a warder's hand reaching down through the priests clothing to finally grab him. Suddenly distant shouting caused his would be captor to drop the heavy wooden lid and make a hasty retreat. Eventually all was quiet again and he knew their search had widened beyond the church grounds. He guessed the search would now take in the whole of Portsmouth, he also knew they would not give up. All he could do was wait until dark. Matcher knew this was his one and only chance to prove his innocence and that to fail was to meet with the gallows.

To the authorities, Matcher's escape had confirmed his guilt. They believed that he would try to get as far from Portsmouth as possible, so all their efforts were put to this effect. The Hilsea Lines* were closely guarded. Ferry ports and train stations were heavily guarded. With police resources stretched to such an extent, Matcher could walk almost freely through the city. He now had purpose and determination, and no one was looking for a man in a priest's hat and robes.

The following evening Nell sat beside Clare's bed. A candle supplemented the inadequate gas light over the old woman's bed that Nell needed to read. Clare had fallen asleep as most of the ward had; working days were long and there was not much else to keep one occupied in the evening.

As Nell read quietly to herself, she heard soft footsteps approaching along the ward. It was Betty.
"Hello love. What are you reading?
"Oh hello! I was just tiring myself out ready for bed. I read for this lady here, but she's fallen asleep."

*Portsmouth's line of defence from the mainland.

"Oh that's nice of you dear. I thought I'd best come and tell you to have a word with your friend Vivien. I just saw her and that little porter they call Bob, going into one of the linen stores. She'll be in hot water if the master finds out."

"But she's only got a few weeks to go surely you don't think she'd...I mean he wouldn't want..."

"Oh get wise girl, it don't make no difference to some blokes. I just wouldn't want to see her get kicked out on the street not when she's just going to have the kid.

"I'll talk to her tomorrow," Nell said. "But I'm not sure it will make any difference. She's a strange one is Viv. Did you know she's going to give her baby away?"

"That doesn't surprise me, a lot of them do that. Well what do you expect? Can't bring a kid up proper in a place like this, 'taint right. Speaking of which, I hear you're having one. It doesn't belong to that lecherous Boswell, does it? I mean, tell me to mind my own business if you like, but I remember what he was like."

"No it's not like that." Nell said without wishing to elaborate.

"Oh, well it wouldn't be the first time he'd got one of his workers in the family way."

"Really!"

"Oh yes," said Betty, pulling up a chair. "It happened when I worked there. Pretty young thing she was too. Dirty bugger was engaged to another girl called Irene Little at the time. Mind you, her family was a bit well to do, so he wasn't going to give her up."

"Yes Irene! You're right that's his wife's name. So, what happened to the pregnant girl? Can you remember her name?" A whirlpool of dates questions and predetermined answers, started to impede Nell's ability to absorb Betty's words.

"Sacked her, what else? Word had it he paid her a lot of money to keep it secret, but we all knew it was his kid. Blimey, the two of them were disappearing out to the stable nearly every day. Some of us would creep out to the washhouse and listen. Blimey! That gal didn't take much coaxing, not from the noises coming out of there."

"Yes but what was her name?"

"Do me a favour love! That was sixteen or more years ago and I hadn't been working there long enough to get to know any of the workers. But I do remember she moved into a house near me, one of those roads off Queen Street it was: Lyons Terrace, do you know it?"

Nell never slept that night. A cascade of questions plagued her, to which answers were not easily forthcoming, and those that were, created anger that would only be suppressed by confronting her mother. She lay there reliving the day her mother had thrown her out. How could she, Nell reflected, for something she herself was guilty of?

Yes, Nell was sure Boswell was her father, it all made sense: Getting a job at Boswell's for which she was not really qualified, Boswell, always touching the younger women, yet never trying it on with her. There were other things too, things that her mother had said. *"Don't let him get too friendly I know what he's like."* Yes, Nell thought angrily she would.

Before daylight came, Nell had made up her mind. She would return home, if only to let her mother know that she'd discovered the truth, and to return some of the verbal venom that her mother had given her.

The following day Viv was back sitting next to Nell having forgotten her tantrum.

"You're quiet Nell what's up?" Viv said, holding out a bag of sweets. Nell took one.

"Nothing that concerns you. Where did you get these?"

"Up the shop."

"I know that! I meant where did you get the money?" Nell sounded annoyed. "You told me you never had any yesterday."

"A friend gave me it. Why are you being so horrible to me?"

"That friend wouldn't be a little man in a white coat called Bob would it."

Viv giggled. "Why would a little man call his coat Bob?"

Nell was not amused. "You know what I bloody well mean," she said, raising her voice.

"Masters!" came the irate voice of supervisor. "Stop talking."
The two girls remained quiet for a while, but Nell looked up to see
Betty staring at her, mouth slightly agape. Nell wondered, had the
calling out of her name jarred the old woman's memory? Or had she
recalled the face of the young woman that Boswell had seduced and
realised the likeness?

Suddenly a siren sounded. Inmates peered worriedly about them
waiting for someone to explain. Someone said it's the prison, while
another argued that it was too far away. The eerie wailing sound
went on for some time. The no-talking rule was ignored as workers
speculated on the siren's meaning. After it stopped, a porter came
into the workroom and whispered to the supervisor. Soon the news
travelled throughout the works that a prisoner had escaped and on
everyone's lips was the name: Oli Matcher.

8
The Return

Nell spent another uncomfortable night dodging horrifying monsters. They chased her relentlessly, ruining what little sleep she managed to get. She awoke long before dawn, realising that all her nightmarish fiends were one man, Oli Matcher, monster. That was how she'd come to think of him, yet the only description she had of him was based on the gossip she'd heard in Boswell's and this strengthened her conviction that he was a monster, a beast that had created this thing inside her. She imagined the child she carried would turn out to be a vile replica of Matcher and the thought of nurturing it as its mother, filled her with revulsion.

Nell had heard a lot of talk, especially there in the workhouse, of how one could abort babies. Most, if not all, the methods were old wives tales but even so, she might have considered attempting one, if not for the bathroom episode on her first day there.

She put the birth out of her mind and tried to concentrate on the questions that needed answers: questions about Matcher.

Did he come back that day to rob the old woman? And had the old woman recovered enough to put up a fight? No, she reasoned, even if the old woman was still alive after falling down the stairs she was in no condition to put up any resistance to a man of his stature and reputation. So, why would he stab a frail old woman, as the rumours suggested? Maybe it was to ensure she never spoke to the police.

But then if the old woman had a fortune hoarded away like everyone said, what did he do with it? It was reported that the police never found it.

Nell started to have doubts about his guilt. Did he just escape to avoid the hangman's rope, she asked herself, or would he come looking for her?

Matcher had always maintained that a young prostitute had committed the murder so he must have really thought that she was there just for the money. He had left her alone in the house with the old woman so for him to believe the old woman's death was Nell's doing was only logical. Where was he now, though? What would she do if faced with his predicament? Maybe lack of sleep caused the answer to evade her.

Early that same morning Vivien Price was shaken from her sleep. She opened one eye to see that Nell was fully clothed, and standing over her.

"Bloody hell Nell! What time is it? Are we late for work or something? Why have you got your coat on?"

"Shush, it's not six yet," Nell whispered. "Have you got any money, I need some tram fare? I would have asked Clare but I didn't want to wake her."

"Oh, I see, but it was alright to wake me, cow!" Viv said rubbing her eyes.

"Well the old lady needs her beauty sleep. But you're past caring," Nell said, grinning.

"Bleedin' cheek. Anyway, where are you going? You are coming back?" Suddenly Viv's own words seemed to awaken her fully. She sat up and grabbed Nell's arm. "You are coming back, Nell?" Viv repeated anxiously.

"Don't worry. I'll pay you back."

"You know that's not what I meant. I just don't want you to leave me here on my own."

"Ok, I promise I'll come back. But there's something that I must do and I don't know how long I'll be." This seemed to calm the older girl.

"How much d-you want. " Viv said, pulling back the corner of her mattress to reveal a sheet of cardboard on which lay a mass of silver and copper coins.

"I don't believe it Viv! How many times have you been in that linen cupboard?" Viv giggled and picked up a fistful of coins. She dropped them in Nell's open palms saying,

"There you go. Now piss off and let me get my beauty sleep or I'll have to drop my rates."

"Oh another thing," answered Nell. "Would you look in on Clare, see if she needs anything."

"Bloody hell! Anything else?"

Nell did not have long to wait for a tram. The streets were crowded with workers at that time of the morning. The biggest problem for tram drivers, was trying not to run down one of the hundreds of cyclists that were all making their way to the Portsmouth dockyard. The biggest hazard to cyclists, though most comical, was when a cyclist caught his wheel in a tramline. Then a whole heap of them would pile on top of each other. Luckily, there was little other traffic on the road at that time.

Twice Nell's tram was stopped by police and searched. On the second occasion, one irate passenger had words with one of the two policemen that boarded,

"Oi mate you're gonna make us all late! That bugger Matcher's long gone by now."

"You're probably right son, but we're only doing as ordered," said the officer as he waited for his fellow peeler to come down from the top deck.

Passengers by now were in no doubt who the law was looking for; the news of the escapee had spread through the city with the speed of a forest fire.

It was 7.15 and almost daylight, when Nell reached her stop. She walked along Queen Street towards Lyons Terrace. Once, she ducked into a doorway when spotting two Boswell employee's walking toward her, presumably on their way to work.

She turned into Lyons Street and started to walk slowly along it. It was nearly 7.30. She knew that her mother left for work around that time and she half expected to see her emerge on to the pavement at any moment. Nell was nervous, every word she intended to say to her mother had been so apt and clear in her mind the previous night, but this was when the sleepless tossing and turning had stirred her anger into fever pitch. Now, in the light of day she wasn't so sure. She practised the intended speech in her mind as she walked slowly along Lyons Terrace, but the words now seemed over harsh and hurtful, and this Matcher business was confusing her.

She walked up to the door and was about to knock, but lost her nerve and walked past it glancing quickly through the front window and into the darkness of the front room. She thought she saw movement but was not sure. It would be unusual for her mother to be in there as it was kept only for special occasions and to receive guests, although she couldn't remember the last time one had called. Nell called it the posh room as it housed the best of their furnishings, such as they were.

She walked on for a few yards then turned back. This time she stopped and raised the knocker. Suddenly the door swung inwards and in seconds, she was dragged, sprawling on the passage floor. The door slammed and Nell found herself looking up at a huge man dressed in a long priests cape.

Nell knew this was the core of her nightmares; the beast that had made her pregnant, but he was not quite what she had imagined. He was far from ugly, though the sheer size of him was enough to terrify any young girl, Let alone one that believed him to be capable of murder.

Where's my mother?" Nell said defiantly, as she looked into eyes that were filled with menace. Matcher ignored the question as he stood with his great boots straddled either side of her. "You're Oli Matcher. You murdered that old woman, and I suppose your going to murder me now. Why not, you've already raped me, you filthy murderous beast?" Nell was surprised at her own doughty defiance. Matcher let out a kind of growl and lifted a boot over her face. Resigned to her fate, Nell closed her eyes and waited to be dealt a quick death.

Moments passed before she realised nothing had happened. Suddenly she felt the skin of her chest being painfully pinched as Matcher grabbed the lapels of her coat with one hand and hoisted her to her feet. He marched her backwards into the front room. Still holding her, he spoke through gritted teeth,

"I never murdered anyone you little bitch, and you know it, what's more I've never raped any female but if I had it wouldn't be a bloody prostitute."

Nell was remembering his voice but even though he was irate and dangerous, he didn't seem as frightening as his reputation had her believing. There was a hint of softness in the dark brown eyes. Nell thought he might even be described as handsome. But she pushed these negative thoughts from her mind, and faced the present situation.

"You're a liar! You raped me and you murdered that old woman." Nell spat the words defiantly at him while trying to pry his fingers from her lapels. Angrily he brought his right arm across in a motion to hit her with the back of his hand. It stopped inches from her face and he let out another growl. Matcher stared at her for a moment before shoving her backwards, forcing her to fall back onto the settee. He then drew the curtains and in the semi-darkness, Nell believed her short life was about to end.

"Now you sit there and listen," he said, to Nell's relief. "People know that I'm here, so I haven't much time. I paid that old woman for a prostitute and that was you! When I left the old woman, she was alive and well."

Nell was only half listening having suddenly remembered why she'd gone there.

"What have you done with my mother?" she shouted, as tears clouded her eyes. Then she heard a meek and frightened voice call out,

"I'm alright Nell."

"And she will be if she stay's put," said Matcher. "Now then, you killed the old woman and took her money hoping that I'd get the blame and it might have worked if I hadn't remembered something the old woman said to me. Now you're going to own up and tell me what you did with the old woman's money. Then you're going to tell the police when they get here, or I'm going to beat it out of you."

Nell couldn't help feeling that maybe this giant was somehow genuine. Maybe he was innocent, but the fact remained that the old lady was stabbed and Nell knew that she had not done the deed. However, it was too soon to make any rash judgments. And if he didn't murder the old woman, she asked herself, then who did?

"Rubbish!" she said with an air of defiance, "You came back after I'd left and stabbed her twice in the heart." Nell could not believe her own nerve, speaking as she was to this giant of a man and most likely, murderer.

Oli looked at Nell quizzically. "Who told you that she was stabbed twice?"

"I don't know. I read it in the paper I think. Or heard someone talking about it. Anyway I know I didn't do it, even though I wanted to stab both of you."

"Why?"

"Why!" Nell echoed indignantly "After what you did? You— you… " With that Nell buried her head in the crook of her arm and cried like she'd done for so many nights in the Workhouse. Oli left the room, he came back moments later and threw her a towel.

"Here, dry your eyes, and stop snivelling. I'm the one with something to cry about. I got the bloody hangman's shadow following me."

"You don't know what I've been through." Nell said trying to compose herself. "I was tricked into going to that house, and that old woman drugged me." At this point Nell saw a slight reaction from the giant.

"What do you mean, tricked?" he said.

"I was told it was the house of my sick friend. When I got there, I was half frozen. The old woman never told me I was at the wrong house. Instead, she took me in and gave me something she said was to warm me up. I don't remember much more." The corners of Nell's mouth turned down in a gesture of contempt as she said, "But you know don't you! I woke up in that filthy room and grabbed the clothes you had torn from me." Nell looked at him with increasing hostility. Oli coloured and shifted about uncomfortably. "I dashed out of that room," Nell continued. "That's when I met the old woman on the landing, she tried to give me money like I was some common whore. When I knocked it out of her hand she started to fall backwards down the stairs. I tried to grab her but her clothes tore. She lay still at the bottom of the stairs. She must have been unconscious, but I thought she was dead, and at the time, I was glad. That's when I left." Nell scowled at Oli again. " But she wasn't, was she? Because you came back and murdered her and I hope they hang you."

Suddenly it was as if the anger had left him as he said. "If you're telling the truth I don't blame you," he said, peering nervously out into the street through a gap in the curtains. "I can see how young you are now, when I get drunk I don't really like myself. For what its worth, I'm sorry. But I'm telling the truth, I never came back."

Nell stared at him long and hard, trying to gauge his honesty. "And I suppose you never stabbed her?" She said sarcastically.

"No! And if the paper said she was stabbed twice, they got it wrong. The examiner testified that there were two puncture wounds, and that he thought it could have been done with partly opened scissors."

Nell sat staring up at him, open-mouthed.

"You still don't believe me, do you?"

"No, I mean yes. But I just remembered the last thing I heard the old woman say. She said: "The Gill's sent this one. They're going to want a few bob". Nell repeated the words just as she remembered them. She could also hear a commotion outside as she watched the frown disappear from Oli's brow. He too had remembered something, something he'd seen less than an hour ago when the Gill sisters had told him Nell's address: scissors, hanging from Rose Gill's waist.

Oli Matcher had no reason to resist arrest. He was not afraid of going back to prison now. He knew that with Nell's evidence he would be acquitted. After a police inspector had a few words with Nell about attending another trial, they led Matcher away.

Violet Masters had heard most of the conversation between Matcher and Nell while tied to a chair in the next room. She appeared to be full of remorse for the way she'd treated Nell. However, Nell did not feel very forgiving. She was not going to brush aside the terrible experience that her mother's spiteful scorn had put her through. There was also the matter of Betty Graham's account of the past, which put a significant question mark by Nell's birthright.

As the Black Mariah pulled away from the house with Oli on board, inquisitive neighbours and onlookers slowly dispersed.

Violet was pleased that Nell was home and she so wanted Nell's forgiveness for her own mistaken assumption of past events. Nell was still full of pent up anger, but her mother was in such a humble and self-critical mood that Nell could not bring herself to air the venomous outburst that she had mentally enacted through her long restless night. Yes, for a while, Violet was sweetness itself and when Nell told her that she was not staying, her mother became tearful, pleading for her to stay. Nell eventually agreed, but Violet's, new found, pleasant disposition did not last.

A week later, Nell was clearing the dinner table:
"Nell, I'm surprised you never told Mr Matcher about his ... you know," Violet motioned and glanced in the direction of Nell's stomach as if reluctant to mention the word, child or baby.
"No, and I don't want him to know."
"Why not? If he's the father, he should take some of the responsibility we're not made of money you know. You never know, he might feel obligated to share the responsibility. He didn't seem that bad, once things were straightened out. I mean, how long am I supposed to keep us both."

For the last week Violet had been the perfect mother: soft-spoken, kind and apologetic, but out of this last statement Nell detected the old Violet Masters returning; the one that would soon be demanding that Nell be out earning, or doing more around the house. The anger that Nell had brought back home had subsided over the last week and now suddenly it was about to spill over.
"Yes, or maybe I could just blackmail him like you blackmailed Boswell." said Nell. Her mother stared at her open-mouthed for some moments before spluttering: "What, Who...are you suggest..."
Nell ignored her blather and continued, "I met a woman in the workhouse," Nell noticed a slight frown on Violet's brow with the mention of the workhouse. "Yes the workhouse! I know you prefer St Mary's House, but that's what it is! The workhouse." Nell repeated. "Where did you think I'd go when you threw me out with nothing, The Queens Hotel? I spent the first night in a doorway and nearly froze to death." As Nell paused to let her words sink in, Violet started to voice excuses.
"But I didn't know, I mean you wouldn't tell me who...."

"Who the father was? No, and now you know why. But you were so quick to label me a whore. And I know why. Because you thought, like mother like daughter."

"Now you stop this…"

Nell ignored her mother's weak retaliation and went on, "This woman I mentioned," Nell said, studying her mother's reaction. "She worked at Boswell's when you were there." Violet's look of embarrassment confirmed Nell's belief and she continued. "It seems that while Boswell was engaged to the woman who is now his wife, he was getting a bit on the side."

"Is this the kind of filth they taught you in that place?" Violet said, but her anger had died and Nell read defeat on her face.

"Oh you'd be amazed at what they teach you in that place, Mother. Ever seen someone try to give them self an abortion with a crochet needle? I have, it's not very pretty. You wouldn't believe how much blood comes away. And did you know; you can actually hang yourself with the springs from a bed? I saw…"

"Stop it," said Violet angrily. "I said I was sorry, I thought you were staying with a friend. You don't have to go into all the…."

"You were the bit on the side," Nell interrupted. "And I was the result. That's the truth isn't it, that's why you were able to get me that job, because Boswell is my real father."

"Look, Nell love, none of that matters now, I mean what difference does it make. You're still my daughter and …"

"Did dad know?"

"What?"

"Did dad know that I wasn't his?"

"Yes." Violet said solemnly. She appeared as someone drained of energy. As if the secret she had carried for such a long time had worn her down. "We were not married when I fell for you. Jack married me to give you a name. For that he got a home, bought and paid for by Boswell. It was a marriage of convenience, but he was a good husband and I came to love him very much. He certainly loved you."

"I know he did." Nell tried to picture Jack Master's face, but anger seemed to be clouding her mind. Tears began to cloud Violet's eyes and her chin started to quiver.

"Can you forgive me, Nell? Can't we start again? This house is really more yours than mine." Nell had never seen her mother look so defenceless or pathetic. Nell fought the urge to embrace her, but couldn't stop herself. They held each other for some moments letting their tears flow freely. When they finally drew apart, Nell sniffed back the last of her tears, saying,

"You're my mother and I love you, but right now I'm too angry to forgive anyone for what I've been through. I can never go back to work in that factory, and now I don't feel that I can stay here. I've made new friends now and I'm going back to them. Maybe I'll come to visit." With that Nell unhooked her coat from the door, kissed her mother on the cheek and said quietly, "Bye Mum."

9
The high life

Nell's popularity was evident as she entered her ward in St Mary's House. The smiles she received made her feel like she'd come home. Viv Price in particular was overjoyed to see her. She ran up and hugged Nell as she came through the ward doors.

"Everyone's been asking about you," said Viv. "Especially Sister Goodman. She was ever so upset when you disappeared and I didn't know what to tell her.

"Why? I would have thought she'd be pleased to have one less on her register."

"I don't know about that, but she said to tell you to go to her office if you came back."

"Oh God! I'm for it."

Nell decided to call on Clare first, to apologise for leaving without saying goodbye. She was surprised to find the old lady still in her bed so early. But her face lit up at the sight of Nell. Nell bent to kiss the old lady's cheek and as she did Clare put her arms around Nell's neck pulling the girl to her. With her face held to the old lady's chest Nell was concerned at the sound of Clare's breathing, she said nothing to Clare but decided to mention it to Sister Goodman.

"You didn't think I had gone for good, did you Clare?"

"I didn't know what to think! No one could tell me anything."

"Well I see you have some new books, who brought…?"

"I did." said a familiar voice. Nell turned to see Sister Goodman standing over her. "Would you come to my office, Nell, I want to talk to you?"

Nell pulled Clare's covers up, and tucking them in, said: "See you later love. Be back for a chat,"

Nell followed the sister to her office wondering just how much trouble she was in. Would they throw her out for going absent without permission Nell wasn't sure what to expect. She was convinced that her reasons for going absent were excusable, but she really didn't want to voice them for obvious reasons.

Sister Goodman closed the door as Nell followed her into her office. "Take a seat Nell."

"Look! I'm sorry," Nell blurted out. "I know I should have asked before I disappeared like I did. But can I just say something, and I don't want you to think I'm interfering but I think a doctor should look at Clare, I've just...."

"That's already being dealt with, her doctor is on his way to see her."

"Her doctor? I don't... "

"Yes I'll explain some other time, and I know you had good reason to run off like you did..."

"You know! How?"

"I'll come to that but that's not why I've asked you in here. You're here because I have an offer to make to you." Nell's bewilderment was self-evident.

"An offer of what?"

"No. Not yet. Before I tell you anymore I'd like you to take a little trip."

The following day Nell found herself once again riding on trams, and this time it required changing trams twice to reach her destination. Her journey was to take her north past the Hilsea Lines to the mainland. Eventually to a familiar setting that brought back very fond memories. She was surprised when Sister Goodman handed her the tram fare and a set of instructions. She had even ordered the kitchen to prepare a packed lunch to take with her. Nell was intrigued with her mission, but for all her questions, all Sister Goodman would say is,

"It will all be made clear when you get back!"

Though still cold, it was a beautiful morning and quite comparable to a spring day. The journey seemed to be uncomfortably long but the view of the countryside was a pleasant change from the smoke stained streets and cobbled alleys of Portsmouth.

The journey gave her time to think about her talk with Sister Goodman, as she looked out at the unfamiliar villages and districts that formed the island of Portsmouth.

She thought how different the Sister had seemed from that first dreadful day at St Mary's Workhouse. Her hard, almost spiteful, manner with which the sister had first received her had gone and though she still spoke in a terse and forthright tone, there was now more than a hint of kindness in her voice.

The tram was well out of the city limits and only one or two passengers were left on it when Nell noticed that the two shires pulling the tram were not finding their task so easy. They were on a steep incline and she remembered Alfie Button calling it Portsdown Hill.

"Big hearts and tiny minds," the conductor said to Nell.

Nell sat at the front of the tram where the driver had been making small talk to her since she boarded. "I often wonder what goes on inside their heads, if anything," he said grinning at Nell.

"Pardon?"

"Bessie and Sal! The horses. I often wonder what they think every time they have to pull us up this hill, the poor brutes. Cold, wind or rain, they don't complain and they never refuse."

"Yes, I've always loved horses," Nell said as she recalled the link with her golden haired Alfie.

Five minutes later and with no coaxing from the driver, the horses came to a halt.

"Yes I sometimes wonder if they need a driver, Bessie and Sal know just where to stop. Well, here we are love, this is the George Inn, where you wanted to get off. Now look, we change horses at Horndean and we're due back here about 11oclock, that's if you're going back with us, OK?" Nell thanked him and watched the tram move slowly down the road on the northern side of the hill where it would pass the villages of Purbrook, Waterlooville, Cowplain and finally, its last stop, Horndean.

Nell stood gazing at the horse trough outside the pub, where she remembered Alfie giving Pegasus his well-earned drink, when a voice said, in a broad Hampshire accent,

"What's up gal, you lost?" It came from one of two elderly men sat on a wooden bench beside the horse trough. Nell guessed they were farmers. They stared at Nell with curiosity.

"No not really, but I'm looking for Clearview House."

"Up the road gal." He said, motioning with the pewter tankard he was holding.

"Taint far," said the other. "Can't miss it gal, it's the biggest house up there. Name's on the wall, beside the gate."

"Nell thanked them and followed the directions by trudging up another short incline. She then followed the road eastward, to her right, chalk hills swept down to the village of Cosham and beyond this, the city of Portsmouth. Nell stopped to drink in the breath taking view, while trying to discern some landmark that she could relate to. It didn't take long before she recognised the four spires of St Mary's church or Portsmouth's coastline where the blue waters of the Solent stretched across to the Isle of Wight.

To Nell's left, large and grand houses stretched along the crest of Portsdown Hill. Each house purposely situated for its panoramic view over the downs and coastline.

She thought how peaceful it was up there, and compared it with the drab, smoke-stained, district of Portsea somewhere out in the distance.

There was not a person to be seen. Nell followed the road as instructed and as she passed houses that could only be described as mansions she gazed in awe through their gates at the beautiful lawns and driveways that fronted them. Finally, she came to a large pair of green painted iron gates that were easily wide enough to drive a carriage through. The name on the brass plaque set in the wall confirmed her arrival: Clearview House.

Nell pulled a large bolt out of the ground and pushed the gate open. She entered and followed a winding shingle path through overhanging willows for a hundred feet or more. The path circled a lawn in front of a huge house to rejoin the path again.

Nell stood inside a large porch facing stained glass panels in double doors. She raised the lion head knocker but as she did, she heard a bolt slide with a clunk on the inside. The door opened and a white haired lady stood there looking somewhat disapprovingly at Nell's humble attire. The woman spoke sharply and in a west-country accent.

"I suppose you're Nell, are you? I expected you earlier, come in."

Nell found herself standing in a huge tiled hall. She stared around her, wide-eyed, at glossy wood panelled walls, and the magnificent semi-circular staircase enclosed by its ornate handrail. She stared with wonder at the feature of modern science that she'd only ever seen in a post office: a shiny black telephone on a highly polished hall table. Nell had only read about such places. She introduced herself apologetically.

"How do you do. Yes, my name is Nell Masters. Sorry if I've caused you any inconvenience." The woman's manner softened.

"That's alright my dear. Mrs Hilda Brough's my name. I'm the housekeeper and responsible for the staff here. Unfortunately, they have been stood down until the mistress returns. That means they get an allowance to be on standby, but I still come in to do a bit of dusting, open windows to keep the place aired, that sort of thing. That's what I was doing when I got the telephone message. My orders were to show you around the place, so I've stayed on special like."

"I suppose it was Sister Goodman that spoke to you?" Nell inquired.

"Oh I don't know about any Sister; it was Miss Pauline that I spoke to. It was nice to hear her voice after such a long time. It reminded me of the old days when she and her sister Sarah were running about the place. Funny though, the way she just told me to show you around."

"In what way, funny?"

"Well I usually conduct the interviews with any new staff, but I wasn't asked to interview you, just to show you the place. Anyway I'm all behind today so enough of the gossiping and lets be getting on."

Nell was becoming more confused by the minute. Could Sister Goodman be a part of this place? If so, why was she working in St Mary's House? Maybe this Miss Pauline was someone else entirely, someone she'd not yet met.

Nell was amazed at the size of Clearview House and complimented Hilda on how nice the rooms had been kept.

"Well it's what we're paid for," said Hilda, opening another door. "Now Miss Pauline especially asked me to show you this room. I don't know why. This was her room and all the servants' rooms are downstairs."

"It's really lovely," said Nell.

"Yes quite small compared with the others though. We call this the pink room. Come and look at the view," Hilda said opening a window. Nell peered out and found the scene breathtaking. The window was high enough to overlook the willows at the front of the house giving a panoramic view of the whole south coast stretching from Gosport to Hayling Island.

"Well it's easy to see why it was named Clearview," said Nell.

"Yes, you're right, but Mrs Rutherford told me that it wasn't the first choice of names. The master, Mr Rutherford, who had the house built, wanted to name it after his young wife. But she didn't like the idea, she thought it was too pretentious so they came to a compromise, and called it Clearview. See! Take out a few letters and her name is still there, Clare!"

Suddenly in Nell's mind a curtain had been opened, and the mysterious reason for her being there had suddenly come a little closer to revealing itself.

Hilda went on to show Nell everything from the stables and paddock to the gazebo at the bottom of the garden.

"What a lovely carriage," Nell said when Hilda opened the stable door. "Oh and what beautiful horses," She said, bounding up to the grey and fearlessly stroking its head.

Nell's short romance with Alfie Button had accustomed Nell to horses, expelling any fear she might previously have had of them.

"Yes they are. That one's called Chevron because of the white marking down his face. Miss Sarah named them. The white one is called Denver. Don't ask me why, but Sarah did spend some time in America with her father.

The Master wanted to have Denver put down after the accident, but the mistress wouldn't hear of it. Mistress Clare said it wouldn't bring Miss Sarah back."

"Are you saying their daughter Sarah died through riding this horse? That's awful."

"Yes. Denver was her favourite. And she rode him so well. That's why it was such a shock that he'd thrown her, especially as she'd ridden him the same route every day. Come, follow me, I'll show you!"

Hilda led Nell outside and to the end of the stable. "Look!" Hilda said pointing down the north side of the hill. "You see that wooded area at the bottom of the hill?"

"Yes."

"That's where it happened, See the gap in the trees where the track goes through?"

"Yes."

"Well that's called Bluebell Copse. Of course, it's too early for bluebells yet. But when Miss Sarah...." Hilda suddenly paused and looked tearful. "Well anyway that's where it happened. Mind you, Thompson said he warned her. She used to ride through those trees like a thing possessed. When Denver came back without her, I think we all expected the worst. Then Thompson came puffing and panting up the hill to tell us the bad news. Come to think of it the lazy man should have been here by now to tend these horses."

"That is very sad. How long ago did it happen?"

"It will be two years ago this May. Mr Rutherford died a year after but I think he started to become ill when Pauline left home. He became almost a recluse, avoiding all the staff and shutting himself away like he did, but I think it was the death of Sarah that really finished him." Hilda was silent for a while as Nell followed her back toward the house, and Nell knew she was remembering happier days. They reached the house and as Hilda's sadness abated, she said, "Well I can see you're not afraid of the brutes. Thompson comes in to feed and check on them, he was supposed to come in first thing this morning."

"Who is Thompson?"

"The driver, dear," answered Hilda as if Nell had just asked which planet they were on. God, he's such a lazy man, I don't know how he's kept the job. I was supposed to get him to come and fetch you, but he wasn't home when I called on him. Probably in The George, I shouldn't wonder. He practically lives in that place since they took on a young barmaid." Arriving back at the starting point, Hilda said:

"Well that's it, dear. What do you think?"

"Oh I think the house is beautiful. And thank you for showing me around."

"So you'll be taking the position then."

"Position! What position?"

"Well I thought that you would tell me! Isn't that the reason I've been showing you over the house? I presumed it must be for an opening of some kind. Have you not been in service before?"

"Do you mean like a maid or something?"

"Yes."

"No never!"

Nell caught the eleven o'clock tram as planned and found Sister Goodman sitting in her office when she arrived back at St Mary's House. She looked up as Nell entered and in her usual terse manner said,

"Well? What did you think?"

"Yes I thought it was beautiful. But I'm not sure…"

"You're wondering what this is all about. Well sit down and I'll explain." Nell sat pensively on the edge of the only other chair in the room. "Clare, the old lady that you've befriended, owns Clearview House." Nell's mouth opened in disbelief even though she suspected a link.

"Why would she be here in…?"

"She's my mother. I talked her into coming here so that I could look after her. She has a serious chest complaint as you have discovered, and she wasn't eating enough or looking after herself. However, I now think that bringing her here was a mistake. She's likely to pick up more ailments if she stays in this place. The only thing that seems to have done her any good is you. She refuses to go back home unless you go with her. So we talked it over and decided to make you an offer."

"Are you Pauline?"

"Yes," the nurse smiled. "Hilda's obviously dropped some names."

"Yes, she also mentioned your sister…"

"Yes, Sarah died. That, and the loss of my father, is what I believe caused my mother's illness; it is the reason this situation has come about. Now you are being offered the position…"

"But I've never… I mean I don't know the first…"

"Of course not, you're very young, and I'll be honest, I think you're too young to be offered this position. However, my mother believes you're intelligent and my mother is usually right. Also, there's little for you to know, you'll do as my mother asks and as the position's title suggests, you will be her companion. In other words just do what you've been doing, be kind to her. Now that my father and sister are gone she needs someone, and I can't be there. The house is taken care of by its employees. Did Hilda show you the pink room? That would be your room because it's next to mothers and it has a bell installed. She'll ring if she needs you."

At this point Pauline got up and with her back to Nell stared out of the window. Her hand went up to her face and Nell thought she might have been crying. After a few moments, she sat back down.

"Can I ask a question?" Nell said.

"Of course."

"Your Mother must be very well off, and you obviously love her very much. Why not give this up and live at Clearview yourself."

"I can't. You see my husband is devoted to this work and I have devoted myself to him, Besides, Clearview would uproot a lot of memories for me that I'd rather leave buried. Now, you will be paid an allowance of ten shillings a fortnight on top of your keep and you will have one day off a week. Your duties will just be to keep my mother happy and do as she asks. She's a kind lady and I'm sure you won't be taken advantage of. If you accept these terms I can have Thompson pick you both up tomorrow."

"Thompson? Oh yes the driver"

"Yes."

"Well it sounds very nice and I am very grateful, but…" Nell glanced down.

"Oh yes, the baby," interrupted Pauline. "My mother and I have already discussed that. We feel that you would not choose to give birth in a workhouse and you will be better looked after at Clearview than you would be in here. Mother has her own family doctor; he will take care of you. You are going to keep the baby aren't you?"

"Yes. I am now." Pauline waited for Nell to say something more but the girl seemed deep in thought. "Is there another problem?"

"Well yes, I think you should know why I came to be here in the first place before you consider me fit to take care of your mother."

"Oh! Now I'm intrigued. What are you going to tell me? You haven't murdered anyone have you?"

"No not quite, but do you remember the Oli Matcher…"

"Alright Nell, you can stop there. You have just given me the best reference one could. You see, when my mother suggested you as her companion I took the trouble to have you vetted. We keep in close contact with the police, as you can well imagine by some of the people we have to deal with at St Mary's House. When you disappeared, I contacted a friend, an inspector at Fratton police station. Then, when they recaptured our Mr Matcher and found you, I got the whole story. The very fact that you were going to tell me all about it, confirmed your honesty. The police say you're going to be needed for the new trial but I think we can cope with that." Pauline smiled for the first time as Nell sat open-mouthed. "As I said Nell, I have my source of information." Nell stood up with a smile. "That's it then Sister. I accept, and I promise to do my best to keep your mother happy."

"I think you can call me Pauline now. Oh! There's something else and I hope it won't change your mind. While you were away, a young man came here looking for you. A fetching lad; he said his name was Button. He also said he would come back on his next day off."

For a moment, Alfie's name filled Nell's stomach with butterflies. She looked down and inadvertently laid a hand on her stomach before saying,

"I really don't want to face him, Pauline. Like you said, some things are best left buried."

Goodbyes were a tearful affair at the Big House, especially from Vivien Price. Even though Nell was her junior, to Viv, Nell was like the mother she wished she'd had. But after convincing Viv that she would visit her frequently, Viv's tears soon subsided.

As Nell said her goodbyes, the carriage waited. Thompson looked majestic in polished gaiters and his smart livery costume. The black shiny sedan shone in the bright morning sunlight. While he stood patiently holding the reins of Chevron and Denver, he stared at Nell.

He was younger than Nell had imagined him to be, about forty-five, she guessed, and certainly handsome with a fine physique. However, the attention he paid her, made her uncomfortable. She was glad when Clare Rutherford appeared, helped by Pauline and one of the porters.

As they helped the old lady board the carriage Nell witnessed an exchange of glances between Pauline and Thompson and in that brief exchange Nell saw what she thought was an intense look of dislike between them.

The forty-five minute ride from the district of Copnor to Clearview House on Portsdown Hill was a most pleasant ride and Nell felt quite the lady when heads turned to see who rode in the magnificent carriage.

"You know Nell, I really am pleased to be going home. I never really liked that place," said Clare.

"No? Well I've no doubt you've stayed at better hotels," said Nell jokingly. "I don't know what ever possessed you to go there."

"Pauline was worried about me. I was losing weight. I went there because she begged me to. She wanted to make sure I was eating. I believe she thought I wanted to die and was starving myself."

"And were you?"

"Certainly not, but I did have a loss of appetite for a while. Anyway, I've got you to look after me now."

"That's right and if you don't eat your dinner you'll get it for supper," warned Nell. Pedestrians stared, with the sound of Clare's laughter.

Life at Clearview was all that a young working girl could have wished for. Nell's highly regarded position as the Mistress's personal companion might easily have caused jealousy among the staff. However, Nell remained the humble girl that befitted her background and she openly sought the advice of the experienced staff whenever prudent. Because of this, they took an instant liking to her. That is—all except Thompson. He resented someone so young stepping straight into the Mistress's close confidence. He had worked for the family for ten years and was still referred to by his surname, and considered it demeaning. No, he did not like Nell, at least not in the platonic sense.

The feeling was mutual though, Nell disliked the way he eyed her whenever they passed each other. When he opened her bedroom door one morning without knocking, she angrily confronted him. He excused himself saying he'd come to change a tap washer in the bathroom and had opened her door by mistake. Nell did not believe him; she had seen the way he hung around the kitchen and was always touching and teasing Betty Frost, the young kitchen maid. Betty was fifteen, a pretty girl with short copper coloured hair; she was a friendly girl, in a loud and overbearing way. Maude, the cook referred to Betty as a bit of a tomboy. Nell liked her and found her to be an able girl, and a very hard worker, but possibly slow in recognising the difference between a man's innocent banter and something more sinister.

Hilda Brough, the housekeeper, tolerated Thompson but thought him lazy; Maude Ferry distrusted him as Nell did, especially around young girls.

Nell soon found her way about the place and quickly learnt what was expected of her. However, her early days were not without mistakes, like the day she wandered down the hill to Bluebell Copse and came back with an armful of the flowers. She found a vase and arranged them on a table in the lounge. Just as she stood back to admire them, Clare walked in,

"Get them out of this house!" Clare shouted, while fighting to get her breath.

Hilda came running in. She saw the vase and immediately assessed the situation. She grabbed the vase of flowers, frowned at Nell and quickly took them out. Nell, having then guessed why the old lady got upset, said,

"I'm so sorry Clare, I just didn't think." Nell put her arm around the old lady and guided her to a chair then hurried to the kitchen to fetch a glass of water. When Nell returned, Clare was breathing normally.

"I'm sorry Nell, it wasn't your fault. You should have been told. You see, when they came to tell me that Denver had thrown my daughter and that she was dead. I insisted on going down there. I'll always remember her lying there, eyes wide open, staring up out of the bluebells. She had such lovely eyes, but the light had gone out of them. I collapsed and they had to carry me back. I told the staff never to bring those flowers in the house, but of course no one told you, did they dear?" said Clare, patting Nell's hand. "Geoffrey never got over it you know. He wanted to have Denver put down but I couldn't let him. What good would that do I told him, it won't bring her back."

"You must still miss him Clare? I know I still miss my father."

"Oh I do! I loved him so much Nell. Though, towards the end I didn't like him. I know that doesn't make much sense, Nell, especially to one as young as you. But to understand, you had to know Geoffrey. God, he was so different when he was young, so romantic. Did they tell you how he named this house?"

"Yes he must have loved you very much," said Nell. Nell looked at the old lady and saw tears in her eyes.

"Yes when we were young." Nell felt for one moment that Clare wanted to tell her more but decided not to, and Nell considered the subject too personal to pursue.

For the first few weeks, Pauline called to see her mother as often as she could. She was still concerned with Clare's health. However,

Clare continued to recover and when the family Doctor complained to Pauline that Nell was calling him out for the least little concern, Pauline's confidence in Nell grew and she became very fond of her.

One morning as Nell returned Clare's empty breakfast tray into the kitchen Maude said:

"Miss Pauline's arrived Nell. She came in here looking for you I think she's in the master's study."

Pauline was sitting in one of the high backed armchairs staring out of the French doors.

"Come and sit down Nell." Nell sat in the matching chair facing her. "How do you get along with the staff?" Nell wondered what was coming. Had there been a complaint, she thought?

"Very well I think. Betty works very hard and…"

"What about Thompson, do you like him?"

"Well I don't see much of him I mean he's…"

"You don't do you?"

"No, not much."

"No, neither do I. Has he…you know…tried anything on with you?" Nell looked surprised. "Well no it's just that… I don't know, it's the way that he looks at me. Like he can see through my clothes, and the way he teases Betty. I don't think she minds but I think that's because she doesn't always understand. He jokes with her and his humour always seems to have…you know…sexual implications, and not really appropriate for a girl of her age."

It was the first time Nell heard Pauline laugh outwardly.

"Just listen to you Nell, seventeen going on seventy. And such big words. Heavens! Has Mother got you reading her the dictionary as well." They both laughed, until Pauline said,

"But your right, about Thompson, that's the way he's always been."

"So why did your father employ him?"

"Oh My father wouldn't have a word said against him. I think secretly, Thompson was the son he always wanted. If we girls complained to father about anything Thompson said or did, he would shrug it off with some lame excuse. When I was about eighteen Thompson tried it on with me, but I quickly put him in his place, and he never tried it again. I've always had my suspicions about him with Sarah, though."

"But she was your sister, surely you would know."

"Not really. We had different interests. She had her equestrian friends and I had my nursing and medical interests. There was one particular incident that brought about my suspicion."

"But Pauline, I don't know why you would want to drag this up now that Sarah's gone, especially to me, I mean you've only known me a short time."

"Because I feel responsible Nell, and I want you to be careful while you're in this house. I just hope that when I've said my piece you will be more watchful and alert." Pauline moved her chair closer to Nell's before continuing. "There was a young girl here by the name of Jenny…something or other. She started working here as a kitchen maid about six months before Sarah died. I never got to know her very well because I had already left home then. Then one weekend when father was away I stayed over. It was a warm, humid night and I stayed awake reading for some time. Even then, I couldn't sleep. I crossed the hall to the bathroom. That's when I heard the stable door open. I quietly opened the bathroom window to see this…Jenny Ryan; yes now I remember, that was her name, Ryan. She came creeping out of the stable in her bare feet and ran across the courtyard where she climbed into her room through the window. I went back to my room but no sooner had I got into bed when I heard Sarah's bedroom door open, then the stairs creak. I crept back into the bathroom, and this time I saw Sarah going into the stable. I heard voices, angry voices that seemed to get louder. I couldn't hear what they were saying but Jenny must have. Her room was right opposite the stable and she couldn't have fallen asleep in so short a time. I'm guessing that this was a row between two lovers, and this young Jenny was the cause. It wasn't long after, that Sarah had the accident and even before the funeral this Jenny Ryan had left."

With that, Pauline smiled "Of course this could all be a figment of my overactive imagination. I do read a lot." Then more seriously she said "But no! I know what I saw."

"You're not suggesting that Thompson, or this Jenny, had something to do with the accident, are you?"

"No I'm not, although I've always thought it a coincidence that it happened to be Thompson that discovered Sarah's body and reported it. It was his day off and he said he was coming back from Waterlooville when he found her. Anyway Nell, as I said, I just want you to be vigilant. And if you hear anything that you think may be relevant to what I've told you, I'd want you to let me know."

Nell promised that she would.

Nell considered Pauline's words, even to the point of letting it keep her awake for the next few nights. Then, while having her lunch in the kitchen one day, she decided to put a question,

"Maude, do you remember a Jenny Ryan who worked here?"

"Aye course I do," said the cook. "Didn't know her very well though. She was a shy young thing, pretty though, and a good worker. Why?"

"Its just that I knew a family of Ryan's that had a daughter around that age." Nell felt a pang of guilt as she lied.

"Well she weren't here that long, and that was a bit of a sore point with Hilda. She gave in her notice just when Miss Sarah's funeral was coming up. Hilda was right peeved about it."

"What was she like?" Nell asked, just as Betty came through the door and started rummaging through one of the cupboards. "I seem to remember this girl having dark hair?"

"Oh no, Jenny Ryan had auburn hair, it was beautiful long hair."

"Huh!" intervened Betty. "You've been listening to that Thompson. I don't think Jenny Ryan is that much to look at." Then finding the tin of polish she was looking for, she breezed out again.

Maude laughed, "Thompson's always ribbing her about how pretty the last kitchen maid was, and I suppose Jenny was, apart from being a bit on the skinny side and the scar. Oh yes, did this girl that you knew have a scar up here," said Maude rubbing a finger above her eye. "Quite a prominent scar, Jenny had."

"Well the girl I remember was a lot younger when I last saw her," said Nell not really liking the pretence, yet feeling that it was necessary for her purpose. "Maybe the scar is more recent. Then again it may not be the same girl at all." Nell paused before saying "But Betty spoke as if she knew this Jenny Ryan."

"She does, they went to the same school."

On her following day off Nell took a trip into Purbrook to purchase some personal items. On her return, she passed the stables and it was here that Thompson confronted her as she made her way through a narrow gap between two outbuildings.

"'Ere, Maude tells me you been asking a lot of questions about Jenny Ryan. Is that right?" The groom spoke in a manner far from friendly and Nell answered with equal surliness.

"Yes. And?"

"What're you wanting to know about her for?"

"Well now I don't think that's got a lot to do with you," said Nell, fully aware of his angry manner.

"You think you're pretty clever don't you," he said. "Coming out here lording it over a bunch of backward country folk and getting your feet under the old gal's table. Well I'm warning you. You better not try to stir things up for me or you'll be sorry."

Nell looked down at his clenched fist and knowing they could not be seen, decided not to respond. She turned aside to brush past him, but as she did, she heard someone enter the courtyard. It gave her the confidence to have the last word. She turned and confronted him again.

"Thompson, if you have a complaint about me, then why don't you put it in a letter and address it to the "old gal" and I'll see that she gets it." Nell started to walk on, then stopped adding, "Oh! If you need any help with the spelling, feel free to call on me."

The following week Nell took the tram to visit her mother and as promised, she called in to see her friends at the big house. Viv ran to greet her as she entered her ward and hugged her.

"Look at the size of you," said Nell "if you get any bigger you'll need a wheelbarrow. When is it due?"

"Its due at any time. But look at you, are you sure you're having one; there's nothing there. Here Nell, guess what? Those people are giving me fifty pounds. I can get out of here and get a place of my own."

"What people?"

"You know! Them what's taking my baby."

"Oh Viv! Are you sure you still want to go through with it. Its not something you should take lightly you know. And how long do you think that fifty pounds will last."

"I know Nell, but what can I do. I can't bring a kid up in here. And besides it will get the best of chances: they got bags of money."

"Yes but it won't have you, will it? You're its mother."

"Oh! Don't make me feel bad about it Nell, not when I haven't got any choice."

"If you did have a choice would you keep the baby?" Viv nodded decisively

"Yeah, course I would. To have a real little person of my own that I could love and that would love me back. Yes I really would, Nell."

The two girls sat chatting for about an hour at the end of which, Nell sat silently biting a nail.

"What are you thinking Nell? Is it about the baby?"

"Look Viv, if you do have the baby soon, like in the next few days, will you promise me that you won't let them take it away until I come back to see you. I've got an idea that might just give you the choice that you've been on about. I'm not making any hard and fast promises, but I'm going to try. I've got to go now, but I should be back by this time next week. Now in the meantime, if the little beggar arrives and those people come round, tell them they can have the afterbirth. Oh! And stay out of the linen cupboard." Nell kissed her on the cheek and left her laughing.

On her way out Nell knocked on Pauline's door.

"Come in Nell. Sit down. Is everything alright?"

"Yes everything's fine, but I had a little run in with our Mr Thompson." Nell explained how after their last meeting she had decided to make a few discreet enquires and how it had led to her confrontation with Thompson. Pauline laughed at the part about helping him with the letter.

"You be careful Nell, I think he's got a temper."

"I will. Oh, I've just been to see Vivien Price."

"Yes her baby's due any time now."

"You know, she intends to let it be adopted."

"Yes, I think it's very sad but it's her decision. And I agree that she's in no position to look after it."

"Well she's changed her mind, at least for the moment. I might have the answer to her problem. So if Viv does have the baby in the next day or so, could you put these people off, at least until I've had a chance to write a couple of letters."

"You know Nell, you don't have to take everyone's problems on your shoulders."

"I know, but Viv's a friend."

Nell left St Mary's House and caught the tram to Queen Street. Seeing Lyons Terrace again with its poor ragged kids and deprived residents made her feel sad, and in a way, strangely guilty, to be dressed in her expensive clothes and shoes. She had experienced both ends of the class scale and realised the power of a good education.

Nell spent the rest of the day cleaning for her mother whom she found to be in poor health.

"Tell me why you feel bad mum, is it your breathing?"

"Yes, partly. And then there's this lump that's come up under here." Nell felt the side of her mother's breast where she had indicated. The lump was distinctly evident.

"I expect it's a boil or a cyst, you haven't banged yourself or fallen have you."

"No I don't think so. Anyway tell me what its like living in a big posh house."

"Oh its like a dream mum. The servants are friendly and the Mistress is a real lady. We get along so well. From my bedroom window, I can see right over Portsmouth. On a clear day you can see Nelson's flag ship: the Victory."

"What will happen when the baby arrives, will you have to leave?"

"No mum, in fact Mrs Rutherford is having a room decorated as a nursery. I think she's more excited over this baby than I am." Violet looked disappointed. "I'll still come to see you mum! Do you want me to bring the baby?"

"Yes of course I do, after all, it is my grandchild." Violet grinned and added, "no matter who the father is."

Nell smiled remembering their terrible row concerning her pregnancy. "I wonder what happened to Oliver Matcher," said Nell.

"They reckon he moved away from Portsmouth after the trial. Neighbours were giving him a rough time."

"I can imagine. Oh! By the way mum, have you seen anything of auntie Annie?"

"Yes she was round here this morning. All she talks about is her Janie. Gets on your nerves after a while."

"Mum! She must be feeling pretty lonely, being on her own now," said Nell.

"Well so do I."

"Yes but when you've lost a daughter and a grandchild...."

"Yes you're right Nell, I must remember to be kinder to her when she comes here. God Nell, you always make me feel so guilty."

"I'm sorry mum I don't mean to. Now is there anything I can do for you before I go?"

Nell left her Mother's house a little earlier than she had planned in order to make another stop before catching the tram home to Clearview.

"Nell! Hello love, come in. Can I get you a cup of tea? Its good of you to come see me, I don't get too many visitors." Nell followed her auntie Annie into her living room.

"No tea for me auntie I can't stay long, I've got a tram to catch. Look I've come to ask you something and I hope you won't be upset by it."

"Best thing to do is try me."

"Okay. Well you know I've been away in St Mary's House."

"The Workhouse! No, I don't believe it. Your mother never told me!"

"No, well I don't suppose its something a mother would be proud of. Anyway I have a very good friend in there, she's not much older than me, her name's Vivien."

Annie appeared pensive, wondering just what was coming. "Now Vivien is about to have a baby any day now."

"What, in the workhouse. You can't raise a baby in the workhouse?"

"I know. That's why she intends to give it away."

"Oh! Nell that's terrible."

"Yes it is, especially when she doesn't want to lose it. That's why I thought of you."

"What are you suggesting?"

"If my friend could find a place where her baby could be looked after during the day, she could get a job. She's a very good seamstress and she'd pay her keep. That would allow her to keep the baby." Annie said nothing for some time, but sat staring at Nell.

"I know it's a big thing to ask auntie, especially so soon after losing Janie and the baby. But I thought that you must be feeling…"

"Bring her to see me Nell! Bring this Vivien to meet me. I don't know if it will work. I don't even know if I will like the girl, but it couldn't do any harm to meet her could it."

Two days later, while Clare was taking her afternoon nap, Nell decided to write the letter she'd been mentally composing since leaving Annie's house. She entered the study to find Betty polishing the brass and silver. Nell sat down at the roll top desk and started to write.

"Do you know Nell, this is my favourite job. Just see how this brass shines."

"Yes and you really do make a very good job of cleaning it Betty," said Nell thinking she was never going to get this letter written. Then a thought occurred to her.

"Betty, did you say you knew this Jenny Ryan girl?"

"Yes, we went to the same school, though she was a fair bit older than me. Matter of fact I saw her in Waterlooville only about a week ago. She reckons she got a good job working for some well-to-do family as a nanny. But by the state of the pram she was pushing I don't reckon they could have been that well-to-do."

"That's where she lives, is it, Waterlooville?"

"Yes, Maypole Square. At least she did when we were at school. Ere, why are you so interested in Jenny? Nothing to do with the accident is it?

"What accident?"

"You know! Miss Sarah's accident. I heard talk about Jenny Ryan getting a right telling off by Miss Sarah just a day or so before the accident. I think they were suggesting that Jenny might have had something to do with it."

"Betty! That's a terrible thing to say! Who was suggesting it?"

"I don't know, I can't remember who said what. They were all there in the kitchen."

"Well people shouldn't spread gossip like that. And anyway, how could this girl possibly have had anything to do with a riding accident?"

"I don't know, Thompson was saying something about a loose strap. Oh and I heard him moaning at Maude this morning, for talking to you about Jenny."

"And why do you think he should get upset about that?"

"I don't know, now that you mention it."

The following Sunday Nell took a trip into Waterlooville. Having no idea where Maypole Square was, she looked about for someone to ask. There were very few people about, but across the road, a ladder was propped against the roof of a shop, above which a man could be seen working on the roof. On the ground below him, a young man was mixing cement. She approached him.

"Excuse me could you tell me...." Nell was suddenly interrupted,

"Hey!"

She looked up to see the older man looking down at them from the top of the ladder.

"Is he shouting to you?" Nell asked.

The boy shrugged. "He's my boss, but I think he means you,"

"Hang on I'll come down!"

Nell still wasn't sure whom he was addressing. He wasn't someone she recognised at least not from that height or angle. Nell was perplexed, was he someone she'd met at St Mary's House she thought. These were the only men she'd become acquainted with. She never had long to wait. The man clambered down the ladder, and was by her side in seconds.

"I never had a chance to thank you or to really say I was sorry." He said gazing at her and smiling at the confused expression on her face.

Nell looked at him for some moments until her mouth slowly opened and she realised who he was. She took a while answering therefore prompting him to remark, "I'm sorry maybe I shouldn't have spoken to you."

"No, It's just that I didn't recognise you. You look so different," Nell said awkwardly. He took her gently by the arm and guided her out of hearing distance of the young man, and although Nell's pregnant condition was hardly visible, she consciously adjusted her coat to hide the slight bulge.

"Oh, yes the beard," he said. "Well it had to go. There were too many pictures of that face around. And what about you, you look positively affluent and even prettier, I must say."

"Thank you. I work as a companion for a lady up on Portsdown hill, a house called Clearview."

"Not the Rutherford's!"

"Yes, do you know it?"

"Yes I renewed some tiles there. Nice old lady as I remember!"

"And what else happened?" Nell said smiling up at his close-cropped hair, and being a little surprised at her own friendliness toward the very man whose illegitimate child she now carried.

"Yes," he said grinning and running his hand over his head. "Maybe I went too far, but lets face it, you didn't recognise me and that's the general idea. Anyway, that was all I wanted to say Nell. If it wasn't for your evidence, I might have been a goner by now. And after the way I ..." There was a long pause and Nell sensed his embarrassment and knew he was trying to apologise.

Nell touched the back of his hand, "It's all in the past now Mr Matcher."

He glanced worriedly toward the young man who was shovelling sand and whispered: "Yes, and by the way, its Smith now."

Nell grinned. "Of course, anyway we just have to put that sort of thing behind us."

"Oh I have. I don't drink any more," he said. Then his mouth stretched to a wide grin, "and I haven't had a real good fight since they let me out of clink. I've come out to the country to make a new start and I owe a lot of it to you Nell. If there is ever a way I can repay you," he said, pointing to a sign on the side of a truck that read O. Smith. Roofers. "Don't hesitate to come and find me."

"Well you could start by telling me where Maypole Square is," said Nell with a smile, and just for a moment, the thought that this man had fathered the child she now carried, was to her, no longer abhorrent.

Nell was hoping to see this Jenny Ryan, although she had no idea at that moment what she was going to say, or how to approach her.

The square consisted of half a dozen farm workers cottages and once one had entered the square, the only way out was to go back the same way.

A little boy of about six, and four younger girls sat in the road drawing with pieces of chalk. Their dirty faces and ragged clothes brought scenes from Lyons Terrace back to her. They all looked up as Nell approached.

"That's nice, is that a boat?" Nell asked the boy.

"A ship." He said as he started drawing another one."

"And what are you drawing. She said to one of the girls."

"A hat."

"Of course you are, silly me I can see it's a hat now. Are you going to write your name on it?"

"Yes, I am."

"I bet I can guess what your name is." Nell said to the boy.

"Bet you can't," he said, coming out of his shyness.

Nell rubbed her temples like she had some magic power. "Its...Jenny!"

"No silly, that's my sisters name." said the boy laughing.

"Oh! I'm always doing that," said Nell. She then closed her eyes and rubbed her temples again. Now she had all of their attention. "But wait a minute I can feel another name coming. "Ryan!"

"That's my other name the boy said excitedly. That's magic!"

Suddenly a window opened and a woman shouted "David! Get in here." The boy got up.

"I've got to go now," he said to Nell. Just then, a baby started crying and a young girl came out of the same cottage to lift the infant out of an old pram.

"Is that your big sister?" Nell asked the boy.

"Yes and that lady with the big mouth was my mum." Nell laughed and followed him up the garden path.

Three lines of washing decorated the front garden along with a broken and rusty mangle and two old galvanized baths'

"My! Your mum does a lot of washing?"

"She gets money for it."

"Oh! I see."

The girl had taken the baby indoors and as Nell and the boy neared the open front door, the boy's mother appeared. Nell still had no idea how to handle the questions she wanted to ask.

"Mrs Ryan?" said Nell.

"Yes!" The woman appeared to be about forty, tall and very slim as was Jenny from the glimpse that Nell saw of her. The woman wore a headscarf tied in a typical housewife fashion. A pinafore hung about her neck. This was holed due to the constant wear against the edge of a washboard. The back door of the house was open and Nell could see more washing blowing in the back garden.

"I wonder if I might have a word with your daughter Jenny?" The woman looked nervous although not as nervous as her daughter when she called her to the door. The girl was just as Maude had described her, very tall and pretty with the loveliest long auburn hair. The only blight on her almost perfect features was the deep scar above her eye. Nell took a deep breath and thought here goes:

"Jenny?" the girl nodded anxiously. "I'd like to ask you a few questions about Sarah Rutherford."

Nell had imagined her statement to bring all kinds of results, anger, or fear, even indifference, but she wasn't prepared for the girl collapsing on the doorstep. Nell called for the mother and together they carried Jenny into the living room and laid her on the tattered settee.

"What's up with Jen, Mum?" asked the boy.

"Go on out David."

"God! Make up your mind," the boy said slinking out the door.

"It's her own fault," said Mrs Ryan, while unscrewing the top off a bottle of smelling salts. "She doesn't eat enough. Mind you, she's not been the same since the attack. What did you say to her?" She waved the open bottle under Jenny's nose and the girl jerked into life.

"I just asked her about Sarah Rutherford."

"Well I'm not surprised. That was about the time of the rape, when those…"

"It didn't happen Mum!" Jenny interrupted her mother as she moved to a sitting position. The girl looked up at Nell. "Who are you?"

"My name's Nell Masters. I work for Clare Rutherford. What did you mean, Jenny, when you said it didn't happen?"

"I knew this day would come, and now I'm glad it has." Jenny looked up at her mother. "I lied mum, I wasn't attacked by a gang of boys. That's not how it happened, but in a way I **was** raped."

"Tell me Jenny," Nell said holding the girl's hand. "Was it Thompson?" Jenny looked from Nell to her mother and nodded.

Mrs Ryan frowned "Who's this Thompson? And why did you make up a pack of lies…"

"I was frightened mum."

"Frightened of what, girl, for God's sake?"

"Of dad, but most of all frightened of Thompson."

"I don't understand any of this. You just wait until your father gets…"

"Mrs Ryan, don't you think it would be better if Jenny told the whole story before you decide if she deserves to be punished. Thompson is the Rutherford's driver, a man of about forty-five. If I'm right, it's he that should be punished. Do you want to start at the beginning Jenny?

"Will they put me in prison?"

"Prison!" Mrs Ryan spluttered. "What ever for, girl?"

"For killing Miss Sarah," said Jenny, meekly

"Oh my God!" Her mother reached for the armchair behind her and almost fell back into it.

"I think you should start at the beginning," said Nell. "And tell us everything Jenny, before you ask any questions," Nell looked worriedly at Jenny, wondering if she shouldn't have just left and gone straight to the police. Jenny told her story while her mother sat quietly sobbing.

"I liked it at Clearview," Jenny began. "It was so grand and they had so many nice things there. Mrs Brough the housekeeper, and Maude were very nice, but they didn't seem to have much time for talking, not to me anyway. I suppose I was too young. Thompson was the friendliest, and at first, I liked him. Any questions I had about my duties or wages, I would ask him rather than bother the women. But he became too friendly, smacking my bum when he passed me. Then the smacking became squeezing or he would come up behind me and kiss my neck. I tried to avoid him but he would come looking for me. Once, when Mrs Rutherford and Miss Sarah were out, he came upstairs while I was cleaning one of the rooms. He grabbed me and threw me on the bed." Jenny paused and looked coyly at her mother. Nell could see the embarrassment on her face.

"It's alright Jenny," Nell said, trying to reassure the girl.

"Well that's when he first hurt me."

"Are you saying he hit you?" asked Mrs Ryan.

"No, not that kind of hurt." Jenny's mother clamped her hands over her face and started sobbing again. Jenny continued. "He warned me not to tell anyone, said that I'd be sorry if I did. He made me meet him in the stable at night. That's when he first did it, proper like. I said I was going to tell the Mistress but he said even if I did get him into trouble, I would still get the sack, and I knew how much you needed the money, mum."

"Jenny did you ever know Miss Sarah to meet Thompson at night?" Nell asked

"Only once. That was the night she heard me coming out of the stable. She guessed what was going on. She went over there and threatened him. They had a real shouting match. I could hear it from my room. He called her a stuck up little rich cow and she called him a filthy lecher. The next day Miss Sarah gave me a real telling off for going to the stable. For a while after that, he left me alone. Then he started again, not in the house because I think Sarah scared him, but he told me to meet him at different places. I kept refusing, until I found that my monthlies had stopped. I really got frightened then. I knew I was pregnant and when he asked me to meet him on his day off down in Bluebell Copse I agreed because I thought like a fool, that I could turn the tables on him, threaten him and make him marry me. I told him I was having his baby. At first, he was nice about it. We sat down on the grass and he told me not to worry, he said he would take care of me. I started to talk about getting married, and he started to touch me and I let him have his way because of his promise to take care of me. Afterwards we lay there for a while then he suddenly starts laughing. I asked him what was so funny. He said you are. I asked him why. He said he'd spent thirty years getting his way with women without having to marry one. And did I think I could net him when all the others had failed. He called me a stupid little cow and that if I ever threatened him again he would give me a matching scar. I became hysterical. I can't ever remember crying like I did that day. I thought of the shame I would bring on you and dad, I just wanted to die. Then we heard it. I'll never forget that sound. It was like the rumble of thunder. I peered through the trees and saw Miss Sarah charging down the hill on Denver. I never meant to hurt Sarah; I just wanted it all to end. I ran out into the clearing, but I ran out too soon. Instead of running me down, Denver reared up and threw Sarah. She hit her head on a felled tree and lay there. Thompson told me to get home and not talk to anyone on the way. He said he would take care of it. The next day he said that I should leave my job. He said if I didn't, they would find out that I killed her.

Mrs Brough wasn't very happy when I told her I was leaving. I told mum I got the sack. What will they do to me, miss? Do they hang girls Miss?"

Nell looked into her frightened eyes and remembered once asking herself the same question.

Mrs Ryan knelt down and put her arms around her daughter. "Oh love I'm so ashamed, ashamed for your father and me both."

"Why mum? I'm the one that did wrong, you've done nothing to be ashamed of."

"Yes we have, we should have been the kind of parents that our kids could bring their troubles to."

Nell stood looking out the window. She watched the children outside play while Jenny and her mother shared a moment together.

When Mrs Ryan got up she said, "I'll make a cup of tea Miss, I think it might help." Nell smiled and watched her leave the room. She then sat beside Jenny and held her hand.

"I'm not sure what will happen to you Jenny, I only know that you have nothing to be ashamed of. Now I want you to think very carefully. Where was Sarah when you left Bluebell Copse?"

"Like I said, she was lying with her head against the log."

"You said her eyes were shut. Are you sure?" Nell said, as Mrs Ryan came in with a tray.

"Does it really matter?" said Mrs Ryan.

"It very well might, Mrs Ryan."

"Shut, definitely shut," said Jenny

"One more thing Jenny. Were there bluebells' growing around her?" Jenny and her mother looked at Nell as though she'd gone mad.

"No, there were none in the clearing. There's too much sunlight I suppose, they only seem to grow among the trees," Nell stood up.

"Well I'm no authority when it comes to the law but I don't think you need worry Jenny. You will probably have to tell your story all over again though. When you do, I think it will be Thompson doing the worrying."

Nell stayed to drink her tea while trying to reassure Jenny and her mother, although Nell was far from convinced they were out of the mire.

On the way back to Clearview Nell got off the tram a stop early. From there, she took a detour through Bluebell Copse. Her curiosity was like an annoying itch that just had to be scratched.

10
A taste of the past

The next day, without explanation, Nell asked Clare for permission to phone Pauline and to take her day off early. She then caught the earliest tram to Portsmouth.

Nell met Pauline in a corridor of St Mary's Workhouse.

"Nell!" Pauline said with surprise, "What is it you like about this place that you just can't stay away?" Nell giggled and came back with,

"Pauline, surely it's obvious. It's your sunny smile, and the way you used to tuck us in at night." Nell waited for Pauline to stop laughing before saying,

"Pauline, I think that what I have to tell you is very serious. There was more to Sarah's riding accident than just being thrown by her horse, and I think you were wrong about your sister and Thompson."

"You had better come to my office."

Nell told Pauline the whole story of her visit with Jenny Ryan, including her reason for taking a short cut through Bluebell Copse.

Pauline sat and listened intently without interrupting. After Nell finished, Pauline explained her own intentions and asked for Nell's assistance. Nell agreed.

"Oh Nell I do hope you're right. I've had this nightmare hanging over me for so long. I hated the thought of Sarah being involved with Thompson. Now I have some phone calls to make. Have you said anything to Mother?"

"No I wasn't sure you'd want her to know; I don't know how she'll take the news."

"Thank you Nell, she will have to be told, I'll take care of it. Anyway, you'd better run along and see Vivien. I told her you telephoned and that you were on your way. Now she's got all spruced up and excited, waiting for you. You shouldn't keep her out too long though. I think her baby is due any time now."

An hour later Nell and Vivien sat chatting and drinking tea with Nell's Auntie Annie.

"Are you sure about this, Auntie?" Nell said. "I feel like I'm taking advantage especially as it's so soon after…well, you know, losing Janie."

"Nell, you're such a worrier. I've thought about this and now that I've met Vivien," Annie said patting Viv's hand. "I really think it might work out for both of us, and anyway, if you're willing to give it a try Vivien, what have we got to lose."

When Nell arrived back at Clearview, she dated the letter that she had already written some two days earlier. It wasn't too long before she received the answer she expected.

It was two weeks since Nell had introduced Vivien to her aunt Annie and now they were back at Annie's house. Vivien's bulbous figure was gone and as Annie sat nursing Viv's baby girl, she wore a smile that she hadn't used for as long as she could remember.

"You don't know how happy this has made me," she said, looking at the tiny bundle. "I thought I was going to lose my mind after Janie died. Now, with Vivien and little Angela here coming to stay with me, its just like I've been given a second chance. And I'm sure Vivien and I will get along fine. Now you two run along and do what you have to do. I'll look after this little mite until you get back."

Fifteen minutes later Nell and Viv were in Queen Street and stepping through the inner door of Boswell's Naval Outfitters.

Mrs Irene Boswell was showing some shirts to a naval officer. She gave the two girls no more than a fleeting glance, obviously not recognising Nell. Ivan Boswell was standing on steps, packing socks into a drawer. He immediately recognised Nell and quickly got down. He was still as handsome as Nell remembered with his wavy hair and greying sideburns, and his clothes were just as immaculate.

He whispered something to his wife, then without a word, rapidly ushered the two girls out of the shop door. As they ascended the stairs leading to the factory floor, Nell heard the familiar sound of industrial sewing machines and whispered mutterings coming from above. Nell physically shivered as memories of the unpleasant times there, came back to her.

Nell looked around and recognised most of the women but she was not surprised to see new girls occupying the Gill sister's seats. Three chairs were empty, however, and it disturbed Nell to see that one of them was Marie's. Recognising Nell, Sadie Drew and Dolly Fields gave her a furtive wave. The room had not changed, except that Boswell had enclosed his work desk to create a little office with glass windows. It would give the women something more to grumble about while they're shivering with the cold, Nell thought to herself.

Boswell ushered them proudly into his office where he directed them to sit on two wooden chairs while he closed the door. He circled the desk and sat facing them from a comfortable leather bound chair.

"Well Miss Masters I received your letter," he said, examining his pocket watch with an air of importance. "And the fact that you are here on time tells me that you received my answer. I take it that this is the young lady in question." He picked up a crumpled piece of paper from the desk, which Nell recognised as her letter. He studied it for a few seconds then looked at Viv. "Miss Vivien Price, is it?"

"Yes. Pleased to meet you Mr Boswell," Vivien said, smiling shyly at him. Boswell's response to Viv was cold and less than friendly. Nell was slowly getting annoyed, she remembered how Boswell liked to make his pompous speeches and belittle his employee's. It didn't take him long to get started. When he spoke, it was loud enough to be heard on the factory floor outside. "Now when I read your letter Miss Masters, I laughed, screwed it up and tossed it in the waste basket. Then I thought to myself, what audacity this girl has. She walks out of here with not a word of explanation. She then expects me to employ a girl on her recommendation. Furthermore, you commend her with little more qualification other than to say, she's nice." He then turned his attention back to Vivien. "Where have you worked before, Miss Price?"

Vivien was now looking very nervous. She looked at Nell for guidance. Nell on the other hand, was not intimidated by Boswell's tone of voice. She shifted to the edge of her seat, leaned menacingly forward and through tight lips, said angrily,

"Vivien has had varied experience in both manual and machine stitching. She did this while spending nearly eight months in the workhouse, after which she gave birth to a beautiful little bastard. A much bigger bastard, who accepted no responsibility, sired the child. Of course, I'm sure you understand how these little accidents happen Mr Boswell,"

Boswell turned red, his jaw had dropped, and he appeared stunned. He then gave a little cough and started to shift about in his seat while staring uneasily at Nell. Nell knew the reason; she knew he was asking himself how much knowledge she had acquired of her own past. Boswell then sat back in his chair and gave a nervous laugh before saying,

"I hardly think that qualifies her for a position in my Company. As you know, Nell, we do very intricate work here."

"That didn't seem to matter when my mother asked you to employ me, and Viv's a far better seamstress than I ever was, even when I left here."

"That was different," he said.

"Why," Nell said glaring at him, "Because you're my father? And because you were afraid my mother might have told your wife if you didn't employ me?"

Viv now started to shift about nervously, while Boswell went pale and glanced through the window toward the top of the stairs. At the workbench outside, faces were turned toward his office.

"Keep your voice down," Boswell rasped, in an angry whisper. "I paid your mother a great deal of money and she promised not to tell anyone, especially you."

"She didn't! She kept her word. But you know why I disappeared. You read the papers. Bloody Hell! You employed Rose Gill. You must have followed the case word for word, and so you know that I went to the workhouse. That's where I met one of your old employees. It was her who told me about your lecherous past with a young girl who lived in Lyons Terrace. I just put two and two together. And guess what? It came up Dad." At this point Nell leaned across the desk and through gritted teeth she said. "Well nothing's changed Dad. You've got empty chairs out there and my friend here has a newborn baby to feed and clothe. Now, if she isn't sitting at one of those chairs on Monday morning on a full wage, I will be back to take the matter up with Irene, your wife."

Ivan Boswell sat back in his chair looking very angry. Viv didn't know where to look while Nell sat staring defiantly back at the man she knew to be her father.

Suddenly, and to both the girls surprise. Boswell's mouth broke into a smile. He leaned across the desk and spoke quietly.

"When you came here Nell, you were such a timid thing. Oh yes, I knew you were my daughter, though I couldn't let you know. However, I suppose I was curious, and if only for hereditary reasons, I took a mild interest in you. I found you to be a disappointment. I saw no special merits in you, no leadership qualities. You let the Gill sisters intimidate and belittle you. Now suddenly this, what happened?"

"I read some books," Nell said, with the corners of her mouth hinting a smile.

"Well I certainly would like to know the titles of these books." he said, smiling back at her.

At that moment it occurred to Nell that she'd never seen him smile before and she suddenly realised how her mother could have fallen for him all those years ago.

"Okay, you're right Nell. I have got a couple of vacancies," he said in a back-to-business voice. "Miss Price, you start Monday; seven sharp. Don't be late."

Boswell ushered them down the stairs and out onto the pavement where Irene, his wife, could not overhear what he had to say. Viv thanked him and as they said their goodbyes, he turned to Nell and there was compassion in his voice as he said, "Nell, I'm sorry about your friend, Marie, I know you were close. It was consumption." Then he took Nell's hand and said. "Be good to your mother, for all my sins Nell, I really did love her." Then to his surprise Nell stood on tiptoe and kissed his cheek.

A fortnight later Jim Thompson sat in the Clearview kitchen joking with Betty and Maude. He was waiting for the kitchen clock to tell him he was off duty, when Hilda came through the swing door.

"You're wanted in the dining room." She said to him.

"Oh no! Not now, I'm just going to the George Inn. She can't want me to take her out now, surely not; I mean, look at the time."

"I don't think the mistress wants to go anywhere," said Hilda solemnly.

"Well what is it then?"

"I don't know, but I do know they're waiting," said Hilda.

Thompson got up. As he edged toward the door he was troubled by Hilda's cold stare as she watched him leave the kitchen. He reached the dining room and knocked.

"Come in," a voice called. Thompson entered and was disturbed by the scene before him.

A long dining table graced the centre of the room, accommodating twelve chairs. Four of these chairs were now occupied.

Clare Rutherford sat at the far end of the table facing him. To her left sat Nell and to her right, her daughter Pauline and to Pauline's right sat an unfamiliar middle-aged gentleman. Behind them was the door that led to the entrance hall. However, what troubled Thompson were the two uniformed policemen guarding it.

"You sent for me Madam?" Thompson said looking uncomfortable.

"Yes Thompson," said Clare in an expressionless tone. "Would you close the door? These people would like to ask you some questions. Please be seated?"

Thompson pulled out a chair as he watched one of the uniformed policemen move around the table to guard the door he himself had just entered.

The man next to Pauline spoke first as he looked at a sheet of paper held in front of him.

"You are Mr James Edward Thompson?"

"Yes."

"My name's Davage and I'm from a Portsmouth branch of the C.I.D." With that, Thompson glared from Pauline to Nell, while Davage studied his notes. The two women stared blankly back at him, giving no clue as to their feelings at that moment. He then looked at Clare hoping for some sign of friendliness, but Clare would not look at him. "Now then, you've worked for the Rutherford family for some years I believe?"

"More than ten, I reckon."

"On the day Miss Sarah died…" Clare suddenly put a hand to her forehead and closed her eyes. Nell took hold of her hand as the Inspector went on. "You reported the accident to the family. Is that right?"

"Aye it is."

"Can I ask how you came to be in this…" Davage paused to look at his paper again. "Bluebell Copse at the time of the accident?"

Thompson didn't hesitate "Short cut, I was taking a shortcut."

"Yes I believe that's what you told the official inquiry at the time. Now, from where were you taking this short cut?"

"Waterlooville." Thompson said with an air of defiance.

"Yes I believe that is also what you said at the inquest, but you would have to come through Purbrook before making this shortcut. I have checked the only two routes from Purbrook to this house and I estimate the route you took to be longer."

Thompson started to rub his hands down his lap. Nell wanted to smile, thinking his hands might be getting a little sweaty.

"Ah well it was a better way to go, more colourful like, after all it *was* spring."

"Are you sure that was the reason Mr Thompson?"

"Yeah, course I am, why else?"

Davage turned to the uniformed officer standing behind him. "Read Mr Thompson his rights Sergeant would you." The officer took a small notebook from his tunic pocket and proceeded to read its words out loud to Thompson.

"Here, what's all this about. I haven't done anything."

Davage ignored Thompson's protests. "Tell us in your own words what exactly happened that day Mr Thompson."

"Its just like I told everyone I came through the copse that day and there she was lying there, dead. The horse was gone, I knew she'd been thrown it was obvious." At this point Clare leaned toward Nell and whispered to her.

"Inspector," said Nell. "Is there any need for Mrs Rutherford to be here for this? It's very upsetting for her."

"No I don't think so. If I need your help Mrs Rutherford I'll have someone fetch you."

Nell walked Clare to the door and up to her room. When Nell came back into the room Thompson was speaking.

"Like I said she was just lying there in amongst the flowers. I could see she was dead, her head was at a funny angle and her eyes were open. Anyway, that's when I ran up to the house and told Mrs Rutherford."

"And that is your full account of what happened is it?"

"Aye it is," said Thompson. Davage once again turned and nodded to the sergeant who opened the door to the entrance hall and beckoned to someone outside.

Pauline and Nell watched the colour drain from Thompson's face as Jenny walked into the room. However, he soon recovered and his expression changed to a sneer as he directed his next words to Pauline and Nell.

"You bleeding bitches been plotting against me, well, you got nothing on me cause I've done nothing wrong, see?" He then pointed at Jenny. "And that little slut will say anything they told her to say. Ask her who got a real telling off by Miss Sarah the day before the accident. Ask her why Denver's girth strap was loose."

"Take a seat Miss Ryan," Davage said, ignoring Thompson's outburst. "And Sergeant, take note of Mr Thompson's comments at the sight of Miss Ryan. Now Jenny has already given us her account of what happened that day and I don't think there's any doubt which of you is telling the truth."

"Yeah, well it don't make no difference what the little tart told you, I've still done nothing wrong and you can't prove I did."

"We think you did Mr Thompson. We think you did something very wrong." said Davage.

"Thinking and proving is two different things." Thompson said with a smirk. Davage turned to Jenny.

"Miss Ryan, What happened to Denver after he threw Miss Sarah."

"Thompson grabbed his reins and managed to calm him."

"And where exactly was Miss Sarah lying when you ran from the copse that day?"

"She was lying with her head against a fallen tree. The one that she fell against."

"Were her eyes open or closed?"

"Closed."

"Were there flowers around that log? Bluebells for instance."

"Oh no sir. They don't grow in any clearing they only grow where it's shady. They were much farther back under the trees."

"Now that's not what you told us is it Mr Thompson?"

"Well it was a long time ago I might have got it wrong." Said Thompson rubbing his hands down his trousers again.

"No you didn't get it wrong Mr Thompson. If you like I can get Mrs Rutherford back in here. She will confirm that what you said is exactly what she saw, but you did make a mistake, James."

Nell wondered why the Inspectors voice had changed to a more friendly tone.

"You see Clare Rutherford agrees with you that there were bluebells surrounding Sarah's body, and that her eyes were definitely open. However, I believe that when you told Miss Ryan to run off home, Miss Sarah was merely stunned: knocked out as it were. That's why Jenny remembers Sarah's eyes being closed. You see, one's eyes do not normally remain open when unconscious James, but Jenny here didn't know that. She thought Sarah was dead and because she had caused Sarah's horse to rear up, she thought she was to blame for her death and was actually coming here today to confess to murder." Thompson was now looking sad and dejected. "But Sarah was not dead was she James? Miss Masters here took it on herself to examine the tree that Sarah fell against. It was rotten, soft as a sponge. Oh, I know it happened a long time ago but that tree has been rotting there for years. That's why Sarah was still alive. She came round after Jenny left didn't she. What happened then James? Sarah had already warned you about molesting Jenny. Did she tell you that she was going to tell her father? Naturally you would have to stop her James, I mean, this meant the end of your job."

Nell and Pauline could see what Davage was up to, He was trying to probe Thompson's sense of reasoning, make him feel that others would understand what made him resort to his brutal action. They could also see that Davage was enjoying it. Nell knew that Thomson's intellect was no match for that of the Inspector and she couldn't help feeling a little sorry for him. Davage continued. "It wasn't fair I mean this stuck up little snob had no right to end ten years of faithful service, just because of a little bit of hanky panky with the kitchen maid. I mean what business was it of hers if you were seeing…"

"She never liked me." Thomson interrupted with a quiet mumble. He looked down at his lap as he launched into a tirade of self-justifications. "Always lauding it over me, she was. I could never do anything right. If I saddled Denver for her, the straps were either too tight or too loose."

"You can easily lose your temper with someone like that, I know!" urged Davage. "What did you hit her with, James. Must have been something pretty heavy, to break her neck like that."

"Didn't use anything," said Thompson. "Didn't need to, when she came round, the snotty bitch got up and just rubbed her head. Then she saw me and flew into a rage. She accused me of raping this little tart. I'm reporting this to my father," she said. "Then she strutted off toward the house. Well it would have finished me. I panicked, before she'd gone a few steps I ran and put my arm around her neck."

"What did you do then James?"

"She started to shout I thought they might hear her up at the house so I put my other hand across her mouth to stop her screaming. But the cow bit me. So I tugged hard on her jaw."

Nell and Pauline watched Thompson's arm go stiff and jerk to one side as he mentally re-lived the breaking of Sarah's neck.

Davage looked at the two women as Thompson inadvertently jerked in his chair, gritting his teeth and repeating his heartless deed.

"I heard it snap and she went all limp, like. I was surprised how easy it was. I started to drag her back to where she fell she was real heavy. Then I thought I heard someone and I panicked. I dropped her amongst the bluebells."

"I suppose that is when you slackened Denver's strap. You thought that if suspicion was to fall on anyone it would be on Jenny. You then slapped his rump and sent him home before running up to the house."

Thompson never looked up. His silence was his admission.

The inspector nodded to one of the officers who took out a pair of handcuffs.

As the policeman snapped them on, Davage stood up. Thompson sounded pathetic as he looked up at him and said,

"I've not slept much, you know!"

"Never mind lad," Davage answered. "That won't be a problem for you now."

11
All good things

The next five years were the happiest in Nell's memory and it seemed like the whole household's spirits had been lifted with the presence of her daughter: Cathleen, running about the place. To Clare she was like the grandchild she'd always wanted. She maintained that Cathy put love and laughter into the house, something that it's rooms had not been subjected to for a long time.

Christmas was only a couple of weeks away and as with any child of Cathy's age, excitement was mounting.

"Will the man bring the Christmas tree tomorrow Mummy?" she said as Nell pulled her blankets back for her to jump into bed."

"I certainly hope so. That's what he said, when I ordered it."

"And can we put paper chains on it?"

"Yes, when you come home from school. Have you written your letter to Father Christmas yet?"

"Yes. I asked him to leave me a doll with shutting eyes and a pushchair to put her in. Oh! And I asked him to take away my blue patch so the boys and girls at school won't make fun of me any more."

"Oh love," said Nell hugging her daughter tightly. "I don't think Father Christmas can do things like that."

"Why not?" Cathleen said pouting.

"Because God put that birth mark on your neck and he outranks Father Christmas. Anyway I told you before, he put it there for a good reason."

"Tell me again what it was mummy."

"To mark you to be one of his angels when it's your turn to go to heaven. So don't you take any notice of those silly children, they are just jealous. Did you remember to kiss Nanny Clare goodnight?"

"Yes of course." said Cathleen climbing between the fresh white sheets with her teddy bear.

"And what have you forgotten?" Cathleen thought for a moment then jumped back out of bed. She knelt beside it with eyes closed and hands clasped. Moments later she jumped back in the bed.

"Mummy, how long will Nanny Clare live?" Cathleen said as Nell tucked her in.

"I don't know love. None of us know how long we will live. That's something only God knows."

"I don't want her to die, ever."

"None of us do love, so I hope you asked God to keep her safe."

"Yes, I always do. How old is she?"

"She's nearly eighty," said Nell. Then as Nell leaned over to kiss her daughter goodnight, she saw the glassy look in Cathleen's eyes. "Now what's wrong?"

"Well the Sunday school man said we only live for three score years and ten, and he said that makes seventy. So if Nanny is eighty, that means..." Nell could see tears forming in Cathleen's eyes.

"Oh, don't cry love. Father Brent was only quoting what the Bible considers an average age. Some people live to more than a hundred, and from the way Nanny's looking I think she could be one of them." This seemed to ease Cathleen's troubled mind as she kissed her mother and snuggled down with her woolly bear.

The next morning, as usual, Nell carried a breakfast tray into Clare's room.

"Come along lazy bones. Time to wake up." Moving various pill and medicine bottles to one side on the bedside table, Nell made room for the tray. "Come on Snowy, you can get up as well," reluctantly the family cat stretched himself then jumped off the bed. Moving to the window, Nell started to draw the curtains saying loudly. "Come along Clare you're not getting out of it. You wanted to go into Portsmouth today, and I've asked Clarence to get the car out." Bright sunlight flooded the room but still no answer came from the old lady in the four-poster.

Nell turned and stood transfixed, gazing at Clare's pale face. The old lady's eyes were still closed and Nell held her breath as she moved slowly toward the bed. Cathleen's words from the previous night prodded Nell's thoughts: three score years and ten. Gingerly, Nell shook the old lady. Suddenly Clare opened her eyes.

"My! That was a deep one, I must have still been dreaming." Nell put her hand to her breast and let out a sigh. "What's the matter Nell you look a little pale. Did I frighten you?"

"Yes you did, I called you twice." Nell sounded irritable. "It wasn't until I shook you that you woke, and what with Cathy crying and getting herself in a state last night…"

"What about?"

"You!" said Nell. "She asked how old you were so I told her. But It seems, that silly vicar's been quoting the Bible's three score years and ten. And she's taken it too literally. She thinks you're long overdue for popping your clogs.

Clare laughed. "Bless her. She does remind me of Sarah you know. She could get very emotional sometimes by just thinking quietly to herself."

"You poor thing," said Nell. "You must have gone through a terrible time after she died."

"Oh! Nell It was awful. But I believe I was the strong one. Gerald just went to pieces. If only he had opened up and let Pauline and I share his misery. But he wouldn't or couldn't, not after that business with Pauline's husband, but I expect she's told you about that."

"She said something about her father and her husband not getting on," said Nell, handing Clare a pill and a glass of water.

"Huh! It's just like her to make light of Gerald's bigotry. He was an American you know, from the Deep South, place called Charleston. His father owned a cotton plantation. That was how we met. My father owned one of the Lancashire cotton mills and Gerald came over here on business. I suppose one has to know what it's like growing up around such terrible prejudices. You wouldn't believe the humiliation those coloured people have to endure. As much as Pauline loved her father, she loathed the bigotry that constantly flowed from him. At the breakfast table, at dinner, the subject of race was a constant source of argument. It was almost as if Pauline was determined to find herself a coloured man just to infuriate Gerald. When he found out she had been meeting one, they had the most furious row and he told her to get out. This only made Pauline more determined to carry on seeing her young man. Inevitably, she broke the news that they were to be married. Pauline came to the house a few times to try to talk to her father but he would just shut himself in his room until she'd gone. Pauline never saw her father again until the day of his funeral." Clare's chin started to quiver and she searched the bedside table for a hanky.

"Now don't go getting yourself in a state," said Nell, fetching one from a linen drawer.

"I'm alright," said Clare, trying to stem the tears, "Hate is a terrible thing, Nell. Even when it has no logical foundation; hate can eat away at a person until there's not a dram of tenderness or reason left in them."

Nell understood only too well. The same kind of hate almost ended her life. Hate without reason described Nell's association with Molly Gill to a word and brought bitter memories back to her.

"As I said," Clare continued, "when Sarah died it finished Gerald, and he died almost to the day a year later. I felt that life was over for me. Its funny you know, I believe that if you give up on life, life gives up on you. I started to become ill. Pauline wanted to come home and nurse me but I couldn't let her do that. She had a husband and her life all planned. That's why I agreed to live in that terrible place, where she could keep an eye on me. I'm glad now that I did Nell. You've been a real tonic."

"Oh stop it, you'll have me blushing in a minute," Nell said laying the tray across the bed.

"Did you meet Pauline's husband while you were at St Mary's, Nell?"

"Mr Goodman? Only once, he seemed a very kind man. Now are you going to talk all day or are you going to make an effort to eat that and get dressed?"

An hour later, they were saying goodbye to Hilda and Betty. Clarence, the chauffeur and most recent employee, helped Clare into her new mode of transport: a Rolls Royce Silver Ghost.

"You know, I still can't get used to this," said Clare as Nell climbed in beside her. "Don't seem natural, not having a horse to look at."

"Well I think it's marvellous," Nell argued, "And I can think of a lot better things to look at than a horse's arse."

Hilda and Betty could hear the sound of Clare's laughter as the car slowly eased down the drive.

Portsmouth, like any English town at that time of year was busy with Christmas shoppers. Clare and Nell became separated as they each browsed around the Landport Drapery Bazaar. Clare was looking for curtain material, while Nell's mind was set on dresses for both her and Cathleen.

Clare Rutherford was well known, respected and liked in and around Portsmouth, and Nell was quite used to people stopping them to make conversation, but above the hubbub of the crowded store came a voice that caught Nell's attention.

"Excuse me but aren't you Mrs Rutherford?"

"Yes I am. Do I know you?"

"Well you probably wouldn't remember me, I'm Irene Boswell of Boswell's Naval Outfitter's."

"Yes of course I do. You have a shop in Queen Street. My husband would not have his shirts made anywhere else. If I remember rightly, we've spoken before. Don't you live at Cosham?"

"Yes you're right. I'm flattered you should remember," said Mrs Boswell

"At my age it's a blessing that I remember anything my dear." Clare then became aware of the little girl half hiding shyly behind the woman. I say, what a beautiful child! How old is she?"

"This is Martia, she's nearly five," said Irene Boswell, as the little girl smiled up at Clare. "Say hello to the lady, Martia." With that, the girl disappeared behind Irene's skirts again. "Needless to say self-assurance is not one of her virtues."

"Well it should be, she is quite striking: such bright blue eyes."

At this point Nell furtively shifted some lace net to get a better view of her old employer and her mystery child.

"My God!" Nell thought to herself, "Clare's right, this child would win any baby show." The child's raven hair shone with an almost blue sheen, yet her eyes were an unnatural shade of blue, creating a beauty rarely seen. However, Nell had seen it before and, as she remembered where, an unavoidable shiver went through her.

"Nell, come and see this little girl," said Clare. Nell came out from behind the net curtains to a very surprised Irene Boswell.

"Well I never! Nell Masters," said Irene "It must be six or seven years since…"

"You two obviously know each other," interrupted Clare. "I'll leave you to chat. I'll be looking at the new sewing machines when you want me Nell. Nice seeing you Mrs Boswell." Clare wandered off to the far side of the shop while Irene's attention returned to Nell.

"I was going to say," Irene continued, "since that awful business with Rose Gill."

Nell always liked Mrs Boswell. She had little to do with the factory girls, as she spent all her time in the shop, but she was always friendly to them as they passed through the shop to use the washroom.

"That must have been terrible for you, going through all that trial and court business."

"Yes it was," Nell said, though only half listening. She was looking at the child who was peering back at her from behind Irene's dress.

Nell's next question was superfluous as she knew the answer, but her curiosity was at bursting point. "Is this your child Mrs Boswell?"

"Yes…well actually, adopted. You remember her mother: Molly Gill. Well, Molly died. I don't think she ever got over seeing her sister, Rose, taken away. It was just after she had the baby that she contracted diphtheria and it wasn't long after that she died. Ivan was there at the end you know and her last wish was for us to look after her baby."

"What about her husband, the girls father."

"Oh she wasn't married, dear, and we don't know who the father was. With that family I'd be surprised if any of them knew who their father was."

"I think I might," Nell thought to herself.

"Molly's mother didn't want the responsibility." Irene looked down at the child and lowered her voice as if the child could understand her next words. "Quite honestly it would have been a crime to leave her with that family. God, it was an awful place."

"Yes I saw some of them at the trial. I can imagine the kind of life she would have had. I think you're very kind to have taken her."

"It's nice of you to say so but its Ivan and I who have been rewarded, not being blessed with any of our own. But I hear that you have a child now don't you?"

It became common knowledge during Oli Matchers re-trial that Nell was raped, and that it resulted in her pregnancy. Although Irene's question could be regarded as insensitive, Nell knew that it was not meant with any malice. However, the subject was embarrassing and Nell dealt with it by ignoring the question and changing the subject.

"Can I ask how my friend Vivien Price is getting on?" Nell said. The ploy worked and Irene coloured slightly, realising her question was inappropriate and an embarrassment to Nell.

"Well as you know I don't have much to do with that side of the business but as far as I know she's coping. Oh, do you remember my sister's boy, Alfie Button? He still looks after our horse." Nell was surprised that after so long, the mention of Alfie still sent a flutter through her. "He mentioned you the other day."

"Did he really?" Nell tried not to sound overly interested when she asked, "I expect he's married now, isn't he?"

"Good Lord no, but he would be if it was up to that awful Brenda Scopes."

"Oh yes, I remember, she was always sweet on Alfie."

"Well, If you ask me, she was sweet on anything wearing trousers and that includes bellbottoms! I've seen her out with a few sailors, and I remember the day she almost got you killed in Queen Street. I never really believed she did that for a joke, Nell. And I know you were seeing Alfie at the time." Nell smiled,

"Well never mind. That's all in the past now."

"Yes I suppose so. He still talks about you though, I think he still has a soft spot for you." Nell blushed and was lost for a reply. "He has his own forge now, you know, Nell. I'll tell him I saw you. Tell me, how come you know Mrs Rutherford? Mixing with the upper classes now are we?"

"Not exactly, she's my employer."

"Really! Well you are a lucky girl. She's such a nice lady."

"I wouldn't argue with that! I do consider myself very privileged." With that, Clare interrupted them.

"If you ladies have finished gossiping, I am starving. Nell I thought we'd stop at Lyons restaurant. Before we go on to Barker's"

"Whatever you say Clare. Who am I to argue with your stomach?" Clare laughed and Irene's open mouth displayed surprised at such light-hearted banter between employee and employer.

"Well goodbye Mrs Boswell, hope to see you again sometime," said Clare while Nell smiled and nodded her goodbye.

Irene watched through the shop window as the two climbed into the Rolls and the car moved off.

Clarence drove on into Portsmouth. After a light meal at Lyons restaurant they made one of Clare's frequent visits to the offices of Barker & Son, the Rutherford's family solicitors. Their offices were situated above Evelins: a very large and popular toyshop in Fratton Road.

Since the death of her husband, Barker& Son had been entrusted with most of Clare's financial and legal affairs which meant Clare was frequently signing papers.

Resigning herself to a customary long wait, Nell sat in the passenger seat chatting to Clarence until the understandable, but persistent curiosity of passers-by became too much.

"Clarence, I feel like a goldfish sitting here. I'm going to look around the toyshop. If the Mistress returns before I get back, please come and get me."

Nell browsed around the shop making mental notes of possible Christmas gifts.

"I'm looking for a doll for my little girl," Nell told the assistant. "It's got to have eyes that open and close."

"Most of the good ones do now, Miss. Babytears is our best example. There's one left in the window. Shall I fetch it?"

"No thank you, I'm a bit pressed for time, but I'll have a look in your window."

As Nell emerged from the shop, she smiled to see Clarence still behind the wheel of the Rolls looking positively bored. She scanned Evelin's shop window for the doll, but before she could find it, she heard the familiar sound of a trotting pony, then a voice from the past,

"Nell! Nell Masters,"

Nell turned without thinking. Her mind and stomach went into turmoil. There across the road was Alfie Button, her golden haired Alfie, still as handsome as her dreams portrayed. He stood proudly holding the reins of Pegasus.

His pony and trap were on the far side of the road and the traffic was too heavy for him to turn. He shouted across the busy traffic, "Wait there, Nell, I'll go to the next corner and turn around." Nell heard him make a familiar clucking noise with his tongue and watched Pegasus quickly break into a trot. Nell waited until Alfie had turned the corner of the next road then to Clarence's surprise she jumped into the back of the car and bellowed,

"Drive Clarence, quickly."

"Where?"

"Just go. Around the block, anywhere, do it now please, quick." Clarence complied with the same urgency, taking them in the opposite direction to Alfie. The chauffer turned at the next corner, and again at the next before Nell asked him to stop in a little back street behind the shops.

"Can I ask what we're doing here, Miss Nell? What if the Mistress returns?" Clarence asked as he turned off the motor. Not getting an immediate answer, He turned in his seat to see Nell crying and obviously distraught.

Clarence was a widower and in the autumn of his years, but quite shrewd in matters of the heart. He waited for Nell to compose herself before saying quietly, "Someone special, was he Miss?"

"What do you mean, Clarence?" Nell said, sniffing the last of her tears away.

"The young man that called out, I saw the way you looked at him, and now the tears. Remembering my youth, I'd say there were some very strong feelings involved. It's many years since any young woman shed any tears over me. I envy him, although why you'd want to avoid him, I can't imagine."

"Yes he was very special to me once, Clarence, but that's all in the past, and all too complicated."

"Would you like me to walk back to see if he's gone Miss?"

"You are a dear, Clarence, but no, I think he'll be gone by now."

They returned to Barkers to find Clare waiting on the pavement.

"Where have you been? Clare sounded mildly annoyed."

"I'm sorry Clare," Nell said, having recovered and dried her eyes. "Clarence needed to pee," she said, grinning at Clarence's image in his mirror.

Christmas came and it was a truly happy one at Clearview. It was Boxing Day and for once, the large dining table served its purpose. It was the one day of the year that dinner included all the staff.

Clare sat at the head of the table. To her right sat Pauline and her husband Neville, then young Betty Frost and Maude Ferry.

To Clare's left sat Hilda Brough, Clarence, the chauffer, then Nell, Cathy and special guest: Nell's mother Violet. Most importantly, the table was graced with a Christmas spirit and good humour, as when Clare addressed Nell's mother,

"Mrs Masters, did Clarence give you a pleasant ride here? I swear, when he's in a mood he tries to hit every bump in the road,"

"Oh no, Mrs Rutherford," said Violet. "Clarence drove real nice, I never 'ad such a nice experience, or such a lovely Christmas dinner. Thank you for inviting me."

With that, Clarence, who had proved to have a droll sense of humour, winked at Nell before putting down his knife and fork. He then dabbed his mouth with his napkin and addressed Clare in a mock servile voice.

"If it pleases Madam, I must apologize that the excursion to fetch Mrs Masters took so long, but I'm afraid Mrs Masters insisted that we drove around her block until her neighbours curtains were seen to furtively move."

Midst the laughter this caused, Clare was called upon to give a speech.

Clare pulled the paper hat from her head and used it to wipe the tears of laughter from her eyes.

"I want to thank you all for making this a special Christmas for me. It's been a very long time since I've had a real sensation of having family around me and I do mean everyone. Neville, thank you for coming, your being here today has made me even more sorry for the many wasted years.

Now I'm feeling a little tired, so I'm going to my room for a nap. I'll see you all for tea and parlour games. Nell would you see me up the stairs."

Nell helped Clare to her room. "I won't get in bed Nell. I'll just lie here until its time to come down," she said, closing her eyes. "Would you just pull the eiderdown over my legs?" Nell did so, kissing Clare's cheek. After closing the curtains she left, quietly closing the door.

Clare Rutherford closed her eyes for the last time.

The staff at Clearview found themselves unemployed, and the house was put up for sale. However, Pauline was more than generous with all of their severance pay. She also asked Nell to stay on, at least until a buyer for the house was found, which Nell was happy to do.

Nell had no idea how long she had to make other arrangements, and having sent best part of her earnings home to her mother over the last few years, her options were limited. She felt that her only choice would be to ask her mother if she could return home. In her mind, Nell had it all planned; she would get a job and let her mother stay home and look after Cathy. Nell believed that Violet would be only too pleased to give up her job. Nell had also been a little worried about her since Boxing Day, although Violet seemed to enjoy the day, Nell felt that not all was well with her.

So, knowing how Violet wanted her and Cathy back home, Nell chose a Saturday to travel to Portsmouth and tell her mother of her plans.

It was now more than a month since that fateful Boxing Day when Clare passed away and that was the last time Nell had seen her mother. As she and Cathleen walked along Lyons Terrace, she could see nothing much had changed. Ragged kids played hopscotch. One little girl pushed a pushchair containing a child hardly smaller than herself. Another sat in the kerb chewing the remains of a dirty apple core. All were passing time on cost-nothing activities. Some paused, and eyed Cathleen with curiosity, due to her expensive clothes, and likewise, Cathleen stared back with equal curiosity at the ragged urchins.

Reaching her mother's house, Nell knocked the door and was surprised to hear a man's angry voice.

"For Christ sake woman can't you get off your arse?" The door opened and a broad shouldered man with a large paunch stood looking down at them. Nell guessed him to be in his late forties. He frowned at Nell and asked gruffly,

"Well!"

"I'd like to see my mother." Nell said with equal terseness.

"Oh! So, you're Nell are you? You better go in then." He said. Then he turned and shouted back down the hallway "It's for you. I'm off out." With that, he brushed passed Nell and Cathleen and strode off down the road.

"Who the hell was that?" Nell said as she came into the living room where Violet stood ironing a shirt on a blanket covered table. Nell kissed her mother, noting the darkness under her eyes.

Violet hugged Nell more tenderly than was usual and kissed Cathleen.

"Jim Collier. He's my lodger," said Violet averting her eyes from Nell. She folded the shirt, and picked another from a jumbled pile of clean washing on a chair. "I'll make you some tea in a minute love and I've got some of Cathy's favourite biscuits." Nell noticed a slight waver in her mother's voice.

"Mum! You don't take lodgers!" Nell took her mother by the arm and gently swung her round until she faced her. She could see Violet was about to cry. "Mum, you've never taken a lodger. Wouldn't trust them, you said! And who was he shouting at when I knocked the door?"

"Oh don't worry about it love he gets a bit ruffled sometimes."

"A bit ruffled! He's a bloody lodger for Pete's sake. You don't have to take that, and you never answered my question mum, why have you taken in a lodger. You had your job, I know I couldn't send you much but…"

"Oh Nell you've been good to me and I'm grateful, but I had to give the job up. I just couldn't cope any more." Violet put her hand under her arm and took a deep breath. Nell read the pain in her face.

"What is it mum, is it that lump? Better let me take a look."

"Oh stop fussing its nothing. If you want to help, go and put the kettle on. And stick that iron back on the gas." Nell obliged, and from the scullery, called out,

"Well I guess that puts paid to my plans Mum. I was going to suggest that Cathy and I come back home. I was thinking I'd go out to work so you could give up your job. But I'll just have to think again now. Where did he come from Mum?" Violet never answered. Nell started to carry the tea tray in before saying: "You don't seem to want to talk about it mum, why is that?" Violet was sitting down with Cathleen on her lap as Nell entered and her face was wet with tears.

"Mum whatever's wrong." Nell said. "Was it my big mouth? I'm sorry I should mind my own business."

"No love, it's not you. I'd love to have you both back here with me, but Nell, I've made a terrible mistake by taking him in."

"Then why did you?"

"Well I've been coming home from my job feeling so ill for the last few weeks, and then one day I heard a couple of women in the corner shop talking about letting rooms. Before I had given it any thought, I'd put a advertisement in the shop window." Violet reached up and took a packet of five Woodbines from the mantle. Her hands were shaking as she put the cigarette to her lips.

"Mum, you've started smoking again!"

"Yes it calms me down." She lit the cigarette and continued. "He seemed so nice when he called about the room. But it didn't take long before he started throwing his weight about." Violet paused and looked away before adding, "and worse. He hasn't paid any rent for two weeks."

"Is that what you meant when you said and worse?" Violet took a while answering. She glanced at Cathy fearing she'd decipher the thread of conversation, but decided it was safe to speak and when she did, her voice was a whisper.

"Nell, I now know what it's like to experience what you went through."

"What do you mean? Oh, Mum! Did he...have you told the police?"

"I can't Nell, he's threatened to kill me if I make trouble. When you wrote to say the old lady had died, and that Clearview was up for sale, I thought...well I hoped that you would come home. I told him that I wanted him to leave but he just laughed. Oh Nell! He knows that I have no one to turn to. What am I going to do?"

"Where has he gone now?"

"He'll be up the pub. He's usually in the Dew Drop Inn on his day off."

"Oh is he! He can buy beer but can't pay his rent. Well just wait until he comes back."

"No Nell, Don't say anything, please, especially after he's been drinking. You don't know what he's like. He'll start on me after you've gone." Nell could see the fear on her mothers face.

"Alright mum but you'll have to put your foot down."

The Dewdrop Inn was doing an unusually good trade of late due to sewage work going on in Portsmouth at the time, and many Irish ground workers were filling the pubs.

Jim Collier propped himself up at the bar downing his second pint of ale, while eavesdropping on a bunch of Irishmen discussing the well known business of prostitution that went on in the surrounding area. Their discussion prompted an idea in Collier.

It was almost two hours after Collier had ventured to the pub that Violet and Nell eventually heard a key being inserted in the front door then heavy footsteps along the hall. Collier came in red-faced and bleary-eyed. "What's to eat, gal," he said, ignoring Nell but winking at Cathleen. Then he almost fell backwards into an armchair. Violet quickly lifted Cathy down from her lap saying, "There's a pork pie in the larder. I'll get it." As Violet hurried into the scullery, Collier pulled Cathy toward him.

"Hello my little angel," he said. "Do you want to come and sit on my lap?" Nell grabbed her arm and pulled her away.

"What's up? I was just being friendly," Collier said.

"If you want to be friendly." Nell said angrily. "Why don't you do as my mother has asked, and leave?"

"Has she been talking about me? I pays good money for my room and I'm not leaving." Violet came back in and placed in front of him four segments of pork pie on a small plate. "It's not as if she overfeeds me, is it?" He said darting a scowl from the plate to Violet. "Got any mustard, pork pies no bloody good without mustard."

"I haven't been to the shops yet." Violet said timidly. Nell began to fidget as her anger surfaced.

"Didn't you say you were waiting for some rent, mum, before you could afford to get some shopping?" Nell said glaring at Collier as she said it, while the fear on Violet's face was a plea to Nell, not to rouse his temper.

"Oh, so you have been talking about me. Well don't worry gal, you'll have your money tonight." With that, he started to laugh, leaving Nell and Violet looking puzzled.

The following day Nell went about her daily tasks at Clearveiw while fretting inwardly about where she would go once a buyer had been found. She also worried about how her mother would cope with this unsavoury Collier character, she'd become encumbered with.

Nell received a reasonable wage while looking after Clearview House, and her only duty was to keep it clean, dusted and ready for any potential buyers to inspect it. Cathleen still attended her school, and would until the place was sold and Nell was given a date to vacate the premises. So far, two families had shown an interest in the house. But no reasonable offer had been made.

Pauline Goodman was the only person to call Clearview by phone, and lately, it was only to tell Nell that some buyer was coming to view the house. The morning after her visit to her mother, however, it did ring and Nell raced down to the hall to quickly pick it up.

"Yes Pauline?" Nell said, anticipating the caller. But there was only silence "Pauline! Hello is that you?" she said louder. There was the sound of someone sobbing, and then a faint voice,

"Nell."

"Mum is that you? Where are you?

"I'm in the post office. Oh! Nell can you come home…I don't know what to do. I've been beaten and…" Nell had never heard her mother sound so desperate Violet could hardly speak her words.

"Oh mum you'll have to get rid of him you can't just let a man come into your home and mistreat you."

"If that were all…" The line went silent.

"Mum are you still there? What were you saying?" Nell could hear her mother trying to control her sobbing. "Mum take your time, just tell me what happened."

"He used me like a prostitute. Nell he brought three men home with him last night. And they…they dragged me… When they left, I saw them give him money. Nell what am I going to do?"

"Go to the police mum. Tell them…"

"I did, this morning, but when I mentioned that I lived in Lyons Street they just laughed and said what do you expect. They know how bad it's become with the prostitution here. When I told them about Collier they said if he's paid rent there's nothing they can do about him. Please Nell, if you were here he might leave."

"I'm not sure he would mum but I'll try to think of something. I'll try to get down to see you tomorrow Mum but I'll have to wait for Cathleen to get home from school. Lock your bedroom door tonight and wedge a chair under the handle."

Nell never told her mother that she already had a plan that might solve her problem of getting rid of Jim Collier; the reason being that her plan was sketchy to say the least. It was a plan based on a promise made long ago.

Nell stepped off the tram and immediately recognised the shoe repair shop where she'd last seen Oliver Matcher working on the roof. She entered the shop, a cobbler sat working at his Last. Nell could see he held nails in his mouth but she asked her question anyway. "Excuse me I'm looking for the man who did repairs on your roof. It was about six years ago."

"Oliver Smith!" the man mumbled without taking the nails from his mouth.

"No his name is…" Suddenly Nell remembered that Oli had changed his name. "Oh yes that's right."

As the cobbler took the last nail from his mouth and hammered it into the shoe Nell said, "do you know where I can find him?"

"I can tell you how to find his house, it's in his builders yard."

Nell followed the cobbler's directions and eventually entered the double gates of a huge builders yard. She found herself staring at crates of roof tiles and vehicles with the name Oliver Smith professionally sign-written on the side of each cab. Just inside the gates was a small shed-like building with the word Office over a sliding window. Nell tapped on it and the window slid open.

"Yes?" snapped a middle-aged woman, seemingly devoid of all friendliness.

"I'd like to see Mr Smith, please."

"Oliver Smith?" the woman showed surprise.

"Yes."

"Why? I mean, is it about a job? We haven't any office jobs," the woman said sharply. "And anyway Mr Smith doesn't give interviews himself."

"No I don't want a job, I just want to see him."

"Well you can't. He's not to be disturbed. What's it about?" Nell could see that this woman did not want to help her for some reason. Nell turned and surveyed the yard.

"Is that his house, she said, ignoring the question and pointing to the grand looking house at the far side of the yard?"

"Yes, but I told you…." Before the woman could complete her sentence Nell hurried off in the direction of the house with the woman following in pursuit. Nell reached the front door and lifted the dolphin shaped knocker just as the office woman grabbed her arm and pulled her away leaving the knocker to drop with a louder clonk than Nell would have wished.

"Just what do you think you're doing?" The woman shouted at Nell as the door opened and a smartly dressed Oli Matcher stood looking down at the two of them.

"Ivy! I told you no one was to knock the door, and my wife was not to be disturbed. What's so impor…" Oli paused as he recognised Nell. He stared at her until the office woman spoke.

"I'm sorry Mr Smith, I couldn't stop her she…"

"That's okay Ivy. You carry on. I know this young lady. I'll deal with this." Then to Nell, "You had better come in." As the woman walked away. Nell followed him into the house and into a small study. He took great care to close the door gently behind him then directed her to a chair.

"My wife is very ill and doesn't get much sleep."

"I'm sorry I didn't know you were married." He merely acknowledged Nell's comment with a faint smile.

"Nell, I heard that Mrs Rutherford died, I suppose you need a job now."

"No!"

"Oh! What then?"

"You once told me that I could come to you if I needed help."

"That's right. Do you need some money?"

Nell looked embarrassed: peering down as she clicked and un-clicked the clasps on her purse. "No I need someone with your strength." Oli looked puzzled, as he waited for an explanation. "I have to leave Clearview, its being sold. My mother is ill and I want to be at home with her, but there's a man lodging in my mother's house. She… I mean we, want him to leave but he refuses to go."

"Have you told the police?"

"Yes, but they think that every woman in Lyons Terrace is a prostitute and they have no time for them. Besides, they say that because he's paid rent there's nothing they can do, even though he hasn't paid since the first week, and he's been there a month."

"And you want me to physically evict him?"

"Well…yes!"

"No Nell, I can't. I'm not that kind of man anymore. I can't get involved in that sort of thing. I'm a councillor now. Can you imagine what the papers would do to me if they found out I'd been throwing my weight about? They would drag up all of my past. On top of this, my wife is very ill. What would a scandal do to her?"

Nell stared back at him and fought back a tear while thinking how stupid she was to ever think her plan would work. She stood up and moved toward the door.

"Yes, I understand. I'm sorry I disturbed you. I'll try to think of some other way."

Reading the disappointment in her voice he said: "Wait a minute Nell." Then from a drawer in his desk, he produced some paper money.

"That's not what we need Mr Smith," Nell said as a tear eluded her effort to stop it running down her cheek. "You see, this man is forcing my mother into prostitution, so I've no doubt money will not be a problem."

At 7pm that same day, Nell stood in Lyons St waiting for her mother to open the door. As she stood there, she noticed one of the bottom door panels was missing and been replaced with a piece of cardboard.

She also sensed the attention coming from several women who were, as usual, out on their doorsteps spreading their gossip or awaiting a customer. Some were known prostitutes, who would view any unfamiliar women seen in their street with suspicion and as a possible threat to their own livelihood.

The door opened. "Nell! Where's Cathleen?" Violet exclaimed, seeing Nell standing there alone.

"I took her to Mrs Brough's house the housekeeper. She's going to look after her until I get back. After what you told me over the telephone this morning, I couldn't let her sleep here, could I?"

"Oh Nell, does that mean you'll stay with me tonight?" Violet put her arm around her daughter and ushered her into the house. "Thank you love, I've been so frightened." Nell could feel her mother trembling and noticed bruises on her arms.

"Where is he mum, where's that fat pig, I want to see him?" Violet could feel her daughter's anger as Nell peered past her into the gloomy passage."

"Nell, calm down, he's not here. Sometimes he comes in about five demanding to be fed. Then he goes to the pub until closing time. That's when I get frightened. I don't want you to confront him, though Nell. He's mad and I'm afraid he'll hurt you."

"Did he do that?" Nell pointed to the door.

"Yes. He has a key, but after that night when he brought those awful men home, I tried bolting the door. He just kicked in the panel, put his arm through, and unbolted it." Violet unconsciously caressed the bruises on her arms as she remembered the beating that he gave her that day. "What am I going to do Nell?"

"I'm not sure mum, but I promise he won't touch you tonight. I'll go to the police tomorrow. If that Inspector Davage is still there, I'll see if he can help. He was very nice to everyone up at Clearview. I know this is not his kind of thing, but he might tell us what to do. It's got to be worth a try."

By 6pm Collier had still not appeared, much to Violet's relief. That evening the two prepared themselves for a siege against whatever menace might threaten them that night. Nell found an old kitchen chair in the garden; She broke off two of its legs thinking they would make perfect clubs should they need them. They took what food was left in the larder upstairs to Violet's bedroom. This, Nell believed, might stop Collier and anyone he brought back from the pub from holding their own siege.

After they made sure of having enough books to read, they fed the gas meter with as many pennies as they could find to ensure the light would not fade and leave them in the dark. They then shut themselves in Violet's bedroom and shifted the double bed against the door. Fully clothed they sat up reading. As pub-closing-time neared, they became conscious of each other glancing at the mantle shelf clock. Nell was concerned for her mother. She was surprised at how quickly her health had deteriorated. Her yellowish complexion and sunken eyes told Nell it was more than just Collier that was causing it. Nell's concern deepened a few minutes later when Violet complained that she was cold and got up to don a woollen cardigan. As she raised her arms, Nell noticed the swelling under her arm. Nell quickly hid the look of alarm on her face as her mother climbed back into bed. Nell laid her book down and turned to her mother.

"Have you been to see the doctor lately mum?"

"No! Why."

"Well I was just concerned. You're not looking very well and I was wondering if that lump you showed me, had got any worse?"

"No, it's nothing," Violet said tersely. "Anyway I haven't got money to waste on…" She paused when they both heard a sound from below their window.

"Don't worry Mum, he can't get in this room, and if he tries he'll get a broken head." Nell picked up the chair leg that rested against the wall next to her, and laid it across her lap. "Besides, it's another half hour until the pubs close." Nell could see she had not quelled the fear in Violet, and was not even sure that she believed her own words. Suddenly they heard a loud knock at the front door.

"Oh Nell!" Violet whispered. "It's him."

"Shh" Nell put her finger to her lips. They sat perfectly still for some moments listening. Then the loud knock again and voices.

"If he's got a key why doesn't he open the door?" Nell whispered, then swinging her legs off the bed she tiptoed to the window.

"No! Don't open it." Violet sounded terrified as carefully and silently Nell slid the window up. Instantly the voices became louder.

"Nell, shut the window. Don't let them see you."

"It's alright mum, you'll be safe now!" With the help of the streetlight, Nell had seen something that had given her confidence. She poked her head out of the window and called out, "Hello who is it?"

"Is this Mrs Master's house?" came a manly voice. Nell could make out the shape of four people stood outside the front door.

"Yes."

"Well are you going to open the door gal? We've come a long way."

"Yes, Oh please wait! I'll be right down." Nell turned to her mother, "Quick mum, help me shift the bed. These men have come to help."

"But Nell! Who are they, and how do you know it's not a trick?"

"Because I've seen the name on the side of their truck. I'll explain later mum." Violet was still confused, but followed Nell's instructions.

Nell welcomed the men into the living room while Violet disappeared into the scullery to make tea for them. Still in their working clothes, the men were all big and Nell guessed that Oli had chosen them for that reason.

"Its very good of Mr Smith to send you all this way to help us."

The largest of them, a blonde haired man with a ruddy outdoor complexion, seemed to be their spokesman.

"Make's no difference to us love," he said, while grinning at the others. "Shifting roof tiles or shifting lodgers! We get paid anyway, but I must admit this has got to be the strangest job we've ever been asked to do. You must be a relative I suppose. I'm Chris Moon, by the way and this is Don, Dave and Rob." The men all nodded as they were introduced.

"The boss said you were having trouble getting rid of some lodger." Chris said, "What's it all about then, and where is this bloke now?"

"It's a bit more serious than that Mr Moon," Violet started to tell her story but broke down in tears leaving Nell to explain her mother's predicament. Nell left out little of Collier's brutal treatment of her mother. And as she mentioned her mother's bruises she saw Chris's knuckles turning white.

"You say he'll be here any minute?" It was Rob that spoke. "Has he got any belongings here?" Nell looked to her mother for an answer.

"Yes," said Violet. "A few clothes, a small case and a box of carpenters tools."

"You better get them, gal," said Chris "We don't want him having any excuse to come back do we?"

Violet looked once more at the clock noting that it was after closing time. She made three hurried trips upstairs returning each time with more of Collier's belongings. As she crammed the last of his clothes in the case, they heard voices and raucous laughter coming from the street. Chris quickly turned the gaslight down and pushed the passage door almost shut.

They heard a key being inserted in the front door. Chris motioned to Nell and Violet to keep out of the way and for everyone to keep quiet. The four men were on their feet ready for any event.

The voices became louder as the front door slammed and Nell felt her mother squeeze her arm. Footsteps could be heard coming along the passage.

"Come on me old shipmates you're in for a good time tonight," a voice could be heard saying. "Money well spent, you might say. She's not one of your regular old pro's I can tell you…"

The living room door suddenly opened and a bleary eyed Jim Collier stood with a startled look on his face. Two, equally worse for drink, sailors stood behind him trying their hardest to remain upright. Ignoring the women, Collier said, "Who the hell are you?" His eyes were nervously scanning the faces of Oli Matcher's four employees, and eventually rested on Chris, the largest.

"Well I am your landlady's brother, and these are three mates of mine. Together we make up your friendly bailiffs," said Chris grinning. "We've come to help you move out. You two sailor boys can leave right away while you're still able to climb into a hammock."

"What about our money? He took our money," said the taller of the two.

"Not my problem. Sorry boys, put it down to experience." The two sailors protested angrily as they shuffled unsteadily back along the darkened passage.

Initially Collier looked stunned and frightened but then found his nerve before saying; "you've got a bloody cheek, coming in here, throwing your weight about." He glanced menacingly at Violet, but beads of sweat were forming around his mouth, and Nell knew that his protests were just bravado.

"We were invited, Mr Collier, but you have outstayed your welcome. Oh, and before you leave, I believe you owe my sister some rent." Chris said, in an almost apologetic voice, while still smiling, but Nell had the feeling that this big man's smile was hiding an emotion far less cordial, and that it could be about to surface. She saw the little secretive nudge that Don gave Dave and something told her that they had seen their friend in this quiet smiling mood before, and knew what to expect. The lie about being her mothers brother amused her and she could see the cunning of it. If Collier thought these men were just hired to get him out of the house he might, after a spell, come back.

"I've paid rent!" Collier started to protest, "I suppose that bitch told..." The sudden slap from Chris across Colliers face was so fast and loud; it made the two women jump and it left Collier reeling back against the passage door, slamming it shut.

"Don't call my sister a bitch!"

"But I paid her rent!" Collier repeated, leering at Violet and Nell while caressing his slowly reddening cheek.

"Oh yes, she told us, seven shillings wasn't it? That was for the first week's rent. And how long have you been here now, about a month? I make that another guinea, plus two pounds for the beatings she's taken. Now I suggest you put the money on the table, pick up your belongings and go."

Collier started searching his pockets, bringing quantities of silver from most of them and placing it on the table.

"But where can I go this time of night?"

"Well you could try paying one of the nice lady's that will be out on their doorsteps about now." Dave spoke, while Chris counted out Colliers money. "Failing that, Victoria Park is not far from here. It has lots of benches." Then Chris, while roughly stuffing the remaining money back in Colliers waistcoat pockets said,

"But if you got any sense you'll get out of this district and never come back, because if I ever see you anywhere near my sister again, I'll put you in hospital at the very least. Rob grabbed the suitcase from the table with both hands and jabbed it viciously into Collier's paunch, forcing him to hold it up with both arms, while Dave and Don piled the rest of his belongings on top.

"Don, would you open the door? Our Mr Collier is leaving."
Chris said sarcastically. Don complied while Chris spun Collier
round and literally pushed him along the passage and out the door
with a sarcastic "Bye."

Violet was so grateful to these men who had rid her of her
nightmare. To her they were knights in shining armour. However,
they declined her offer of more tea or food, insisting that they had
wives to get home to.

After waiting a short spell to make sure Collier did not attempt to
come back, Nell and her mother said their goodbyes to the four men
at the door. As they climbed into their lorry, Nell said to Chris,
"Would you please thank Mr Smith for his kindness, and tell him
I hope his wife recovers soon."
"OK love, but I'm afraid Mrs Smith is not expected to recover,
but you both take care now." The four men piled into the cab of
their truck and were soon gone, leaving Nell to explain to mother's
utter astonishment that the mysterious Mr Smith was none other
than Oli Matcher.

A week later Nell received a phone call from Pauline to say that
Clearview had been sold and that she had a week to vacate the
house, but Pauline added something else that Nell found rather odd.
First, she asked where she would be staying, when Nell said with
her mother, Pauline asked for the address. She then said, "expect a
letter soon" and rang off.

Nell moved back to Lyons Terrace and soon had Cathleen settled
in a local school. However, Nell found it hard to find adequate paid
employment that would keep her mother from having to work.
Then Nell received the letter.
The letter was from Barkers and Son: Clare Rutherford's
solicitors. It requested her to be present at the reading of Clare's will
the following week.

"Oh Nell," said Violet. "Wouldn't it be nice if Mrs Rutherford has left you something in her will?"

"Yes it would but I wouldn't count on it, mum. Clare had a lot of nice things in her jewellery box that Cathleen loved playing with. It may just be that Clare's left her a brooch or something."

When Nell arrived at Barker's she was shown into a waiting room where she was surprised to find Maude Ferry the Cook and Hilda Brough the housekeeper.

The three embraced each other and Maude shed a few tears for the memory of Clare.

The three sat in a waiting room. They talked about the happy time they'd spent together at Clearview. And like Nell, Hilda and Maude expected to be left some little trinket that Clare may have remembered that they'd admired. A young man eventually appeared, introduced himself, and ushered them into another room where they were surprised to see Pauline smiling at them. Mr Barker sat behind an enormous desk. He was a man in his seventies and father of the young man who had ushered them in.

" Please take a seat ladies," he said, looking over the top of his spectacles. He nodded toward the three chairs lined neatly in front of his desk. Pauline and young Mr Barker sat at each end of the desk where they could face both Mr Barker and the three women. "Now I expect you have a good idea that you have been left something in Mrs Clare Rutherford's will, and you'd be right. Now, because of your length of service Mrs Brough and Mrs Ferry, Clare Rutherford has bequeathed to you, two thousand pounds each."

"Oh my God," said Hilda, turning pale, while Maude had fainted and was starting to slide off her chair. Young Mr Barker dashed around behind her and pulled her back to a sitting position, while his father poured her a glass of water. With Maude partially restored, Mr Barker went on,

"Now we come to you Miss Masters. Now it seems that Clare Rutherford was a very fair minded woman, for even though you had not been in her service for very long she has left you the considerable sum of five hundred pounds." Nell put the back of her hand up to her face but a determined tear betrayed her emotion. Their problems at home were solved.

"Thank you Mr Barker," said Nell with a broad smile. She then stood up and made ready to leave.

"Please sit down Miss Masters I've not finished. And you haven't received your cheque yet."

Across the desk, he pushed two cheques towards Hilda and Maude. "If you ladies are happy that you have the correct names on your cheques, that concludes our business. It only leaves me to wish you well and to say spend your good fortune wisely." The two women kissed Pauline, thanked the old man and said their goodbyes. Young Mr Barker showed Hilda and Maude to the door.

"Now Miss Masters, apart from her direct family, that is Mrs Pauline Goodman here, there is one other person that Clare Rutherford wished to include in her will and that is your daughter, Cathleen. However because of Clare's age when this will was made, she realised that Cathleen would most certainly be too young to be entrusted with it. Therefore, she has left it for you to invest in your own way, but with Cathleen's welfare in mind." He opened the desk drawer and took out another cheque. "This includes your own five hundred pounds," he said as he pushed it towards her. Nell picked up the cheque and looked at it. Her mouth opened but emitted no sound.

"Invest it wisely Miss Masters," said Mr Barker. "And it will look after you and your daughter for the rest of your lives." Nell looked at Pauline.

"But this can't be right Pauline. Do you know how much this is made out for?"

"Yes Nell, it's ten thousand pounds."

"But this is yours. You're her daughter."

"Nell, I don't think you knew just how much mother was worth. Another ten thousand added to what she left me would not make any difference to me. Besides, in a way, you filled those last empty years of her life that Sarah's death had left. You became her missing daughter and Cathleen, the granddaughter she always wanted. Mr Barker read the will as mother asked him to do. This was for the benefit of Hilda and Maude and to save you all embarrassment, Hence the five hundred pounds. No, the cheque is yours to spend as you see fit. Mother had every faith that you will invest it wisely."

Nell's mother's failing health was Nell's first priority. Within a month of moving back to Lyons Terrace, Violet's health had deteriorated to a new low. Her breathing was now affected, resulting in hospitalisation. Nell tried her hardest to find a specialist who could treat the malignant growth that had started the decline of her mother's health. Unfortunately, knowledge in the treatment of breast cancer was limited, and a week before Cathleen's seventh birthday Violet Masters died.

In the few short months that Nell spent nursing her mother at Lyons Terrace, she was surprised at how many friends her mother had made in the street; it was doubly surprising that most of them were ladies of the night. Nell found them to be caring and kind with regard to Violets illness and was touched by the number of them who attended her mother's funeral. Talking to some of these women had started a train of thought in Nell's mind. This, and something Clare had said to her some time ago, gave her the possible answer to securing both Cathleen's and her own future.

Allowing herself a reasonable amount of time to mourn her mother's death, Nell then re-engaged in life's challenges. With the words of Mr Barker still fresh in her mind about investing wisely, and the financial advice that Clare was always giving her, Nell wasted no time in looking for a solicitor with whom she felt comfortable. One who would advise and act on her behalf with regard to the plans she had in mind. Her search resulted in engaging a young solicitor by the name of Cox.

"Yes I can see the reason why you should want to invest your money in property Miss Masters and I'll be happy to do the transference on these two properties, but I'm wondering why you have chosen these particular houses, you do realise that the district has a certain reputation?"

"I should, Mr Cox, I grew up there." Nell judged her chosen solicitor, William Cox, to be no more than 35 years old and still young enough to be embarrassed when confronting the subject of prostitution, especially with a woman as young as Nell. "You see Mr Cox I could buy houses in better districts but I couldn't always be sure of finding tenants for them whereas in Lyons Terrace I can."

"But you realise that your tenants are likely to be…"

"Prostitutes Mr Cox? Yes, I am aware. In the last few months I've come to know some of them, and a kinder bunch of women I've yet to meet. It seems to me that few of them would have chosen their way of life, given the choice, and as the saying goes, there but for the grace of God, etcetera. They say its one of the oldest professions, did you know that, Mr Cox."

"Yes I'm sure it is Miss Masters," Cox said in a disapproving manner. "However living off immoral earnings is frowned upon, regardless of mitigating circumstances, and whether you approve or not Miss Masters." Nell smiled,

"I think you are mistaking my intentions Mr Cox. You see, all I'm concerned with, is securing my little girls future."

"I'm sorry I didn't mean any disrespect…"

"These two houses," Nell interrupted, "that I wish to buy, and I hope to buy more as they become available, will hopefully rise in value or at least keep pace with the value of the pound. Meanwhile their rents will supply my daughter and I with an income. A reasonable rent will be charged, and collected by an agent. This, I would also like you to arrange. Hopefully I will remain anonymous. I do not intend to become a Madam if that is what you were thinking and I do not intend to get involved in my tenants' business whatever form that business takes."

"Well I must say you're certainly not obtuse when it comes to financial affairs Miss Masters, especially for one so young. I'm sorry I misinterpreted your intentions; would it be impertinent to ask where you were schooled?"

"Well as your question is put as a compliment, no. Most of my financial knowledge came from a place called Clearview House."

"That's not a college I'm familiar with, however, I will be glad to handle any business that you care to put my way Miss Masters, starting with the two properties in Lyons Terrace."

Nell left William Cox's office smiling to herself, and confident that she was about to start a new chapter in her life with the help of an honest advocate.

12
Enemy

Nell was content to keep her life simple. She had experienced the luxury of living in a grand house and she knew that most women, given the choice, could not have willingly regressed to her present living conditions, which, by comparison, was a hovel. But living through the distressing times of her mother's illness and nursing her through the last painful months, had a way of rendering her poor impoverished surroundings as unimportant. By the time her mother died, it was as if Nell had never been away. She had succumbed to her old environment: the little terraced house where she was born. Her only real concern now was the welfare of Cathleen, who was at first, and understandably, confused at being suddenly subjected to living in such lowly conditions.

For a while, and with the promiscuous activity going on around them, Nell wondered if she'd made a mistake. She pondered over her own shrewdness in bringing Cathy up in such depraved surroundings. *"I profoundly disapprove",* she could imagine Clare saying to her. Maybe she should have moved out of the area, she thought, but there were now disadvantages to moving: Cathleen had settled into the local school and was doing well there. Then there was Aunt Annie, who was now engaged to a hard working lodger she'd taken in. Nell considered Annie to be the only relative she had left. Living just around the corner, Annie was a good listener, and was always there when Nell needed a friendly ear.

Then there was her old friend, Vivien, whose sense of humour matched her own and with whom she enjoyed spending her mornings, either shopping or just sharing a cuppa together. On Nell's advice, Vivien rented a house of her own, right next to Annie. Little did Viv or Annie know that Nell had recently become the new owner of both their houses, and that their rent was purposely kept to a minimum.

Vivien's daughter: Angela, and Cathy had also become close friends, another reason Nell did not want to move.

No! For the moment, Nell would stay put. She decided, however, to try giving their little terraced house at least some of the refinements to which Cathy and she had become accustomed while at Clearview.

She hired professional painters and decorators; she paid carpenters to renew doors and window frames, bought expensive antique furniture, usually and whenever possible, with investment in mind. She bought new drapes and bedding; even the tiny garden was given a facelift with a little pond and flowerbed. Six-foot fence panels were erected around its walls. This was not so much for privacy, but to curtain unsightly back yards of her less than tidy neighbours.

Nell did not fraternise too deeply with her fellow Terrace dwellers, though she was equally cordial with them all: single men, working families, ladies of the night, her courteousness was non-discriminative. There were some married women on the street that, in stopping to pass pleasantries with Nell, would try to draw her into their practice of slating one of their neighbours; whether it be a prostitute, or just someone whom they considered socially unwholesome and possibly on the verge of becoming one. These gossiping women had no idea that they were, at times, talking about Nell's own tenants, and of course, Nell would not agree with them, or comment on any such propaganda. Consequently, these women soon lost interest in these one-way conversations, and eventually stopped coming to Nell with their tittle-tattle.

Nell became content with her life at Lyons Terrace and the years slipped by, practically unnoticed. The earlier niggling temptation to move to a grander place had faded. Concern for more important things took precedence, such as making the right investments to safeguard their future.

It was not until Cathleen and Angela reached their early teens that Nell noticed marked difference in the two girls' personalities and interests. Like most young girls, they had liked to experiment with cosmetics. They would spend hours in Cathy's room, playing music on a windup gramophone, dressing up and discussing boys.

To a point, Nell considered this natural and girlish as far as Cathy was concerned. Angela, however, started to be seen with boys much older than her. She began blooming, physically: becoming a young woman much earlier than most parents would consider ethical or healthy.

Maturing at such an early age, Nell feared would exacerbate the girl's likelihood of getting into trouble.

At fourteen Angela would apply powder and lipstick at weekends and stay out far later than was deemed proper. It wasn't until one of Nell's tenants told Nell that she'd seen Angela out with a sailor that Nell took up the subject with Vivien. She tried to persuade her to restrain Angela's habits. But Vivien either wouldn't, or couldn't get Angie to listen to reason. Nell visualised the dangerous path Angela seemed intent on taking, and was afraid that Cathy might also be coaxed along the same path.

Eventually, Nell discussed the subject with Cathy, asking that she sever ties with Angela. Nell was surprised when Cathy told her that she and Angela had already fallen out with each other for that very reason, so Cathy put up little resistance and agreed not to associate with Angela.

A week later on a Sunday morning Nell answered the doorbell to see Vivien standing there. Without even a greeting, Viv came straight to the point,

"What's my Angie done to upset you?" she said in a, louder than necessary, voice.

"First of all, hello Viv how are you, would you like to come in?" Nell said jovially.

"No I wouldn't!" Viv said, with the anger in her tone becoming more noticeable. "Why is Cathy not allowed to see my Angie?"

Nell could see that her own cheery manner was not going to smooth over the mood that Viv was in, and therefore decided to be blunt. "Because she's a bad influence. I told you Viv, didn't I? Your Angie will get herself in trouble if you don't stop her behaving like an eighteen-year-old. Now the whole neighbourhood is talking about her and I don't want Cathy tarred with the same brush. Now, do you want to come in for a cuppa or not?"

"No! And I think you're a stuck up cow. And you needn't bother to knock my door for any more tea in future, either."

Nell expected Viv to get over her tantrum within a couple of weeks, but months passed and still there was no sign of Viv. Nell took to visiting her Aunt Annie more often, hoping that she would bump into Vivien. Nell dearly wanted the two of them to air their differences, but stopped short of knocking Viv's door.

Feeling that she now needed something more to occupy her time, Nell decided to go ahead with an idea she'd been nursing for a while.

She bought a small shop and turned it into a second hand dealership. She learnt the business the hard way, having no one to show her the ropes. At first, she bought the wrong things at the wrong prices but she soon caught on, and learning to run the shop gave her an interest she needed.

More than a year passed since Vivien had called. Then, distressed and almost in tears, she knocked at Nell's door.

"Viv! What's the matter?" This tipped the scales and Viv burst out crying. "You'd better come in!" Nell ushered Vivien into the small living room and sat her down at the table.

"Oh Nell I know you're going to call me stupid. I should have listened to you, my Angie's got herself mixed up with a bad lot, and I don't know how far it's gone."

"What do you mean Viv, you're not making much sense at the moment?"

Viv paused a while, biting her lip and Nell could see that what Viv had to impart was not easy for her.

"You know you had a go at me about letting Angie stay out late, well it got worse. She started coming home at one and two in the morning. When I asked her where she'd been, she just told me to mind my own business. Anyway, one evening I followed her. She went to a house in Crane Street. I took note of the door number ready to make a few inquires about the place, that was Monday evening. I waited up for her that night. She rolled in about midnight and Nell, her breath reeked of gin."

"Oh Viv, the girl's only fifteen. Who are these people and what did you mean when you said you don't know how far it's gone?"

Midst another outburst of tears, Viv blurted out the full account and the cause of her anxiety.

"I went back to Crane St the next day Nell; I wasn't even sure why, or what I was going to do, but I was so worried. Before I got to the house, I met a woman I worked with at Boswell's. I stopped and we chatted. I asked her if she knew who lived at number 28." Viv paused, dabbed her eyes and stared solemnly at Nell.

"And?"

"Elsie Craven, the woman said. Then she said that lately the place was like a bloody brothel with women and blokes coming and going every night. She said she thought the husband was away, because she hadn't seen him lately."

Nell took Vivien's hands in hers, squeezing them gently, she said, "Oh Viv I am sorry love, you've got to get Angie away from there! Did you go to the house?"

"No. She said this Craven woman was trouble and that even her husband is frightened of her. Anyway I wouldn't know what to say Nell, I was hoping you would come with me."

"Alright Viv I'll come with you, but how did Angie get involved with this woman?"

"Well she's got this young good looking nephew. They say he works down the market, and I've been told that's where Angie's been hanging out. I'm sure that's the connection."

It was raining when Nell and Viv knocked the door of number 28 Crane Street. They were both huddled together under one umbrella as the door opened and a very slovenly looking young woman, aged about 30, stood there with an enquiring look on her face.

"Are you the householder?" Nell said.

The woman turned and shouted into the darkness of the passage behind her,

"Elsie!" Light flooded the passage as a door opened and a heavily pregnant woman shuffled her way toward them.

"Okay Greta," said the pregnant woman, on reaching the front door. Greta turned, squeezed past her and disappeared through a side door of the passage. The Elsie woman eyed her two callers with a cold look of suspicion. Without a word she jerked her chin upward in a, what's-your-business, gesture. Viv opened her mouth to speak but Nell was first with,

"Are you Elsie Craven?" The woman nodded. "I believe a young girl by the name of Angela left your house late on Monday night. Is that right?" It was raining much harder now, and the water running down the back of Nell's legs was trying her patience.

Nell could see this woman had no intention of asking them inside, she also felt the woman had guessed why they were there. Elsie's mouth dropped at the corners as she slowly shook her head,

"Sorry love, don't know any young girl by that name."

"You're a liar!" Vivien shouted. "I saw her come in here." As if Viv's loud outburst had rung a bell, a shaft of light reappeared at the far end of the passage, and a man, around the same age as Elsie, came toward them, followed by a handsome boy who looked to be in his late teens.

"What's all the shouting about Else?" the man asked in a quiet manner as he stood beside her. The restrictive width of the passage forced the boy to peer over their shoulders. Now all three were in the clear light of day, Nell allowed her own power of assumption to have its way.

The boy, she guessed, was about nineteen, the barrow boy, Angela was besotted with. The man would be Elsie's husband, good-looking, yet frail. Nell deduced by the way Elsie ignored his question, that he did not wear the proverbial trousers.

"You ought to watch your mouth gal!" Elsie said to Vivien. "What's it to do with you anyway?"

"I'm the girls mother!" Viv said angrily.

Elsie ignored her and refocused on Nell, "You're that woman from Lyons Terrace. You own them brothels!"

"No!" Nell said angrily "You're the woman with the brothel. I just own houses. What my tenants do is their business. Now you listen to me Mrs Whatever-your-name-is. My friend here, tells me her girl has left this house at gone midnight smelling of gin. Now there's only one reason you'd want to get a young girl in that state."

"Who is she talking about Else, what girl?" said the man.

It then occurred to Nell that maybe this man knew nothing of what was going on in his own house.

"Its nothing for you to worry about, Sean, love," said the woman. "It's all a misunderstanding. Go in and put your feet up, love." Sean glanced once more at the two women standing out in the rain, and then retreated along the passage.

As the passage door closed, Elsie answered Nell in an angry, threatening whisper. "Now look, you, you've got it all wrong. I don't know what you're talking about and before you start accusing people of Lord knows what, you better get your facts right. My old man's just come out of hospital and he don't need the likes of you two coming round here causing trouble."

Up until then, the boy had said nothing, but now he decided to add his own input to the dispute, "Yeah, we know the law, do you think we'd be stupid enough to get a fifteen-year-old girl on the game?" Elsie looked at him like she wanted to throttle the boy.

"Why not." said Nell. "You're stupid enough to mention her age. Something in Elsie's eyes suddenly gave Nell a warning sign causing her to take a step backwards pulling Viv with her.

"I've only this left to say on the matter." Nell continued. "If you let Angela in this house again, you can expect the law to follow close...."

The door slammed shut before Nell finished her sentence, but she knew her message had struck home.

Vivien kept a close eye on Angela for a while but when the girl came home from the market crying her eyes out, Viv knew that Elsie's nephew had given her the brush off, and that Elsie had probably taken heed of Nell's warning.

Angela's promiscuous ways abated, much to her mother's relief, and they were both a lot wiser from their association with Mrs Elsie Craven. However, unbeknown to Nell, the paths of Elsie Craven and herself were destined to cross again.

Part Two

Chapter 13
Hasty words

It was early summer, 1929 when Jane Gough: wife of a wealthy industrialist, sat gnawing nervously away at a ragged fingernail while she leaned farther out of the bay window of the grand coastal house. The house overlooked Canoe Lake close to Portsmouth and Southsea's sea front. From here, Jane scanned the multitude of people, strollers that the warm summers day had coaxed to parade along the sea front and around its popular Canoe Lake. She was searching the faces of young men wearing straw boaters, particularly ones that were escorting young ladies. It was among these that she hoped to spot Henry, her son.
In an armchair across the room from her, her husband Ben sat reading a day old newspaper.

Jane was worried, and not without good reason. Damn this Martia Boswell that Henry had got himself mixed up with. She was the cause of all this worry. Oh, why did the silly girl have to find out now? Jane reasoned to herself. In a few weeks, the three of them would be finished with Portsmouth and be back living in Scotland. It wouldn't have mattered then. This last thought jabbed at Jane's conscience. How would the girl have managed, all alone and pregnant with Henry's baby? And how would it have looked in the newspaper? Jane visualised the headlines: Young girl made pregnant, then deserted by son of wealthy industrialist. No, she mused. It was a stupid thought anyway. But how could Henry be so stupid, now of all times? Yes Henry! Jane thought. After all, she couldn't just blame the girl. It takes two.

A mile or so along the promenade Jane's son Henry, and his young lady Martia, occupied a chair near the top of a Ferris wheel. The wheel came to a halt making the chair swing gently to and fro, and the sea far below them sparkled in the warm afternoon sun. Henry Gough looked lovingly at the back of Martia's head. He moved his face closer, taking in the scented smell of her raven black hair and asked himself how his father could not forgive his son's actions when he sees this beautiful girl? Anyway, what man of his father's age wouldn't relish the idea of a grandson or daughter? Yes, Henry was sure Dad would forgive him and see things differently when he saw Martia. Everything would work out.

He pulled at the gold chain that hung from his waistcoat pocket. The time on the Half Hunter told him that this would have to be the last fairground ride before they walked the promenade to Canoe Lake.

"How much higher before we see it Henry?" Martia said impatiently. The fairground was packed that day and the Ferris wheel, being a popular new ride was slow moving.

"How much longer you mean, at this rate we're never going to get to my parents!"

"Well I don't care if we never get there," said Martia, "I'm really nervous about meeting your Mum and Dad, especially now with the baby. I mean, what a way to greet your future in-laws"

"Don't be daft. Nobody's going to bite you. Besides, Dad's away so you'll only have to face Mum and she already knows. That is if we ever get down off of this blasted Ferris wheel."

Martia suddenly lunged forward grabbing the safety bar. Their seat rocked violently causing Henry to grab Martia by the waist.

"There it is!" She shouted. "But I can only see the masts."

"Hell, Martia! I wish you wouldn't keep jumping up like that; I'm the one that's getting nervous. Yes, I can see it."

"But I thought it would be bigger than that," said Martia.

"You funny little Hampshire hussy." Henry said, grinning.

"Here, who are you calling a hussy? Better not let your mother hear you call me that; she might not think you're joking."

"Well, it is some distance away and small or not if it were not for that little ship and one brave little Englishman, my mother might have been getting snails ready for our tea. You know I can't believe you've spent all your life around Portsmouth and never seen the Victory."

"Well we lived in Cosham, and mum and dad were always too busy to take me anywhere."

"Looks like that's about to change. I only hope you're going to like Scotland."

Fifteen minutes later Jane Gough was still peering out her open window. She craned her neck to peer one way then the other but the For Sale sign on their front lawn blocked her view.

She glanced back into the room at her husband, Ben, half expecting him to be looking at her, reading her thoughts, but no, Ben was still absorbed in his newspaper.

Oh, why did he have to come home a day early, she thought, he'd never done that before. He always came home on a Monday whenever he went on one of his Coventry trips. Now, when it really wasn't convenient he had to break the habit. I've got to warn Henry that he's home, she mused. But why, Ben is going to find out anyway; it was only a matter of time, and Henry was not worried about telling his father anyway. No, he wasn't worried, but I am, she mused. Oh! Not of Ben's temper, although that was something to behold. It was more for the disappointment that she knew it would cause him.

Suddenly Ben Gough's harsh Scottish accent startled Jane as it boomed out from behind his paper. "Bloody fools! They're going to get burned!"

"Who dear," said Jane, trying to sound interested, while still trying to peer farther down the street?

"Those blasted Yanks! You can't keep pushing the price of shares up if Companies are not worth it. Something's got to give."

"I know I've heard you say so before dear. I only wish I understood it better."

With an unintelligible mumble, Ben turned the page, and noisily shook the paper to straighten it as if to emphasize his annoyance.

"Why are you hanging out of that blasted window again? Can't you get that girl to make some tea or something?" Ben said referring to their maid.

"Its cooler by the window dear, and I like to see what new dresses are being worn this year," Jane lied, and giving herself an imaginary pat on the back for such a prompt answer. "Besides it's a bit early for tea, and Bessie's busy upstairs." Jane did not want to leave the window; she wanted to somehow warn Henry that his father was home, although what good that would do she wasn't sure.

Jane had not seen her son for a fortnight, as Henry did not live at home. Since he finished his spell with the Army, things had become a bit strained between him and his father. Nothing serious, but Ben did not like the late nights Henry was keeping. So, when one of Henry's friends offered to share his flat, Henry moved out. The move was good: the relationship between Henry and his father became more amiable. Moreover, each time Henry came to visit, he and his father would discuss business plans for the future and Henry's eventual directorship in his fathers Company.

Jane had told Henry to wait until his father was on one of his trips before bringing the girl to meet her. They would be able to discuss the problem between the three of them and how to break the news to Ben. Today was the day. It was all arranged, but Ben had cut his trip short. He'd come home a day early. How would Ben take it, Jane thought, he had such high hopes for his son. Gough & Son, Precision Engineers, it was what Ben had dreamed of seeing above his factory gates.

Scotland was Jane's birthplace, where she had met Ben, where they were married and where Henry was born.

Ben had inherited the first factory from his father. Since then the business had flourished. Ben opened a second factory in Coventry and a few years later, the couple took their thirteen-year-old son and moved to Portsmouth where Ben opened a third site.

Henry reached school leaving age and expected to be given a position in his father's business, but Ben did not want the boy to be mollycoddled by his workers, or for Henry to take advantage of his name. However, he did want his son to one day take his place and therefore learn as much about precision engineering as possible. With no help from his father, Henry applied and received an apprenticeship with a small engineering company. Then, for a while he carried on his skills with the Army.

As much as Jane loved the south coast, she was an only child and the health of her elderly mother back in Scotland was giving concern.

Ben had promised her that when Henry had finished his apprenticeship and their Portsmouth plant was in running order they would return to Scotland. The opportunity had now arisen. Things were now running smoothly at the Portsmouth plant, so Ben saw this as a good time to fulfil his wife's wishes and move back up north.

The house was sold and Henry had quit his job. The plan was to stop on route at the Coventry site where Henry would be introduced to, and start working with, the manager there.

"Jane. Jane! **Jane!**" At the third shout of her name, Jane was severed from her thoughts.

"Oh sorry dear, I was miles away."

"I was saying where's that son of ours. Has he been round here lately? I haven't seen him for weeks. He did give his notice in didn't he?"

"Yes I think so. Yes I'm sure he has."

"I hope he's not going to leave all his packing until the last minute."

"Yes dear I think he may be calling in this afternoon."

"Bet he's got some little filly in tow," Ben said with a chuckle. "Well, he'd better not get too serious. I don't want anything spoiling our plans now. We're off in a few weeks you know." Jane started biting another fingernail.

Turning back to the window she said,

"Why haven't they taken that sign down yet? I thought as soon as the house was sold they would take it down."

"Why, does it bother you?"

"No not really it's just that…" Suddenly Jane jumped up and dashed out of the room leaving Ben looking puzzled until he heard muffled voices in the hall.

"Mum this is Martia," said Henry, grinning widely as Jane studied the young lady that stood beside her son on the marble steps outside. "Isn't she a beauty?" Henry said, while giggling at Martia's obvious embarrassment.

"How do you do Mrs Gough? Pleased to make your acquaintance."

"And she's even prettier when she changes back to her normal colour." Martia giggled but felt less embarrassed for Henry's little witticism.

Jane took only moments to assess Martia's social status. She formed the opinion that the girl was of working class, although she had tried to create a good impression. Her shoes were well worn but polished, and the dress was modern but of a cheap material. She also guessed that the Grecian style hat Martia wore, had been borrowed, and that it was clearly too large for her.

There, the criticism ended. Jane felt that she had not seen a more beautiful girl, and was especially taken with the combination of her pale blue eyes and raven black hair. Jane lightly took the girl's arm and led her into the house.

"*Henry your fathers home!*" Jane whispered nervously as Henry entered the reception hall.

"Oh Good. Have you told him?" He asked in a quite audible voice.

"Told me what, my boy?" Ben said, emerging from the lounge. "Hello! What have we here." He added, forgetting his question as he ogled Martia unashamedly.

Again, Martia blushed at the elderly man's over zealous stare. She held out her hand and repeated her well-rehearsed introduction. "And yours my dear, and yours." Ben answered. "Well this is a surprise. You are both staying to tea I hope," said Ben, still holding on to Martia's hand.

"Try and stop us dad, what are we having?" said Henry as his straw boater made the perfect landing on the hall hat stand.

Ben and the young couple entered the lounge while Jane went to arrange tea. It was as she made her way back to the lounge that she momentarily paused with fear.

Raised voices coming from the lounge told her that Henry had broken the news to his father. As Jane entered the lounge, all three were standing.

"Did you know about this?" Ben almost bellowed at his wife. Jane could not remember Ben sounding or looking so angry.

"I was going to tell you Ben, it's just that…" Jane was not given time to finish.

"Was going to! When?" Ben shouted. "When she went into bloody labour I suppose," he said sarcastically.

Martia started to cry.

Henry intervened "There's no need to shout at Mum. It's not her fault Dad. Look I'm sorry, I know we made plans…"

"Yes and we are bloody well going to carry them out," Ben intervened. "The girl can have the child if that's what she wants and we will pay her maintenance, or she can have it aborted; its of no consequence to me. I have contacts and I will pay whatever it costs." At this point Ben's face twisted into a snarl as he pointed at Martia. "But this…this…conniving trollop is not going to ruin my plans."

Henry started to take threatening steps toward his father until Jane, who was now also crying, stepped between them.

"Don't you dare talk to her like that!" Henry snapped angrily. "She doesn't deserve to be spoken to that way. She is nothing like the trollops that you associate with."

"What the hell do you mean?" Ben started to colour, feeling Jane's attention turn to him.

"You seem to forget that I visit your factory and speak to the men. You know dad, you shouldn't boast so much to them about your exploits on your trips up north. And before you say any more, this trollop, as you spitefully called her is my wife, and has been since last Friday."

The room went quiet. Ben felt for the arm of the chair behind him and eased himself down into it. He looked pitiful and pale as he buried his face in his hands.

Henry had lost his temper and now he realised that in so doing he had not only disgraced his father, but had caused his mother so much pain. He tried to take his mothers hand in a gesture of regret for what he had said, but she slowly pulled it away. Henry felt sick inside and wished with all his heart that he could retract his outburst. He turned once more to his father and his voice sounded desperate.

"Believe me Dad, I am sorry. I didn't mean it to happen like this, but it doesn't have to make any difference. We just have to plan things a little differently."

Henry waited for some response from Ben but none came. Henry's next words took a more quiet and sombre tone. "We do love each other dad; getting married just seemed to make sense. It's not the way we'd have chosen to be married, but I knew what your response would be, and you have just proved it Dad...Dad?"

Ben said nothing, but sat hunched over with his face in his hands.

"I think it best if you both leave now," said Jane quietly.

14
Lyons Terrace

Henry was deeply troubled over the incident with his parents. He tried several times to call on them, but each time the maid told him they were out. Henry knew they were avoiding him. He stayed away for a while hoping time would at least quell their anger, but it didn't help. When he called on them, a month later, new owners of the house told him that they had left for Scotland and left no forwarding address.

Four months passed, but still Henry's rift with his parents and feelings of guilt were making him miserable. Now, when he thought of how much his words must have hurt them, he wondered whether either of them would ever wish to see him again. He tried not to dwell on it by pushing his mind onward with thoughts of a family life with his Martia and maybe a son of his own. His unborn child and Martia: they would now be his life, his one and only concern. He found employment in the Portsmouth dockyard. The wages were not high but at least it was more than the job he'd left.

Lack of money and the impending birth of their child brought into question their present accommodation. As far as Henry knew, Martia had no family left to turn to. One of Henry's Army buddies had let them use his flat, but it was totally inadequate for a couple with a baby on the way. Finding affordable accommodation was proving to be a problem. Henry had very little money saved, and the wages from his job in the Dockyard would not run to a mortgage. Even rented accommodation seemed more than they could afford.

It was while they were on one of their accommodation seeking trips that a strange and tragic incident occurred, one that was to leave their minds and memories with deep and nightmarish scars for many years.

Martia and Henry had turned the corner on Fratton Bridge and started to walk toward the railway station. Henry kept looking back over his shoulder. As he did, a young man came into view holding the hand of a little boy. The infant looked to be about five, and his little legs had to run to keep up with the man.

"I don't believe it," said Henry. "He's still following us, are you sure you don't know him?"

"No." shouted Martia angrily. "How many more times? And don't keep looking back at them."

"But he said something to you. What did he say?"

"I don't know! You heard him, maybe he's mental or something, coming up behind me like that."

"I only heard him say something about being free, but I thought he knew you." Henry said peering over his shoulder again. "He's still there."

The couple entered the station and bought their tickets. The platform was crowded and Martia ushered Henry through the crowd and away from the entrance. Henry noticed how Martia kept darting nervous glances towards the platform entrance. After a few moments, the man and boy appeared again. Henry watched him search the mass of faces. Suddenly his eyes found Martia and his face changed to a smile.

"You must know him!" Henry exclaimed. With that, the stationmaster came along, pushing people back from the platform edge, and repeating,

"Non-stop Express, move back please". As the great steam engine came racing into view, people were craning heads to view it. Everyone except Martia: she had her hands up to her face, and was looking along the platform in the opposite direction. Henry followed her gaze and in one terrible moment, realised what was about to happen. The stranger had the boy in his arms now and was grinning insanely at Martia. He'd moved to the edge of the platform again, closer than anyone else. The noise of the express grew louder, and Henry wanted to run toward the stranger, to pull him and the boy back from the edge. But his legs would not move. Then it was too late. Even as the man leapt, he seemed to be smiling at Martia. One woman, who had been standing close to the man, screamed, and then fainted. Others who saw the tragedy were physically sick. Those who saw nothing, milled around, questioning others that had. Martia's legs started to buckle under her, but Henry grabbed her and helped her to a bench seat. The Express did not stop or even brake. Neither the driver nor footman could have known that anything was wrong. The stationmaster rushed to his office telephone as Henry sat down beside Martia and put his arm round her.

"Are you alright, love?"

Martia slid her hands down to expose her tear soaked face and red rimmed eyes. But she couldn't speak.

"You did know him didn't you?"

"I don't want to talk about it," Martia sobbed.

"Alright love. Lets forget it. At least I don't think they'd have known much about it, the infant certainly wouldn't. Poor lad couldn't have known what was going to happen."

Another week passed and the memory of the station tragedy had started to fade. The couple still had not found suitable accommodation and both were feeling miserable. Henry had grown up around wealth with hardly a care in the world. Now he felt alone and vulnerable, unsure if he could carry the burden of a family.

A few weeks after the train incident, Henry's luck changed. It happened while he was at work.

"I hear you're looking for a place to rent." The thickset Scotsman was shouting above the sound of noisy machinery in the dockyard machine shop. His broad Scottish accent set him apart from other men in the factory, so much so that his red hair and ruddy complexion seemed to overemphasise the obvious.

Henry responded by pulling a lever on the front of his lathe. A long flapping belt shifted to another overhead pulley and the work piece in his machine stopped revolving. He had seen the man around, but the workshop was enormous and never knew him by name. Wiping his hands in a cloth Henry offered his hand. "The name's Henry Gough, and yes, you heard right. I have been looking for a place, but my wages don't match the places my wife thinks we can afford."

"I'll probably be wasting my breath then," said the man, shaking Henry's hand. "Ken McFee's the name."

Henry winced with the big Scotsman's grip. "What makes you say that, what were you going to say?"

"Well I was going to say the cost depends a lot on the district. If you don't mind being surrounded by a lot of whores, you could take over the rent on my place in Lyons Terrace."

"Really! That's very ni…," Henry paused, he was suddenly reminded of the row with his father. "What do you mean, whores?"

"You know, whores, prostitutes, I rent a house here in Portsea, just off Queen St. The area is crawling with them. Well, if you're going to live near a naval port, what can you expect? Still, they've never bothered me and the rent is reasonable. Anyway, I'm off back up to the Clyde at the end of the month so if you are interested why not come round and take a look, and if you want the place I'll take you to see the agent. He should be pleased to let you take it over; it'll save him the trouble of finding another tenant." Just then, a bell sounded, indicating tea break. "I'll bring my tea over," said the Scot. We'll have a chat while I write down the address."

When McFee came back with his tea and found an oil drum to sit on, Henry said, "Why the move if you don't mind my asking?"

"You see, I married a Portsmouth girl. I met her while I was stationed down here with the Marines but it didn't work out and recently we split up. There's nothing to keep me here now and I miss my family. I have a brother back home and we keep in touch. We both did our apprenticeships at the same firm back home, a place called Gough Engineering. Hey! That's a coincidence?" Henry said nothing, and McFee continued, "Anyway, he wrote to tell me that my old job was vacant, so I wrote to the manager. He remembered me, and what do you know, I got the job. It'll be good to see the family again." McFee invited Henry round to see his house on their way home from work that day. Henry was quite taken with the place, considering the low rent. It was untidy, however, Henry felt that it could be made to feel quite cosy with a woman's touch. So Mc Fee arranged for Henry to collect the key from the agent on the following Saturday.

In the short time that Henry and McFee worked together, they became friends. However, Henry never mentioned that Gough Engineering belonged to his father, and for no other reason than not wanting to be reminded of the last visit with his parents. He certainly did not want to explain to McFee why, when having such an affluent family, he was not in a better financial or social position.

McFee said goodbye to Henry and his workmates on the Friday and left for Scotland that same evening. Henry and Martia set out for Lyons Terrace the following day. Henry wasn't sure if Martia was aware of the district's reputation, and because it was the only affordable place they'd found, he had not mentioned it to her. It was for this reason he wanted to avoid the surrounding neighbours; he did not want Martia to prejudge the place.

As they turned the corner into Lyons Terrace, Henry's heart sank. The street seemed to be full of gossiping women. Four of them were directly opposite Number 12, the house they were about to view. Ken McFee's words came back to him: *Whores, prostitutes the place is crawling with them.* Henry eyed some of the women thinking how apt McFee's description was.

Raggedy ten-year olds pulled nailed-together go-carts along the road while others played hopscotch on the narrow pavements. Henry wondered how many of them were the by-product of these women's sordid trade.

This was Saturday and with new neighbours in mind, Martia had wanted Henry and herself to look their best. She insisted that Henry wear his best suit, while she looked radiant in a navy blue and white dress with matching blue and white high heels. One might have said she looked altogether too stylish for this particular neighbourhood.

A group of scruffy children stopped pushing their cart to stare at the well-dressed couple. One small boy saw fit to comment.

"Cor! You look a bit of alright Miss." Martia and Henry could not help but laugh.

As the couple neared number twelve the four women opposite could not contain their curiosity. They stopped talking and just stared.

Reaching the door of number twelve Henry searched for the key. As he did, one of the four women spoke in an unnaturally loud voice. It was obvious that her words were meant for the young couple's ears.

"Here Maisie! You're not going to get many customers with a skinny cow like that living just up the road. Reckon them sailor-boys won't want to pass number twelve to get to your house." With that, the women's laughter rang out causing Henry to fumble even longer to find the key; then he cursed it for not turning in the lock. He felt himself blushing and knew that Martia must be feeling even more uncomfortable than he.

"Hurry up love. This is awful." Martia whispered urgently. But the women opposite were enjoying the couple's embarrassment. Now it was Maisie's turn. She was the largest of the four women.

"Don't you worry about that gal, my customers prefer something with a bit of meat on them. What about him! Do you reckon he might like a change? You know, something that don't rattle." The laughter that followed exacerbated the young couple's humiliation.

By now, Henry just wanted to get away. It was in his mind to return the key and tell the agent that he didn't want the place. He pulled the key out of the lock and turned to Martia.

"Come on love I don't think..." Henry stopped short when he saw what looked like the eldest of the four women coming toward them. Henry's first impression was: nice looking. Her arms were folded and she was smiling as she crossed the narrow street. She was dressed in a clean pinafore and a headscarf, tied in a typical housewife style. Henry, having prejudged all the women in Lyons Terrace, thought this woman seemed somehow out of place. There was a kind of relaxed confidence in the way she smiled. Casually, she took the key from Henry and inserted it back into the lock. She then faced Henry and made a show of pulling it slightly out before turning it. The door opened and as she handed the key back to him, a smell of expensive perfume wafted around him. Henry felt a strange attraction toward the woman, which left him slightly confused. There was warmth in her eyes when she smiled and her presence within these surroundings seemed incongruous. He guessed the woman could be in her mid thirty's yet could, he believed in the right clothes, pass for a much younger woman. She smiled at Martia, turned and nodded toward the three women across the narrow street, and in a voice loud enough for the women to hear, said,

"Take no notice of them love, they've got no manners." The women laughed out loud, then dispersed to go their separate ways. The woman then addressed Martia. "They're not so bad really, not when you get to know them. It's just that seeing a pretty thing like you around here makes them nervous. They think you're a threat to their livelihood, you see," she said grinning. Martia glanced at Henry with a bemused look and he wondered if she was waiting for him to say something.

"What do you mean?" he said haughtily. "This is my wife! And she's not a—a—Henry stammered, unable to finish his sentence.

"Oh don't get so uppity," the woman said with a chuckle. "I know that! I can spot a girl that's on the game a mile off." Then jabbing a thumb over her shoulder added, "Trouble is, they can't."

"Surely they can see that my Martia is not a…a, you know." Henry stammered again. There was a pause as the woman stared for some moments at Martia before she finally answered with,

"Don't be afraid to say it love. I'm sure the little lady's heard the word prostitute before. No, you see, when a couple like you two move in down this street, all these women see is a pretty young thing who, with the aid of her young pimp, is going to put them out of business. But don't worry; once they know you're straight, they won't bother you. And no matter what you may think of their trade, there is another side to their character. Some of them are nice people and would give you their last penny if they thought you needed it more than them. Look, I'd like us to get off on the right foot, I know how hard it can be when you're just starting out, and I have a couple of second-hand shops in the town. There's not much I can't get hold of in the way of furniture, and probably a lot cheaper than you can. Don't forget now, I'm right opposite in number eleven, the name's Nell Masters.

"How did you know about the key?" Henry said, having calmed down a little. Nell grinned and answered by touching the side of her nose with a forefinger, then started to walk away, but suddenly stopped. She turned back to stare curiously at Martia. "Have you always lived in Portsmouth, love?"

Martia glanced at Henry, surprised at what seemed to her, an odd question.

"No, but I was born here." Nell then said, "Can I ask what your maiden name was?"

"Boswell, Why?"

Nell stared silently for some time at Martia before saying,

"Oh nothing, nothing at all."

Suddenly. The door of a house opposite had opened and a barrage of foul language came from a female voice inside. This was followed by the appearance of a small boy around seven years old. He backed out of the house after slamming the door. He glanced around, frowning at Henry and Martia as if they were intruding on something private. Then as if having an afterthought, he went back into the doorway, put his mouth to the letter flap and shouted down the passage, "You're a bleeding thief, that's what. And I hope you die!" Nell beckoned to the boy as he came out again. He sauntered across the road and stood looking dejectedly up at Nell. His short trousers were in tatters, his feet were bare and his face looked like it had not experienced the feel of soap for some time.

"Here! That's no way to talk to your mother Jimmy; now what's all the shouting about?" Nell said, wiping the lads tears with her pinafore.

"She spent my larking money," said the lad. "The old cow! It took me all morning to earn that, now I can't go to the bleeding pictures, and its Robin Hood." Henry and Martia were shocked but fascinated by the boy's swearing.

"Well you shouldn't talk to your mother like that," Nell said calmly. "If she took your money she must have had good reason. Now how much do you need for the pictures?"

"Sixpence," said the boy.

"OK Jimmy. You run a couple of errands for me, later and I'll give you thrupence,"

"Yeah, but you can't get in the pictures for…"

"Hang on a minute I haven't finished. I will let lend you another thrupence to make up your picture money, but the next time you work the flats you have to pay back the extra thrupence. Do you understand? I'm not a charity; I don't give something for nothing."

"Yeah, thanks Aunt Nell, I will, I promise." The boy stood on tiptoe to kiss the woman on the cheek and ran off down the road.

"You're his aunt?" Henry said with surprise.

"Not really but all the kids know me as Aunt Nell down this street. Anyway, don't forget, number eleven!"

"Wonder what he meant by larking," said Martia as they watched Nell return to her house. As she reached her door, Henry saw someone move back into the shadows of Nell's hallway. He glanced at Martia and guessed that she had also seen the shadow.

"Begging," said Henry as he ushered Martia inside the house. "They call it mud larking, but I call it begging; haven't you seen them on the mud flats down by the harbour station?"

"Oh! So that's what she meant by working the flats, mud flats. Oh, yes I've heard about the mud larks," said Martia, stepping inside the house. She opened the first door inside the dark passage and scanned the room. Henry waited for her to comment, thinking for sure that the undesirable neighbours and the episode outside would have already disillusioned her. He wasn't at all sure, now, if he wanted to live there.

"I wouldn't let a kid of mine go mud larking it's downright dangerous. A kid nearly drowned there, a few years ago," said Henry, still waiting for her opinion on the lounge. Henry had already seen the house but was surprised at how clean McFee had left it.

Closing the door, Martia brushed passed him. She reached the end of the passage, and ascended the stairs with Henry in tow. She opened each room in turn, saying nothing. Henry was becoming more disgruntled with her non-committal silence, especially as he felt that she was certainly going to reject the place.

The inspection did not take long. Finally, they stood looking at the last aspect of the house, the tiny back garden.

"Well?" said Henry, sure of a negative response.

"Yes I think this will do us nicely," Henry just stood mouth agape. "Of course we're going to need some furniture, like a bed for a start." Martia added. "Maybe that Nell woman can help us out."

"You mean you'd live here, after that business with those-those... and you'd ask that woman for help?"

"Oh don't be so stuck up!" Martia said abruptly. "Live and let live. Anyway, like she said, they acted like that because they thought I was going to take their trade away." Then squeezing Henry's hand and nuzzling into his neck, she added. "And you better be nice to me or I might."

"You know, you never cease to amaze me," said Henry, hugging her to him.

"Well you said so yourself, beggars cant be choosers, and it won't be forever. We have to start somewhere, and it is close to your job."

Less than a mile from the Gough's little three bedroom terraced house in Portsea was the Naval dockyard. About the same distance in the opposite direction, were the Naval barracks, thus forming a coexistence between the Naval fleets of the world and Portsea's ladies of the night. However, these women's activities did not bother the young couple; they had a baby coming into their lives. This and financial pressure took all their attention. Henry was soon to find out that Martia was a spender; one who lived for the moment with little thought for tomorrow. This caused most of their tiffs in the early months of Martia's pregnancy, like the day Henry came home from work just two weeks before Martia was due to give birth.

"Nell stopped me in the street, Martia. She told me that her shop in Arundel Street has had a real nice pram just come in. What do you say we go down there and take a look at it this weekend if it's still there?"

"No!" Martia snapped.

"Why not. Have we got something else on?"

"No, It's just that I'm not pushing my kid around in a second hand pram."

"Hell, Martia! Have you seen the price of a new one? You're the one who's always telling me beggars can't be chooser's. Or does that only apply to the meals you put up."

"What do you mean by that?"

"Well that's what you say if I complain about cheap meat or sausages."

The arguments became more frequent as the time of Martia's parturition came closer. After she gave birth to their baby girl: Janice Elaine, Martia's temperament changed, she was no longer argumentative, but morose and distant. She showed no affection for the baby and arguments only occurred when she had to feed her.

Henry became worried about Martia. He confided in married work associates, who told him that her condition was normal. He was not convinced. He called on Nell, telling her that he thought Martia was in a trance. Nell assured him that postnatal depression was not unheard of, and that most women eventually recovered with time.

Martia did recover, however, and it did take time, but her feelings toward baby Janice never changed. It was almost as if she hated the infant. For the next two years, Henry found that he'd almost become father and mother to their daughter.

It was on Janice's second birthday that two new women came to live, or more to the point, "solicit" in Lyons Terrace. And to Henry's annoyance, Martia became friendly with them. Martia had in fact become friendly with most of the known prostitutes in the street, but Henry found these two were somehow different. It was as if they made an effort to befriend Martia, whereby the others, while being friendly, seemed to respect the fact that she was a married woman.

Walking home from work along Queen Street one day, Henry happened to see Nell Masters. She appeared to be leisurely window-shopping in the company of three other women. One woman was around Nell's age while the other two were much younger. They were discussing the contents in a dressmaker's window. As Henry approached them, it was one of the two younger ladies that attracted Henry's attention. He knew he'd seen her in Lyons Street before. The girl was smartly dressed, Henry guessed her to be around Martia's age, her early twenties. She wore a white blouse and a dark tweed two-piece suit that showed off a shapely, though slightly full figure. Her shoulder length auburn hair hid part of her face, but what was visible, told Henry she was very pretty. She looked at Henry and immediately took the arm of her young friend and ushered her into the deep-fronted shop doorway and out of Henry's line of sight. Henry was sure this was a deliberate ploy to avoid their meeting. He felt, however, that in that first exchange of glances there was a look of recognition, though he felt sure he'd never seen her before.

"Hello Henry," said Nell "How's Martia and our little Janice?" Before he could answer, Vivien beamed at Henry, saying,

"Ere Nell where you been hiding him then?"

"This is my friend Vivien, Henry and those young ladies are our daughters," said Nell, nodding towards the Angela and Cathleen. "We've known each other years. Viv's man-mad so take no notice of her," said Nell laughingly.

Henry smiled at Viv and received a seductive hello from Angela while Cathy remained hidden in the doorway.

"Yes, after two years, we're gradually getting sorted Nell. Oh! Thanks for putting us onto that wardrobe, it's ideal, problem is, Martia will want some clothes to put in it now. Anyway I suppose I'd better get home to the little woman." Before Henry could walk off, Nell said,

"Henry I know it's none of my business, but I saw Elsie Craven going into your house a couple of times this week. Don't get me wrong. I'm not running Elsie down, live and let live, but it may not be a very good idea for Martia to spend too much time around her."

"I think I know what you mean Nell, I think that applies to her friend Debbie, too." Nell pulled Henry to one side, leaving Viv with the two girls. Keeping her voice down to a murmur, Nell said,

"Look you ought to know that Debbie works for Elsie as do one or two others in the street. I've had dealings with Elsie before and I've never trusted her, even when her husband was about."

"She's married?"

"Yes, or was. I've not seen her husband since she came to Lyons Terrace. When I first met her she was pregnant, but that was years ago. Maybe she lost the baby, or maybe he left her and took the child with him. However, she seems to be on her own now and I think she's out to make big money from soliciting. She gives her girls a rent free house and helps to supply their clients. The girl's pay her a percentage, a very high percentage from what I hear. It's more than she pays in mortgages and certainly more than she would get from an average rent. Now I'm not supposed to know all this and if you tell anyone else, you and I will fall out. Elsie is an up and coming Madame and she is always looking to recruit more girls, especially if they're as pretty as your Martia. Now you'll understand why I'm telling you this."

"Yes I do, and thanks Nell, I'll sort it out with Martia." Henry was surprised at what he had learnt and it had certainly given him cause to worry as he walked the short distance home.

Henry was far from happy with their accommodation in Lyons Terrace. He felt that it would take some serious saving to bring them out of what he considered poverty. Sadly, Martia was no saver and Henry's enthusiasm to escape Lyons Terrace was not something she shared.

After leaving Nell, he was annoyed to get home and find Elsie Craven in the living room. Elsie was sat at the bare dining table, carefully painting her nails, while the baby, Janice, sat unwashed on the floor, sucking on a filthy crust of bread.

He could hear Martia in the scullery, but there was no smell of cooking.

Acknowledging Elsie with the briefest of nods, he hung his knapsack on the coat hook behind the door before picking Janice up to give her a hug and kiss.

"Hello, Henry." Elsie said without looking up from her intricate task. "Been working hard on your little lathe have you, love."

Henry answered in an over-polite voice, "Yes as a matter of fact I have, Elsie. Oh probably not as hard as you. What with all that painting and decorating, but then I don't suppose you do all ten fingernails in one day do you? Hell, you'd never have time for any clients." Elsie stared at him open mouthed, not sure whether to laugh or be offended."

"Take no notice of him Elsie," said Martia, carrying in two mugs of tea and glaring angrily at Henry. "He often comes home in a mood. There you go love, two sugars wasn't it?" Martia said putting a mug down in front of Elsie. The second mug she banged down in front of Henry spilling it on the wooden table. Henry retaliated, his voice raised to match Martia's,

"I wouldn't come home in a mood if just once, I came home to a cooked dinner."

At this point Elsie got up from the table. "I think I'd better go Martia, I don't want to be the cause of trouble."

"Don't be silly Elsie," Martia said. "Stay and drink your tea," then to Henry. "You're not going to tell me when I can or can't have a friend in."

"OK, fine," Henry said, angrily. "You stay Elsie, I'll get something to eat up Sid's Café. I'll take the baby with me too; I think she could do with a little more than a dirt sandwich." With that, Henry put Janice in her pushchair and left, slamming the front door.

When Henry came home later that evening, he'd calmed down enough to try a more diplomatic approach in getting across his feelings about Martia's friendship with Elsie and Debbie.

"All I'm saying is, its one thing to talk to them in passing, but if people see them coming and going from this house, they might get the wrong idea."

"Like what! Like I'm on the game, you mean?"

"Well... yes."

"That's just too bad. Because it's bad enough being stuck in this bloody hole all day with that little brat, without being told who I can or can't have as a friend. But don't worry, if any blokes come knocking on the door, I'll tell them I'm not open for business. How does that suit you?"

Henry could tell by Martia's mood that he was wasting his breath.

"I'm going to bed."

The following morning was Saturday. It meant two days off for Henry and with the sun shining he was in a better mood. Martia was ironing in the living room when Henry tried to strike a normal conversation.

"I saw Nell in Queen Street yesterday," he said, while scraping his burnt toast with a knife over the sink before bringing it in from the scullery to the dining table. "I thanked her for the wardrobe, looked like she was shopping with a couple of friends. Those shops of hers must be doing okay, she always seems to be well dressed," he said, cutting off a strip of toast, and dipping it in his egg. "Is it just furniture she sells?"

"I think she owns more than one shop, according to Elsie. Who were the two friends? Do I know them?" Martia asked. Baby Janice stood rattling the side of her cot in anticipation at the sight of the tasty egg soldier.

"The one she called Vivien looked about Nell's age." Henry said, feeding the toast to Janice.

The other two were more your age I suppose. One seemed a bit shy, sort of slunk off when I approached."

"Oh, that'll be Nell's daughter! You remember: the ghost?" Henry looked puzzled for a moment.

"Oh! Yes, I remember. She was in Nell's passage on the first day we came. How come I haven't seen her since?"

"She doesn't live there, she only visits. She's a nurse. Anyway she's not shy, she's just embarrassed about her birthmark. Apparently, she has a mauve birthmark on her neck. She tries to cover it up with her hair."

"How do you know all this?"

"Elsie and Debbie told me all about her."

"They are just walking libraries of information, those two, aren't they? I bet they could even tell you the date that the next American ship is due to dock, and more important, how many sailors will be on it."

"Are you going to start that again?" snapped Martia, unimpressed by Henry's witticisms.

"Sorry! Anyway I never noticed a birthmark."

"No, because you were probably looking at her legs."

"Now that you come to mention it," Henry said, grinning.

A week later, Martia took an evening job as an usherette in a nearby cinema, while Henry looked after the baby. It was decided she would do this to bring in some extra cash. This pleased Henry, not only for the financial help, but it meant Martia spending less time around Elsie and Debbie.

Henry carried out his fatherly duties with the patience of a saint. This was just as well, as he'd now well established that Martia was not the home loving maternal type. One whom he had once hoped and imagined his future wife would be.

When Janice started teething, Martia would often scream at Henry, threatening to do the baby harm unless he took her out. Henry would spend hours, even late at night walking her in her pushchair, just to get her to sleep and keep her out of Martia's way. Arguments and rows became commonplace, most of them over money. Even so, Henry took the optimistic view that in a short time Janice could be looked after by a babysitter, and Martia could get a full time job, something to which he now knew she was more suited, rather than that of motherhood,

But this was not to be, at least not, for some time. Janice was only two and a half when Martia announced to him that she was pregnant again. Henry's mire suddenly became a bottomless pit.

Very little changed for the Gough's over the next few years except that Martia grew even less tolerant now that they had another child: a boy they named William.

With encouragement from Elsie Craven, Martia took to smoking which created more ammunition for arguments in the Gough household.

Henry was promoted at work to Leading Hand, but financially they still found life a struggle. Even when Henry had the chance to put in overtime, Martia could never make the housekeeping last the full week.

Henry started to think about how things might have turned out if he had not met Martia, how life might have been if the plans that he and his father had often talked about, had materialised. The more he dwelt on it, the more dissatisfied he became with his life. He wrote several long letters to his parents. He would tell them amusing little things about Janice and Billy, and every letter carried a message of apology for his outburst at their last meeting.

Henry had no idea where in Scotland his parents were living. He addressed the letters to his father's factory, but getting no reply, left him wondering whether his father had received them, or if he was still unforgiving. Henry became irritable and remote toward Martia.

Billy's birth had put even more strain on their marriage. Poverty became more pronounced, while rows and arguments worsened. The consequence of this was that Martia had taken to physically ill-treating Janice. The first evidence of this was when Henry came home unexpectedly one morning. Before he opened the door of the little living room, he could hear Martia shouting foul language. Janice was crying out in obvious pain. Opening the living room door, he found Martia with Janice over her knee. Martia was holding a hairbrush and a guilty look showed on her face. The infant's naked backside was covered in red welts while milk, cornflakes and broken pieces of a breakfast bowl lie on the floor.

"What the hell do you think you're doing?" Henry bellowed at Martia. "Look at her backside, it's red-raw." Martia quickly recovered from her look of guilt.

"Well look at this mess. She did this on purpose just because I wouldn't let her get down from the table. The little cow's getting out of hand, and she has to be taught a lesson, you spoil her."

Henry lifted Janice up and patted her back while she sobbed on his shoulder.

"I see you're teaching her some new language too, from what I heard as I came down the passage, but then I suppose it goes with the neighbourhood. You seem to be fitting in very well."

"Shove the sarcasm. It doesn't impress me." Martia said with bravado, but something in Henry's manner kept her out of arm's reach.

"If I catch you hitting her like that again, I'll leave an impression on you." Martia was sure Henry meant it.

By the time Janice was seven, women who appeared mainly after dark, occupied most of the houses in Lyons Street. Martia remained friendly toward Elsie and Debbie, although they were now reluctant to call when they knew Henry was home.

Martia was darning some socks one evening while Henry was reading a book. The children were keeping themselves amused with crayons and paper when Martia casually remarked,

"You should have seen Elsie today, Henry, She had a knew outfit on. She didn't half look nice."

"Hmm. It won't help," Henry said without looking up from his reading.

"What do you mean," said Martia thinking it a strange answer.

"What I mean is, I wouldn't care if she wore the crown jewels. I still wouldn't like her. She's got a mean look about her; I never did like thin lips on a woman and I wish you wouldn't spend so much time in her company."

"I don't know what she's done to upset you. I think she's very friendly. Why have you got to be nasty to her?"

"How can I be nasty to her when I don't even talk to her. I just don't want to associate with that lot."

"What do you mean? That lot!"

"You know, Her and that Debbie those…those," Henry looked down at Janice and chose his words carefully, "You know what I mean, those women. And some of the blokes I've seen them with look a bit shady."

"Well I just wish you would be a bit more talkative when they come here. It's embarrassing the way you ignore them." Henry looked at her over the book he was reading. "I can't help it. I just don't like them, or most of the other women in this street."

"Why not, you don't seem to mind talking to Nell."

"Nell's different!"

"Why is she different? Did you know she owns houses in this street? I know for a fact, at least one is a brothel."

"Who told you that?"

"Elsie!"

"Oh well in that case it must be true," said Henry with a cynical laugh.

"How come you're so fond of Nell? It wouldn't have anything to do with that daughter of hers would it?"

"Don't be stupid I've only seen her a couple of times, and never up close. Anyway I wish you would stop inviting that Elsie and Debbie in here, you'll be getting a reputation next."

"As what?" Martia snapped.

"For Christ sake! How many times have we had this argument? You know what they are: prostitutes."

"Bloody hell! I'm not a kid, of course I know." Martia gave a false laugh, "Did you think I didn't know that? Why should it matter to you? Have you seen some of the women you're talking about? I'd like to be able to buy some of the clothes they wear. Elsie's the smartest dressed woman around."

Janice suddenly interrupted without looking up from her drawing.

"I think she's a witch!" She said. Martia scowled at her.

"You mind your bloody business!" She snapped. "No one asked you. You're getting to be a nasty little busybody"

"Don't speak to her like that," Henry retaliated. "For Pete's sake! She's only seven,"

"Well I wish she would act it, and keep her nose out."

Janice and Billy stopped drawing and stared worriedly at their parents as Henry and Martia's voices became louder and more frightening.

"You're always snapping at her. Why don't you give her a break?" Henry said.

"Well why don't you tell her to keep her nose out. You'd let her get away with murder, and anyway she shouldn't be listening."

Jan started to cry. Henry slammed shut the book he was reading.

"Does that matter? I don't suppose much goes on in this street that she doesn't understand, moreover if she doesn't she soon will. To listen to you, anyone would think these women were running a respectable business. God knows what kind of upbringing you had!" His last remark hit the spot and Martia's voice went up a pitch.

"One that taught me to mind my own bleeding business!" She shouted. "What those women get up to has nothing to do with you. They perform a service for which they get paid. The point is they're not hurting you, are they." Now Billy started to cry and seeing the children upset, made Henry even more irate. He got to his feet.

"Are you stupid?" he said. "Those women spread disease, or don't you understand that?"

"Sure I do and so do their clients, but that's their problem. It doesn't affect you, does it? Or maybe it does. Maybe you've seen one that you fancy, and you're jealous because on your paltry wage you couldn't afford her."

Almost before the palm of Henry's hand had reached Martia's face, he was once again regretting his volatile temper, but it was too late. Martia reeled backwards under the blow while Janice started to cry out,

"Stop it daddy, stop it." Henry saw his terrified children huddled in the corner of the room. Billy was trembling. Janice's face was wet with tears. Henry knelt, and embraced them both as his rage subsided and he fought back his own tears. He then linked their hands, saying to Janice,

"Take him up to bed love and let him sleep in your bed tonight."

The next day Henry found it difficult to concentrate on his work and in a moment of carelessness cut his hand severely. The First Aid personnel did a temporary dressing but the cut needed stitches and he was driven to the Portsmouth Royal hospital. After giving his name and address at a reception desk, he was directed to a crowded waiting room.

As he sat there he started to analyse his eight years of marriage. He remembered how lucky he'd considered himself when he met Martia, but now he wondered if love really had anything to do with their partnership. He realised that until now it was something that he had not even considered. He believed that when a man was as besotted with a woman as he was with Martia, it must be love. But if it was, how could he ever bring himself to raise a hand to her. Maybe her beauty had blinded him, and it wasn't love at all.

His thoughts turned to Janice and Billy and he physically smiled. That was different, how could a father not love them? He realised it was the kids that kept their marriage going. It was them that he looked forward to coming home to, every day. He asked himself, was it fair to subject them to the fights and hostility that had surrounded their young lives?

A slender hand suddenly broke Henry's train of thought by gently lifting his damaged hand.

"What's your name?" said the young nurse.

"Why is everyone so obsessed with names around here? Can't you see I'm bleeding to death?" Henry said jokingly.

"Well the desk need it for their records, but I just want to know what to call you. Does it hurt?"

"Like hell," he said, looking up at the pretty, hazel eyes above him. "The name's Henry."

"Right then. Come with me, Henry."

As Henry followed the young nurse, his eyes followed her form. He had never liked black stockings and flat shoes on a woman; normally he found them to be sexually unattractive, a complete turn off. He had even remarked on it to Martia one day as they strolled along Queen Street behind a couple of Wrens, yet somehow this young nurse seemed to be changing his mind.

She led Henry from the waiting area to a small room with a sink. There, she ordered him to sit on the only chair in the room. As she unwrapped the blood-soaked bandage Henry noticed she wore no wedding band. As he looked into her face, she fleetingly pulled her hair forward, partially covering a large purple birthmark that marred part of her neck. Henry immediately realised that she was Nell's daughter. That fine form that he had just followed down the corridor was the same one that disappeared into the shop doorway, and the same one that tried to melt into the shadows of her mother's hall on that first day in Lyons Terrace. Jesus! All that time ago, he thought, and they had not recognised each other today for the same reason; him in overalls and her in a nurses uniform. But now Henry had the advantage.

"So, what have we been up to then Henry?" she said.

"We?" Well I don't know what you've been up to, but I've been cutting my hand open." he said looking up at her and holding his grin until she acknowledged it.

Trying to keep a straight face, she said. "I can see that. I meant how did it happen?"

"I don't know. But I know *why* it happened. I was thinking about a woman when I should have been concentrating on my job."

"Oh I see! Think about women a lot, do we?"

"No not **we**. Me!"

This time she smiled. "Yes alright you've made your point. I can't help it, it's a habit." The last fold of dressing had stuck to the dry blood around the cut and Henry let out a hiss of pain as she pulled it away.

"Oh that is nasty. I hope she was worth it." She started to disinfect the cut.

"I used to think so." Henry said in a more sombre tone."

"Oh, fallen out have we"

"There you go with the **we** stuff again." This time she giggled. Henry liked the sound, and when their eyes met it seemed like time, for both of them, paused.

"Never mind, there's plenty more fish in the sea." she said, colouring slightly and forcing her eyes from his as she redressed his hand.

"Not if you've already made your catch and find you soon have two more little fishes"

"Oh! You have two children?" Henry detected disappointment. "Then you shouldn't be thinking of other women," she said as she cleaned the cut with less gentleness.

"Ow! That hurt! I never said I'd been thinking of *other* women, at least not until now."

She felt his eyes staring at her and knew she was blushing again. Desperately, she searched for something to say. "Do you live around here?" she said, and then wondered if she had sounded too brazen. "Not too far. What about you?"

"I used to. My mother still does."

"Can I ask what your name is?" He said, as she re-bandaged his hand.

"Why"

"Well, just in case I do decide to think about another woman, I'd like to have a name to go with the face, and it is a very pretty face."

"There you go, all finished. You can go now," she said, ignoring his question yet feeling quietly exited by his compliment.

Henry stood up, thanked her and said goodbye. Leaning against the sink with her arms crossed she watched the door close behind him. She was still staring at the door a few seconds later when it reopened and his grinning face appeared,

"Well?" he said.

She giggled again. "It's Cathleen."

"Well thanks again Cathleen, Oh, give my best to your mother, Nell!"

"Oh yes, I wi…" The door closed just as the proverbial penny dropped.

15
The neighbour

Conviviality continued to decline at No 12 Lyons Terrace, although Henry tried hard to make things as pleasant as possible for his children. He tried his best to keep Martia happy. He'd come to realise that keeping her in a good mood meant less suffering for Jan and Billy. For that reason he even tried being pleasant to Elsie Craven, which put a strain on his powers of self control.

As time went on Martia interpreted Henry's attempts to please her as weakness on his part. This put Henry in a no-win situation. The more he tried to please Martia the harder she made it for him to do so.

Janice was eight and Billy, five when Henry broke the news to Martia that he was rejoining the army. Apart from being concerned about managing financially, Martia showed little concern when Henry left to rejoin his old Army unit. From then on, Henry was away from home for long periods.

It was during one of these spells that number 14: the house next door to the Gough's, which had been empty for some time suddenly became occupied. This became apparent to Jan and Billy one day while they were playing Hide and Seek in their back yard.

Because the yard was far too small to find enough places to hide, Jan changed the rules to add spice to the game. The rules were that the seeker was armed with an elastic band and paper pellets, and could not claim a find unless the hunted was hit with a pellet before they could reach the home base.

The game usually ended with Billy in tears; nevertheless, it was always Billy who suggested the game.

The game had started and Billy had hidden behind the shed. As Jan crept up behind him, paper pellet at the ready, they both heard a child's giggle. Forgetting their game, they approached next-door's low wall where a small boy had been watching them.

"Hello!" said Jan "Do you live there?"

"Yes, and my mummy."

"My name's Janice and this is my brother Billy. I'm eight and he's five. What's your name?"

"George, I'm five too."

"You can play with us if you like," said Jan.

George looked a little worried. " Do it hurt?" he asked, pointing to Jan's elastic band.

"Only for a little while," chimed in Billy. "Look!" he said proudly pulling his shirt collar down to reveal a red mark on his neck. "I didn't even cry."

"OK," said George nodding eagerly. Billy clapped his hands, a habit he'd acquired when excited. Jan struggled, but managed to lift the boy over to their side of the wall. The game restarted with added zest until George's young mother came looking for him. Panic was evident in her voice as she called his name.

"George is over here playing, Miss," Jan said politely, while George slunk out from behind an old galvanized bath.

"How did you get over there?" George's mother said angrily. "I told you about climbing in those shoes." she said angrily.

"He didn't climb Miss. I lifted him over," said Jan meekly.

Meanwhile, Martia was in her scullery. She had heard the woman's irate voice and so, made her way along the garden path.

"Well you had no right," the young woman was saying. "He's not to leave this garden, do you hear?"

"What's the problem?" said Martia, though seeing the infant George on her side of the wall and hearing the young woman's last sentence, she had already deduced the problem.

"Your girl's the problem," the young woman said angrily. "She's taken my baby without my permission."

With a smile, Martia said, "I would hardly call him a baby. He must be four or five, and I don't think she intended to kidnap him. Never mind," Martia said, lifting George back over the wall. "It won't happen again."

Martia heard nothing from the young woman next door for several weeks, and so far she'd not seen a man enter or leave number 14 either. This left Martia guessing that the young mother's husband may have been in the Service. Then, one day whilst in her kitchen, she heard the young woman calling to her. Martia walked along her garden path and peered around the high privacy wall that separated their back doors.

"Oh Mrs Gough I know you are going to think I'm impertinent for asking, and I wouldn't blame you if you refused, but I want to ask a favour.

Martia was quite taken by the young woman's polished enunciation and guessing her age to be no more than twenty, Martia wondered how young she must have been when George was born.

"Ask away!"

"Well my George has not been well. I've been using a croup kettle in his room but his cough doesn't seem to be getting any better. He keeps talking about your Billy and I thought it might do him good if your boy could come over and keep him company, he hasn't any other friends."

Martia felt sorry for the woman for having to swallow her pride after their little set-to. "Of course he can. I'm sure he'd love it. He can stay the night if you like. Just send him back when he starts to get on your nerves." Then, deviously, Martia added. "That's if you're sure his dad won't mind."

Without elaborating the girl just said, "no there's only the two of us." Martia thought that this little ice-breaking event would create a more sociable air between them, but this was not to be. Martia was sure that when seeing her young neighbour in Queen Street a week later, the woman purposely crossed the road to avoid speaking to her.

Billy slept at Billy's that night and the two became very close friends. For the next couple of weeks Billy slept next door almost every night, and still Martia and the young mother had no more than a nodding acquaintance. Billy loved staying over at George's house, not only because they enjoyed each other's company, but also because he was free of Martia's almost constant bad temper, even though most of her venom was directed at Janice.

George's health picked up and the boys remained good friends. They started their first day at school together and left each morning holding each other's hands.

On nights when Billy didn't sleep over with George, they would often call softly to each other from their bedroom windows across their narrow back yards.

Martia put her young neighbour's un-neighbourly attitude down to her age and shyness. She asked Nell Masters if she knew anything about her, but Nell's response was,
"I think your friend, Elsie Craven, is the best one to ask."
However, Elsie seemed evasive when Martia asked her about her young neighbour. Martia thought this a little strange. Elsie was not normally averse to talking about, or slating anyone in the Terrace. She certainly knew about everyone's business.

A few weeks after the new neighbour had moved in, Billy awoke one night with the sound of a sharp crack against his bedroom window. This did not surprise him. Throwing things at each other's window had become a regular way for he and George to communicate. Jan was asleep in the next room.

Billy threw his bed covers back and kneeled up against the window. He struggled to slide the window up far enough to lean out. It was almost a full moon and he could see his friend clearly; George was leaning out of his window, and peering down into his own back yard. Cupping his hands to his mouth, Billy called softly,
"What's up?"
"Listen!" Billy knew immediately what George meant. He heard raised voices coming from the living-room window of George's house. "They've been shouting like that for ages," said George. "I can't sleep."
"Who's your mum shouting at?"
"I don't know." Suddenly the voices became louder as the kitchen door opened and light flooded the yard. Instinctively, George and Billy faded back into the shadows of their rooms, but from Billy's vantage point, he could still see George's back door. A thin man leaned against the doorframe, smoking a cigarette. As he blew smoke upwards into the night sky, Billy saw his face clearly.
More noise came from inside like furniture breaking. At one point, Billy heard a scream. The tall man suddenly flicked his

cigarette stub at the adjoining wall sending sparks swirling into the darkness. Billy watched him re-enter the kitchen before the door closed.

It was the following Monday and the children were at school when Martia experienced her next encounter with the young Mrs Moody.

Martia was in the back yard, hanging out washing when she suddenly heard a voice say,

"Don't get involved." Martia waited, expecting to hear another voice, thinking her neighbour had company, but there was only silence. Martia peered round the high privacy wall toward her neighbour's back door,

"Sorry, were you speaking to me?" She was surprised to see her neighbour with her arm in plaster. She was struggling to feed wet clothes between the rollers of an old mangle outside her back door. "What happened to your arm?" Martia said. The girl ignored the question and avoided looking up as she spoke.

"I saw you talking to that Craven woman. You shouldn't get involved with her," she said, turning the mangle's handle.

"You mean Elsie! Why, what do you mean?" Martia said, while thinking the girl's shabby appearance did not match the elegance of her enunciation.

"She's not the kind hearted person she would have you believe. Heed my word," the girl said in a bitter tone of voice.

"Would you like me to help you with that?" said Martia, seeing something white fall from the mangle to the ground.

Ignoring Martia's offer she said, "I'm just warning you." Martia could see that she was becoming frustrated with her own awkwardness. "Don't borrow from her," The girl went on. "In fact don't let them do you any favours. Their favours will have a price."

Martia wondered what Elsie had done to upset the girl and why she had changed the word "her" to "them." Then the girl looked up at Martia revealing the worst black eye that Martia had seen. "There's something very wrong with that Craven woman," said the girl. Martia thought she detected a sob in the girl's voice as she watched her throw the last garment on top of the basket of washing.

"Wrong?" repeated Martia. "In what way?"

"Up here," said the girl, touching her temple.

Martia expected her to bring the pile of washing down to peg it on her line, but she retreated into her house. With one foot inside her door, she turned to face Martia again. Martia could clearly see her tears as the girl said finally. "She'll get you too. Take my word!"

Billy was nearing his sixth birthday, and the excitement over whether his present would be the clockwork train that he'd asked for had kept Billy awake late into Saturday night. Just when sleep had started to win the battle, and his thoughts were turning to dreams, he was hastily brought back to consciousness, by Georges signal: the sharp crack against his window. Throwing back his bedcovers he got to a kneeling position and quietly slid his window up. A cold breeze blew away the last strands of sleep.

"What's up?" he called softly.

"Those men are back, can you hear them?"

"Yes. Are they shouting at your mum?"

"Yes, I'm scared. They hurt my mum bad the last time they came. Can you come over, Billy. I'll be alright if you're here."

"I don't see how I can. My mums down the pub, so I can't ask her. Anyway what would those men do if I knocked your door?"

"You don't have to. They're out the back in the kitchen. I can let you in the front door."

"What if my mum looks in my room when she comes home."

"That's easy, remember that film that your Jan took us to see, when that man put his pillow under his bed covers to make it look like he was asleep?"

"Oh yes, I remember," Billy thought this all sounded like a Famous Five adventure, which his teacher had been reading to his class. He now felt like one of those children in the story, but then he didn't remember any of them having a mother with a temper like his mother. "No George, I'd better not." Billy started to slide the window down.

"Oh! please Billy, please!"

Six-thirty Sunday morning, Jan was awakened by the chink of small stones hitting her bedroom window. She looked out and was surprised to see Billy at the door in his pyjamas. She crept downstairs and opened the door. Billy stood shivering and looking pale.

"Does mum know you slept next door?" she whispered.

"No, and don't you dare tell her."

The two crept upstairs and got into bed without waking their mother. An hour later Jan took Martia a cup of tea telling her that the tide was out, and that she and Billy were going winkling down in the harbour.

An hour after the children had left a loud clanging of bells prompted Martia to leave her bed and peer out of her front room window. Two police cars and an ambulance were below her window and a crowd had started to form outside. She started to dress as someone knocked her door. It was Elsie Craven.

"Elsie! What's going on? What's all the excitement about on a Sunday morning?"

"Oh, bit of trouble next door to you last night. Did you hear any noise?" Elsie looked worried as she nervously toyed with a bunch of keys in her hand.

Martia could not deduce the meaning behind the expression on Elsie's face, but could see she was certainly not her usual calm self.

"Like what?"

"Anything! Did you hear or see anyone at her front door last night."

"Hell no! I heard nothing. Mind you, I'd had a few. I slept like a log. Why, what's happened?"

"Don't suppose you've heard then, have you, girl?"

"No. For God's sake Elsie, tell me!" Martia said, standing on tiptoe to peer over Elsie's head at the gathering crowd.

"It's your neighbour, Helen Moody. She hanged herself last night."

"Oh no!" Martia said through cupped hands. "She was only talking abou…" Martia suddenly paused realising the delicacy of the situation, and took a moment to collect her thoughts.

"What," Elsie said with concern. "You were going to say she was talking about someone."

Instinct told Martia to use caution and to think quickly.

"Yes, about little George, only a couple of weeks ago, about how well her George and my Billy got on together. Helen! Was that her name? God, I never even found out her name. "

"Well don't blame yourself for that, girl. After all, she was a bit of a strange one. Yes, moody by name, moody by nature, as they say. I think she must have had one bad mood too many."

"Anyway, I was the one who called the police. Didn't really surprise me, you know. That sort was never cut out for it."

What Elsie meant by her last comment Martia wasn't sure, and she could hardly believe the callous way in which Elsie referred to someone who had just died so tragically. However, she did stop talking just long enough for the ambulance men to carry out a white sheet-covered stretcher. They watched the crowd part to let the men slide the body in the back of the ambulance. Then the slamming of the ambulance doors seemed a signal for Elsie to continue.

"Little George found her when he got up for school this morning, the thoughtless cow, fancy letting your kid wake up to that. He woke me up. Came along and banged on my door."

"Why?"

"What do you mean, why?"

"Why did he come to your house?"

"Well I suppose he knew I was the landlady and…"

"Are you saying you own this place next door?"

"Well, not outright, but yes, I thought you knew. Anyway, do you know what the poor little mite said? Mummy's got herself all tangled up. He sure got that right. Did it under the stairs she did. She made a good job of it, too. When she kicked the chair away, it went the length of the passage. She really meant it this time."

"Are you saying she's tried it before?"

"Oh sure, the last time she jumped in the Bunny."

"The what?"

"The Bunny, it's in Old Portsmouth, you know, Sallyport. Some people call it the hot walls. It's where the generating plant pumps hot water into the sea. The silly cow couldn't have picked a more popular place, lots of people swim there, even in the winter, because of the warm water. Anyway, someone saw her and dragged her out. But all that happened before I let her move in here."

"What did you mean by her not being cut out for it, cut out for what?"

"You know," said Elsie, nudging Martia while emphasising the "know".

"You don't mean?" Martia's mouth went agape. "What, on the game. Well I never would have thought she was the type!"

"Yes exactly! That was her trouble. The stuck up cow was too fussy. Never made enough to manage, yet you never saw her go out to work did you?"

"Now you come to mention it, no I can't say I did, but if I had known she was on the game I would never have let Billy sleep over with little George like he did."

"Well think yourself lucky he didn't..." Elsie paused, and with concern, said. "He didn't sleep there last night did he?"

"No, I don't think so, he couldn't have. Jan took him out with her first thing this morning."

"Good! No telling what nightmares little George is going to have after waking up to that."

Elsie stopped talking when a police sergeant and a plain-clothes man emerged from next door. The two women watched them get into the Riley Pathfinder and slam the door. The ambulance pulled away and the crowd waited for the car to follow, but instead, the car door opened again and the man in plain clothes leaned out of the door and called out,

"No one's to enter this house until we've finished in there, Mrs Craven. Is that clear?" Elsie nodded. The car door slammed again and the car pulled away.

As the police car reached the end of the road and turned out of sight Martia was the first to speak.

"He called you Mrs, but you're not married are you Elsie?"

"I was." Martia surmised that Elsie did not want to elaborate on the subject and didn't pursue it.

"Course," Elsie went on. "She came from money people you know, no doubt about it, but the silly cow got herself pregnant by some young shit who promised to marry her; how gullible can they get eh? Anyway, he disappeared as soon as she told him about the baby. After that, she ran away from home. I suppose she was too ashamed to tell her parents, whoever they are. God knows where she had been living until she gave birth to little George. Anyway, Debbie and me found her begging outside a pub. She was in trouble; she had no money and nowhere to stay so I helped her out. I let her move in here. I told her how she could solve her problems. I sent a few clients to her, but no, too bloody stuck up, that was her trouble. You help the silly cows out, and then they don't want to play the bloody game."

Martia was beginning to get the picture.

"Still, you've got to feel sorry for her, bringing up a baby all on her own. It must have been hard," said Martia. Elsie suddenly became tense.

"Hard?" Elsie said. Martia thought she was going to laugh out loud. "Hard?" She repeated even louder. Martia saw the insane look in her eyes but could not have known just how profound that insanity was.

"She never knew the meaning of the word," Elsie continued. "No, she got herself pregnant with her eyes wide open, among other things." Martia started to smile at Elsie's lewd joke but refrained when Elsie's face came within an inch of her own. "I'll tell you what's hard gal," she sneered. "Hard is when your mother's a drunken pro that lets her filthy clients come into your room and interfere with you when you're only ten years old. No! Don't you talk to me about having it hard."

Martia was intrigued, and wanted to ask her more, but a quiver on Elsie's chin told Martia she was about to cry. In an attempt to save her from embarrassment, Martia quickly asked another question.

"What about little George, what's going to happen to him?"

Elsie took a deep breath to gain her composure.

"Well he's in my place at the moment. Poor little sod seems to have lost his voice. That stupid CID copper can't get a word out of him. I expect the police will get in touch with old Father Crowley and he'll be taken to the orphanage. Anyway, if the police question you, just tell them that you heard and saw nothing. They won't bother you again."

Having collected a considerable amount of winkles that morning, Jan and Billy sat on the shore watching the mud larks below the causeway. They were amused by their antics, and how they enticed the people above them to part with their coins.

Jan poured their collection of winkles into one bucket and as she looked into it, she said,

"Billy, you know that bracelet in the shop window we were looking at? Billy didn't answer. He sat gazing out to sea with his arms around his legs and his chin resting on his knees.

"You know! In that pawn shop." Jan went on. "I think if we sold all these down our street we might have enough to buy it." Still, there was no answer from Billy. "You know! For mums birthday."

Still, Billy seemed in a daze.

"**Billy**!" Jan prodded him.

Ignoring Jan's question Billy said quietly: "You don't only get ogres in fairy stories, do you Jan?"

"Of course you do. That's why they're called fairy stories. I mean fairies are not real, so ogres can't be real, can they. What a funny thing you are; what made you say that?"

"I think I saw one last night!"

"Oh that was just a dream."

16
When the cats away

The children arrived home around midday with the proceeds of their morning's work. It had taken them over an hour of knocking doors to sell all their winkles. Martia said nothing to them about the happenings next door, only that George and his Mum had gone away for a while. She surmised that Billy would get used to George not being around by the time the street's gossip eventually filtered down to him.

Due to Henry's past training and engineering background, he was quickly promoted through the ranks. Unfortunately, the more responsibility his position held, the less time he spent at home. This meant the less the children saw of him.

This was of little consequence to Martia, but she was surprised at how often Nell knocked her door now that Henry was away. She seemed to find lots of excuses to do so.

"I've made some bread pudding," she would say, "thought you and the children might like some." Or, "I wondered if Janice wasn't doing anything she would pop down the shop for me."

Martia, in fact misinterpreted the meaning of Nell's frequent visits and said to her one day,

"You don't like Henry very much, do you Nell?"

Nell looked surprised. "Whatever do you mean? Of course I do. Henry's always been polite to me. Well, except for that first day we met. Do you remember when he couldn't open the front door? I thought he was going to bite my head off. But no, Henry was always the first to stop and chat if we met in the street."

"Oh! Well it's just that you never seemed to come over here when he was home," said Martia.

"Well a young couple don't want some busybody knocking the door all the time. But now you're alone so long with the children, I just like to think I can help."

"Oh you do, Nell, and I am grateful."

Unbeknown to Martia, Henry had asked Nell to keep an eye on Jan and Billy now that he was spending so much time away from home. This was the reason for her frequent visits.

Martia was pleased with her newfound friend, simply because she found Nell to be a convenient baby sitter. Nell could be relied upon to mind Jan and Billy when Martia wanted a night out. And since Henry was now away most of the time, her nights out were becoming more frequent.

Nell enjoyed having Jan and Billy over. With her daughter, Cathleen, having her own flat and only paying short visits, Nell found the children to be good company. She taught them card games, or they would play board games and Nell would always come out with some edible treat during the evening. Yes, the children came to appreciate their mother's nights out.

"Martia! Come in love. I'm just making a cuppa." Nell said, on opening her door one Saturday morning.

"I expect you know what I was going to ask, Nell."

"Well if it was to have the children I'd be glad of the company." Nell led Martia down the passage and into her tastefully furnished living room. "Have a chair love, I'll just put the kettle on." Then before disappearing into the adjoining kitchen, Nell said, "You're in luck. I was going to the pictures with Cathleen my daughter, tonight, but she popped in to say that she's got to work. Apparently, they're short staffed. So, where are you going, anywhere nice?"

"It's Elsie's birthday and she's invited me out for a few drinks." Nell didn't answer. Martia waited until Nell came in with a tea tray before saying,

"You don't like Elsie much, do you Nell?"

"Lets say we don't care much for each other." Nell sat facing Martia as she poured the tea.

"Is that because you're competitors?"

"Whatever do you mean?" Nell sounded annoyed.

"Oh I didn't mean to be rude. It's just that I know you both own houses in the terrace and I thought…"

"Oh I see! You're adding two and two and coming up with the same answer for both Elsie and myself. No! You've got it wrong. I have an agent that manages my properties. I insist that he collects a fair rent. If a woman, who happens to be on the game, rents one, that's her business. Lets face it, it's kind of expected around here, but I don't live on immoral earnings, the rent is the same no matter who the tenant is, male or female. I don't think any less of my tenants whatever their lifestyle. One of my best friends was once a prostitute and a kinder woman you couldn't wish to meet, but I don't judge her, or think any less of her. As you know, I also have a couple of second hand shops run by trustworthy managers so I have no need to live off immoral earnings. Yes, both Elsie and I have houses in the terrace and yes, prostitutes occupy some of them, but that's where the similarity ends. If you want to know how Elsie runs her business you'll have to ask her."

"I didn't mean to offend…"

"That's alright love. I suppose people think that if you own half a dozen houses around here you must be doing something illegal. Anyway, enough about that, how's Henry and when is he coming home?"

"I don't know Nell, when he does come home, we always seem to start quarrelling. He thinks it's easy looking after two kids on an Army allowance."

"Yes, sometimes you just need someone to tell your troubles to." Nell then saw her chance and pushed the question she'd been longing to ask for so long. "What about your parents Martia, where are they?"

"Gone, well mum is. Dad is in a home. He kind of lost it after mum died. She kept him in check when they ran the business together. You might remember it! Boswell's in Queen Street." Nell showed no sign of recognising the name and Martia continued, "When Mum became ill he started gambling. Card schools, he just couldn't keep away from them. He lost a lot of money. I think that is what started his drinking. I kept finding empty whisky bottles around the house. He borrowed money against the business and lost it. Eventually he couldn't pay his workers and the bank closed him down."

"That's very sad. Do you visit him, or is it too far to travel?"

"Oh no! It's only at Copnor, in St Mary's House."

"Your father's in the workhouse!" Nell tried to hide the shock and wasn't sure that she'd succeeded.

"Well, I suppose if you want to be blunt. Do they still call it that?" Martia said, like she'd been accused of abandoning him.

"Oh I'm sorry, I didn't mean it to sound like an accusation," said Nell.

"Anyway it was his own fault drinking and gambling like he did. He was weak. He had a good business and he squandered the profits all because mum wasn't there to keep an eye on him. I went to visit him once, to tell him I was getting married, but it's a horrible place, so I've not been back since. Anyway they weren't my real parents." Martia said, like it justified abandoning her father. Nell dearly wanted to tell her the truth about herself. That Ivan Boswell was her real and biological father, but without divulging the truth about her mother and the sordid Gill family, she couldn't.

"But does that matter!" Nell said. "I mean, if they brought you up?"

"I know it sounds callous, but I couldn't forgive him for squandering all that money."

"All the same don't you feel anything? I mean, knowing he's in that place with no one to visit him."

Martia thought about it for a moment. "No, not really. Anyway I expect Alfie still goes to visit him."

Nell felt a sudden stirring within her. Of course! She'd forgotten the connection. Alfie Button was related to Ivan Boswell's wife and she remembered how close he and Ivan were. Nell wanted to bombard Martia with questions about Alfie, like, was he married, was he still handsome, where did he live, but Nell wanted to keep her past a secret, at least from Martia, so she made do with a simple,

"Alfie?"

"Yes, Alfie Button. He's like a cousin, although we're not really related. Funny name isn't it, Alfie Button? He always looked after mum and dad's horses. He came to live with us for a while when his parents died. I was about nine or ten then. Boy, did I have a crush on Alfie. I used to say to him. (Wait for me to grow up, Alfie, then we can get married). I think he's still a blacksmith. Last I heard he owned a forge somewhere near Fratton Road."

It was around seven that evening when Nell opened her front door to the knock she was expecting. Jan and Billy stood there with Martia behind them looking beautiful yet angry. Nell could see that she was dressed up and ready for her night out. She could also see that Jan had been crying as the girl was still sniffing the last of her tears away.

"Hope you don't mind Nell, I brought them over a bit early cause this one's been getting on my nerves," said Martia, poking Jan sharply in the back.

Nell cradled the two children to her. "No I don't mind, what's all the tears for, love." Nell said, lifting Jan's chin to look into her face.

"Same old story Nell," Martia intervened, before Jan could get a word in. "Money! Apparently, her school is running a trip to Southsea. There's going to be some sort of a show on Southsea Common. You know the sort of thing: farm animals, dog and flower show, that sort of thing."

"Oh yes! My Cathleen's promoting the Red Cross tent out there. Should be fun."

"Well anyway," Martia continued. "She brought a note home from school saying that the kids in her year can go if they can come up with the fare and spending money. Well I'm not paying out for that sort of thing. I mean, like Elsie said: What's all that got to do with education anyway?"

"Yes well you run along Martia, they'll be OK with me," Nell said, biting her tongue for fear of saying something she might regret and not wishing to argue the comparison of Janice's welfare with that of a few gins on a night out.

That evening Nell produced a stack of indoor games and toys she'd saved from Cathleen's childhood, and although Nell tried to keep the pair amused; Jan's underlying sadness remained evident. Nell enjoyed the children's company. She baked them shortbread biscuits and joined them in Cathleen's old table games. In a way, it brought home to Nell the realisation of how lonely her life had become.

At around 8pm Nell was surprised at the arrival of her daughter, Cathleen.

"Hello love, I thought you said you were working tonight." Nell said on opening the front door.

"I know I did, but I swapped shifts to do one of the girls a favour."

"Well it's a bit late to go to the pictures now. Anyway I'm looking after Jan and Billy Gough from over the road." Cathy followed her through to the living room where Jan and Billy were playing draughts.

"Hi-ya-kids, what are you doing with all my toys?" Cathy said, grinning at them. "And I was worried about you being lonely mum, that's why I came over. Never mind. Now that I'm here, maybe we can all play a game."

"Ooh yes," Billy said, clapping excitedly. "Can we play snakes and ladders?" Nell got out the box and the four of them sat round the table. The mood of the evening was cheerful, as the game got under way, until Cathy suddenly remarked that Jan looked like she'd been crying.

"That's cause Mum won't let her go to the Southsea show on Saturday," interrupted Billy

"Oh, that's a shame," said Cathy. "Why can't you go Jan?"

"Mum says she can't afford it, and because she says it's got nothing to do with education."

"Oh but of course it has…"

"Cathy!" Nell interrupted her daughter sternly. "We mustn't interfere."

"No, you're right Mum." There was a lull in the conversation until Cathy said, "Would your mum let you come to the show with me, and help us with the Red Cross tent. It wouldn't cost her anything and I'm sure you could help out?"

Jan's face lit up. "Really! Do you mean it?"

"Of course. But only with your mum's permission." Cathy saw the look of anticipation on Billy's face. "Yes alright, you too if mum says it's okay."

The following week felt, to Jan, like the longest week of her life. She polished both hers and Billy's shoes, washed Billy's best shirt along with her white school blouse. She sewed up the lining in the only coat she had to wear, and made sure Billy's attire was also fit to be seen out with Cathleen. When she was sure she could do no more it was still only Thursday.

Cathleen, having received word from Nell that Jan and Billy could go, turned up bright and early on the Saturday to knock at number 12 Lyons Terrace. Martia opened the door looking very fragile and as if she'd just awoken.

"Hello Mrs Gough. I've called to collect Jan and Billy, are they ready?" It was the first time Cathleen had seen Martia at close quarters, and even though Martia appeared to be emerging from a drunken stupor, Cathleen thought how beautiful she was, and could see why Jan and Billy had such beautiful blue eyes.

"What?" Martia looked puzzled at first as she tried to run her fingers through her matted hair. "Oh yes, you're Nell's girl. Sorry I've got a bit of a headache. Yes, they've been ready for days; it's all they talk about. Are you sure you want to take them, they can be a handful you know, especially Jan?"

"Well, they're always well behaved for mum, and anyway I couldn't disappoint them now." With that, Jan and Billy arrived at the doorway, with a shiny just washed look and grinning with excitement. "Ready kids? Right lets go."

"It couldn't have been a better day for such an event; the sun shone and Southsea Common was bustling. Tents were advertising all kinds of attractions: Dog shows, bird shows, flower shows and among the various tents were merry-go-rounds and other fairground amusements. Jan and Billy were wide eyed with excitement from the moment they arrived.

Cathleen told them to look for a tent or an army lorry with a Red Cross on it. Billy was the first to spot it. There were three other nurses already there. They were laughing as they struggled with the task of pitching the Red Cross tent. Recognising Cathleen they greeted her and the children with smiles.

"Okay girls, help has arrived." Cathy said jokingly "These are the two I told you about, Janice and Billy. They have come to help us out. "

"The nurses made a great fuss over the children making them feel very welcome and, more importantly, useful. They helped the nurses turn their site into a mock wartime operating theatre, with wounded dummies laid out on stretchers. Jan asked if she could help with the collection tins and was thrilled when Cathy produced an extra Red Cross apron for her to wear. Immediately, Jan decided she wanted to be a nurse when she grew up. As the morning wore on, Southsea's common became more and more crowded. Suddenly one of the nurses turned to Cathy and asked,

"Where's Billy?" Cathy looked about her,

"Jan, did Billy go to the toilets?" Scanning the crowd, Jan replied,

"He must have, but he never told me he was going."

"Well I think we should look for him, I don't like him wandering off like that. I'm supposed to be looking after him."

The two of them meandered in and out of the various attractions, making their way toward the public toilets on the far side of the common. They reached it just as a man came out,

"Excuse me sir," said Cathy, "did you see a young boy in there?"

"No, sorry miss, no kids in there." Cathy grabbed Jan's hand and the two hurried back to the common. They wandered in and out of tents and as Cathy became more anxious, her fear was transmitted to Jan. They came upon a small crowd of people gathered in a semi-circle beside a huge lorry. The crowd's attention was drawn to something that the pair could not see. Jan tried pushing through the crowd to see if Billy was in there but didn't get far and went back to where Cathy waited for her.

"I couldn't see him in there Cathy. What are we going to do? Mum will kill me if I go home without him."

Cathleen thought Janice was about to cry. She put her arms around her, saying,

"We're not going home without him love, and he won't have gone far. What is this crowd looking at?"

"I'm not sure, but I think I saw a horse. Maybe we should go back, he might be back at the tent by now."

Cathy looked down at Jan's worried face and knew that her tears were about to overflow. "Don't fret love, we'll find him. I expect you're right. I bet we missed him on the way to the toilet. He's probably back at the tent. Come on let's hurry." She took Jan's hand and was about to walk on when a burst of laughter came from the crowd. Jan dug her heel in the ground, pulling Cathy to a jolt.

"He's in there Cathy! I'd know his giggle anywhere." Jan forced her way through the crowd, ignoring angry looks as she pulled Cathy along with her. On reaching the front of the crowd, they were filled with relief. There was Billy proudly standing there, holding the reins of a huge Shire horse, while a man gave a demonstration of changing one of its shoes.

Then they witnessed the reason for the laughter. As the man pulled nails from the Shire's hoof, the horse turned his head and nibbled the man's cap. The crowd started to laugh in anticipation of what was to come. The farrier looked up at Billy and in a serious voice said.

"Now what did I say? I asked you not to let him eat my hat. I mean that's why I picked you to hold him, because you looked like the strongest bloke in the crowd." The crowd were laughing at the man's act and none more than Billy.

Cathleen laughed along with the crowd, and recalled a childhood story of how a young golden haired boy had stolen her mother's heart, a boy that had his cap eaten by a horse. Could it possibly be? Cathy asked herself. The man could be about her mother's age. He was certainly broad and handsome and his hair was fair and wavy, though not long, as her mother had described. But the horse nibbling his hat was too much of a coincidence.

She tried to recall his name; a funny name, she thought. But as much as she tried, she could not remember. She craned her neck and peered over the crowd. There it was, painted on the cab of the lorry: *A.Button*. Yes, that was it, Alfie Button.

Peering out from the cab was a young woman. She appeared to be about the same age as herself and assumed the girl to be his daughter. Cathy felt sad for her mother and decided not to mention this to her.

It was a fortnight after Helen Moody's body had been taken away, before Janice learned the details of what had happened to young George and his mother. That same night Martia went out, leaving instructions for Jan to put Billy to bed. As Jan tucked in his bedclothes, Billy said,

"How much longer will George be gone Jan?"

"I don't think he will be coming back Billy, not after what I heard today."

"What?"

"That his mum died."

"You're not supposed to joke about things like that Jan. God will punish you," said Billy, voicing the phrase his mother constantly threatened them with.

"I'm not, honestly! Lily Shelton, across the road, told me she committed suicide. She said that Creepy Crowley *(The neighbourhood children's nickname for the local catholic priest)* came and took George away."

Knowing Jan was always playing tricks on him, Billy looked warily at Jan, trying to read humour in her eyes, some hint that would tell him she was joking, that tomorrow he and George would be trotting off to school together like always. But there was no glint of humour and Billy knew Jan was telling the truth. "He will be looked after, Billy," Jan said, seeing Billy's eyes filling with tears. Billy turned away to face the window where he had spent so many hours talking to George. "They say the boys get lots to eat in them orphan homes," said Jan, trying her hardest to cheer her brother up. Billy didn't answer. Jan started towards the door, leading to her room and as she raised her hand to turn off the light, Billy's muffled voice came from under his covers.

"Leave the light on please Jan. Just for tonight."

When Nell was not out with her daughter Cathleen, she started to become a regular shopper in Fratton Rd. She told herself that it had better shops and was more convenient. But she knew in her heart that she was lying to herself, and that it was really in hope of seeing Alfie once again. I probably wouldn't even recognise him, she told herself. But two or three days every week Nell spent walking the length of Fratton Rd without so much as a glimpse of Alfie. It didn't seem to matter though. Somehow, just the thought that he was somewhere close by, gave her a warm feeling. The thought that he might suddenly turn a corner for them to meet was enough to keep her shopping there. It was on one of these shopping trips that she happened to be passing a dray being unloaded, and seeing its Shire horse, prompted her to question the driver,

"Excuse me, but do you know of any blacksmiths' around here?"

"There's one in Sandringham Road lady, opposite the Troxy." Nell thanked him and crossed over the road. Now her heart beat faster thinking that she could soon be laying eyes on the only man that she had ever loved. But as she neared the corner of Sandringham Rd, doubts started to enter her mind. Would he be married, she thought? Yes, how could some lucky girl not have snapped up a golden haired boy like her Alfie? Would he be disappointed at how she'd aged, and more importantly would she see the disappointment in his face. That would be something she couldn't bear.

A young woman brushed passed her, dressed in the latest clothes and Nell considered how nice she looked. She stopped and looked at her own reflection in a shop window. She stood there wondering how long it had been since she'd bought any new clothes or visited a hairdresser. Hell, its not as if I can't afford it, she thought. Suddenly Nell knew what she had to do. She retraced her steps toward Arundel Street and caught the next bus home.

A week later, she returned to Fratton Road dressed like the Lord Mayor's wife, and feeling ten years younger. Turning heads told her she was now ready to receive Alfie Button. Nell entered Sandringham Road.

Even before she had reached the blacksmiths, the loud clank of hammer against steel told her she was close. Gradually the smell of the furnace confirmed it, and sweet memories of her childhood came flooding back.

On reaching the double wooden doors of the forge, Nell peered inside. She saw three men working but none of them resembled Alfie. Of course, he is a lot older, she thought, and he may not have the same beautiful long golden hair. But none of these men looked…"

"Nell! Nell Masters." The voice called from behind her.

Nell had been unaware of the man who had followed her from some distance behind, along Sandringham Rd. She turned and felt her legs go weak as she looked into the same blue eyes that for years she could only dream about. "Alfie?"

"Got it in one gal."

"How did you know it was me?"

"I'd know them gorgeous legs anywhere gal. I've thought about them enough." Alfie stood holding a large paper bag in one hand and a half eaten doughnut in the other. Grinning, he offered the bag to Nell, saying "Doughnut?"

Nell laughed, "No thank you, Alfie." This was her Alfie, just as she remembered him, no airs or graces, just the unpretentious gentle giant that filled her dreams on so many lonely nights.

"What you doing around here anyway?"

Nell was ready with her answer, which was honest to a point. But before she could speak one of the men working inside shouted:

"Hey! Alf, where's them doughnuts." Alfie acknowledged him with a wave of his hand and then turned to Nell.

"Look, Nell. Have you got time to come up the corner café for a cup of tea? I've got so many questions."

" I'd love to," said Nell.

"There you go lads," Alfie said plonking the bag on an anvil. "You can have mine as well. I'll see you later." Chuckling at his men's carefully chosen, but sexually tainted witticisms, he said, "If I'm not back by five, lock up, Bye.

Nell felt she was in a dream as the two of them strolled towards Fratton Road. Yes, this was Alfie, Oh, not her golden haired boy that she lay with on Portsdown Hill all those years ago. No, this was a mature handsome man with shoulders like an ox, yet a man that had stolen Alfie's laughing blue eyes.

"What happened to the hair, Alfie?"

"Ah well, a man's got to grow up sometime and I got fed up with women giving me funny looks. Probably thought I was a nancy-boy or something."

"It's more likely they were jealous." They reached Fratton Road and turned northward.

"Anyway, you never said what you were doing here?" Alfie asked.

Nell was ready with an answer that was only a half-truth. She certainly wasn't prepared to tell him she'd been walking the length of Fratton Road twice a week for the past month just for the chance of seeing him after all these years.

"Well someone told me that Ivan Boswell was in St Mary's House and that you visited him. I was doing a bit of shopping in Fratton Road so I thought I would ask you how he is. Where did you say we were going?" she asked.

"Just along here to the Bay Tree Café. I usually have my lunch there. It's cheap and cheerful, but I like it," said Alfie. Then out of the blue he said, "It doesn't surprise me that you should ask about Ivan Boswell, you're Ivan's daughter aren't you?" Nell was taken by surprise.

"How did you find that out?"

"He told me." They reached the café and went upstairs to a quiet corner. The waitress took their order for tea and cakes and as she left them Nell said:

"But he always tried to keep that a secret."

"Yes I know, but I don't think he worried about it after Aunt Irene died. He didn't even ask me to keep it secret."

"Yes I heard that Irene died, she was a nice lady I am sorry Alfie, I know you were close."

"Yes, though Uncle Ivan took it a lot harder than I thought he would." Nell found it strange to hear this strapping man refer to the Boswell's as aunt and uncle, yet it somehow matched his gentle personality.

"But why would he tell you about my being his daughter. I mean why would he think you'd even be interested?"

"It was something that I said, that brought it about." Alfie turned his head and stared out of the window as he spoke. "I started to discuss the Oli Matcher case with him, and I think he knew how I felt about you." With that Nell put her hands over her face but Alfie reached out and gently taking her wrists parted her hands and said, "Nell, you had nothing to be ashamed of. You were a victim. You were drugged, and there was nothing you could do about it." Nell searched her handbag and found a handkerchief. "Anyway, that's when he told me you were his daughter." Then Alfie laughed, "He also told me about how you blackmailed him into giving your friend a job because she had been left with a baby. Ivan laughed about that. He said she turned out to be the best worker he had. He also told me not to make the same mistakes that he had. Not sure what he meant by that. Anyway, he said that if I really wanted you, then I should come after you. I took his advice. I went to the workhouse to find you. I was told you were away on an errand. I went back a week later and a nurse told me you had left and didn't want to see me. Why was that Nell? Hardly a day has gone by when I didn't ask myself that question."

Nell's tears were close to flowing as she answered "I couldn't face you, Alfie, I was carrying Oliver Matcher's baby"

"For crying out loud, Nell! I loved you too much for it to make any difference?"

The waitress brought the tray and Nell buried her face in her handkerchief to hide her tears. The waitress emptied the tray and left.

"Alfie I'm so sorry, but I was afraid to face you, afraid you wouldn't understand. I feel like I've wasted our lives."

"You and me both, Nell. I got married and that's been a disaster." Nell's heart sank with Alfie's last words, and from then on, the conversation seemed to become more formal. They talked of their younger days, of the picnics and pony trap rides, but to Nell, all promise of reconciliation had dispersed with the mention of his marriage, and Alfie did not insult Nell by suggesting any future meetings.

Nell told him of her intention to visit Ivan Boswell and the two eventually parted with talk of a possible chance meeting at St Mary's House. They said goodbye with nothing more intimate than a gentle clasp of hands though they could not hide the love reflected in each other's eyes.

It was August 1939 when Henry received another promotion, but was almost immediately given a posting in France. The following month, Britain's Neville Chamberlain announced his failure to achieve a peaceful solution to the problems in Europe and that his talks with the German Chancellor had been a waste of time. Britain was now at war.

It was about then that life started to change for Martia, but more so for Janice and Billy. Elsie Craven enticed Martia to spend more time in pubs on weekends and Martia soon developed a craving for alcohol. A lot her housekeeping was spent on drink and the more she drank the more abuse the children could expect from her, especially Janice.

Martia came home earlier than usual one evening. She was in a foul mood, having run out of money before drinking her fill at the corner pub. The children were sat at the living-room table with a jigsaw puzzle. Martia ignored them and went into the scullery. From there she called out,

"Janice, come here!" Jan came gingerly to the kitchen doorway. Her mother stood with arms folded in front of the gas cooker. "Who was the last one to come out here, and remember, God will punish you if you lie?" Martia's especially calm and composed voice rang a warning bell. Past experience had taught Jan that it was usually a sign of trouble.

"I don't know mum, it might have been me." Jan said nervously, knowing that she had just made Billy and herself a cup of cocoa.

"But there's two cups in the sink. Who do you think could have put them there?"

"I don't know mum."

"Oh, I think you do my girl. Come here." Jan moved nervously toward her mother. "Give me your hand."

"What did I do wrong mummy?" Tears started to fill Jan's eyes. Billy appeared at the kitchen doorway.

"Give me your hand!" Martia said through gritted teeth. Slowly Jan held out her arm. Grabbing her daughter's wrist, Martia prized opened Jan's fingers. "Now you know I'm always telling you how expensive it is to keep putting pennies in the metre and to always turn the gas out?" Jan's eyes darted towards the four gas burners on the stove. None of them were alight.

"Yes Mummy." She said nervously,

"Now then, did you remember to turn the gas off?"

"Yes Mummy."

"Good, then the metal won't be hot, will it?" Martia started to pull Jan's hand toward the gas burner,

"Don't Mummy please. I'm sorry." Jan repeated her cries as the puny weight of her thin body tried to resist the strength of her mother.

"Stop it! Stop it!" Billy cried, dashing up to his mother and pummelling his fists into her thigh. Jan felt the heat radiating from the metal even before her skin had touched it. That night Jan's pitiful scream echoed long into Billy's dreams.

A week later Martia had just risen and was still in her dressing gown. She sat with elbows on the wooden tabletop in the tiny living room. It was Saturday morning and she had consumed a lot of gin the previous evening. Her head was buzzing, her hands covered her face as she sat cursing the empty gin bottle staring back at her through the gaps of her fingers.

Janice came into the room followed by Billy. They stood waiting for their mother to acknowledge them. Their features, like their mother's were striking. The dark brown hair accentuated by pale blue eyes was enough to distract one's attention from their shabby clothes. Jan looked at the empty bottle, determined her mother's mood and was half tempted to creep back out again.

Martia didn't look up but felt their presence as they stood watching her. "What do you want?" she mumbled through her hands. It was not the first time Janice had seen her mother like this. She knew it was not a good time to approach her with any kind of request, especially one that involved money, but needs must, and in a timid voice, Jan blurted out. "It's Saturday, Mum" There was a pause while Martia tried to work out the significance of her daughter's words. What was special about Saturday? She asked herself, but it was no use; trying to concentrate just made her headache worse, along with her temper.

"So what? For Christ's sake," she shouted. "Just tell me what you bloody well want!"

Being head and shoulders shorter than his sister, Billy nudged Jan's leg. Jan looked down to see him silently mouth the words, "Go on."

"It's about the school games next week mum. Do you remember I asked you about some plimsoll's?" Jan bit her lip in anticipation of her mother's angry response, but Martia was slow in answering so Jan went on, "You said I could have the money to buy some Plimsolls today, for the school games next week, Billy and I was going to..." Jan paused as her mother turned to face them.

Jan was shocked to see the puffy dark swelling under her mother's eyes. Martia practically hissed her next words and shook her head spitefully. "Yes, Yes, alright I remember, but do you have to get them today, can't it wait until..." Martia stopped mid sentence, "Where are your sandals?" She was looking down at Jan's bare feet. "Are you trying to make me feel guilty or something?"

The palm of Jan's right hand was still sore from her recent burn. Now she feared she was very close to another burning sensation: from a slapped face.

"No Mum, honest, its just that one of the buckles came off. I was about to sew it back on, but Billy was hungry so I thought I would make him some toast first."

"How come, when we got no margarine?"

"There was some dripping in the pan, Billy likes it on toast."

"Well what's wrong with your sandals, why can't you run in them?"

"Well yes I suppose I could, it's just that the other girls at school..." Billy suddenly pointed an accusing finger at his mother,

"You told a lie," he blurted out. "You promised Jan some plimsolls."

"Shut up Billy," Jan said.

"No!" Billy persisted. "She's always saying God will punish us for telling lies."

"Billy shut up," Jan shouted, embarrassed by Billy's loyalty to her and afraid that Martia would turn her anger towards him.

"Don't talk to him like that," Martia snapped. "I wouldn't be surprised to find you put him up to it."

"Oh no she didn't," said Billy, now gaining confidence.

"Oh for God's sake! Jan, take him out somewhere will you. I've got a splitting head, we'll talk about plimsolls later."

"Yes, okay Mum, thanks," Jan said, happy that the meeting was over, but disappointed that she failed in her goal, and been fobbed off again with another false promise.

"Where are we going Jan?" Billy asked, as his sister practically pulled him along Queens Street.

"We'll go down to the harbour and watch the boats." Jan was now short tempered. Disappointment over the plimsolls made her a little terse with Billy when he asked,

"Can we catch a bus?"

"Don't be so lazy it's not far and besides what would we use for the fare?"

"Will we see those boys again?" Billy said, while having to run every few steps to keep up with Jan. "What boys?" Jan said, as she spotted two girls that she recognised from school. Embarrassed by her shabby weekend clothes, she pulled Billy into the deep porch of a pawnshop.

"You know!" said Billy, not knowing why they had stopped. Those dirty boys."

"Dirty? Oh, you mean the mud larks. Yes I expect so." Seeing the two girls turn a corner, Jan then pulled Billy onward. The sound of seagulls became louder and the foul smell of sun dried seaweed and rotting sea life filled their nostrils. They were nearing the main dockyard gates and harbour. Reaching the end of Queen St, they were now in sight of the harbour. Jan said,

"Shall we watch some trains come in first, Billy?"

"I want to see the ferry," Billy argued. He liked to watch the docking of the Isle of Wight Ferry."

"But we have to pass the station, we might as well…."

"Ferry, ferry, ferry." Billy repeated loudly. Jan hated Billy causing a scene and Billy knew it.

"Oh alright. Shut up you little monster!"

Jan preferred the station, she liked the smell of steam engines and to watch the passengers alight from the London trains. On non school days, she would sit for hours on the station seats, watching the incoming passengers from the London to Portsmouth train. She would read imaginary stories into the endless array of faces. In Jan's mind, London, though she'd never been there, seemed such an exciting place. She loved to see the new hairstyles and the modern clothes of some of the young women that arrived. She would look into their faces and conjure up stories about their lives especially if some handsome young man accompanied them.

The children could now see that the tide was out, although the smell had already confirmed that fact. They followed the sea wall until they reached the causeway. The harbour causeway was a road bridge, built on steel supports, like that of a seaside pier. It stretched from the main road across the mudflats to the harbour train station and ferry berth. All rail and ferry passengers had to cross it. The causeway was at that moment almost deserted, but this was normal between train and ferry arrivals.

The children were halfway across the causeway when they heard a voice call out.

"Chuck us a penny mister!" Jan looked over the railings. Below her, small boats lie drunkenly on their sides in the mud, awaiting the incoming tide to right them again. Also sank in the mud was a small boy looking up at Jan.

"Sorry Miss, heard footsteps, thought you was a bloke." The harbour was foul smelling; its black and oily mud came up to the boy's knees. He was naked down to his waist, and apart from his platinum-white hair and sunburned face, Jan could see that the upper part of his body had also been under the black mud, though most of it had dried to a dirty grey colour. The boy didn't seem much older than Billy, but from twenty feet above, it was hard to tell. "You got any money, gal?" he called out.

"No I haven't. What's it to you, anyway?" Jan could tell now by his voice that he was older than Billy.

"Well that's obvious gal? I'm a mud lark. You throw's down a coin and us mud larks jostle and fight to try to find it first. That's what larkin's all about."

Jan could feel Billy yanking at her dress. "I want to see," he said in earnest. Jan lifted him up for Billy to gain a foothold in the railings.

"Who's we?" Jan called back to the boy. "You're the only one down there, so who's going to throw money down if there's no one for you to jostle with,"

"Well some do. Anyway its early yet, I expect more kids will be here before the tide changes." With that, the boy suddenly disappeared under the causeway. He then reappeared shaking a tin can that sounded quite laden with coins. "See, you don't always have to jostle for it, you just have to get muddy. You get more if you can make 'em laugh, that's what larkin's all about," he repeated.

A notion started to form in Jan's mind; she suddenly pictured a new pair of plimsolls.

"What's your name?"

"Colin. What's yours?"

"Janice! And this is my little brother, Billy. Can anyone do it. I mean could I do it?" Jan said.

"Do What?"

"You know! mud lark."

"Yeah, course you could. Got to watch the tides though, it can be a bit dangerous if you don't, and I don't think you'll get as much as a boy."

"Why?"

"I told you, sometimes you got to fight and jostle for the money and some boys gets a bit rough, especially if it's a bit of silver, say like half a crown,"

"What about you, Colin, do you get rough?"

"Not if we share what we make. Still, you got to put on a show. Know what I mean?"

Jan looked at Billy.

"You know how you like to make mud pies in the back yard Billy?"

"Y—yes." Billy dragged the word, unsure of what he might be letting himself in for.

Jan hurriedly led Billy back along the causeway. She climbed over the sea wall where she lifted Billy over onto the pebble-stoned shore. There she gave him instructions to look after her dress and shoes. Then, dressed only in vest and knickers, Jan gingerly made her way across the mudflats. Her thin arms waved about like those of a tightrope walker, as she tried to keep her balance and not fall headlong into the black ooze. Her progress was slow and unpleasant. The black oily mud became deeper, sucking at her legs and feet with every step, each new cavity that her feet made, emitted an ever-stronger stench causing Jan to fight back the urge to vomit.

"What do I have to do now Colin?" Jan said as she reached the fair-haired lad.

"First you got to find yourself a tin or something to put your money in. I think I saw one over there." He pointed under the causeway. "Better hurry up though, there's a train coming in."

"How can you tell from down here?"

"Put your hand here." Colin laid his hand on one of the steel supports. Jan did the same.

"It's shaking, she said, looking surprised.

"That's how you can tell so find something to put your money in quick, and when you hear the passengers walking over the bridge, be ready to shout out loud, *chuck us a coin gov.* "

It was early evening by the time Jan and Billy made their way home.

"You wait!" Jan said, tugging at Billy's hand angrily. "When mum sees you, she'll go mad," Billy was struggling to keep pace with his sister. "And don't you dare say a word! I'll tell her we were walking along the shore and you fell in the mud."

"Why?" Billy asked, skipping every two steps.

"Why! Are you daft? Just look at the state of you!"

"Its only mud! Anyway, you told me to make mud pies."

"I didn't tell you try eating them, look at the state of you. what did you do, take a bath in it? I just wanted you to play on the shore, so you wouldn't get in the way, or get drowned,"

"Can't drown in mud," Billy said, cockily.

"Don't argue, anyway, it's not you who'll get a hiding. You could have washed it off like I did."

"How many did you get?" Billy asked, bored with the subject of mud.

"You mean how much, not how many." Jan stopped abruptly spinning Billy round to face her. She crouched down and hugged him, then shaking her tin and grinning, she said. "More than enough for plimsolls, in fact enough for you and me to go to the pictures tomorrow, and get some sweets."

"Wow, really?"

"Yes as long as we go to the Troxy." Billy frowned, knowing the implications of Jan's words. He knew it meant he would have to be lifted through the cinemas toilet window to unlock the side door for Jan.

"What film is it?"

"Snow White."

"Wow! Great. But I thought you said you had enough to pay, and you never pay when we go to the Troxy. You always push me through the window."

"We can pay if you like, but then we won't have enough to get sweets. And when we come out, you won't get your hot bread at the Co-op bakery on the way home, so it's up to you."

Billy thought about the warm bread that Jan had bought from the Co-op bakery on their way home from the cinema. They would stand in the doorway breathing in the wonderful smell of freshly baked buns and bread. They would wait for the loaves to emerge fresh and hot from the oven, ready to be sold in the morning. Jan would then ask the man to sell her one, and although it meant him breaking the rules, so far she'd not been refused. Jan would tear the hot loaf in half and they would eat it on the way home. Billy thought about it now and for one moment, thought he could actually smell it.

"Okay I'll get through the window."

"Right that's settled then." Jan then frowned at Billy and in a stern voice she said, "But only if mum doesn't find out how I got the money. Now I mean it! If mum finds out I've been mud-larking, she will beat me and keep me indoors for ages and there will be no pictures for you or me. Do you understand?" Copying Jan's serious frown, Billy nodded,

Jan felt it was her lucky day, when they arrived home the front door was open, Jan knew this was a sure sign her mother would either be across the road in Nell's house, or at Elsie Craven's house. This allowed her to hide her money and get Billy and herself cleaned up.

In the weeks that followed the harbour mud flats became very familiar to Jan and Billy, especially when they were hungry. This was usually when the pantry took second place to their mother's bottle of gin. Jan became adept in the art of mud larking and Billy nagged her to let him help in the quest to fill their, so often, hungry stomachs. However, she would not let him, fearing for his safety. Their mud larking remained a secret for some time until the day Jan became careless.

She arrived home from school one Monday. The smell of boiled bacon put a smile on her face as hardly a day went by of late, when she and Billy were not hungry; it told her that her mother had not only bought food for dinner but had stayed sober long enough to cook it. With any luck, Jan thought, she might even be in a good mood for a change. She hurried through to the little scullery where her mother stood watching over a pot of boiling potatoes. Billy sat in his favourite spot, on top of the copper boiler that stood beside the cooking stove. Here he could watch his mother on the rare occasions that she decided to cook a meal.

"Hello Mum, yummy that smells good." Jan said, trying to influence her mother's mood.

"We're having bacon, Jan," said Billy excitedly.

"Well, it should be good," said Martia." It certainly cost enough, and I hope you're both hungry because its quite a big joint." The children both nodded vigorously.

"Right, you two can start laying the table." Billy jumped down off the boiler and the two got busy in the living room. As they laid out the knives and forks, Martia called out to Jan. Jan went to the scullery door. "How come Billy came home on his own today? You always come home together!"

"Yes I know mum but we had netball today and it finished a bit late."

"Well I hope you didn't scuff those shoe..." Martia's words finished abruptly as she stared down at Jan's feet causing Jan to do the same. To her horror, Jan realised she'd forgotten to change back into her sandals at school, and her new plimsolls glared brazenly up at them.

"Where did you get the money to buy them?" Martia said menacingly. Jan was lost for words. She stammered guiltily and before she could string together a plausible sentence, "You stole it didn't you? I thought I was missing money from my bag." Jan started to step back into the living room as her mother moved towards her.

"No, honest mum I wouldn't touch your..."

"Then where did you get the money to buy those?" They were now, both in the living room and as Jan backed away, her mother stooped to pick up the poker from the fireplace. Billy was looking pale and frightened. He then started to cry and as Martia drew the poker back to strike Jan, Billy shouted,

"Mud larking!" The poker in Martia's hand stopped on its downward swing and Martia turned and frowned at Billy.

"What did you say?" said Martia, staring open mouthed at Billy.

"Shut up Billy. Its none of your business," interrupted Jan, thinking Billy would only make matters worse.

"No! Come on Billy," Martia said. "Let's have your version."

"Jan never pinched your money," said Billy sniffing back the tears. "She got them with her mud lark money because you wouldn't buy them. Because you're too mean."

"Oh so now you've taken up begging have you?" Martia turned her attention back to face Jan, who now, fearing reprisals from Billy's well-meaning, but damning, statement, cowered in the corner of the room with her arms wrapped defensively around her face and head. "Answer!" Martia shouted, whacking Jan's bare arm and making her cry out in pain. Billy tried to stop the onslaught. He jumped up and with all his strength, held on to his mothers arm, forcing it, and the poker downward, all the time shouting at the top of his voice.

"Stop it! Stop hitting her!" This only had the effect of heightening his mother's temper. Martia simply took the poker in the other hand and flung Billy to the floor. Turning her attention back to Jan, she said.

"Now I suppose you're happy, you've got your little brother to stick up for you. I suppose you made him go down in the mud flats to beg for your precious plimsoll money, you selfish little cow?"

"No Mum, I wouldn't let him do that, he…" Jan paused when she noticed Billy wasn't getting up, and seeing the sudden new look of concern on Jan's face, prompted Martia to turn and look at him.

"Oh my God! He's hit his head on the fireplace. Now see what you've made me do," said Martia.

Jan's timid defensiveness suddenly changed to anger. She got up and pushed her mother aside, knocking the poker from her hand. She knelt down beside Billy and helped him sit up. Blood ran from a cut on his forehead, but he seemed to be gaining his senses. Jan returned her mothers stare with a look of defiance and disgust, a look that forced Martia to turn away.

With Henry being away, Martia became more irresponsible. She spent even more time in Elsie and Debbie's company. Most weekends would find them all in one pub or another. Martia's Army allowance never seemed to quite last the week out. If this wasn't enough to depress her, news from the children's school that the children were to be evacuated, made matters worse. Not because of their absence, or that she would miss them, but she felt sure that their school would demand money for something or other and the thought of more expense, annoyed and depressed her. She was reading the school letter explaining their evacuation when Elsie knocked her door.

"Martia, guess what?" Elsie said. "Its Deb's birthday. We're going to see Max Miller at the Coliseum tonight and you're invited."

"Thanks Elsie, but I can't afford it."

"Look, this is on us. So just get your glad rags on tonight, ready for the first house. I expect we'll be going for a little drink afterwards."

"It sounds nice Elsie. But I've got no one to mind the kids, I don't like to ask Nell again, she looked after them last week."

"Oh come on Martia it wouldn't be the first time you've left them on their own."

Later that morning Martia called on Nell.

"Nell, I've been invited to a show tonight…"

"Yes of course I will," Nell said, anticipating Martia's next line. "Send them over when you're ready. I suppose you're going with those two." Nell said nodding in the general direction of Elsie Craven's house. "What are you going to see?"

"Max Miller."

"Oh yes, need I have asked! Come in love." Martia followed Nell along the passage and into the little living room. All the houses in Lyons Terrace were identical in design but seeing the interior of Nell's house showed how having money could make such a difference. The place was beautifully decorated and furnished.

"Like a cup of tea while you're here, love?"

"No thanks Nell I've got to nip up the school to see about this evacuation business."

"Oh yes. I heard about that. Well look, I didn't want to talk on the doorstep and you can tell me to mind my own business, but I just wanted to warn you about the company you're keeping."

"You already did Nell."

"I know I did, but with Henry away I wouldn't want to see them taking advantage of you, those two are in with a very nasty bunch."

"Okay Nell I'll be careful."

Martia dismissed Nell's words almost as soon as she'd left her house, putting Nell's warning down to "sour grapes" because Elsie knew how to enjoy her life, while Nell never seemed to go anywhere. Maybe the fact that Elsie was catching up with Nell as a property owner added to her jealousy, Martia thought.

The variety show at the Coliseum theatre was a welcome break for Martia; however, to her way of thinking she deserved it, having to manage on what she considered her paltry Army allowance, let alone the everyday-headaches of feeding and looking after two selfish kids. Yes, she convinced herself that she deserved a night out now and again.

Janice and Billy enjoyed their evenings with Nell. They played their card games and listened to Nell's stories. She kept them laughing and entertained for most of the evening, until a particular subject was mentioned.

"Don't you get lonely, living here on your own, Aunty Nell?" Jan said.

"Well I have my daughter. Cathleen comes to see me quite often. Oh by the way Jan, did you know she's being made a Staff Nurse soon?"

"What's that Aunt Nell?" Billy asked.

"That's like a head nurse, isn't it Nell?" said Jan.

"That's right love, I'm very proud of her. Anyway, apart from Cathleen I have two very good friends called Jan and Billy as well as my tenants."

"What's a tenant?" Billy said.

"They are people that rent my houses."

Billy took that in, then remarked, "I get lonely aunty Nell!"

"Do you love? Oh that is sad."

"Yes, now that George is gone. He was my best friend."

"Yes, I know, but I expect he's being well looked after. I can't help thinking about his poor mother and what possessed her to do such a terrible thing."

"What thing?" asked Billy. Nell immediately wished she'd not mentioned George's mother.

"Well its something we don't talk about, Billy, Do we Jan?"

"What Nell," said Jan who had been only half listening through concentrating on the playing cards in her hand?

" You know, we don't mention rope." Nell said, making faces at Jan to signal that she did not wish to elaborate in front of Billy."

"Oh. Yes, that's right," said Jan.

But the mention of rope triggered something in Billy's head. Something dark and chilling that he didn't wish to remember.

"It doesn't matter Billy," said Jan seeing a disturbed look on Billy's face.

"No, and anyway, lets not be miserable," Nell said, as she brought out a familiar cardboard box from a cabinet. "Lets play my favourite game of Monopoly, It's all about owning property."

The three women left the theatre later that evening and hailed a taxi, which delivered them to a pub called The Blue Anchor. The place was crowded. Elsie guided Martia to a bench seat behind a table.

"Wait there, love, we'll get you a drink." Debbie came back with two drinks and sat with the young mother. They sat with their backs to a window, facing the bar. Elsie seemed to have disappeared among the noisy crowd at the bar. Most of the clientele were men and Debbie introduced some to Martia. Men thronged around Martia offering to buy her drinks.

"Wait there, love, got to spend a penny, I'll bring you back some crisps." Martia watched Debbie push her way through the crowd, apparently headed for the ladies toilet, but in fact, she had joined Elsie who was in deep conversation with a handsome and smartly dressed young man up at the bar.

"Where is she?" The man said to Debbie.

"I left her over by the window." The man stood on tiptoe and craned his neck to see over the crowd.

"Hey, she's a real looker!"

"Yes," said Elsie, "but so is her old man, so it might take more than just looks to hook this one Danny. I just hope you're as good as you think you are."

"I've not met one yet that I couldn't win over, unless she's a bit the other way, if you get my meaning. Don't you think you ought to go back and sit with her, Deb? She might get suspicious."

"Not yet," I've arranged a little test for her. We'll see what happens. I'm just going to the ladies."

Martia couldn't remember how many drinks she'd had, but she became very giggly, laughing at anyone's remarks even when they weren't meant to be funny.

Occasionally Martia would catch a glimpse of Elsie or Debbie through the crowd and wondered why they had deserted her. She was wishing she were home in bed as she felt more than a little light headed. So much so that she was hardly aware of the two men that had slipped in behind her table, either side of her. How many gin and oranges Martia drank that night she never knew, but they seemed to keep coming. She heard Elsie's name a few times above the blend of voices and half audible conversations up at the bar.

"Nice one Elsie, you'll do okay with her gal," someone at the bar shouted. "She'll make you a few bob, Elsie," another added. Martia was too drunk to realise the comments were aimed at her and even if she had, she was far too intoxicated to decode their meaning. Whenever someone spoke to her, she found it easier to just giggle, rather than try to think of an answer.

She was even unaware that the two men had moved closer to her. The one on Martia's right had introduced himself as Les and his friend as Bob. Les was quite fat and rosy faced: a would-be comedian who persisted in telling crude jokes, whether they were appreciated or not. As he whispered his vulgar stories in Martia's ear, she was aware of his sickly smell of perspiration.

The most prominent features of the second man were a few wisps of hair stretched across a near bald head and a mouth full of rotting teeth. Martia noticed that he made a constant sipping noise due to his inability to refrain from dribbling. He kept leaning across Martia to listen to Les's jokes. Martia was not sure which was the most offensive, the smell of Les's sweat, or Bob's bad breath, but Martia felt trapped sitting between them. She looked up and through the smoky haze, she saw that the crowd at the bar had thinned out and she could now see Elsie talking to a young man at the bar. Martia wished that she would come and rescue her from between her two obnoxious bookends.

Debbie had wandered off into the crowd to find herself a likely client for the night, while the young man talking to Elsie, lit a

Woodbine from a packet of twenty, then offered the open packet to Elsie.

"What's happening in the terrace?" He said. "Are the C.I.D still sniffing around?" There was anger in Elsie's voice as she answered.

"Not at the moment Danny, but I feel much better knowing you're worrying about it."

Danny ignored the remark. Through a space in the crowd, he caught another glimpse of Martia. "I've seen her before, Else. She's a bit of alright, don't she live next to...you know?"

"Can't bring yourself to say her name, can you Danny." Elsie said as she lit her cigarette.

"Don't drag that up again. I told you. It was an accident. And don't sit there criticising, as though it had nothing to do with you, we were there on your orders."

"Yes, some accident. You let that bloody idiot, Bunny shake the girl so hard that her neck snaps, and you call it an accident. I don't know why you employ that bloody ape. I'm sure he's not all there."

"Yeah, but he does whatever I tell him, that's why I keep him on, besides, if I got rid of him, where would he go and how do you know he wouldn't go blabbing his mouth off to someone? At least I can keep an eye on him."

"Well it's a pity you didn't keep it on him when you told him to rough up Helen Moody."

"Bloody hell, Else! Keep your voice down." Danny stubbed out his Woodbine and nervously looked about to see if anyone was listening. Elsie lowered her voice.

"God! I couldn't believe it. The way you and that ape tried to make it look like a bloody suicide. You even messed that up! Didn't it occur to you that one can't commit suicide by hauling themselves up by the neck and then while they are slowly turning blue, carefully tie the rope to a coat peg."

"Yeah okay, you already made that point. Don't rub it in."

"Don't rub it in! Christ, if I hadn't gone in there and placed that chair on its side after you left, even that stupid C.I.D, Davage, would have known it couldn't have been suicide."

"Okay you made your point, Elsie, but you weren't there. You don't know what it was like. I panicked when I saw she wasn't breathing. Then I heard a noise from upstairs. I reckon her kid must have heard us. I thought the game was up. We had to get out of there quick. Anyway, let's give it a miss now, shall we, it's yesterdays news."

"Not quite, Danny. Apparently, our Inspector Davage is asking questions about the rope. It seems it had engine oil on it, and he wants to know where it came from. He must know by now that nobody in the terrace has a car."

"Don't worry there's no way they can tie it to us. Hey! Get it… rope…tie it to us? Oh please yourself." Danny said, swinging around on his bar stool to feast his eyes once again on Martia. "Bit classy to be one of yours, Else."

"You watch your mouth and get serious, I want this one Danny, and I don't care what it takes to get her. I suggest you get her working at the café for a start, then you'll have plenty of chance to work your charms."

"I'll give it a try but if she don't want to play…"

"No! You're not listening. Use the same method, do you understand?" Elsie pushed a small brown bottle in Danny's top pocket. "I got these off Sandy, slip them in her drink when you get the chance. Get in touch with Sandy at the hospital, He'll help you, and don't forget! Use the camera. You know the kind of pictures I want."

"Blimey! What's she done to upset you, I've never known you to go for a married one before?" said Danny.

"I got my reasons, but that's my business. Anyway, I want her earning, is that clear? Don't worry I'll pay well for this one." Danny glanced in Martia's direction again, saying,

"You may not need me if those two old lechers get their way with her."

"Oh yes, this is Debbie's little test. Knowing what those two are like, they're bound to try it on. Lets just see how she reacts."

The two men with Martia were becoming bolder, shifting closer to her. As fat Les delivered the punch lines to his endless stream of bad jokes, Bob would pat Martia's leg and laugh excitedly. This went on for some time; Martia giggled with each joke, unaware of the amount the two men were encouraging her to drink.

Then gradually through her haze of drunkenness she thought of Janice; feelings of shame nagged at her as she thought about her treatment of the girl. This however was nothing new to Martia, this was just the effects of the drink. In the morning her conscience would take back stage and Jan would once again become a victim of Martia's abuse.

Suddenly a booming voice invaded her thoughts.

"Oi! You three. Out!" The man was huge and the scowl on his face established his anger. Martia had seen him serving behind the bar and assumed him to be the landlord. She followed the direction of his eyes, downward below the table's surface until the reason for his anger became obvious. Bob, who had been slapping her leg, had worked her dress up over her knees and his hand was high inside her thigh.

Martia's shame had an instant sobering effect. She grabbed Bob's hand and before he had time to pull it away, Martia sank her teeth into his wrist to the extent of drawing blood. The man screamed before snatching his hand away. The pub went quiet as Danny turned to Elsie and whispered, "It won't be easy."

17
The weakening

Martia's drinking habit was now such that one or two pub jaunts per week were not enough and with Henry being away in France, lack of funds were the only control over her habit. She started frequenting the corner pub in the evening with enough money to buy one drink; she would then fraternize with the customers, hoping they'd buy her more. Sometimes she would drink at home. Her rent and food money started to find its way into the till of the corner off-licence, causing the children's welfare to suffer even more.

Jan and Billy became more ragged in appearance. They were sent home from school one day with head lice. Nell found them sitting on the pavement outside their house. Jan had been crying. After some coaxing, Jan explained to her why Billy and she had been sent home. Billy wasn't sure what it was all about, but Janice told Nell she was upset because her friends knew why they'd been sent home. The school nit-nurse as the children called her, told Jan to ask her parents to buy de-lousing treatment from the chemist, but Jan came home to find Martia in one of her morning-after conditions. Jan was too frightened to tell Martia why they were sent home and even more scared to ask for money to buy the chemical treatment.

Nell immediately gave Jan some money and sent her to the chemist to buy Quassia chips.* When she returned Nell washed their heads in the medication.

"I don't want you to mention this to mum, Jan," said Nell. "She hasn't got much money and she'll only be embarrassed if you tell her."

The nights Jan and Billy went to bed hungry, became more frequent, due to their mother's often inebriated condition and an empty pantry. To make life worse for the children, the more financial trouble Martia found herself in, the more punishment they would suffer.

*Bitter tasting wood chips, once used in the treatment of delousing hair.

It was a Saturday morning when Martia knocked Elsie Craven's door. The door opened and a very embarrassed Martia said,

"Elsie, I'm sorry to bother you and I know I already owe you five shillings, but I've got the rent man coming back today. I told him I would have some money for him."

"Well, you should have asked me first, because I don't think I can. What about your snotty friend over the road, have you asked her?"

Martia was surprised at the venom in Elsie's spiteful outburst. "No I haven't, and I don't think she's home anyway, but it doesn't matter. I can see you're in a mood, I'll just put him off for a few days."

"Oh forget it, I'm just having a bad day and looking for someone to take it out on. How much did you want?"

"Well I was thinking ten shillings. It would keep him happy until I get my next Army pay."

Elsie appeared thoughtful for a moment, and then said, "Look why don't you come in and have a cuppa, I've got someone here that I'd like you to meet. He might just have the answer to your rent problem. Come on, come and meet him."

Martia followed Elsie along the passage. On entering the living room, Martia encountered a slim man of about her own age. Martia recognised him immediately. She had often seen him at Elsie's door and recalled Henry referring to him as a spiv. She also remembered him as the man Elsie had been talking to at the Blue Anchor. Martia thought him to be very good looking in a coarse and flashy way. He wore a thin moustache that was made popular by certain film stars of the day. His double-breasted pin-stripe grey suit was pressed neatly, and his cravat was tucked into a crisp white open-necked shirt. He'd taken off his trilby hat and his dark hair shone with hair cream. It was neatly parted on one side, but the shape of his hat had left its indentation, giving his head a rather comical shape. He sat at the dining table fiddling with the trilby's hatband. He made no apology for the lecherous way that he eyed Martia up and down. Elsie quickly introduced them.

"This is my young nephew, Danny. Danny, meet Martia." Elsie then mumbled something about tea and disappeared into her scullery.

"You're that gal from down the road aren't you? I've seen you before," said Danny.

"Well it's a while since anyone called me a girl," Martia said, "but I do live down the road." Then louder for Nell's benefit, "at least until the rent man calls back." Martia grinned hearing Elsie's laughter coming from the scullery.

"Yes I've seen you before too. Blue Anchor wasn't it?"

"Yeah." He said, grinning. "If I'm not at my café down the market, you can bet I'll either be in The Blue Anchor or The Air Balloon."

"Really! Got a café have you?" Martia sounded impressed.

"Sure have. Don't want a job do you? The barrow boys down Charlotte Street wouldn't mind being served by a tasty piece of fluff like you."

Martia secretly welcomed the compliment but felt compelled to complain about its crude delivery.

"Ere you got some nerve. I'll have you know I'm married. If my Henry was to hear you call me a…"

"He'd need to have pretty good hearing. I was told he's in France."

"You seem to know a lot about me. Here, Elsie," Martia called out. "What have you been telling him about me?"

"Only the nice bits love," came a giggled answer from Elsie as she entered with two mugs of tea. "No need to get all bitter and twisted gal. I was just telling Danny that you were finding it a bit tough now that your old man's away."

"Talking about being away," Martia directed at Danny. "How come you're not in the Army, doing your bit for England?"

"Dodgy feet, gal. Can't march, you know how it is," he said grinning. "Well, how about it? I'm offering you a job."

"Danny's got a café in Charlotte Street," said Elsie excitedly. "Yes, so he said."

"Only thing is," said Danny, "you might overhear things, you know, deals that won't concern you, and you got to learn to keep your trap shut. Ration books don't play much of a part in my business, know what I mean, love?"

Martia felt annoyed that this villain, for that was what she had already made him out to be, seemed to take it for granted that she would accept his offer. She found his vanity irksome and felt that it was time to put him in his place.

"Oh don't worry, your little secrets are safe with me because I've already got a job."

"Oh yeah, at the Classic," said Danny in a mocking tone.

The Classic was one of the smallest cinemas in Portsmouth with a reputation for attracting unsavoury and perverted clientele. Danny said its name as if it left a bad taste in his mouth, and Martia chalked it up as another insult.

"I'll up your pay, and if the kids are a problem you can work part time."

"So you know about my kids as well! You seem to know quite a lot about me." Martia said while giving Elsie a black look.

"When I see something I fancy, I go for it," Danny said.

"Oh I see, and I'm the *it* am I?"

"Yeah, you could say that," he answered with a smirk.

"Well you can fancy all you like, I'm married." Martia started toward the passage door. "I'll see you later Elsie. Don't worry about the money I'll think of something."

"Don't be silly Martia. It's a chance to get yourself straight," said Elsie.

"You still need the job." Danny said.

"I'll manage!" Martia stepped into the passage and closed the living room door. Elsie and Danny could hear her retreating along the passage. Elsie quickly whispered something to Danny and just as they heard Martia open the front door, Danny called out,

"I'll double what they pay you at the Classic!" He and Elsie looked at each other, while waiting in anticipation to see if Martia would respond. They heard the front door close, then nothing. Elsie looked at Danny and he read the anger on her face. Then the living-room door slowly opened again and Martia's face reappeared.

"Double?" Martia said, grinning.

"Yep," said Danny cockily lighting a cigarette, while pulling a roll of one pound and ten shilling notes from an inside coat pocket, "and just to show good faith, how much are you behind with the rent?"

With Portsmouth being of such strategic importance to England's Naval defence, it became a major target in Germany's night bombing raids. On one such night, the eerie wail of sirens had sent Pompey's inhabitants hurrying to their nearest shelters.

In their tiny back garden Martia and the two children were huddled in the little Anderson shelter that Henry had erected. The ground inside the corrugated hut had been dug out just as the authorities had advised. This insured breathing space, in the event of the shelter being crushed by falling debris?

The three sat in silence, staring out at the beams of searchlights as they crossed and uncrossed, searching for enemy aircraft. Every few minutes the ground would shake as another bomb exploded and Billy would tighten his hold around his mother's waist.

When the sirens started, Jan had grabbed her father's greatcoat, which he'd left to supplement the insufficient blankets on her bed. She sat alone with it now wrapped around her in the little steel shelter.

Martia sat opposite on an equally worn out armchair with Billy on her lap and a blanket wrapped around them. As the droning of planes became louder, Janice pulled Henry's heavy coat tightly around her and the scent of her father brought her more comfort than its warmth.

"When will Dad be coming home mum?" Jan said loudly, in an attempt to muffle the frightening sounds. Billy nestled closer to Martia and added.

"Jimmy Gimble says that his dad is coming home soon. When will Dad come home for a holiday mum?" Billy said.

"Soldiers don't have holiday's," Janice intervened solemnly, and then cringed as the familiar whistling sound of a bomb started.

"Martia squeezed her eyes tightly shut and held Billy closer to her, as the whistling became louder. "She's right love. Soldiers don't have holidays, not when they're at war. But sometimes they get some leave, and that means they can come home for a rest," said Martia with relief. The whistling had stopped without the sound of an explosion. "That's one for the bomb squad," she said.

"Do you think they will give Dad some leave Mum?" said Janice.

"We'll just have to wait and see won't we?" Martia said, without emotion.

The following two weeks went well for Martia, she even found herself easing up on the gin. Giving up her job with the cinema, paid off. Danny kept his word, and her wages doubled. Martia quite enjoyed the change of managing Danny's little café.

Elsie was also pleased. Elsie had plans of her own, and they were starting to take shape. One morning her plan had an unexpected boost. Martia had been working at the café a fortnight when on the second Friday morning she knocked Elsie's door.

"Elsie could you do me a favour. The gasman's arrived to empty the meter. I've let him in, but I'm late for work. Do you think you could see him out, and shut the front door when he's gone?" Elsie said she would, and went along to number twelve, while Martia hurried off to work. Elsie waited for the man to leave and as she was about to close the door, the postman arrived. He handed her two letters. Checking to see that no neighbours were watching, Elsie stepped back inside the front door and pushed the door closed. She could see by the familiar envelope and postmark that one was from Henry, this one she put in her apron pocket. The second letter made her curious. After establishing the Scottish postmark on it, she also slipped this one in her pocket before leaving.

Martia had enjoyed her first two weeks at the café, though she spent much of the time warding off Danny's over active hands. She secretly enjoyed his advances; his earthy sense of humour made her laugh.

She thought it strange that Danny did not drive a car, yet he spent hours being driven around Portsmouth to various business establishments in a shiny black Vauxhall. The reason, she surmised would be non-ration-book related. The driver was a large apish man and Martia found it hard to determine his age. Danny called him Bunny and said he was about thirty.

Martia took an instant dislike to Bunny. Not just because of his ape-like stature, or the fact that kept staring at her. Martia was used to being stared at by men, but not like Bunny stared. It was not a look of admiration or even lust, but a dark look of hate that was alien to her. Her repugnance of the man was not even for anything he'd said, as he hardly spoke to anyone.

If Martia asked Danny where he went on these car journeys, he would just tap the side of his nose with his forefinger and say. *What you don't know can't hurt you.* She also became curious about a locked door behind the café's counter. This obviously led to the flat above the shop, as it was the only possible way up there.

"You could expand the business by having more tables up there," Martia said to Danny one day.

"Forget it! The door stays locked. I need it for storing stuff."

"What stuff?" Danny touched his nose and Martia said, "Yes alright, what I don't know and all that rubbish."

Martia's duties were light. This was mainly serving tea and making sandwiches for the market traders. The takings were meagre and caused Martia to wonder what other dealings enabled Danny to produce the roll of notes he always had about his person.

But Danny was not a demanding employer and Martia, not wanting to bite the proverbial hand that fed her, learnt not to ask too many questions. "Got to see a man about a dog", he would say, and off he and Bunny would go, sometimes for hours. Often, he would bring her back flowers or some little trinket from one of his market associates.

Martia not only became tolerant of Danny's advances, but sometimes encouraged them. He had the ability to make her laugh, even when she was feeling down, or depressed. In addition, his little gifts gave her a feeling of importance that she had not felt for a long time. Yet, however much Martia had warmed toward Danny, she had drawn the line at accepting his offers to take her out for an evening.

One morning, Elsie dropped in on Martia. It was a busy Saturday and Martia was finding her job more demanding than usual.

"Just doing a bit of shopping, my lovely," said Elsie. "I thought I'd come and have a cup of tea with you. How are you managing on your own?"

"Things are a bit hectic at the moment Else," Martia said, pouring her a mug of tea. "But most of the time I can cope."

"Seems to me you could do with a break."

"Oh! I don't think Danny could afford to take anyone else on, besides, it's only busy like this on a Saturday."

"That's not what I meant. Danny popped in this morning; he was saying you wouldn't go out for a drink with him. Why is that, don't you like him?"

"Sure I do, he's a real comic, but it's not right. You know, me being married and all."

"Your Henry doesn't need to know does he? After all, he shouldn't expect you to sit on the garden gate and just wait until he comes home. I mean its not like he was called up is it. He chose the Army."

"Yes, that's true I suppose."

"I can keep an eye on the kids for you. You deserve a break, where's the harm in having one night out? Anyway you owe it to Danny."

"What do you mean?"

"You know, for the job and for helping you out of trouble."

"Just what do you think I owe him Elsie?" Martia sounded annoyed. "And why are you so concerned? Did he ask you to talk to me?"

"No, I just feel that Danny's been good to you, that's all, and it wouldn't hurt to show a bit of appreciation." Martia looked thoughtful for a moment.

"Maybe I have been a bit mean," she said. "I suppose there's no harm in just going out for a couple of drinks, is there."

"Course not, that's what I've been saying. What about telling him you'll go out with him next Saturday then?"

That night Portsmouth suffered one of its most devastating air raids. Sirens screamed their warning. The sound of running feet told of peoples fear and desperate attempt to reach the relative safety of any air raid shelter.

The war up to that point had been an impersonal thing to Martia, a situation that only concerned politicians. When it started, she, like most people, believed the word of the media: that the war would end quickly and people would soon get their lives back on track, but time was proving them wrong.

Now, as the drone of aircraft filled the night sky, once again Jan and Billy huddled close to their mother in the tiny air raid shelter. At that moment, Martia was wondering if she would be alive to see the conclusion of the war. She also found herself thinking about Danny and not Henry. She thought about nights out, and the fun they could be having. After all, she thought, as a nearby explosion shook the ground, life can sometimes be short.

When Danny asked Martia to go out with him the following Saturday evening, he didn't seem surprised when she answered,
"Okay, where are we going?"

Outside St Mary's House Nell Masters paced up and down in front of the great arched doors that had appeared so frightening to her as a teenager. Strange how they didn't seem as large as she remembered them the first time she came to the workhouse. They were, however, just as formidable.

Should she knock? She asked herself, and what kind of reception would she get if she did? She certainly wouldn't see the friendly face of Sister Pauline Goodman. She was told that Pauline and her husband had moved up north to take care of the family business after Clare's will was read. Nell looked up at the high walls and wondered just how many poor souls had perished inside them since she was last there.

"Why had she felt compelled to visit St Mary's Workhouse again?" She asked herself. There was certainly pity for Ivan

Boswell, the man she knew to be her father; that handsome man who had strutted so proudly around his team of seamstresses in his immaculate suits. But wasn't it more than that? In her heart, she knew that it was. Could her visit possibly lead to a chance meeting with Alfie? But that was silly, she told herself. There could be no reconciliation with Alfie; he was married now and all this silly love business was in their teens.

In a moment of bravado, Nell picked up the large lion's head knocker and dropped it. The single clunk brought a miserable face to the sliding window.

"I've come to visit someone," said Nell

"Relative?" The wizened faced man snapped nastily. "Can only see relative, it's rules."

"Yes, my father."

The beady eyes squinted back at Nell for some time as if to determine the truth in Nell's words. Then with a considerable amount of mumbling that contained the word rules several times, Nell heard a bolt slide back before one of the doors opened.

Nell stepped inside and waited, while this strange little man who seemed to talk in shorthand, closed and bolted the door. He gestured and she followed him towards the same room that she remembered being taken to on her first visit. She remembered the first gatekeeper; St Peter, as everyone jokingly knew him. She remembered how he always wore a dog collar and tried to get her to undress before Pauline stopped his little game. This little man was very much like him, minus the collar. Nell wondered what happened to St Peter. It crossed her mind that the workhouse might have a storeroom full of these funny little men, replacements, for whenever one popped his clogs.

"Who's in charge, is there a matron?" Nell said as they entered the room.

"You sit, I get. It's rules," said the man, shuffling out.

Nell looked around her. Little had changed. Facing her were the linen cupboards where the grey and white striped uniforms were kept. She looked down at the cold stone floor where, in her teens she stood shivering on that first day at St Mary's House. The inner door suddenly opened.

"Nell Masters! I don't believe it."

"Nell looked up and could hardly believe her eyes. "Pauline! How! What?" With that, the two women started laughing while they embraced each other. "But you left and went to Lancashire to run the business," said Nell.

"I know, couldn't stand it. My husband wouldn't give this place up, and I missed my job here. So I left a manager in charge and came back to be with him. It's so good to see you Nell. How's Cathleen?"

"Cathy's fine. She could soon become a Matron you know."

"Oh Nell! That's wonderful. Is she Married? Any children?"

"No, I think she's too wrapped up in her nursing to get involved in that way."

"Never mind, it'll happen one day. What about your mother and do you still see Vivien, how are they both?"

"Mother died some years ago, it was a growth."

"I'm sorry."

"Anyway, Viv's doing fine. She rents one of my houses; got herself a nice man, don't stop her chasing the others though!"

Pauline laughed. "That was a very shrewd move buying up those places, Nell"

"Yes it was, but I can't take the credit. Your mother was always giving me financial advice. I never knew why. I had no money, yet she was always saying, Nell, buy property, you can't lose; she never let on that she was going to be so generous in her will."

"Well I'm just glad that you spent it wisely, but you obviously haven't come to see me, not if you thought I was in Lancashire."

"No, I came to see my father."

"Your father?" Pauline looked puzzled.

"Ivan Boswell?" Nell said, like it was a question. "He is here isn't he?" Pauline still stood open mouthed. "It's a long story Pauline. Maybe one day I'll have time to explain, but I've only recently found out that he's here."

"Right, yes he's here, and he's been here some time. We've done the best we could for him, Nell, but I'm afraid too much whisky over the years has left its mark. He's in better condition than when he arrived, though. We thought he only had one daughter, and I think she's only been to see him once. He does get one visitor though, a man. I'm not sure who he is, but I have a feeling I've seen him before. Anyway, come, I'll take you to see our Ivan."

They reached the ward where Pauline pointed to a white-haired man, sat staring out of a window, then Pauline left Nell at the entrance. As Nell approached him, she wondered just how she would be received. Would he even remember her? He looked frail sitting there. Nell suddenly realised he must now be in his seventies. She stood beside him, waiting for him to feel her presence. Slowly he turned his head and looked up at her. The whites of his eyes were yellow, as was the colour of his skin and Nell knew that his kidneys were failing.

"Nell Masters! Is it really you?" he said, holding out a trembling hand. "Why…" The word faded on his lips as if he'd forgotten what he'd started to say.

"Why have I come to see you? Because you're my father, isn't that what daughters are supposed to do?"

The faintest of smiles drifted across his mouth and he spoke slowly, pausing often, to take a breath. "I'd like to help you Nell, God knows I owe it to you, but I've nothing left."

"Oh! I see. You think I've come to ask for money?" said Nell pulling up a chair and sitting beside him.

"Well, that's what Martia always came to me for, but that was a long time ago, when I still had a business. She came here once to see if I had any money left. She thought I might have hidden some somewhere, but I couldn't really remember. She got annoyed with me and left. She never came back. I don't suppose I'll see her again, now that she knows I'm broke." He reached out and took Nell's hand and, turning to stare out of the window, he said "Is your mother still, I mean is she…"

"She died some years ago." Nell remembered the last time she saw her father and how he told her that he had loved her mother. Ivan was silent for a while. He stared blankly through the window, out at the cemetery beyond the workhouse grounds.

"Did you know Nell, that you can love two people at the same time?"

"Can you Dad?" Nell just felt that she should let her father talk; it was really all she could do for him.

"Yes, its true, and I never knew it. Oh I knew that I loved your mother."

"Yes I remember. You told me," said Nell. It seemed strange that she now felt close enough to this man to call him Dad.

"I spent my married life thinking that your mother was the only woman that I would ever love. I married Irene for her money, you know. God! I've been a wicked man, Nell. For years, I was unfaithful to Irene. Do you remember Molly Gill?"

"How could I forget her Dad?" It suddenly occurred to Nell that this must be what it was like to be a catholic priest in the confessional box.

"Oh yes, Molly and her sister gave you a bad time, as I remember. Well, Molly had my child, a little girl we named Martia. I never told Irene the truth. When Molly died, I lied to Irene about the baby. I told her that Martia's father was an American sailor and that Molly's dying wish was that we adopt her. That wasn't true Nell. Molly's mother knew I was the father and threatened to tell Irene unless I paid her a hundred pounds and took the baby. So, I invented the whole story. Poor Irene!"

"It doesn't matter now Dad, I know all about it."

"You do? You see, that's how stupid I've been, I've lied and cheated over the years Nell, but I wasn't deceiving anyone except myself."

Nell was touched to see her father's face was as wet with tears as her own. She was remembering this once smart, upright man in his immaculate suit, hair meticulously groomed. Ivan Boswell now sat here broken, his hair matted and the evidence of his last meal staining the front of a frayed shirt.

"Yes Dad, it seems like all your life somebody's been threatening to tell your wife something or other." Ivan chuckled while Nell wiped the tears from his face.

"You certainly got that right, Nell. Funny thing is, Irene knew all the time. Do you know what she said to me before she passed away? She said: "look after Martia, Ivan, she's your flesh and blood". Ivan gave another little chuckle. "Yes, Irene knew all the time, and can you believe it? Only then, I realised I had always loved Irene and how she must have loved me, to endure all that I'd put her through. All those wasted years, chasing what was already in my grasp." Taking hold of Nell's hand, Ivan then said, "Love and be loved Nell, remember that. It's really all that matters. Dreams are for children." Nell stooped down and kissed his cheek, and he squeezed her hand. "I tried to grant Irene's wish, by looking after Martia, but I even failed at that. I confused looking after her with spoiling her. I gave her everything she wanted. She was so demanding. In her teens, she made my life hell. Not that I didn't deserve it, mind you, but she stayed out until all hours. She played around with married men and was always demanding money to buy new clothes. I got depressed and started gambling. Did you know that you could lose a business on the turn of a card?" Nell didn't answer, but dabbed the wetness from her own eyes with a small hanky. "That led to drinking," Ivan went on, "now that it's all gone, she doesn't even visit me."

"Well you have more than one daughter Dad, and I would like to visit you."

Ivan smiled and patted her hand. "Yes I'd like that very much"

"Is there anything you need? Anything I can get you?"

"If you only knew how strange that sounds after years with your half-sister." That sounded peculiar to Nell. Until that day she'd hardly thought of Martia as a half-sister. "No, it's not necessary Nell, I have someone that brings me what I need." Then, as if he'd remembered something, he asked: "Are you married, Nell?"

"No Dad, I'm afraid it just never happened."

"Never mind, it still might. I would like you to come to see me again. I'd really like to hear what you've done with your life. Do you think you could come on Sunday? That would be best for me."

"I'm afraid it will have to be Sunday week Dad, my daughter has some time off and she I have planned a weekend in Brighton."

"Of course, I forgot. I'm a grandfather. It was as if Ivan Boswell had just awakened. Nell wanted to tell him that he had three wonderful grandchildren. She wanted to tell him about Janice and Billy, but wasn't sure it was her place to do so. It was something that needed thought. "What's she like Nell, is she as pretty as you?"

"Prettier Dad. Would you like me to bring her?"

"Of course, of course." Ivan repeated excitedly.

Nell promised that she would, and kissed him goodbye.

18
The softening

The following Saturday was Martia's night out with Danny. Elsie Craven had volunteered to look after Jan and Billy. It was an understatement to say that Jan did not like Elsie Craven and she refused to take Billy and herself along to Elsie's house.

"Why can't we go over to Nell's house?" Jan argued.

"I told you yesterday, Nell and her daughter are away for the weekend."

"Well I'm not going up there to that Craven woman, said Jan. Billy doesn't like her and neither do I."

Martia was only half listening; her concentration was centred on the wall mirror and getting her lipstick on straight. "I don't know why. She's always been good to you. I remember when she took you both to Southsea beach for the day."

"Yes, so do I," said Jan. "Why do you think Billy is so frightened of her?"

"Oh for God's sake, are you going to harp on about that little boating incident?"

"You weren't there! You didn't see the look on her face when it happened."

Jan was remembering the time when Elsie had volunteered to look after them both. The occasion had left a stain on her young mind and caused her many sleepless nights. She remembered that her mother and father were away somewhere for the whole day and for some reason Billy and she could not go with them. Henry and Martia had argued the day before about whom they should ask to look after them. Elsie had already offered but Henry wanted Nell to have them. Jan remembered that her mum had won the argument as she usually did.

The day had started fine; Elsie had taken them to Southsea and for a while, it had been fun. Then she took them out on Canoe Lake in a rowing boat. Billy was being a pest that day. He kept asking to row, but he was much too little. And Jan was surprised when Elsie gave in to him saying, "Come on then Billy come up here and take the oars". Billy stood up in the boat and Jan never forgot the expression on Elsie's face as she grabbed the sides of the boat and with the weight of her body, pitched the boat sideways. Jan screamed as Billy disappeared over the side. Luckily, a young man heard Jan's cry. He wasted no time, but waded out and lifted Billy back in the boat.

When they got home that day, Henry was working out in the yard and Martia was alone in the living room. Explanations were made why Billy's clothes were wet. Elsie's version of events differed vastly from the way Jan recalled them. She knew Elsie was lying and was furious. Jan blurted out the true account of what happened, placing the blame squarely on Elsie, but her mother and Elsie just laughed, saying she had a colourful imagination. Jan slunk off feeling humiliated and belittled. But she was sure of what she had seen that day and the crazed look on Elsie Craven's face.

"Fine," said Martia. "If you don't want Elsie to look after you, you can bloody well stay home on your own, but God help you, if you're not in bed and asleep when I get home."

While Martia had her night out with Danny, the children stayed home alone. Except for an hour spent huddled together in the shelter, when the sirens wailed out their warning, Jan and Billy spent that evening amusing themselves with Draughts and Ludo on the living-room table. At 9.30, Jan started to put the dice and counters back in their boxes.

"Come on Billy, Mum said we had to be in bed and asleep before she got home."

"Just one more game?" pleaded Billy.

"You said that after the last game." Jan gave in to Billy, but the next time she looked up at the mantelpiece, the clock said 10.05 "Come on Billy, it's me that gets it, if we're still up when she comes home," said Jan.

"Okay, but will you sleep in my bed with me, and can we leave the light on?"

"I'll come in with you until you go to sleep, but why do you want the light on?"

"You know!"

"Oh don't be daft, a mouse can't hurt you." Jan said, remembering how Billy had jumped into her bed the previous night because he heard scratching. "Besides, leaving the light on won't make any difference. If he wants to come out he will, light or no light."

"Well, I'm not taking my shoes off down here, not until I'm sitting on my bed."

"Why not?"

"Because he'll get my toes."

"Yes, well that's probably because of your cheesy feet, anyway please yourself," Jan said, indignantly.

Ten minutes later the two children climbed, shivering, under Billy's thin blanket. They settled down to sleep with Jan's arm around Billy and his backside snuggled firmly in her lap.

Hardly any time had passed when Jan heard a scratching sound. She felt Billy go tense and knew that he'd also heard it. The scratching stopped and some moments later, just as Jan was dropping off to sleep she heard what she thought was a whisper,

"Jan," then louder. "**Jan**."

"Go to sleep Billy," she answered, "It won't hurt you."

Billy quickly sat up.

"That wasn't me! I never said that," he said.

 Forgetting the mouse, Billy jumped out of bed and ran to the window. Quickly he slid the window upwards and craned his neck out into the cold night air. Immediately he recognised his father's cap and uniform.

"Daddy!" he shouted with excitement. Tears of joy clouded Jan's eyes as she hurried to the window.

"Shh! You'll wake the neighbours," whispered the shadowy figure. "Come down and let me in."

Jan and Billy raced down the stairs to open the door.

Ten minutes later, Henry sat at the dining table with Billy on his lap. Jan sat facing them. With her elbows on the table, face resting in both hands, she gazed lovingly at her dad. Her head was full of

questions about his escapades abroad. Both children especially
wanted to know about the walking stick that he now used and why
his bandaged foot was wearing a piece of rubber tyre instead of a
shoe. The children gave a sharp intake of breath when Henry
explained to them that his bandaged foot was the result of a rifle
bullet and that he'd lost a couple of toes.

"But the good news is, it got me home to see you two," Henry
said.

"Christ!" Billy exclaimed, "that must have hurt Dad!"

"Who taught him that kind of language?" Henry said frowning at
Jan.

"All the kids down the mudflats talk like that, dad." Billy said,
unaware that he was fuelling Henry's anger at the things he was
learning and finding his children left alone.

"I hope that doesn't mean what I think it does," Henry said,
looking sternly at Jan. "Have you two been mud larking?"

Jan looked sheepishly away from her father's angry gaze. "We
only did it when we had to dad," said Billy.

"What does that mean?" Henry snapped, then feeling annoyed
with himself when he saw Janice flinch.

"When mum had no money."

"You mean she sent you down there?" Henry was becoming
more irate.

"No Dad, but if Billy or I want something special, we can
usually make enough money down on the flats to get it, and we
don't have to ask Mum for it."

"Something special! Like what? What is it that's so damn special
that my kids have to go begging for it?"

"Plimsolls." said Billy, truthfully. Janice could have slapped
Billy knowing how his innocent, though truthful, answers were
stirring more trouble.

"Plimsolls?" Henry repeated angrily.

"Oh, and food." Billy added, making Jan screw up her face in
sheer frustration. This time Henry said nothing for some moments,
but looked thoughtfully at his two under nourished children. He
then launched into his own tirade of questions, like why the pair of
them had become so thin, how Jan got the bruises on her arms, why

their Mother had left them alone in the house and where the hell was she?

Jan, anticipating the angry confrontation that seemed inevitable on her mother's return, tried to smooth over her answers. Billy, however, was having none of it and in his innocence, painted a bleak, but honest picture. Henry's inspection of the pantry convinced him that very little was spent on food and that several empty gin bottles gave him a clue as to why. He looked at the clock. It was 11.30pm.

"Right, you two, I want you in bed and asleep before she comes in."

Martia and Danny's evening had started with a Variety show at the Theatre Royal. Martia wore a new outfit complete with fine nylons and high heels that Danny had acquired on the black market. Elsie had arranged for one of her girls to do Martia's hair and she was looking most attractive. The show was interrupted only once with an air raid warning, which turned out to be a false alarm, and in no way marred their entertainment.

After the show, they dined at a restaurant, where they were received with importance. Martia guessed that this had more to do with Danny's shady black market dealings than his riveting personality, nevertheless Martia couldn't help feeling special and was somewhat impressed.

From there, Danny took her by taxi to three of his favourite haunts. In each pub, Danny seemed to be a popular figure.

Martia had the feeling she was being shown off, like some new prize Danny had acquired. By the fourth gin and orange, she was feeling pretty good and in no way disappointed with the evening so far; quite the contrary: Danny's good looks were made more evident by the attention he received from the female clientele in each of the pubs they visited, thus giving Martia a feeling of superiority.

Yes, in all, Martia felt she had had a good time. Danny had been the perfect escort and she found him fun to be with.

The last Public House they visited was Danny's favourite, The Blue Anchor. By now, Martia was over her normal liquid limit; she had lost count of the drinks she had downed. The pub was crowded and to Martia, things were starting to look quite hazy. Danny found her a seat in a quiet corner and after placing another full glass and a packet of Smiths Crisps in front of her; he excused himself with some mention of business.

Martia sat listening to the mediocre talent of a pianist giving his rendition of "I'll Be Seeing You." While through half closed eyes, she watched Danny laugh and joke with a group of his acquaintances. There was only one person there whom she recognised, the one that seemed to shadow Danny wherever he went, Danny's driver, Bunny or ape-man, as she'd come to think of him. At that moment, Bunny was staring at her and it made her uneasy, forcing her to look away, but each time she glanced back, Bunny's beady eyes would be on her.

It was close to closing time when Martia noticed two newcomers talking to Danny and what looked to be a large sum of money being handed to him by one of them. When Danny came to tell her they were leaving, he seemed excited.

"Here, how do you fancy a few days up the Smoke?"

"London! When?"

"Next week. We'll go up Thursday, I'll get my bit of business out of the way then I'll show you the sights."

"Yes, I bet you would too."

"Don't be like that, I've behaved myself tonight haven't I?"

"Up to now," said Martia, taking hold of his hand and transferring it from her knee to the table.

"Well there you are then. Ever been to Madam Tussaud's waxworks?"

"I've never even been to London."

"That's what we'll do then. And maybe see a show, what do you say?"

"What about your café and my kids?"

"I can shut the café for a couple of days and don't start getting a conscience over your kids. After all, who's looking out for them tonight?" Martia looked angry for a moment, then said,

"Yes, I suppose you're right."

It was gone midnight when Bunny stopped at 12 Lyons Terrace.

Laughing loudly, Danny and Martia, lurched drunkenly from the back seat of the Vauxhall.

Danny mumbled something to Bunny and the Vauxhall's engine died. Martia stood in the porch, fumbling in her coat pocket for her key. As she stood against the sidewall of the shallow porch, Danny pressed himself against her. She felt his warm breath against her neck and felt strangely excited by the smell of its beery aroma.

"Are you going to ask me in for a little nightcap, gal?"

Martia giggled, "Don't be daft you'd look silly in a nightcap."

"You know what I mean." He said, slipping his hands inside Martia's coat and round her waist.

"What about your pet gorilla, don't you have to get him back to the zoo?" Martia said, giggling.

"He'll wait. He's used to it."

With that, Martia turned the key in the lock and Danny followed her in.

Martia flicked the passage light switch but after an instant of light, they were in darkness again. "Damn! That's the second bulb that's blown this week," she said as she felt her way along the dark passage.

"Don't worry," Danny said, laughingly grabbing Martia round the waist as he shuffled behind her, "We don't need to see. Not for what I've got in mind."

"Shush! You'll wake the kids." Martia then noticed a strip of light under the living-room door. "That little cow's left the bloody light on. She'll know about that in the morning," Martia said.

With that, the living room door suddenly opened wide and light flooded the passage. The couple's eyes slowly adjusted to the light, and through Martia's gin-clouded vision she recognised Henry's broad silhouette filling the doorframe.

"Yes I would think at least a beating with the poker," said Henry who had heard Martia's last words. "Or maybe you could burn her other hand, that might be a suitable punishment."

Danny's face took on a stupid grin. His chin rested on Martia's shoulder and on seeing Henry he giggled drunkenly. Martia suddenly sobered up, quickly pulling Danny's hands from around her waist, as Henry calmly said, "You know, your list of failings as a mother was quite long, even before I left. Now we can add child beater and drunken slut to the list."

Danny decided to intervene. He tried to stand up straight.

"Hold it there, soldier boy…" he began, until Henry cut him short.

"Martia, tell your spiv client, its time to leave."

"That's it," said Danny loudly. He made to push passed Martia but she stopped him by putting her arm out and grabbing the doorjamb. Martia, having recovered from the shock of having to confront Henry in such an excusable pose, finally found her voice,

"No! Leave it Danny. Who cares what he thinks anyway." Then to Henry, Martia said. "You're pathetic. I can see through your game, skulking home without so much as a postcard. You were just praying you'd catch me…"

"Well if that were the case," interrupted Henry. "I wouldn't have to pray very hard. However, I did write to say I'd be home today. Maybe you were busy with a client and it got overlooked."

"Right, that's it," said Danny. With that, he pushed Martia aside and with his head down, rushed headlong at Henry. Calmly and with one movement Henry stepped to one side and pulled Danny by the hair, aiding his momentum. Danny went sprawling across two chairs and ended in a swearing heap on the floor, blood pouring from his nose. Ignoring him, Henry turned back to Martia,

"When I left here I at least thought the kids would be safe. Hell, was I wrong! I should have guessed it wouldn't take you long to fit in with the rest of the whores in this street once I was out of the way."

"Well at least I didn't run off and leave them, like you did, you selfish bastard."

"Yes you're right and for that I'm ashamed, not so much for leaving them, but for leaving them with an uncaring slut like you. Anyway that's about to change because I've decided to leave tonight and take them with me." Henry moved towards her, making for the stairs.

Martia tried to block the doorway as she cried out. "Danny do something, he's going to take my kids!"

"Go and get Bunny!" Danny shouted as Henry pushed Martia aside. Henry could hear Martia's high heels hurrying toward the front door as he made his way up the stairs. He had no idea where he was going to take Janice and Billy, only that he had to get them away from that house.

He decided to get Billy dressed first. He switched on the light and looked around for his son's clothes. He gathered them together while wondering whom, or what the hell was Bunny. He propped Billy up on the edge of the bed, where the infant sat only half awake rubbing his eyes. Henry knelt down to dress him, unaware of the ape-like figure, making his way silently up the stairs. Henry pulled Billy's vest over him, and as the boy's head appeared through the garment Henry saw a look of horror on his face. Henry started to turn just before the light in his own head went out.

"Go back to sleep love," Billy heard his mother saying, as he felt her tuck his bedcovers in. "It was just a bad dream." Meanwhile in the dark street below Bunny and Danny were bundling an unconscious Henry Gough into the back seat of the Vauxhall. Suddenly a voice startled them.

"What's going on?" Danny jumped, banging his head against the car's doorframe. He then looked up to see Elsie Craven's head peering through the offside front window.

"Christ, Else! You scared the life out of me," he whispered, while rubbing the back of his head. "Do you know we came home to find her old man waiting for us," said Danny.

"Yes but what's wrong with him, is he drunk?"

"No he's knocked out, Bunny hit him. "

"Is that his blood on your shirt?"

"No it's mine, I think he broke my nose. We had no idea he was home."

"I did." Elsie said calmly

"You mean you knew he was in there and you never warned us. Bloody hell! Why?"

"I wanted him to catch her with you," she said, unperturbed by Danny's anger. "I didn't want her knowing he was coming home." Jabbing a thumb over her shoulder towards Martia's front door, she added, "Why do you think I pressed her to go out with you tonight?

This should be enough to make him leave her for good. Then she's mine." She looked at the limp body of Henry lying across the back seat with his legs still outside the car door. Bunny lifted his legs and bundled them inside, and closed the door. "This has turned out better than I thought," Elsie said. "Where are you taking him?"

"Well I thought we would leave him on the hospital steps for someone to find," said Danny. Elsie thought for a moment, before jabbing a thumb over her shoulder, saying,

"What's she doing now?"

"She's getting her kid back to sleep."

"Have you arranged, you know…what we talked about?"

"Yeah, don't worry, it's all arranged. I'll do it when we get back from the Smoke."

"Camera, pills?"

"Christ, how many more times. Yes, I said I'd fix it."

"Well you better get back in there with her. Bunny can handle him." Danny did as Elsie instructed, telling Bunny to pick him up later. Danny went back inside the house and as he closed the door, Bunny came round Elsie's side of the car to take the driver's seat. As he brushed by her to open the door, she whispered, "It doesn't really matter if he doesn't come round Bunny! Know what I mean? In fact, it might be better for all concerned if he didn't.

The day Nell promised to visit Ivan Boswell, it rained. It was raining when Nell woke that morning and it rained all that day. Nell would normally have stayed home on such a day, but she had made a promise and Nell prided herself on keeping her promises.

After breakfast, Nell spent an hour grooming herself for her visit. Her perm had been freshened up the previous day with a set and she looked her best.

She gazed out of her window and as she contemplated the question of an umbrella and a taxi, Cathleen pulled up in her little Austin Ruby. She got out and ran round the car with a raincoat held over her head while Nell held the front door open for her.

"What are you doing here," said Nell. "I thought you were working today."

"I was, I did the early shift. Hey, don't you look stunning? What are you all dressed up for?"

"I'm going to see my father." Cathleen started to laugh then realised that her mother was serious.

"But I thought you were supposed to keep that a secret."

"I was and I have. You and Viv were the only ones that knew, but now it doesn't matter. His wife died and I don't think he's got long to live."

"Well I don't wish to sound callous mum, but do you feel that you owe him anything. I mean he's never wanted to know…"

"What is it with you Cathleen?" Nell sounded annoyed. "Why do you think that every deed has to have a price? I'm going to see him because I want to, and because I was born out of the love he shared with my mother. Even if a percentage of that love was lust, I'm here because of him, and so are you; for that reason alone I would like to be able to say I knew him."

"You're right mum. You're always right," Cathleen said with a smile "Come on I'll take you. After all he is my granddad I suppose."

"Well I'm pleased you said that, because he got quite excited when I told him about you. Are you sure you want to? Its not a very nice place."

"Hey, if its good enough for my mum to have lived in, its good enough for me to visit." With that, they went out the door laughing.

Nell was disappointed to learn that it was Pauline's day off. She so wanted her to meet Cathy. However, having talked their way passed the strange gatekeeper Nell led her daughter through the maze of corridors that she knew so well.

"How much farther mum?"

"It's just around this next corner." Nell suddenly stopped at the corridor that led to her father's ward. Sat outside the ward was Alfie Button.

"Come on love, there's someone I want you to meet." As Nell and Cathy approached Alfie Nell thought he appeared upset,

"Hello Nell,"

"Alfie, This is my daughter, Cathleen."

Alfie took Cathleen's hand in both of his. "Yes I can see it Nell, she's very pretty." Alfie paused and studied Cathy's face. "Have we met somewhere?"

"Briefly. Do you remember the little boy who held your horse at the Southsea Show?"

"Of course, Billy! You were the young lady who came to collect him. How is he?"

"Getting taller, last time I saw him. So you're the famous Alfie Button that I've had to hear about since the day I was born?" Alfie smiled.

"If that were only true." He turned to Nell "Nell I've been waiting here to tell you that Ivan is gone. They called me out last night and I stayed with him until he passed away this morning. I couldn't let you just walk in there and find his empty bed, so I waited. If you intend to come to his funeral I will let you know the details as soon as I can." Cathy read the sorrow on her mothers face and put her arm around her.

"Cathleen, do you think I could have a word with your mother alone," Alfie said. Cathy smiled and strolled back along the corridor.

"How did you know I would be coming?" Nell asked.

"Apparently you had just left, when I came to visit him the last time. He told me that he had arranged it for my sake. You see he knew I only came to see him on Sundays and he's known for years how I felt about you. Do you know what he said to me last night? He said if you and I were to become united through his doing, maybe God would knock some of the bad points off his record."

Nell smiled, "And so he might have, but you're married."

"Not for much longer!"

"You're getting a divorce? Alfie, its got nothing to do with me has it?"

"No Nell. The marriage has never really worked. I married Brenda, as I was led to believe, to give our daughter a name. That was a mistake, I only recently discovered it was only to give Brenda's daughter a name, if you know what I mean."

"Oh Alfie, I am sorry…you said Brenda. That wouldn't be…"

"Brenda Scopes, yes of course, you know her. You should do, she almost got you killed, as I remember."

"Yes, but never mind, that's all in the past, but I am rather surprised."

"At what? That she and I … yes, well I suppose it was kind of a rebound thing, bit of a weak moment just after the matron here told me you didn't want to see me. Brenda was there and you weren't."

"I know, Alfie and hardly a day's gone by, that I haven't wish things could have turned out differently. Among my very good fortune, I seem to have been dealt some bad blows too, and losing you was one of them. But what about this divorce business. No chance of a reconciliation?"

"Not a chance Nell, not after what's happened." Alfie then grinned, saying, "but I'm too much of a gentleman to bore you with the sordid details, only that it will be on the grounds of adultery and I'm not just talking about Lily, our daughter."

"Oh! Like that, is it?"

"Afraid so, maybe I'll tell you about it one day. Anyway, life's too short, time to move on. I take it, you will come to Ivan's funeral, Nell?"

"Of course. And I would like to take care of the costs."

"No Nell, that's something he arranged himself some time ago."

"Can we drop you off somewhere Alfie?" Cathleen said. They heard the workhouse doors close behind them as they reached Cathleen's car.

"No thanks Cathy. I have my own transport."

Nell smiled, "Its not a pony and trap is it Alfie?"

"No love. You have to keep up with the times. Anyway, I'd like to see you again, what do you say Nell. Would you come out for a drink or a meal one night?"

"Won't that complicate matters for you? You know, with regards to your divorce?"

Alfie thought for a minute, "Yes it might, okay, what about when it's final." Nell looked at Cathleen as if to ask her advice.

"Alfie, she'd love to," said Cathleen searching her handbag for a pencil. Nell and Alfie watched her scribble on a piece of paper. "Look, here's the address." She handed him the piece of paper.

Alfie grinned at them both. "She's quite bossy Nell," Alfie said grinning at Cathleen. "I bet she'll make a terrific Matron." Alfie looked at the paper. "Nell. You're back at Lyons Terrace!"

"Yes, why so surprised?"

"Well it's not…well, you know," Alfie began to blush.

"Not what, Alfie."

"I think what Alfie is trying to say mum, is that Lyons Street is not a very desirable neighbourhood for a lady to reside. Is that what you meant, Alfie?"

Alfie looked uncomfortable, "Well, what I meant to say was, the place has developed a reputation that it never had when you were a girl Nell."

"Oh don't be such a snob Alfie," said Nell. "It's always had a reputation. It's just that we were too young to realise it. Live and let live, that's what I say. Some of those girls are very nice when you get to know them."

"Mum, those very nice girls are prostitutes and I don't suppose Alfie wants to get to know them. Alfie, I've been trying to get her to move out of that street for years, she won't listen. That's why I moved out. Mum, I never told you how many times I've been approached in that district." Alfie smiled and slipped the paper in his top pocket. "Anyway Nell, when I'm free I'll call on you, if that's alright, but if it isn't tell me now and I won't bother you again." Nell smiled, squeezed his hand and said,

"You call! Alfie, please."

As Cathleen drove her mother home, she asked, "Why did you hesitate when he asked you out mum. I've had to listen to you harping on about Alfie Button since I was a little girl, like he was the only man on this planet. Then when you finally get the chance to win him back, you go all coy."

"I know. It's just that I'm nervous. I've lived alone for so long, I'm not sure I can handle a man coming into my life now. I know it sounds daft, but it worries me that I might frighten him off, I couldn't bear to lose him a second time. What did you think, Cathy, did you like him? Was he what you expected?"

"Mum I thought he was a lovely man. And I could see by the way he looked at you, that he's yours for the asking. Don't wrap yourself in cotton wool for the rest of your life, mum. Don't be afraid to trust or love someone. If you do, you'll end up a lonely old woman."

"Yes, I know you're right. Hell, why did I have to give birth to such a know-it-all?"

19
The Smoke

The same hour that Ivan Boswell took his last breath, Jan burst excitedly into her parents bedroom. Her broad smile, generated by the thought of having her father home, changed to one of surprise when she found her mother alone making her bed.

"Where's Dad, Mum? He's not downstairs, I've looked, and he's not in Billy's room."

"I told you," said Billy, tagging behind, "A monster took him away."

"Oh, tell him mum! He's getting on my nerves with his silly stories."

"Yes, shut up Billy, we don't want to hear about your silly dreams this morning. Your father should have told you both, he had to leave early this morning. He had to get back to his barracks. Now maybe you'll believe me when I tell you he's not the bloody wonderful father you both make him out to be."

"But he didn't have to go back, they sent him home because of his foot," argued Jan. "He wouldn't leave without telling us." Jan was almost crying now as she said, "there's a case upstairs on the landing, so he must still be here."

"Well, you're wrong. The case is for me. I've just got it down from the wardrobe, see?" Jan wiped her tears in her dress.

"But what would you want a suitcase for?" said Jan.

"Are you going to be vacuted [sic] like us," attempted Billy?

"No, I'm just having a break from you two, for a few days."

"When, where!" Jan sounded alarmed as she wiped the tears from her face.

"Next Thursday. I'll be back before you leave on the Monday. Aunt Nell's only over the road. Any problems just pop over and knock her door. You'll be alright, it's only for a few days and I'll be back before you know it."

Martia tried to make light of what she was contemplating, like leaving them on their own, was something all parents did. Jan, however, saw through her play-act and challenged Martia over the seriousness of her intentions.

"But you can't, I mean mothers don't just leave their children on their own. What if something happened?"

"Oh don't be such a baby. You're old enough to look after Billy and I need a break, so don't be so selfish. If you're both good, I might bring you back a little something from London." Martia tried avoiding Jan's eyes, knowing she would see the accusation that she deserved; that she was exactly the unfit mother Jan was suggesting she was.

"Why are you going? Why are you leaving us?" Jan blurted out the words and being unable to contain her emotions any longer, started to cry. This affected Billy, if Jan cried, Billy cried.

"Now you both stop that, I'm just having a little break, that's all. I work every day to put clothes on your back, don't I deserve a break?"

"Why can't you take us?" Jan blurted out. "You're going away with that horrible Danny Clark, that's why, isn't it. I'll tell Dad when he comes home."

"Don't you dare threaten me," Martia said angrily.

"I wouldn't be surprised if you haven't already slept with him. You're just like the rest of the whores in this street." Jan's fear of being deserted had now turned to anger, but even before Jan had finished the sentence, she knew there would be repercussions. She took a resounding slap across her face. But even as Martia delivered the blow, she knew that Jan's words were nearer to the truth than she had previously admitted to herself.

"You little cow, don't you dare spread accusations about your own mother."

Jan stood defiantly still, fighting the need to nurse her burning cheek. Instead she tightened her arm round Billy. It helped, not only to alleviate the pain, but to hide any sign of weakness.

"I don't have to," Jan came back. with even more determination. "You only have to listen to what they're saying on the street." Billy tried to pull his sister away to save her from further punishment.

"Rubbish!" Martia said. Then after a pause, "What are they saying?"

"I heard that Mrs Bragg talking about you when I walked by her house the other day."

"Go on then, tell me what she said?"

"I don't think you really want to know, and if I tell you you'll hit me again."

"I'll bloody well hit you if you don't," said Martia, raising her voice.

"She said that Gough woman is just another terrace tart."

"Well that's just gossip from a jealous dried up old hag. She couldn't get a man if her life depended on it."

"Maybe, but Mrs Carter's not like that," argued Jan. "She stopped me in Queen Street yesterday. She said "I hear your mothers working for that Danny Clark. Why is he not doing his bit for his country"? Then she said, "He's a wrong-un if ever there was one". And then she said, "Bet you're missing your dad, aren't you love"? That was her exact words. They're not stupid, they can see what's going on." Jan finished her word-for-word account of Mrs Carter's comments, fully expecting another angry retort.

"They're just nosey busybodies that's all, and you're getting to be just like them. Danny's a decent bloke and he would have gone in the army. He just wasn't fit enough to march. Anyway, I've done nothing wrong and there's no law that says I cant have a break from being lumbered with you two brats all the time, so save your breath, I'm going."

That same morning, Doctor Neville Colwell and the duty staff nurse, Cathleen Masters, strolled slowly through the Accident and Emergency wing of the Portsmouth Royal Hospital. They stopped at the third bed in the ward. Dr Colwell unhooked the chart hanging from the bed end and examined it. He slid the note addressed to him from under the bulldog clip and read it before turning to the nurse. "What do you know about this chap, nurse?" The young nurse looked at the sorry figure in the bed, his eyes were shut, and a blood-soaked bandage covered the top of his head down to his ears.

"Not enough, Doctor. When the night shift handed over, they told me he was wearing an Army officer's uniform and that they think he'd been in a street fight. Said they found him unconscious on the hospital steps and that he smelled of whisky.

"Yes, it says here that he was found in the early hours of this morning. We should have had some response from him by now, unless that wound to his head is more serious than the late shift suspected. Find out who was on duty when he was brought in, would you, maybe whoever bandaged his head can tell us more about him. Meanwhile, we had better get an x-ray. Oh, and do try to find out where he is stationed. Wartime is no time for a serviceman to go absent without leave, men have been shot for it you know."

"I will try to find out, Doctor, but I think he's on sick leave."

"What makes you think that sister?"

"Well, we checked the dressing on his foot. He has two toes missing and the wound appears to be recent."

The Doctor moved to the side of the bed and lifted the patient's eyelid. "You better change this dressing too and arrange an x-ray. If he does come round, let me know right away."

A very different Martia Gough peered out from behind the net curtains of number twelve Lyons Street the following Thursday morning. One that had not looked so glamorous or smartly turned out for a long time. Elsie stood behind her brushing her coat while Jan and Billy stood sullenly waiting to see their mother leave. Her suitcase was ready at the front door.

"How do I look Else, are my seams straight. Not too over-dressed am I?"

"No, you look smashing. London won't know what's hit it!"

"I ought to wait outside but I don't want Nell Masters to see me leaving."

"Oh, don't worry. I saw her go out earlier with a shopping bag. Anyway, its none of her bleeding business what you do."

"I know, but I always feel guilty when I'm around her. Right, well, their gas masks are in their little boxes, all packed ready for Monday, but I should be back in time to make them a sandwich to eat on the train. They got to be at the station by ten the letter said."

"Yeah, poor loves," Elsie said, ruffling Billy's hair and receiving a look of contempt for her trouble. "Do you know where they're going?"

"Yes, Janice is going to a family in Liphook, and I think the letter said Billy was going to…er." Martia struggled to remember

Billy's destination, while Jan rolled her eyes in a gesture of scorn and disapproval." With Elsie there, Jan knew she could enjoy impunity from a slapped face.

"Haslemere." Jan said, sighing to confirm her disgust.

"Yes alright. I would have thought of it," snapped Martia, giving her daughter a look that bordered hatred.

"Well anyway, they won't be away for long." Elsie said. "The war will be over in no time. You mark my words." It was then that a shiny black Vauxhall pulled into Lyons St. "Here comes your lift." The car stopped at number 12 as the children followed Martia out the door. Jan stood with her mouth agape as the spectacle of Bunny's great ape-like figure emerged from the car. The enormity of his size and weight were affirmed by the recoil of the car's springs, as he stepped off the running board. As Janice watched him, she called to mind pictures on her classroom wall, illustrating Darwin's theory of evolution and how it depicted the transition from ape to man.

Elsie opened the rear door as Martia nudged Jan hard, prompting her to close her mouth and to stop her from staring at Bunny. None of them noticed that Billy had made a hasty retreat back along the passage and into the living room. Bunny made a fearful figure, having a neck that appeared to have the same girth as his head, and his shoulders giving the impression that he could wrestle a bull. As he reached for Martia's case, he looked at Jan through eyes that were canopied by a protruding brow, small humourless eyes, void of any sign of kindness. Jan backed away from him.

With no more than a nod in Elsie's direction, Bunny picked up Martia's case and put it inside the car. Martia kissed Jan on the forehead saying,

"I hope this doesn't smudge my lipstick. Where's Billy gone? Oh, it doesn't matter. Keep an eye on them Elsie. Bye." Then climbing into the back seat of the car, she gave a wave and was gone.

Bunny was his usual silent self as they started the short journey to the station, but Martia had a burning question on her mind.

"Well, what did you do with him? Did you take him to the Royal like Danny told you to?" Martia waited for his response as she watched him in the driving mirror, but he never answered and the grin on his face made Martia uncomfortable. Danny was waiting as promised, at the harbour station. Martia stepped out of the car and he kissed her cheek. As he did, she noticed Bunny was still grinning while unloading her case.

The look on Bunny's face was still troubling her as their train steamed its way out of the Portsmouth Harbour Station. It was this thought that prompted her first question to Danny as they entered an empty carriage.

"Are you sure Bunny took Henry to the hospital?"

"You were there when I told him!" Danny said as he struggled to push her case up on to the rack. "Why? Are you starting to get a conscience? Maybe you care more about him than you're letting on."

"No it's not that. It's just that I don't trust that Bunny. I mean if Henry was just unconscious, like you said, then he should have been back by now, bashing my door down. What if Bunny never dropped him off at the hospital? What if he's done something to him?" Martia said anxiously.

"What if this, what if that! Bloody hell, give it a rest! Bunny does whatever he's told to do, and I told him to drop your old man on the hospital steps. Anyway, who cares? Look at my bleeding nose!" Martia examined the large scab, forming on the side of it, as Danny went on, "I don't expect it will ever straighten up properly so don't expect me to feel sorry for that bastard. And anyway if you were that worried about him you wouldn't be here now so just leave it out!"

"Yes I suppose you're right, but do you think they found Henry alright. I mean Bunny could have taken him inside to make sure he got attended to."

"Oh sure, and have them asking questions."

"Yes, I suppose you're right, though I'm not so sure that the hospital will believe an Army officer would get drunk enough to knock himself out with a fall. He didn't even smell of drink."

"Oh, don't worry, I poured some whisky over him when we loaded him in the car, besides, these service blokes are always getting into fights."

Danny's last sentence seemed to end the subject of Henry. Martia seemed content to stare out of the train window for a while, until she finally said.

"Is your friend Bunny all there? I mean is he exactly sane?"

Danny chuckled. "Oh sure, I know he's a bit strange. Why?"

"Because, he doesn't answer when I ask him anything. I just don't think he likes me. I'm not even sure he can talk."

"Oh he can talk, but you're right, he doesn't like you," Danny said, casually. Martia looked at him in disbelief.

"Why, what have I done to upset him?"

"You get too much of my attention and Bunny hates anyone that I take a liking to."

"Are you saying he's queer?"

"No, just a bit odd, I've known him since we were kids. I did him a favour once and I don't think he's ever forgotten it."

"Must have been some bloody favour!"

"Not really. We were about thirteen at the time. I came out of school one rainy day to find Bunny curled up on the wet ground with four kids kicking him. You know how kids can be with someone that's a bit different. Anyway, being the hero and without thinking, I got stuck into them."

Martia giggled. "I hope you did a better job than you did with my old man."

Danny was not amused and gave Martia a blank stare before continuing. "As a matter of fact they gave us both a good kicking. Bunny lost some teeth and I had two black eyes, but the point is, Bunny's never forgotten it. In later years I found out he could drive. I couldn't, so I gave him a job. He has the use of the car and I pay him enough to get by each week. For that, he runs me around and does anything I ask. Mind you, I think he would anyway, even if I didn't pay him."

"Well I don't like the way he looks at me. He's always grinning as if he knows something that I don't. Maybe he's jealous of what you pay me."

Danny laughed, "I doubt it, money don't interest Bunny. Look, he might be a bit slow on the uptake, but he's a good driver and strong as an ox. I can't drive so I need him."

"Huh! Strong as an ox, built like an ape! Is there anything human about him?" said Martia, still visualising Bunny's grinning face. Martia became bored with talk about Bunny and changed the subject "This hotel we are staying at, you did book two rooms didn't you?"

"…Yeah, course I did. Don't you trust me?" Martia didn't answer.

Martia and Danny's train journey to London's Waterloo Station was painfully slow and soon became very noisy with evacuees, mostly school children, all making their escape to the safety of the countryside. They made her think of Jan and Billy who would be leaving on Monday morning, and a slight feeling of guilt pecked at her conscience.

"We will definitely be back by Sunday night won't we Danny? I told Elsie I would be back to see the kids off."

"Yeah, Yeah, sure. I told you, don't worry about it."

Martia had never travelled outside of Hampshire, and to her, the thought of seeing the capital was quite a thrill. When they finally stepped outside of Waterloo Station, Danny said,

"Right, the day is all yours. We'll get these cases dropped off at the hotel, and then I'll take you wherever you want to go. What would you like to see first?"

"Well I've always wanted to see Buckingham Palace."

"Good as done, gal."

Martia had no idea what districts the taxi passed through, only that some of the streets were looking very scarred from the bombing raids, yet people seemed to be getting on with their every day routine in a seemingly life-goes-on manner.

The cab pulled up at what, to Martia, appeared to be a back street hotel, and not at all what she expected.

"You wait in the taxi. I'll only be two ticks," said Danny.

After watching him carry their cases into the building Martia spoke to the driver through the glass partition.

"It doesn't look a very posh hotel." Martia said, hoping the driver, would quell her fears and tell her that the inside was like a palace.

The driver gave her a knowing grin, "Well it depends what you want it for, know what I mean love?"
Martia knew exactly what he meant and indicated so by slamming shut the glass partition.

"Did you see the rooms?" she asked Danny as he got back into the taxi.

"Er, no not yet. I just asked them to mind the bags. Take us to Buckingham Palace driver." Danny spared no expense. After Buckingham Palace, it was on to Regents Park Zoo, then Madam Tussaud's waxworks. Finally, a meal at Lyons Corner House and Danny's wit had kept Martia amused all day. It was only when they returned to the hotel that Martia's mood took a downward turn. The interior of the place was as drab as the outside had indicated. Danny went to the reception desk. There he spoke to an overweight middle-aged man in a tattered pullover. The man sat behind a reception counter on an equally tattered armchair. Meanwhile, Martia strolled around the foyer looking at the dust covered wall paintings.

"I booked a room earlier those are our cases." Danny whispered to the fat man, while peering round at Martia, hoping she was out of earshot.

The man struggled out of his chair. "Name?" he said, opening the register.

"Clark," said Danny, impatiently. "You know that, for God's sake, I was only in here a few hours ago."

"Oh, yes. Here it is, Mr and Mrs." Said the man loudly, while grinning widely at Martia. Martia glowered at the man before following Danny up a shabby carpeted staircase and along a dimly lit passage. He stopped and put a key in the door, saying, "This is the one."

"What do you mean, the one! And what's with the Mr and Mrs? I hope you don't think we're sleeping in the same room!" Martia took a step backwards as if afraid of the darkness beyond the open door.

"Don't be silly gal, I've saved a lot of dough by booking one room. It gives us a better time while we're here." Danny felt inside the door for the light switch. "Look, there's a nice settee, I can sleep on that. You can have the bed."
Martia moved hesitantly towards the door and peered into the room. The double bed looked inviting, and it had been a long day.

"Why did you lie? You said we would have two rooms!"

"I didn't. I mean I did book two, but I've been a bit short of readies lately. When one of my deals didn't come off in the week, I cancelled one of the rooms. I thought I'd save a bit of money. If I had told you, you wouldn't have come."

"You're dammed right. I'll give you the benefit of the doubt this time, but you'd better not try any funny business."

"Don't worry. I'm too tired to try anything, funny or otherwise. Anyway, I got to be up early tomorrow. I've got to see this bloke down Petticoat Lane, so you are on your own for part of the day. I'll leave you some dough and you can have a mooch around Oxford Street."

Martia took some time getting to sleep that night. She lay awake, listening intently for the sound of movement from the settee, until sleep won her over. Then with the morning, came the realisation that Danny had been true to his word. She was relieved, yet couldn't help feeling somewhat rejected.

A blanket had been left untidily crumpled on the settee, and two white five pound notes had been left beside a scribbled note.

(Get yourself something nice. Be in Magic Teapot, Oxford Street at 2 pm.)

In Portsmouth's Royal Hospital, Cathleen Masters waited patiently. Her head tilted to one side with a look of curiosity while a junior nurse removed the last loops of a bloodied bandage from the unconscious officer. Slowly Cathy's head straitened and her perplexed look changed to one of recognition.

"Henry" she murmured, louder than intended.

"Do you know him, Sister?" the nurse asked.

"Faintly," Cathleen answered, while examining a deep cut on the side of Henry's head. "Look I'm going to leave you to clean that cut and put a fresh dressing on it. I have to make some phone calls."

Early the next morning, Cathy's little Austin Ruby turned into Lyons Terrace. Nell happened to be cleaning her front window and recognised the car immediately. It was rare to see any car in the terrace, apart from Danny Clark's Vauxhall, or occasionally when a doctor might call on someone. But Nell knew this particular car at a glance; she had helped Cathy choose it.

To Nell's surprise, Cathleen stopped on the opposite side of the road. With a smile and a wave to her mother, she knocked at number twelve. Getting no answer, she crossed the road. Kissing Nell on the cheek she said,

"Hi Mum, still keeping guard on the neighbourhood?"

"Someone's got to, love. Why are you not at work?"

"I'm here on a mission," Cathleen said, glancing across the road. "Have you seen Mrs Gough today?"

"No, odd you should ask, though. I haven't seen her for a couple of days. Mind you, I've been out a lot."

"With our Alfie Button no doubt," said Cathy, grinning.

"If only. No, I've spent some time at the cemetery, but I haven't seen Alfie since my father's funeral. Surly Martia must be home though, because I saw Jan and Billy go off winkling with their bucket this morning, and it's too early for her to have gone to work. She might be out back, hanging washing or something. Did you knock really hard?"

"Yes."

"Anyway, is it important?"

"Well, I'm not really supposed to talk about hospital matters. You know how fussy they are about giving out information to non-relatives. So keep this to yourself—Martia's husband is in the Royal."

"Henry, in hospital! Don't be daft. He's in France."

"Believe me mum, its him."

"Oh God, does Janice and Billy know… no of course, they can't know. Is it serious?"

"Mum, being in a coma is always serious. But it's strange, I don't think his wounds have anything to do with his time in France, not his head wounds anyway."

"What do you mean?"

"Well apparently, one of the night staff found him lying unconscious outside the hospital entrance. There was a walking stick beside him and the handle was covered in blood. We think this was used to beat him. Some thug might have robbed him we won't know until he comes round, or should I say if?"

"Of course he'll come round. Don't say that!" Nell said worriedly."

"I hope so. The hospital is doing their best. He also had a bandaged foot, hence the walking stick. We think that's the reason he's been sent home. When we removed the bandage, we found he had two toes missing. However, his foot was well on the way to healing, so I'm guessing Henry was treated in a field hospital, and then sent home on sick leave. Maybe he never reached home. We will only know that when his wife turns up."

"Mm, I see, first names is it," Nell said frowning.

"Now don't go making something out of nothing, Mum. And I don't want you asking questions up and down the street. I'll come back later and try again."

"But how did he… I mean…"

"Mum, you know as much as I do. For the moment, it's all a mystery. We'll just have to wait until he comes round."

With her last Army allowance payment and Danny's generous donation in her handbag, Martia had the spending time of her life. After an hour in a hair salon, she felt alive again. Her raven hair shone as it had not done for years and its latest style gave her a feeling of youth. As she toured the clothes shops, she thought about her marriage and how dull it had been with Henry. Then her mind turned to Danny. She remembered the crumpled blanket on the settee that morning and thought to herself how uncomfortable Danny must have found it. She had warned him not to try anything in the night, but inwardly hoped that he might, hence, his negative response was niggling her. Yes, her feelings toward Danny had started to hold something more than just gratitude. She knew he was a rogue, but that just amused and excited her.

It was a quarter past two when Martia struggled through the door of the Magic Teapot Café, wearing a new outfit and carrying two shoe boxes and a large shopping bag. Danny sat alone at a corner table. Martia saw at a glance, he was not happy.

"Where the hell have you been?" He snapped. "I told you, 2 o'clock and I don't like to be kept waiting."

"Oh come on Danny, you should know it's a lady's privilege to be late," Martia replied flippantly.

Danny leaned towards Martia until their faces almost touched, there was a wild look in his eyes as he hissed at her through gritted teeth,

"You ain't no bleedin' lady! When I tell you to meet me at a certain time, you bloody well be there!"

Martia was startled by this sudden change in him. She'd not seen this side of Danny and it made her nervous. She tried to apologise, but his mood seemed to be set for the rest of the day. Nothing Martia said seemed to cheer him up. They stayed for lunch in the café, which they ate in silence. As they made their way back to the hotel, Danny said, "We might as well pack up and make our way home."

"But why? It's only Friday, and you said we would get a late train on Sunday."

"I know I did, but the bloke I came here to meet has already met with one of those bloody buzz bombs. He's dead, so the deal is off. There's no money to be made, so there's not much point in hanging around London." Martia felt sorry for Danny. He had spared no expense showing her a good time on the strength of this deal coming off. Now he found that he could ill afford what he'd already spent. Martia now understood why he was so annoyed with her. However, she did talk him into staying another night.

Martia lay awake in the darkness. She could hear Danny turning one way then the other as he tried to fight the discomfort of the settee, but she felt that his restlessness was due to more than just discomfort.

"Danny." she called out softly. His fidgeting stopped and she knew he was listening. "This man you went to see, how was he going to help you make money?" There was a long pause before Danny answered.

"I was told to keep it quiet, but I suppose it doesn't matter much now, cause it's not going to happen. The bloke was involved with naval supplies. You know, truckloads of stuff coming in to Tilbury docks, tinned food, fags, you name it, and a lot of it gets transported to Pompey Dockyard. For a price, he was going to slip me some information. Delivery times, lorry number plate, the route it would be taking and what it would be carrying. The load wouldn't have been hijacked before it reached Pompey. The gang financing this will not be happy. I've got to get their money back to them soon as possible or I'm a goner."

"Well I'm glad," Martia said.

"Oh, that's nice! Some poor sod's dead, I'm in trouble with a gang that'd cut a blokes throat as soon as look at him and what do you say? I'm glad. Thanks that's just great!"

"No I didn't mean glad he was dead. I meant, what if it all went wrong and you got caught?"

"Am I hearing right?" Danny said. "Are you saying you actually care?" There was a pause before Martia answered,

"Well, lets put it like this, I've pulled the bed covers open, do you really need any more invitation than that, or do you want to spend another night on that settee?"

20
The Air Balloon

It was long into Saturday afternoon when Martia and Danny boarded the Portsmouth bound train at Waterloo Station. The couple had the carriage to themselves for a good part of the journey, but little conversation took place. Danny seemed preoccupied with his thoughts.

When they reached Guilford, Danny left the carriage to buy a newspaper. It was here that two passengers entered the carriage making the couple's chance of conversation even less likely.

Danny became absorbed in his paper, while Martia gazed unseeingly at the fleeting countryside. Her thoughts dwelled on her previous night of adultery. She stared at Danny, wondering why he'd become so distant, why his manner had changed toward her. Was it because he was worried about his business deal, or was it her? Had she given herself too easily? Did he now regard her as no better than the prostitutes he associated with, or was it, that she was no longer a challenge? Would he drop her now, like some cheap whore?

Maybe it wasn't this at all, she told herself. Maybe the reason for his moodiness was his own sexual performance, or lack of it, she thought. Maybe that's what had made him so irritable. His lovemaking was certainly a disappointment. It was nothing like the wild and steamy set-to that she'd expected.

Danny had often boasted to her about the amount of women he'd had. He usually did this when he was the worse for drink, not caring how crude or graphic his stories became. He'd put names to the women in his stories, though Martia sometimes wondered if they actually existed. She was sure it was all part of his ploy to entice her into bed. His boasting inferred that only women he'd gone all the way with, were especially beautiful and worthy of his unique lovemaking. But Martia called to mind his last night's performance. It was a disaster. Danny had accepted her invite and climbed between the open sheets. She had already taken her nightgown off to make it easy for him. She remembered how cold and bony his thin legs were. She tried to kiss him on the lips but his fumbling to get her knickers off made it impossible. He'd pulled them down only as far as her knees, making it impossible for her to open her legs. Then the prodding and poking started. Danny went at it like a mad thing; Martia likened it to being attacked by a blind and demented gynaecologist. He hit every spot but the right one. As his useless attempts failed, she recalled some of his stories and at one point started to giggle. Danny got annoyed, rolled over on his back and sulked.

Martia felt sorry for him, she apologised and had to coax him into another attempt. This time she decided she'd better help him or they might not get to sleep at all that night. She put her hand beneath the sheets in order to guide him but this only took his excitement to new heights and only, resulted in soiling the sheets and leaving her unfulfilled.

Now Martia sat in the train carriage looking sideways at Danny as he read his paper. She wondered, after his pathetic performance, if she could still be accused of adultery; however, she felt unclean and unquestionably guilty.

Fleeting thoughts of Henry jabbed at what little conscience she possessed, but this was no match for her self-forgiving excuses, like: Henry shouldn't have left her, especially with two kids, or he didn't have to re-enlist, that was his choice, and last night wouldn't have happened if he had stayed with her. Psychologically, the excuses for her adultery continued as the train slowly made its way south. Then Martia started to think about the early days with Henry, and how wonderful and unselfish their sex life had been. But when Janice and Billy came along, gradually, it all went sour. Henry seemed to want her less and less. There was one occasion more recent though, when she remembered Henry making love to her. She smiled as she relived that special night. She remembered it well. It was the time of his accident at work. The day he'd cut his hand.

Unbeknown to Martia and Danny, at that very moment, Portsmouth was suffering the worst daylight air raid of World War 2. Between the sirens and the warden's shouts of all clear, Nell Masters crossed the street to knock the door of number twelve. She received no answer and was concerned about Jan and Billy. She had seen them go out early that morning, but it was now three in the afternoon and still no sign of them, or Martia. There was a nagging suspicion at the back of Nell's mind that Elsie Craven was somehow involved in Martia's absence and with Henry in hospital, Jan and Billy was now giving Nell a great deal of concern.

Reluctantly, and as a last resort, she knocked at Elsie Craven's door. As she waited for the door to open, Nell remembered the blazing row they'd had the last time they spoke to each other. Ironically, that was over a young girl that Nell believed Elsie Craven was trying to entice into her world of prostitution.

The door opened and Elsie stood looking at Nell without saying a word.

"Elsie, I'm worried about Martia's children. Jan and Billy went out early this morning and they're not back yet. Do you know where Martia is?"

"No!" came the harsh reply.

"Only, I've not seen her for a couple of days," Nell said, ignoring the hostile look on Elsie's face. Then, trying to sound as pleasant as she could bear, Nell went on, "I've really banged the door hard, do you think she's alright? I mean she wouldn't still be in her shelter, but she could be ill or something." Heeding her daughter Cathleen's words, Nell stopped short of mentioning Henry being in the Royal Hospital.

"Well if you saw her kids going out this morning, don't you think they would have told one of us if something was wrong?" Elsie said, bluntly.

"Yes, I suppose you're right," said Nell. With that, Elsie's irate manner seemed to mellow slightly.

"Look, I think Martia had some idea that she might be away for a few days; she asked me to see that her kids get to the station on Monday for their evacuation if she didn't get back in time."

"...I don't believe it! Are you saying she's just gone off and left those kids by themselves? And you just let her go?" Nell started to forget the niceties, believing that Elsie had a hand in Martia's disappearance.

"Now don't you go getting on your high-horse, I'm not her bleeding keeper."

"Maybe not on your own, but where's that slimy Danny Clark? I'd bet the two of you have got something to do with it," said Nell.

"Look, I don't need any lectures from the likes of you." With that, Elsie slammed the door.

Nell walked back to her house and as she reached her front door, she was relieved to see Janice and Billy turn the corner into Lyons Terrace. They were carrying their cockling bucket between them. Nell crossed the street to meet them. She wondered if she should tell them about their father, or should she wait for Cathleen to come back as she said she would. No, Cathy was right, she thought, it would only upset them, and what could they do about it anyway.

"Look, Aunty Nell," shouted Billy, as he and Jan got closer. "We got lots of winkles and money. We've been mud larking."

"I can see that, look at the state of you. Your mother will go mad when she sees the pair of you. You've been gone all day. How come you stayed out so long?"

"We had to go down to the air raid shelter for a long time," said Billy "and mum's gone to London so we don't care."

"And left you two on your own?"

"We'll be OK Nell, we can look after ourselves." Jan said.

"Well, if you want anything, come over."

Martia was still trying to forgive herself as the train pulled into Haslemere. Here, a wedding had just taken place and the platform was covered in confetti. A crowd, dressed in their best clothes were having photos taken. This severed Martia from her sordid thoughts. She stood up and pulled down the window to get a better view of the happy throng outside. She smiled at the young and pretty bride in her powder blue two-piece outfit, and the handsome young groom in his sailor's uniform. Martia was remembering her own wedding and wondered if this innocent looking girl had the sense not to make the same stupid mistake that she had made this weekend.

Excited guests, in their best outfits, milled about the happy couple on the platform; some were trying to get their own perfect photos before the young couple boarded the train. The official photographer, who appeared more and more flustered, amused Martia as he tried to adjust his tripod while trying to shout instructions to two uncooperative guests who seemed to delight in ignoring him. Eventually he seemed happy with his results, which ended with photos of the couple waving from the next window, as the train pulled away.

Of the Haslemere passengers that boarded, two chattering middle-aged women entered Martia and Danny's carriage. They sat opposite them, and by their conversation, it was obvious that they were teachers. They were excitedly discussing what must have been a recent news bulletin. As the two women talked, one of them constantly stared at Martia and having just deliberated her own recent sins, Martia found the woman's interest in her, more than a little discomforting.

"It could easily have been me, you know," one woman said. "My husband wanted me to catch the earlier train and my daughter lives just off Lake Rd. I always walk past the Princes Theatre whenever I visit her."

"Well one thing's for sure, you won't be passing it again," said the second woman, still staring at Martia "I only hope my house is still standing. I'm glad my boy lives out here in the country. Could you imagine turning up at school on Monday to find one or more of your pupils had been killed. I don't think I could cope with that."

"No, I suppose we should both be grateful for that." It was at this point that Martia seemed to lose her self-control.

"Am I annoying you or something?" she said glaring at the woman who was still staring. Danny dropped his paper.

"Martia, what the hell's wrong? Have you gone mad or something?"

"No, it's alright young man," said the woman. "It's my fault. I was staring and I do apologise; it was very rude of me. It's just that your wife, er... Martia is it? Well it's so unusual to see such blue eyes with such beautiful dark hair. I couldn't help staring. Will you accept my apology?" The woman held out her hand to Martia, who blushingly took it saying,

"I feel so stupid now."

"Nonsense, It's me that should feel stupid, I made you feel uncomfortable." Danny rescued them both from their embarrassment with,

"Did I hear you say the Princes Theatre in Lake Rd has been bombed?"

"It has, according to the BBC," said the first woman. "Hasn't it Gwen?"

"Certainly has. Portsmouth has taken a terrible battering today. It happened this afternoon in broad daylight. I can't believe how bold these German pilots are getting." said Gwen.

Martia sat upright as the two women shared what news they had.

"Do you know if many were hurt?" asked another man who had just entered the carriage.

"Not really, they said the number of fatalities are not yet known. I suppose they have to count those at the other sites first before they can announce how many."

"What other sites?" Martia asked, with concern.

"Well they mentioned a street, can't remember the name though. Oh, and a public house. I think it was called The Anchor."

Danny and Martia stared at each other then turned back to the woman, and as one voice queried.

"Blue Anchor?"

"Yes I believe it was."

The train took its time over the last few miles. Stopping, it seemed, every few minutes. The passengers' consensus put the delay down to the Portsmouth air raids. It was gone 7pm when the train reached Fratton Station. The last of the people in Danny and Martia's carriage left the train and as it pulled away, again Danny stood up and pulled their suitcases from the rack.

"We've got another stop to go yet," Martia said.

"No, I want to get off at the town station." He patted his inside breast pocket. "I've got to get this money back to where it came from before they come looking for me."

"What about my kids? I ought to get home to them."

"Look these blokes paid for information that they're not going to get. If I don't get their money back to them quick and explain why the deals off, I won't live more than a week. Besides, you didn't even know we were coming home today, so don't start getting all motherly now."

Martia's gaze dropped to her lap, embarrassed by her own lack of scruples.

"How will you find them, if the Blue Anchor is gone?" she said.

"Well, if they're not dead, they'll be in the Air Balloon, and the Town Station is the closest."

If there was the remotest urge for Martia to rush home to her children, this was soon expunged by the thought of a large gin and orange. The couple were soon stepping into the public bar of the Air Balloon.

With her favourite drink, a cheese sandwich and a packet of crisps, Martia sat quietly in a corner, while Danny mingled with the clientele. It was Saturday night and the pub was busy with people debating the day's air raid. Occasionally Danny would refill her glass and spend five minutes telling her what he had learnt about the air raid, then someone would soon catch his attention and Martia would find herself either alone again, or talking to some stranger.

It was around a half hour to closing time when through the pub's bluish haze of tobacco smoke, Martia saw two familiar faces. Danny was talking excitedly to them; one was a young ginger-haired man with deep pockmarks covering both cheeks. He wore a cloth cap and giggled in a girlish manner. Martia remembered Elsie calling him Sandy. She said he was a nurse at one of the local hospitals and that he was homosexual.

The other was the unmistakable Bunny, with his bull neck and gorilla-like posture. She was reminded of the way he'd grinned at her as they left him at the Harbour Station and her thoughts went to Henry once again. Was he all right? Had the hospital found him? She looked up and saw Bunny. He was grinning at her now, unwavering, almost mask-like. Danny seemed to be doing most of the talking. He would, pause now and then while Sandy's girlish giggle rang out. Martia wondered if she was the topic of their discussion. She blushed, while convincing herself that her last night in the London hotel was part of their conversation. Her embarrassment gave way to anger as she saw Danny nod in her direction, which resulted in a burst of laughter. Martia stood up with the intention of confronting Danny in the presence of his friends. She intended to turn the tables on him and say something appertaining to his sexual inability or his inadequate manhood. However, as she stood, her head started to swim. She tried to recall how many drinks she'd had; it didn't seem that many. She dearly wanted to cause a scene and make Danny pay, before walking out; as it was, she found just enough strength to stay upright and make it to the exit door.

Outside the cool air increased her giddiness. She leaned against the pub wall in an attempt to regain some normality. As she stood there, trying not to slip into unconsciousness, she could see the faint outline of someone familiar standing across the street.

She remembered, as a young girl, a picture above her bed. It depicted a man holding up a lantern. Above his long hair and bearded face, was a shining halo. She remembered the caption below. "I am the light". Somehow, this mysterious person across the street reminded her of that picture.

Martia strained her eyes, trying to make the vision clearer. As she did, the apparition grew. As it came closer and clearer, Martia started to giggle as she realised that she'd mistaken her holy vision for that of a young sailor. What she'd mistaken for a halo was the rim of his white cap, perched on the back of his head.

"Hello Miss. Are you, hic, feeling alright?" The hiccups in his speech, inferred that he was as inebriated as Martia. Giggling at the thought of being addressed as Miss, Martia said,

"Hello sailor boy!" Even in her condition, she could see that he was a mere youth, slight in build and maybe just out of his teens. She tried to push herself away from the wall to stand upright, only to slump back again. She giggled while slurring her words:

"Nope, Don't think I am! And you cant help, cause you're not Jesus."

The Sailor laughed. He put his hands on Martia's shoulders, more in an effort to steady himself than to help Martia stand upright.

"Well maybe I'm not Jesus, but God knows you need as much help as I do. Where do you live?"

As the sailor finished his sentence, the noise from inside the pub became louder as the door opened and the light from inside, spewed across the pavement. Someone had opened the pub door. Martia could hear the landlord calling time as Danny stepped into the street, closely followed by Bunny and the character they called Sandy.

Danny's eyes fell immediately on Martia and the young seaman. Peering up and down the darkened High Street, Danny sidled up to the couple. His two companions moved in close behind him.

"Mmm. He's nice!" Sandy said, with a girlish giggle. Danny ignored the comment.

"What's going on then, mate? That's my girl you're mauling!" Danny said in a calm voice. The sailor took his hands from Martia's shoulders and as he stepped back from her, Danny moved closer. Martia seemed to sober up with the fear of impending trouble. She imagined how it must have looked to Danny, seeing the sailor standing so close to her.

"It's OK Danny he was only..."

The sudden sharp pain across her cheek cut Martia's sentence short.

"Shut it!" Danny shouted while nursing his stinging knuckles. Shocked and in pain, Martia cowered back against the wall, cradling her burning cheek. Under different circumstances, she would have retaliated, but she was feeling too ill, and vulnerable, especially after seeing this new side to Danny's character.

"Hey, there's no need for that," the sailor protested. "I just thought she was..." His words trailed off, realising that to finish his intended sentence might cause him even more trouble. There was no disguising the fear in his voice and Martia felt sorry for him.

"You thought what?" Danny said. "You thought she was on the game. That's what you were going to say wasn't it." Danny's hand reached into his trouser pocket as Bunny grabbed the sailor's arms from behind. There was a loud click and a shaft of light from a crack in the pubs blind, reflected off the knife's blade, in Danny's hand.

"Cut him Danny!" Sandy cried excitedly.
Martia tried to shout her protest, she opened her mouth, but her throat would not produce a sound. There was a pause as Danny amused himself by stroking the young seaman's face with the cold

blade. Then there was a second click, as Danny snapped the knife shut and slipped it back in his pocket.

"Watch her," he said. Taking hold of the sailor's arm, Danny pulled him some distance away from the others, until they were out of earshot.

They talked at length, while the three looked on. From his hand movements, it appeared Danny was doing most of the talking. Although Martia could only make them out as silhouettes, at one point the sailor appeared to produce money from the hip pocket of his bellbottoms. Danny took the money and this concluded their conversation.

"Bunny. Get the car," Danny said, roughly pulling the sailor back to rejoin the others. Bunny disappeared into the darkness to return five minutes later behind the wheel of the black Vauxhall.

Sandy sat in the front next to Bunny. Danny pushed the sailor and Martia into the back seat, and then squeezed in beside them. They drove for a few minutes through the deserted streets, before stopping outside Danny's Café.

"Where are we? I've got to get home to my kids." Martia said, slurring her words. She turned to the sailor. "And what about you," she giggled. "Don't you have to catch a boat or something?" The sailor never answered. He avoided looking at her by staring out into the darkness. Bunny turned the ignition key. As the engine died, Danny's door opened. "Come on then!" He said. All four men got out of the car.

Martia still sat repeating her protest, but her words became tangled and made no sense. Danny knelt on the back seat and leaned across to Martia. The keys to the café were in his hand. With his face up close to Martia's, he stroked a key across her bruised cheek. Quietly, but with menace he said "Now don't be a spoilsport, I promised my mates a little drink on the way home, and that's what we're going to do, so get out of the bloody car."

"Just leave me here...I'll just...have a little slee..." Martia slid slowly sideways until she lay horizontal, unable to finish her sentence.

Danny gestured to Bunny and Sandy. They lifted Martia out of the car while Danny opened the door of the café. As the two carried her inside Danny noticed the young sailor was slowly edging away from them along the café front.

"Not thinking of leaving I hope; are we Jack?" said Danny sarcastically. Reluctantly the sailor entered the café.

Inside, Bunny and Sandy propped up Martia, who was now incapable of standing unassisted. Danny pulled down the blinds on the shop front. He flicked a switch, and as light flooded the café, the two men sat Martia down at one of the dozen small tables. Immediately her head flopped onto her arm as she sprawled across the table. "Come on girl, it's not time to sleep yet." Danny said, as he pulled Martia to her feet again. Martia mumbled something inaudible and slumped in Danny's arms.

"Bloody hell! Those pills don't usually work that fast," said Sandy.

"What are you saying?" The sailor said, looking at Sandy's worried face. "Have you been slipping her pills? I don't want anything to do with this. You said she agreed." The sailor moved toward the door.

"Oh no you don't!" said Danny, barring the way "You're going nowhere until you get what you paid for." The sailor looked frightened.

"But you said she knew! You said she'd done this before. I didn't know it would be like this. Look, keep the money. Just let me go I won't make trouble."

"Maybe." Danny said, smiling at his two friends. "But, you're in it as deep as we are now. So maybe you'll think twice before you decide to rat on us." Danny unlocked the door behind the counter. He turned to the other two, and nodded towards the unlocked door. "Sandy, help Bunny get her upstairs!"

The two men hoisted Martia up by her arms while she mumbled another trail of unintelligible protests. They half walked, half dragged her behind the counter to where the door had been wallpapered to match the cheap décor of the café. They struggled awkwardly to get Martia through it and up the narrow stairs that led to the room above the shop.

The two men could be heard grunting and panting as they slowly manhandled Martia up the stairs. Meanwhile Danny pulled a bottle and some glasses from under the counter.

"Lets you and me have a little drink, while we're waiting. What do they call you? Apart from Jack, that is." Danny said, smiling at the young sailor.

"Jason." The sailor answered bluntly. Danny lit a cigarette and leaned nonchalantly across the counter. He poured whisky into two glasses and pushed one toward the sailor.

"Well you see, Jason. They are just getting her ready for you. I mean you paid good money and I want you to leave here happy," Danny said grinning sarcastically.

"But why? I don't care about the money. You can keep it. Just let me go? I promise I won't tell anyone."

"Jason, Jason." Danny whispered, patronisingly. "You don't seem to understand. You see, you just happened to be in the wrong place at the right time."

"What do you mean?"

"Well you see if it hadn't been you, it would have been someone else." At this point Danny spoke as if thinking aloud. "Maybe another sailor, in fact yes, I think a sailor is a good touch. It will look better."

"I don't understand. What will?"

"Don't worry about it. It doesn't concern you. Come on. Time to go up."

The staircase was little more than two foot wide and as Jason was reluctantly jostled up the narrow stairs he realised why the two thugs had struggled so noisily getting the young woman up there. He was not sure what to expect as he turned the handle of the narrow door at the top.

Seeing Martia across the street earlier that night, had sexually aroused the young seaman. Then Danny and his two thugs entered the scene and a sense of foreboding had doused all his amorous feelings. As he swung open the door, the sight of this beautiful, scantily dressed young woman should have aroused him again. But seeing her, so vulnerable in the hands of these corrupt men, he could only feel pity for her.

"Go on then, get on the bed," said Danny, nudging the sailor in roughly in the back.

"I cant. Look, just let me go! Why are you making me do this?" Danny looked at his two friends and gave a deep sigh then with clenched fist hit Jason in the stomach. Jason doubled up in pain and fought to regain his breath. Danny waited for Jason to compose himself.

"I know what it is! He's shy," said Danny, grinning at the others. "Okay, you two, lets give our new friend some privacy." Bunny and Sandy moved towards the door, grinning at each other. "And have yourselves a drink while you're down there," he said loudly as the door closed behind them. "Is that better? Now we haven't got all night, so get on with it." Danny pushed Jason onto the bed. The bed shook but Martia never murmured. One side of the bed was against the wall and Martia lay on top of the covers with her back to them facing the wall. Apart from her undergarments, her clothes had been removed and she appeared to be asleep.

"Go on for Christ's sake, get on with it" Danny said angrily. Trembling with fear, Jason took off his cap and placing it at the bottom of the bed, he tried to unbutton his tunic.

"No, don't take anything off yet. Just get on the bed next to her." Jason complied.
"That's it, now move up close and put your arm round her." Behind Danny, stood an old dressing table, Danny moved slowly backwards feeling behind him for the handle of the top drawer. He pulled the drawer silently open.
Martia lay with her back towards the young sailor. "Good now turn her over to face you."
Jason was puzzled. Was this thug intending to give him detailed instructions on how to perform sex with this woman? And if so, why? Jason was young but not completely naïve with regard to matters of a sexual nature, his short time in the Navy had assured that. Maybe this was how this thug of a character got his excitement, he thought.

"Hurry up for God's sake."

Jason gently pulled on Martia's shoulder. It felt much colder than he expected. Slowly he turned her towards him. Even with her eyes closed, Jason was in awe of her perfect features.

"That's great now put this on her head. It'll make her look like she's enjoying herself," said Danny, tossing Jason's white cap to within his reach of him. Jason was even more confused by this and turned to face Danny, only to be temporarily blinded by the flash from Danny's camera. "Okay, that was great, now for a close up," Danny said as he replaced the burnt out flashbulb. "She'll have no trouble recognising herself. Now do as I said, put the cap on her. Oh, and I think we'll have the bellbottoms off for this next one."

"Look. What's going on? What's the camera all about? You lot are up to something and I want to know what it is. If you're trying to blackmail me, you're wasting you're time. I got no money and I'm not married." As he spoke, Jason started to move off the bed. Danny turned his head toward the door and called out,

"Bunny!" Only seconds passed before the door opened. "Sort him out will you. I want the trousers off. This has got to look good. You know what Elsie's like. She won't pay for a third rate job." Bunny approached the bed just as Jason swung his legs off. He grabbed the front of Jason's tunic with his left hand and with his right fist swung a punch. Again, Jason saw a flash of light, only this time, it was not from the camera.

Sandy's feminine voice came through the swirling mist of Jason's semi-consciousness.

"Oh don't spoil his face, Bunny! I'm sure he'll cooperate now." Jason felt himself being lifted to a sitting position. He heard Sandy whispering in his ear. "Come on young man just make it look good for the picture you don't have to do it for real. Then Danny will let you go. Come on, let Danny take one of the three of us." Sandy sprawled on the bed, put his arm around Jason and propped Martia's head onto Jason's shoulder. "How's this?" he said to Danny, grinning widely.

The camera flashed again.

Although events had erased the alcohol's effects, Jason's head was still swimming from Bunny's punch. He was faintly aware, however, of being undressed and manoeuvred into various positions while intermittent flashes of light came from around the room. Slowly as his head cleared, he found himself lying on top of Martia;

her arms were around his neck yet they hung limp. He placed his hands each side of her in an effort to push himself away. It was then he felt something wet and sticky. The camera flashed again and he saw that it was Martia's vomit. He looked into her face. Her eyes were not fully closed and she did not appear to be sleeping. There was another flash from Danny's camera, and it was as if it blasted away the final cobwebs from Jason's head. As he stared into Martia's face, the truth dawned on him.

"She's dead!" he said quietly. Then as if his own words had alarmed him, Jason pushed himself quickly away from Martia, stared at Danny and this time shouted, "she's dead!"

"Don't talk stupid, she's asleep. Come on, one more picture and..."

Sandy had moved up and was leaning over Martia.

"Danny, she's not breathing!" Sandy started to whimper.

"Shut up, both of you." Danny sat on the bed and took Martia's hand. Sandy leaned over him and watched in silence as Danny listened for her breathing. He slapped her face and as her head flopped to one side, more vomit oozed from her mouth.

Jason quietly slipped his clothes on, while the others were preoccupied.

"Is she? Well is she?" Sandy sounded like he was about to cry, Only Bunny remained unflustered.

Danny slowly got to his feet. "She must have choked on her own sick."

"Bloody Hell! Danny, what are we going to do? That's it we're finished now. This is murder. I told you, I warned Elsie about those pills."

"Shut up Sandy!" Danny shouted, "I'm trying to think. It's not murder if it was an accident."

"It is if they trace them bloody pills to me. Christ, the police are already suspicious of you over that other girl," said Sandy.

"Shut it!" Danny shouted. "I told you not to mention that again," There was silence as they stared down at Martia's pale form.

Eventually Danny said. "Elsie will know what to do. It was all her idea anyway, so she'll have to come up with an answer. I'm not taking the blame on my own." Bunny's expression remained unchanged, while Sandy stared worriedly at Danny, praying that he was right, that Elsie would have the answer to their predicament. Danny suddenly glanced about the room.

"Where's that kid? Bloody Hell! He's gone. If he gets to the police...."

The three rushed to the door and down the stairs. The café was in darkness; the door to the street was open wide. The three dashed out of the shop, peering in all directions. Seeing no sign of the young sailor, Danny slammed the café door shut, and all three jumped in the car to speed off in search of Jason.

As the sound of the Vauxhall's engine faded, Jason moved out of the darkness, from where he'd been hiding at the rear of the café. He made for the door with one thought in mind: to get away from these maniacs. As he reached the door, another thought occurred to him and he turned back.

It was almost 1o'clock when Danny and his two accomplices drove through the deserted streets in search of the young sailor. They headed south along Commercial Rd, thinking he might try to reach the naval barracks. They drove slowly, peering in dark doorways, guessing that Jason would try to hide if he heard the sound of their car. The three had just turned a corner into Edinborough Rd, when Sandy cried out,

"Over there, Danny! Someone just moved back into that shop doorway!"

The car pulled into the kerb level with the doorway. Danny wound his window down and called softly into the darkness of the deep shop-front.

"Come on out Jason. We know you're there. We're not going to hurt you." Getting no response, Danny got out of the car and walked up to the darkened doorway. "Okay kid, let's go. I'm not going to tell you..." Danny never finished the sentence. A fist came out of the darkness sending him sprawling across the pavement. Holding his, already damaged, nose that once again oozed with blood, Danny looked up into the bearded face of a huge sailor.

"Yeah, that should teach the Peeping Tom a lesson," came a woman's voice from behind the sailor. "Go on give him another one for me, Jack."

It became clear to Danny that he'd encroached on a prostitute in the middle of plying her trade. However, the giant of a sailor did not have time to follow out her last request. Danny quickly scrambled back into the car, as fast as he could. "Get moving!" He shouted at Bunny.

A minute or so later, the Vauxhall pulled up alongside the railings of the naval barracks. There was not a pedestrian to be seen. The road was deserted. "He couldn't have made it this far already," said Sandy. "Not on foot. Maybe he took a different route, if that's the case all we have to do is wait." Sandy's voice suddenly raised an octave as a more worrying thought struck him. "But what if he's not coming back here to the barracks? He might be on leave for all we know; he might not even live in Pompey, then we'll never find him."

He turned to look at Danny, waiting for some guidance but it seemed like he wasn't listening. Danny stared through them as if in a trance while nursing his nose and the growing lump where his head hit the pavement. Eventually he said,

"Who turned out the lights in the café?" Bunny and Sandy looked at each other blankly. "The lights." Danny repeated angrily. "If you were doing a runner, would you stop to switch off the light? When we came down the stairs the lights were out, and the shop door was open. But I left the lights on when I brought the kid upstairs. Now try to remember, when I called you back upstairs, did either of you turn them out?"

"Not me!" said Sandy, while Bunny shook his head.

"The crafty bastard must have turned them out, then opened the door to make it look like he'd scarpered. Shit! He was still there all the time. Quick, get us back to the café."

The three arrived back at the café to find the front door wide open and the interior in darkness. Danny closed the door and switched on the lights.

"He's gone. That's it now. We're finished," Sandy whined, like he was about to cry.

Danny never answered, but dashed through the door behind the counter and up the stairs. Bunny and Sandy stood there waiting, tense, listening to Danny thumping about upstairs.

"I wonder if she's moved." It was the first time Bunny had spoken since they left the pub. "If she's still…"

"Dead?" Sandy shouted at him. "Is that what you were going to say? You f------ idiot, who do you think she is, Jesus Christ? When you're dead, you're dead." With that, Sandy started to sob like a woman.

"Keep the noise down," said Danny, appearing through the stairwell door, "There are wardens about."

Danny was looking even more worried and pale. The shiny lump on his face gave him the appearance of a child with mumps. "What was all the noise about up there?" said Sandy trying to control his emotions:
"I was looking for the camera. It's gone."

"Oh my God! That's it then, we're finished. He could hang us all with those pictures." Sandy sounded like he was about to cry again.

"You don't think he'd be daft enough to show them to the police, do you. Don't be stupid, he's in every photo, so shut up snivelling like some bloody great girl. Help Bunny get her down the stairs and in the car. We'd better go see Elsie. She'll know what to do, but what ever you say to her, don't mention that bloody sailor."

21
The truth outs

By 1.45 Sunday morning, Danny Clark and Sandy Smith were sitting at Elsie Craven's dining table. Outside in the silence of the blackout, Bunny Warren waited as usual in the car. However, this time he was hoping that Danny wouldn't make him wait too long. Not very much worried or flustered Bunny, but at that moment, a half moon and his internal mirror allowed him to see the lifeless form of Martia Gough propped up in the seat behind him. Her eyes were not completely closed and Bunny was experiencing fear like never before.

A few minutes earlier, a warden had passed on the opposite side of the street and Bunny slid lower down in his seat, afraid that the man might cross over to look through the car window. To Bunny's relief, the man quickly passed by.

Elsie had gone to her front room cabinet to fetch a bottle of whisky and some glasses. Danny and Sandy were surprised at how little concern Elsie had shown when they told her of Martia's death, especially after the fuss she created over the Moody girl.

"Accidents happen," she repeated for the third time, as she laid the tray on the table and started filling glasses. "People have died all over the city in yesterday's air raid; people were still digging them out before it got dark, another one can't make any difference. For God's sake! Look at the two of you; you're white as ghosts. Here get this down you, it'll steady your nerves."

"Accident!" Sandy exclaimed in a falsetto voice. "No! Maybe the Moody girl was an accident, but then what do you expect, when you let a bloody gorilla loose on a slip of a thing like the Moody girl. But not this, blimey Elsie, how can you be so calm? If it was those two pills that killed Martia I'm bloody sure a jury wouldn't see it as a bloody accident."

"Hey, wait a minute!" Danny said, getting to his feet. "Elsie, you told me to give her four."

"Four!" squealed Sandy "Bloody Hell! No wonder she's dead, with all that drink inside her. I specifically told Elsie, no more than two!" Danny had gone quiet and was glaring threateningly at Elsie, who deliberately avoided his stare as she sipped her drink.

Danny suddenly grabbed her viciously by the jaw, and forced her to face him.

"You bloody well knew, didn't you?" Danny said, his eyes blazing. "You wanted this to happen. That was all lies about wanting her working the streets for you. You wanted her dead, why?"

Elsie knocked his hand away from her face and stood up. She turned her back on them and for some moments stood staring at an old photograph on her mantelpiece. The picture was of a handsome young man holding a baby. After some moments she quietly said, "Because she deserved it. An eye for an eye, that's what the good book says." The two men glanced at each other, unsure if the wildness in her eyes and the grimace on her face meant she'd lost her mind. "Yes, you didn't know that did you?" She continued. "You had no idea that she was a murderess. You don't believe me, I can tell, but its true. She killed my husband and my little boy. Don't make faces at him Danny, I'm not mad. Twelve years ago my husband, Sean, held my little five-year-old boy in his arms and jumped in front of an express train."

"Oh God, I remember that," Sandy said. "That was terrible."

"I don't believe it, Elsie!" said Danny. "You told me Sean left you. You said he took little Raymond with him."

"I know, it was easier for me at the time, I couldn't take all the finger pointing and blame. Everyone knew him as Sean, but his first name was Arthur, the name they printed in the paper. That's why nobody linked him to me, and the way I wanted it. Anyway, that was her doing. She chased my Sean, knowing he was married, and when she had him hooked, she threatened to drop him unless he left Raymond and me, and he did, but then she threw him over anyway. He tried everything to win her back, until in the end, his mind snapped. I never should have let him take Raymond that day. Sean acted strange and I should have seen it coming, but I suppose I never imagined that he could hurt Raymond. He loved him so much. Sean was a weak man but gentle, kind, and the only man I ever really loved."

Elsie looked emotionally drained as she took her drink and slowly eased herself into her armchair. The room was silent, and for a while, Danny and Sandy were lost for words. Elsie took a sip from her glass, sat back in her chair and staring at the ceiling, she continued,

"As far as the law goes, she was guilty of nothing, but she as good as pushed them off that platform and I was determined to see that she paid for her crime. My only dilemma was deciding what the punishment should be."

Elsie reached down and put her glass on the tiled fireplace. She turned to face Danny and they could see her tear filled eyes. "Do you know I almost did her kid in?" Danny and Sandy looked at each other. "Its true! That's what she did to me. I almost drowned the poor little mite in Canoe Lake. I was thinking about my little Raymond and I wanted her to suffer like I had. Anyway, some bloke pulled him out and I'm glad he did now. Do you know why?" Elsie paused, staring into her drink. Danny and Sandy looked at each other, unsure if they were expected to answer. "It wasn't enough punishment for that bitch." Elsie went on. "What was the point? She's never cared for those kids, not like I loved my little Raymond, so I had to find another way. Then we met you, Sandy, a nurse at the hospital, it didn't take me long to size you up for the greedy little tyke that you are. I knew that you would come in useful."

"Hey! Now just a minute. Whatever I am, I wouldn't knowingly take part in murder. I was just doing you a favour when I gave you those pills."

"Yeah! A favour that cost me a fiver; you knew they were dangerous but as long as you got paid, you didn't care what I was going to use them for." Sandy looked embarrassed. He started to splutter out a protest, but Danny intervened with,

"How come she never cottoned on to you, after all this time?"

"She had never seen me, but I knew who she was. You see I'd suspected Sean of being unfaithful. I had him followed, the bloke supplied me with photos I found out she lived in Cosham with her father. I intended to go there and tackle her in front of him, show her up for what she was. But then Sean's mood changed and I knew she'd thrown him over. I thought that had put an end to it so I decided to leave well alone, But Sean was not the same he started acting strange. I confronted him about that bitch and got the whole story. Apparently she'd given him an ultimatum. If he left me she'd go back to him. I could see he was besotted with her. Then, I heard that a For-Sale notice was seen outside her fathers house and that the house was empty. They were gone and I hoped Sean would get over her. Sadly, he found her again, but now she was married. It was just after that Sean killed himself, taking Raymond with him. I lost track of her for some time after that. Then, out of the blue, I spotted her in Queen Street one afternoon. I followed her here to Lyons Terrace. But by then, things had changed. I'd had time to get my head straight. I wasn't going to throw my life away by getting caught pushing her under a bus. There were other ways to make her pay for what she did; more profitable ways, but this was going to take some planning, so I bought this place. It took a while before I could approach her. I was afraid I'd break down and strangle the cow where she stood. Anyway, as far as I'm concerned, Sean and my little Raymond has been avenged, she's paid for her crime."

Elsie got up and refilled her glass. The two men were silent for some time. Only the distant voice of an Air Raid Warden could be heard repeating, "Lights out."

"But why all that rigmarole with the camera," asked Sandy.

"Well, that was plan two. If the pills didn't work, I would have ruined her marriage with the photos, you did get some photos?" Elsie looked from one to the other. "Did you get the photographs? We'll have to get rid of the film." Sandy darted a frightened look at Danny, but Danny was ready for just such a question,

"Yes. Sandy stood in. I took the snaps of them together on the bed, but after we found she was dead, I burned the film."

"Well good for you! Goes to show, you can do something right if you really try. Yes, as I was saying, plan two was to ruin her marriage like she ruined mine, and it wouldn't have taken me long to get her on the game."

"Okay, so you paid her back," said Danny. "But it doesn't solve our problem. You seem to have forgot, there's a corpse sitting out in the car."

"Actually, there's two," said Sandy, emitting a girly giggle. "But one of them has to drive." This only resulted in him getting a cold stare from Danny.

"I was coming to that," said Elsie "First of all, how many people have seen her, Danny, since you got off the train?"

"Just about everyone in the Air Balloon, I suppose."

"I mean people that she knew, apart from Sandy and Bunny," Danny thought about it for a moment. "None, I think."

"Good. Now if you do exactly as I tell you, we'll all come out of this clean as a whistle."

Around 9.30 that morning, Nell Masters crossed the street and knocked the door of number twelve.

"Hello Jan, love, I take it your mum's not back yet?"

"No, not yet Aunt Nell."

"Doesn't matter, it was you and Billy I wanted to see. Can I come in?"

"Yes, sure you can."

"Nell followed Jan down the passage and into the living room. Billy sat at the table, spreading margarine on toast. "Now look kids, I know you can look after yourselves, but before your dad rejoined the Army, he asked me if I'd keep an eye on you. Now with your mum being away I think this gives me a good excuse to invite you to a Sunday roast. How about it? Would you like to come over about 1oclock?"

Jan and Billy looked at each other, grinned and in one voice said, "Yes please."

Dinner at Nell's was a real treat for Janice and Billy. Apart from voting it the best they'd ever tasted, their mother was not there to shout at them, or hit their knuckles for the least reason with whatever cutlery came to hand.

After helping with the washing up, the three settled down to play cards until there came a knock at the front door.

"Where have you been?" Nell said opening the front door to Cathleen. "You said you were coming back yesterday!" Cathleen didn't answer but appeared to be distracted by something happening along the street. "Cathy!" Nell said loudly.

"Oh! Sorry Mum. I was looking at that woman wandering down the street. She seems to be looking at door numbers, I was just wondering who she might be looking for. I thought maybe you could help her."

Nell stepped out of her porch and followed Cathy's gaze. The woman had obviously knocked a door because she was talking to someone several houses along. Nell thought the woman looked familiar, but was too far away for Nell to be sure. "Well, it looks like she's found the house she was looking for," said Nell. "So are you coming in, or are we going to stand out here all day?" Cathy followed Nell inside.

"Yes mum, like you said, I meant to come back yesterday, but that was before we had that terrible air raid. Oh mum, you wouldn't believe some of the injuries we've had to deal with. Anyway I've just knocked at number twelve again..." Cathleen's voice trailed off as Nell put her finger against her lips and gestured for her to go into the front room. Before following her, Nell called out.

"Deal me out for a while Jan. I just want a word with Cathleen." Cathleen waited for Nell to close the door before speaking,

"Don't tell me their mother still isn't home!"

"No, Can you believe it? But at least, Jan and Billy's had a dinner today. What about their dad, have you seen Henry, how is he? Are you going to tell the kids about him?"

"I called in on him before I left the hospital this morning. I was hoping to give them some good news, but he's in a bad way. He has a fractured skull. He regained consciousness for a while but he wasn't making much sense. His doctor ordered him to be sedated, he's been sleeping ever since."

"Yes, but are you going to tell the kids?" Nell repeated.

"I don't think I should. I mean what can they do it'll only upset them. I came to tell his wife. It would be up to her to tell them."

"Did you know they're being evacuated tomorrow?"

"Well, there you are then," said Cathleen. "If I told them now they'd have to leave thinking about their dad lying in hospital. I suppose she will, at least, be back to see them off."

"I wouldn't bet on it. Apparently, she's asked Elsie Craven to see them off if she's not back. I tell you, some people shouldn't be allowed to have kids. Anyway, come and say hello."

Cathleen followed Nell along the passage and into the dining room. While Cathleen and the children said their greetings, there was another knock at the front door.

"Hell, it's like Piccadilly Circus in this street today," said Nell. Talk to Jan and Billy while I get the door, Cathy."

Nell opened the door again and instantly recognised, not only the face of the woman caller, but also her look of hostility; Nell had seen it many years ago. Nell also recognised the piece of paper in the woman's hand, she said nothing but waited for recognition to dawn on the woman's face.

"Nell Masters! I might have known."

"Brenda Scopes. Well I never!"

"It's Brenda Button, actually. But then you knew that, didn't you?" Brenda said sneering. "So, you're the one he's been seeing. You don't give up do you? Still trying it on with my Alfie, are you? Someone told me they saw him out with some tart. Then I found this address in his pocket. I couldn't quite make out the number at first."

"Been through Alfie's pockets, have you Brenda? Nothing like a marriage built on trust is there?"

"Don't you try to get funny with me, Nell Masters. I'm warning you to keep away from Alfie, or..." Brenda's chin started to quiver and she was having difficulty finishing her sentence.

"Or what, Brenda? You'll push me under a tram? Look, what I'm going to tell you is the truth, something, it would appear, you're not familiar with, from what I've been told." Brenda's eyes blazed angrily. "I probably was seen with Alfie once. I actually went looking for him when I discovered where he worked. You see, even after all these years I still love him."

Nell suddenly realised that she was admitting to her old enemy, something she'd tried to hide from herself all these years. "At that time," Nell continued, "I had no idea whether he was married or not. I found his place of work and we had tea together in a little café. That was the extent of Alfie being seen out with a tart. It was then that he told me he was married and I decided not to see him again. But then, as fate would have it, we did meet again by accident when we both visited Ivan Boswell, you see, he was my father. That was the day Alfie told me he was getting a divorce and the reason for it…your adultery.

"Oh, and I suppose you believed him!"

"Now that I know who his wife is, yes, every word. It looks like your lies and deceit have caught up with you Brenda, and if you can remember what you and Molly Gill did to me, you'll understand why I couldn't be happier. Goodbye Brenda."

Jan and Billy enjoyed the next hour in Nell and Cathleen's company, until there came a third knock at the front door.

"I'll go! It might be their mother." Cathleen stepped into the passage closing the living-room door behind her. After a few moments, Nell and the children heard the murmur of voices. Not wanting the afternoon to end, Jan hoped with all her heart that it was not her mother.

The voices became louder as if in an argument, then seconds later they heard,

"Mum, would you bring Janice."

As Nell and Jan made their way towards the front door, they could see Cathleen out on the pavement. She was looking upward talking to someone just out of view. Jan reached the door first and was disturbed to see Cathy was talking to a policeman.

Parked on the opposite side of the street was a police car. A uniformed policewoman sat in the back seat. Jan looked at Cathleen and her expression told her it was bad news.

"Hello young lady." The policeman said. "Are you the daughter of Martia Gough?"

"Yes," Jan said, nervously.

The policeman crouched down and held Jan gently by the shoulders. "Well, you see the lady in that car over there? I want you to go see her. She has something to tell you. I'll stay and look after your little brother until you come back." Nell and Cathleen watched Jan cross the road and the back door of the Riley open for her to get in. Nell looked at Cathleen's watery eyes and guessed the worst.

"Don't worry Miss," said the constable to Cathy. "WPC Phillips was picked for this. She has a way with kids. She's had a lot of this to do lately. If anyone can break it to her gently, she can. This is the forth address we've been to today. A lot of people died in that air raid yesterday.

"What is it Cathy, what's happened?" said Nell. Cathleen was unable to control her emotions sufficiently to speak to her mother and just ran back in the house. The constable was about to openly tell Nell why he was there, when he realised Billy was standing within earshot, just inside the door. The constable took Nell by the arm and gently pulled her a few paces from the door.

"It's their mother." He whispered.

"Martia! What about her?"

"She was in the Blue Anchor when the bomb struck, yesterday afternoon. They must have missed the body when they first searched. They only found her this morning. I'm afraid she's dead."

Nell slumped against the wall, and then, feeling faint, eased herself down to sit on the windowsill. After a few moments, she recovered.

"Rubbish," she said to the policeman. "Martia went to London for the weekend. You ask her daughter. I don't know who it is you've found but it must be someone else."

"No," he argued. "If she did go to London, she must have come back before Saturday's air-raid. It's definitely her; her employer, a Mr Clark has identified her. Anyway, if it isn't, then where is she?"

Nell looked across the street to see Jan's tear soaked face looking back at her.

22
Two into one won't go

It was unusual to see the little railway platform at Liphook, Hampshire, so alive with activity, but not unique. In 1940, small country railway stations throughout England were experiencing much the same amount of activity.

Noisy children, evacuees mostly, from Portsmouth had practically commandeered the Liphook platform, having just disembarked from the Portsmouth to Waterloo train.

Portsmouth was, as expected, a critical target of the German Luftwaffa and evacuees from that stricken city were numbered in the hundreds.

Carriage doors slammed, while children leaned out of carriage windows shouting their farewells to school friends before the train moved on, leaving some of its freight of frightened and bewildered children behind; children who fretted at what fate had in store for them in their new, though temporary, homes.

Belching out its white steam, the engine pulled its carriages slowly onward to other small villages where it would drop off more nervous and frightened children. Meanwhile, here at Liphook, organisers of all descriptions were on hand, trying to create some kind of order from the noise and bustle.

Teachers, parents and porters, even a local policeman tried to link luggage with labelled children. Slowly they'd arrange them into some kind of marching order, ready to move them to the village hall. Once there, they would be distributed to their temporary families.

On one of the benches, Janice sat with her arm around Billy. Her coat was far too short to cover her thin cotton dress, and her shoes, though polished, were coming away at the soles. Dark swellings underlined the girl's pale blue eyes. Billy turned to Jan saying,

"We will be able to stay together Jan, won't we?"

"I hope so Billy, but the trouble is, these people are only expecting me. You were supposed to stay on the train until it got to

Haslemere." Janice lifted Billy's chin, and looking into his sallow face, detected fear in his eyes. Quickly, she added: "But if we stay together, this Mr and Mrs Webster might take us both."

"Well, they bloody well better," said Billy, haughtily.

"Now, you can stop that swearing, or no family will want to take you, do you hear me,"

Billy ignored Jan's scalding with another question, "Well what if they won't?" Jan was lost for an answer, but then a ruddy-faced and portly police sergeant interrupted Billy's question,

"Come on you two, get in line. People are waiting at the village hall you know! The sooner we sort you kids out, the sooner you'll get fed, but more importantly," he said, grinning, "I'll get fed." The two children looked up at him and it was Jan that spoke,

"I don't think we're supposed to get in line sir. Someone is coming to get us here at the station." If the tender politeness in Jan's tone had not softened this local Bobby, then the sadness in her eyes surely would. He crouched down so that his face was level with theirs.

"Looks like you've been doing quite a bit of crying young lady." he said softly. "Now look, Liphook's a nice village with nice people and a nice school. This war can't last long and you'll be back home before you know it. Now, lets show your little brother how brave you can be and lets have no more tears."

"She do get on your nerves," Billy said to him. "She's been crying all night, mister."

The constable ruffled Billy's hair. "Well she's not going to cry any more, are you love. Now then, who's coming to pick you up?"

"Mr Webster's his name sir." The policeman was captivated by Jan's manner and charm. Jan had made up her mind to use these same attributes to win over the Webster's in the hope that they would take Billy as well.

"Well, aren't you the lucky one's. What's your name's?"

"I'm Janice Gough and this is my brother Billy." Running a finger up and down the clipboard he was carrying, he said. "I've not got a Billy on my list; has Mrs Bromwell been to see you?"

Jan guessed that he was referring to the tweedy dressed woman she'd seen questioning children. The woman also carried a clipboard and Jan could now see her along the platform organising a line of twenty or more children. The woman looked agitated as she darted looks between the policeman and the station clock.

"Yes," Jan lied. "But it's okay, she knows all about us."

"That's alright then. You're a lucky pair. I know the Websters; they're a bit well- to-do, but they're very nice people. So you'd better not play them up, or you'll have me to deal with." Jan thought the severity of his threat did not bear out the kindness in his eyes. As if to substantiate Jan's observation, his tone changed and his face beamed as he added: "The Webster's have a young lass about your age, so at least you'll have some company, young lady." Then looking at Billy he asked "Are you sure the Webster's are taking both of you?"

"Yes," Jan said quickly, before Billy could answer. Jan held her breath as the policeman started to re-check his list. Then the tweedy woman started to make her way toward them. Jan tried to sound calm as she quickly said, "I think Mrs Bromwell is getting impatient."

"Oh right. Well good luck to you both and I expect I'll be seeing you around the village." He reached the line of children just as they began marching out of the station. Soon the platform was deserted.

"Come on Billy, let's wait outside. My teacher said that Mr Webster's got a Bentley car. We've never been in a Bentley car before. We can watch for it outside."

"You don't have to say Bentley car, every time, silly; it's just Bentley. Everyone knows that a Bentley is a car. Anyway what for? They won't let us stay together, you know they won't." Billy's bottom lip had put on its severest pout. "Why did we have to come here? And how will mum know where to find us?"

This last question brought more tears to cloud Jan's eyes. She took hold of Billy's hand, while, with the other, wiped the wetness from her face.

"Don't worry about that. Look, its safer out here in the country; you know how frightened you were the other night when the bombs were dropping. Well, you won't hear any of that here and we won't have to sleep in that horrible shelter again."

"But why didn't Mum come to see us off like the other kids. Where is she? And why did that police lady make you cry yesterday?" This time, Billy glanced at his sister's face too quickly for her to hide the fresh wetness around her long dark lashes. Billy waited for an answer.

"Billy, do you remember what Dad said to us about looking after each other if we were on our own?" Jan said, sniffing back the tears. Billy nodded slowly. "Well, that police lady came to tell us that mummy was in the Blue Anchor when…"

"Liar!" Billy shouted the word, in an attempt to drown out what, in his heart, he knew to be the truth. He then emphasised it with an even louder, **"Bloody liar."** The echo reverberated along the now deserted platform. Billy knew about the bombings on that terrible Saturday afternoon. He and Jan had to run, like everyone else, to the nearest shelter. He had heard people talking about the Princes Theatre and the pub called the Blue Anchor. A direct hit, that's what people had said. Everyone down the shelter had been talking about it, and he had often heard his mother mention the Blue Anchor.

Even with all these details, Billy refused to allow his thoughts to dwell on the possibility that his mother could have been one of Saturday's many casualties, yet in his heart he knew. It all made sense: the police car coming to Aunt Nell's, the policeman whispering to her, so that he wouldn't hear. He recalled how Nell almost fainted and how she looked at him afterwards. Yes, deep down he knew, yet he wasn't ready to accept it. Now his sister, Janice was trying to force the awful truth on him. Billy sat with his back to her, fighting back the tears. He sat for some minutes until the noise of an incoming train broke the silence.

Suddenly he stood up and faced his sister. Jan could see that he was trying hard not to cry. He shouted at Janice above the noise of squealing brakes, as the southbound train pulled alongside the opposite platform.

"You're a liar Jan and you know what Mum said! God will punish you." Jan's tears ran freely. Her feelings toward her mother, were they to be questioned at that moment, were anger and hate. Anger, for driving her father away, hate for the beatings and degrading clothes she had to wear to school, but most of all, anger for her weakness in allowing Elsie Craven to cause them such misery. Jan was convinced that Elsie Craven was behind all that had gone wrong in their lives; especially her mothers drinking and the reason she was found in the ruins of the Blue Anchor. She almost felt that Martia had died to escape her responsibilities, just as she had always evaded them.

Nothing could now hide the distress she was feeling. Tears blurred her vision as she tried to stop Billy pulling away from her. She became almost hysterical as she pleaded with him.

"I'm not lying Billy, you know I'm not. Mum's gone and she's never coming back, but we've got to stay together like daddy said."

"Yes, until they put me somewhere else!" Billy sneered. "No! I won't stay here. I'm going home."

Voices could be heard as passengers met friends and relatives on the far platform, while a muffled voice announced the train's destination: Portsmouth's Harbour Station.

"Billy, there is no home to go to! If you go back they will put you in an orphanage."

"No they won't. I'll go to Elsie's so mum can find me." Billy broke free from Jan's grasp and ran towards the footbridge leading to the far platform.

"Billy, come back!" Just as Jan was about to dash after him, she felt someone grab her arm. She turned to face a tall man whom she guessed was around her father's age. With him was a smartly dressed young girl.

"Are you Janice?" asked the man.

"Yes."

"How do you do. I'm Mr Webster and this is Deborah, my daughter. Who was that boy?" he asked looking in the direction of Billy, now running across the bridge.

"Its my brother." Jan tried to pry the man's fingers from her arm. "I've got to stop him before he gets on that train!"

"You wait here. Deborah, stay with her." The man set off with alarming speed, but before he'd reached the top of the bridge, train doors could be heard slamming on the opposite platform. The girls watched the man sprint across the bridge and down the steps on the far side until the train carriages obscured their view of him. As the train moved off, Jan prayed that Billy would be still be standing on the platform; wearing the silly grin, he used so often to goad her.

The train picked up speed until Mr Webster could be seen shrugging his shoulders. Billy was gone.

Deborah did not stop talking on the short journey to the Webster house, but most of her words fell on deaf ears as Jan could think only of Billy.

Only the crunch of gravel could be heard above the almost silent engine of the huge Rolls Bentley, as it turned through two tall white pillars that formed the entrance to the Webster's property. Inside the ornate gates, fully-grown shrubs and fir trees lined neatly kept lawns. The car pulled up outside a large house, where a smartly dressed woman allowed Deborah to make the introductions.

"Mummy, this is Janice. Isn't she pretty? But she's very sad because her little brother has run away." Delia Webster was thirty-five, an attractive woman whose modern attire matched the elegant surroundings of her home. She lifted Jan's chin gently, and looking into her gaunt and tired eyes, said,

"You are in a sorry state. When did this happen?"

"Just a few minutes ago," interrupted Steven Webster. "At the station, I tried to stop him but he jumped on a train. He's probably half way to Portsmouth by now."

"Well don't you worry Janice, we'll get on the telephone to the Portsmouth police. I'm sure they will find him. How old is he?" Delia asked.

"He's only six," sobbed Jan. "And they were sending him to Haslemere on his own. He was so scared, so I let him get off the train with me, but he was afraid you wouldn't let him stay. That's why he ran away, to get home."

"That's terrible. Of course we wouldn't have sent him away, would we Steven?" Steven Webster was getting back in the car and did not answer. Delia assumed that he had not heard. Anyway, don't you worry we'll get your Billy back. Deborah, why don't you show Janice around the grounds before dinner? "

It was early afternoon when Bunny Warren followed Danny Clark along Elsie Craven's passage towards the front door. Before

Danny reached to open it, he heard a faint knock. He opened it and immediately recognised Billy who stared up at him. The boy's face was dirty except where tears had left their tracks. The familiar little cardboard box carried by child evacuees, still hung about his neck. Even before Danny spoke, Billy knew he was the cigarette-smoking man from George's back yard. Then Danny laughed when he saw Billy cower at the sight of Bunny's apelike figure.

"He won't hurt you, kid." Danny said, grinning. "He's already had his dinner today."

Danny turned and shouted down the passage. "Elsie, you got a visitor!" Elsie's slippers could be heard flapping along the dark passage until she appeared.

"Billy! What are you doing here? You should be in Haslemere."

"I can't open the front door," he said, ignoring the question. "I called through the letter box, but mums not in." Billy said, as Bunny opened the door of the Vauxhall.

"Your mum's not there any more love, and its all locked up, so you better come in. I'll get you something to eat and we'll see if we can get you sorted out." Elsie whispered, something to Danny before he got in the car beside Bunny and the car pulled away.

An hour later, as Billy sat at Elsie's table there was a knock at her front door.

"Wait here Billy," said Elsie disappearing down the passage. When she came back in the room she said, "Billy do you remember little George who lived next door to you?" Billy nodded slowly as he looked up into the stern face of a tall man in a black cloak. The man peered down at him from over Nell's shoulder. "Well, this is Father Crowley, he's been looking after little George and now he's going to look after you."

Deborah Webster was seven years old, an only child with doting parents who saw she lacked nothing. However, her childhood had been lonely. Only at school did she have the chance to mix with children of her own age, but even there, her parent's affluence had its affect. Her fellow classmates did not befriend her easily. However, with the arrival of Janice, Deborah felt like she'd been blessed with a sister.

As instructed, Deborah had shown Jan around the grounds while waiting to be called to dinner. The girls now shared a seat in the gazebo at the far side of the grounds.

"Will you still stay here with us even if your brother doesn't come back? I hope you will." said Debbie, pulling an old weather-beaten doll from under the bench seat. Not really wanting to talk, Jan said abruptly,

"I don't know!" Debbie ignored Jan's brash manner, and asked another question while plaiting the doll's hair,

"I suppose Billy will go home to his mother, won't he?" she said. "When he gets to Portsmouth, I mean."

Since being told of the death of her mother, Jan had slept and eaten little. This alone had made her feel physically ill. Now that Billy had run away, she felt that God was punishing her. Martia had told her this so many times and with all that had happened, Jan felt she must have been wicked in some way. She thought about the last argument with her mother over leaving them alone. She remembered telling her that neighbours were calling her a terrace tart. Was this the reason God was punishing her, Jan asked herself? Yet in her own defence, she concluded that she'd only told the truth. She looked down at her thin shabby dress and worn out shoes, and compared them to Debbie's embroidered collar, velvet dress and patent leather shoes.

"He's six!" Jan shouted. "Where the bloody hell do you think he'll go? He'll go home of course, you stupid girl." With that, Jan snatched the doll and threw it. It hit an overhead beam of the gazebo then fell to the floor where its face broke in half. Debbie ran crying towards the house leaving Jan to her own tears and misery.

At that moment, an argument was brewing inside the Webster's drawing room.

"But he's only an infant, Steven," said Delia.

"That's not the point. Look at the way the girl is dressed and the way she speaks. Goodness knows what habits she'll be teaching Deborah even as we speak; now you want her brother here! If only I'd known more about the district they were from. The police certainly knew about the place, when I told them the address. Its a breeding ground for ...well you know!"

"But they're only children. They know nothing of that side of life." It was then that Debbie came through the door, crying.

"Janice called me a bloody stupid girl," she blurted. Steven gave Delia a knowing look.

Janice wanted to get away from the Webster's and return to Portsmouth. All she could think about was finding Billy, with whom she could at least share her misery. She looked about her. High walls surrounding the grounds meant she would have to pass the house to get out. While contemplating her escape, she was suddenly interrupted by a loud and harsh voice from behind.

"Janice!" Delia Webster was angry, and Janice knew why. As Delia approached, Jan instinctively put her arm up to defend herself.

Delia saw Jan's fear and her anger abated. Sitting down beside her, she said.

"I hope you didn't think I was about to hit you!" Jan didn't reply. "We don't do that sort of thing here, and we do not swear, so what was all that unpleasantness about with Debbie?"

"I want to go home," said Jan, avoiding the question. "Please! I want to find Billy."

"Janice, my husband has spoken to the police in Portsmouth. They are looking for him this very minute. We can't let you go chasing about on trains as well, but you can help; the police need to know where he might have gone. Don't worry, they will find him."

"There's only two places that he might go," said Jan "Elsie Craven at number twenty Lyons Terrace, or Nell Masters at number eleven."

"Good. Come on then, let's go ring them again. I'm sure they are quite capable of finding him without the need for you to go traipsing around Portsmouth. Meanwhile, I think some dinner, a bath, and a good night's sleep will make you feel better. Big fat problems always lose weight overnight."

That night, sleep overcame the terrible anxieties that had haunted Jan for the last two days; she slept long into Tuesday. When Debbie came home from school, Jan apologised for swearing at her and the two girls agreed to make a fresh start. That evening the two of them sat playing Draughts, while Jan waited patiently for news of Billy. The phone rang at 8pm; Jan's heart thumped as Mr Webster went into the hall, closing the door behind him. Five minutes later, the door opened and a worried looking Steven beckoned to his wife to join him in the hall. Delia followed him, closing the lounge door behind her.

"The police have found him," whispered Steven. "A Father Crowley has taken him to a Catholic orphanage."

"Poor Janice, now she's really going to be upset. I suppose she will want us to go there and get him back, but why didn't he go home?"

"Well that's not the worst of it! The police said that their mother was killed. Apparently, she was in a public house last Saturday when it was bombed."

Delia covered her open mouth with both hands, then said, "Why didn't Janice tell us. Oh God! Do you think she knows?"

The Webster's returned to the lounge. Janice looked up at them, fearfully expecting the worst.

"We've got some bad news Janice," Delia said.

"They can't find him can they?" said Jan, about to cry.

"Well, they know that he's alright." Jan sniffed back her tears and gained control.

"How do they know?"

"Because they said a priest named Father Crowley has taken him to a Catholic boys home." Steven and Delia waited for Jan to respond. Then for the first time they saw her smile.

"He's with little George, he'll be okay now." Jan said, turning her attention back to the draughts board. Steven and Delia stared at each other, bewildered.

"But there's something else, Janice. And it's more serious. Its about your mother."

"I know what you're going to say," said Jan, jumping two of Deborah's kings. "She's dead."

Billy had sat quietly beside Father Crowley as the little Standard Flying Nine made its way through the city.

"I expect you're hungry Billy, aren't you, with all that dashing about on trains? Never mind. I expect we'll just be in time for some tea. Do you like lardy cake? I think that's what's on the menu today," he said grinning at Billy.

"Will George be there?"

"Who's George?"

"My friend, George Moody."

"Oh yes, I remember, tragic suicide. He's been having trouble at night, shouting in his sleep. The lad has a vivid imagination. I'm not sure if he's still with us, or if he left with the last batch of evacuees. You see, I'm not there all the time Billy, I have my church to look after, but there are a lot of young boys there, maybe your friend George will still be there."

The car stopped at some tall wooden gates set in a ten-foot wall. Over the top of these Billy could see what looked to him like an unwelcoming grey stone building. Father Crowley got out and pushed a button that was set into the wall. He got back in the car and they waited some two or three minutes before a man, also dressed like Father Crowley opened the gates. Billy thought he might have been as tall as Crowley if not for the way he was bent over and the terrible hump on his back. As Father Crowley drove in, he called out through his open window,

"Leave the gate open Michael, I won't be stopping." As the car stopped at the main door of the building, Billy saw half a dozen young faces appear at a window. They stared at him and for a moment, Billy thought he saw George. Then some of them turned their heads and Billy guessed they had been told to get down, as they all disappeared. The gate man hurried up the drive to open Billy's door.

"Hello little one! And what's your name?" the man asked.

"Billy Gough."

"Yes, Billy seems to have lost his way, but I think we can sort him out," said Father Crowley. "This is Father Michael, Billy. He will see that you get cleaned up and fed."

"Yes I will," said Father Michael. "I can see you've been doing a lot of crying laddie. My! He's got beautiful eyes."

"Billy's mother was one of the casualties of last Saturday's raid," said Father Crowley.

"Oh! Well, we'll have to be extra kind to…"

"Is my friend, George Moody here?" Billy interrupted.

"George? Yes George is here. That'll be nice for you both won't it?" Michael said, while practically pulling Billy out of the car.

"Well I've got to go," said Crowley. "Take care of him Michael. I'll see you later." Crowley pushed the gear lever into reverse and the car started to move backward. Suddenly it stopped again and Father Crowley leaned out of his window; in a stern voice he said, "Oh! And Michael, he doesn't need a bath. Just see he has a wash." Father Michael coloured up as he acknowledged Crowley's instruction.

Father Michael led Billy through a maze of corridors only stopping to reprimand one small boy for running, in the corridor. Finally, Billy was led into a cold, bath-come-washroom with a stone floor.

The room was rectangular, measuring approximately twenty feet long by twelve wide. Entry and exit was by one door, this was central at one end of the room. Either side of this, were two locked cupboards. From the doorway, one could see a white ceramic sink set in the far wall. Above it, the only window, this was fitted with obscure glass. To the right of the sink, a draining board that held a stack of small enamel washing bowls. Along the length of the flanking walls were two slate covered shelves, these were held up by several wall brackets, but the room's overbearing presence was the large enamel bath with its huge boiler, this sat squarely in the centre of the room.

"Right now Billy, listen carefully," said the priest. You will use this room to wash each morning. There will be lots of other boys in here, so the quicker you get here when the morning bell rings, the quicker you'll get your breakfast. Take a bowl, fill it half way at the sink then place it on one of the shelves. You can do that now while I get you a towel and some soap." He unclasped a bunch of keys from the belt around his waist and unlocked a cupboard. From it, he took out a small towel and a tiny tablet of soap. "Right, Billy, take this clean towel and soap; you will keep them in the locker by your bed.

You can change the towel once a fortnight on a Friday at which time you can have a new tablet of soap. Now I want you to wash yourself while I find you some clean clothes." The bent-over priest disappeared, leaving Billy to wash his face and hands. He was drying himself when Father Michael came back. "There you are," he said, laying a shirt and a pair of elasticised short trousers on the shelf beside his bowl. "When you've finished, get yourself dressed and then..." The priest's attention suddenly went to the towel Billy used to dry himself. Frowning he said, "Did you do that?"

"What."

"Dirty that towel?"

"I don't know, I might have."

"Might have...Might have!" Billy edged away from the irate priest. "I told you to wash the dirt off, not wipe it off with a clean towel. Come here" he took hold of Billy's ear and pulled him toward the window. Billy cried out with the pain. "Now lets have a look." He scrutinised the back of Billy's ears. "They're absolutely filthy, you are not sitting down to food in that state. Now you had better strip off and I'll see to it that you are washed properly."

Billy wondered what happened to the Father Michael who was going to be extra kind to him. He started to get undressed. As he struggled to get his pullover over his head, the priest moved silently to the door and locked it. "Right, now the shirt and trousers."

"But its cold," argued Billy, though he was more embarrassed than worried about the temperature.

"Well the sooner you get washed, the sooner you get dressed. Come on, get it all off." The priest said, turning on the cold tap and filling another basin in the sink. Billy stripped and piled his clothes on the shelf beside his bowl, then he stood naked and shivering whilst keeping his genitals covered with his hands. "Oh come on boy, you've got nothing I've not seen before," said the priest, lathering his hands in the sink basin. "Come here boy." Billy moved slowly and reluctantly toward him. He pulled Billy in front of him, pushing his head forward over the bowl and forcing his chest against the cold tiled shelf. "That's it Billy now we'll start on your hair." He started to massage the soap first into Billy's hair then down around his ears and neck. Gradually he worked his hands down Billy's naked body and only stopping to add more soap to his hands. The priest's breathing turned to mumbling, while Billy, in his innocence, became more frightened. The priest's hands stopped lathering and his arms held Billy tightly to him. The mumbling became more audible and louder: "Holy Mother of God, Holy Mother of God," Billy was cold, totally confused and covered in lather when the priest finally relaxed his hold and said, "Okay, rinse the soap off and get dressed. The tea bell will be ringing in a minute I'll show you where to go.

Billy had no idea what had just taken place in that washroom. But he was determined that he would not let it happen again.

Father Michael guided Billy to a large dining room where several boys were queuing to be served soup and bread by two more priests. The room consisted of six long tables with twelve places per table. Not all the tables, however, were full. Billy heard a familiar voice calling his name. It was George Moody, his face beaming with the sight of Billy. He beckoned Billy to sit with him.

"Looks like you found your friend," said Father Michael, go on, get your bread and soup, then go sit with your friend. He's saved you a seat."

"What are you doing here Billy? This place is for kids with no mum or dad." George said as Billy put his plate of soup on the table beside him.

"I know. They said my mum got killed, and no one knows where my dad is. Jan's gone to some people in a place called Liphook, but I didn't want to stay there. How come no one here is vacuted,[sic]"

"You mean evacuated, don't you?" came an educated young voice from the end of the table. "Some have been evacuated, but only to make room for more boys. The orphanage has its own underground shelter."

"Tough luck kid," said an older boy, sitting on the other side of George. "I know how you feel, my mum and dad copped it the very first raid. Bleeding Jerry flattened our house. Lucky for me I was in hospital, having me tonsils out."

"This is Ernie Baxter, Billy," said George. "He knows all about this place. He's helped me a lot."

"Hello Ernie," Billy said, smiling at the boy. Billy looked around. Not a boy was eating. "Can we start yet?"

"No, not before grace."

"When does she start?" said Billy seriously. Both Ernie and George laughed out loud.

"Shh quiet now," said the priest who served Billy with his soup. "Father Clive will say grace." A little man, whose face was red with spots, stood at the end of a table and recited from a book; he then led all the boys into the Lord's Prayer. As the prayer finished, the boys tucked into their bread and soup as though it was a week since they'd last eaten.

"Yeah, I know all about the pervies in this place too," said Ernie." You'll soon find out, kid," said Ernie, finishing his soup. Then in a discreet whisper- "Like old humpty Michael, who just brought you in. You don't want to let that dirty old sod get you alone. 'Ere! He didn't bath you when you came in did he?"

"No, but he twisted my ear. Then he washed me after I'd already done it myself."

"Well, if that's all he did, you were lucky. Don't let the dirty bastard lock himself in the bathroom with you."

"Why?"

"Just don't, that's all."

"Yeah, and Ernie, tell him about spotty Clive," said George.

"Oh don't encourage him George." The perfect enunciation came again from the small boy at the end of the table, who had corrected Billy's attempted: *evacuation*. "You know how he exaggerates, and he'll only get these young chaps into trouble." Billy was fascinated by the boy's diction. The boy appeared to be about his own age. He wore a smart maroon school blazer with gold piping around the lapels and his, almost silver, hair was parted neatly on one side.

"Oh listen to la-de-da Cuthbert," said Ernie. "Maybe they don't try it on with you, because your mummy knew someone important and they're afraid you'll go blabbing your mouth off. Or maybe they've already tried it on with you and you liked it, you little ponce!" The boy blushed and did not pursue the matter.

"Nothing to tell about old spotty really," Ernie went on. "Except that he's always playing with himself under that cassock. Anyway, you just got to watch yourself around these blokes, Billy. If he's wearing one of those long black dresses, watch your arse cause he's probably a pervie."

"What's a pervie?"

"You know, Billy. A pervert," said George, having already become wiser since entering the orphanage.

"Oh!" Billy said, pretending to understand, because they made him feel that he should.

"But they've all got long black dresses on!" Billy observed.

"Yeah, now you're learning kid," said Ernie. "Just try not to get caught in a room on your own with any of them. I reckon Crowley's the only straight one amongst them." Ernie could see by Billy's frown that he still didn't fully understand the implications of his warnings.

Two weeks later Sister Cathleen Masters entered Henry Gough's ward to find a new patient occupying his bed. Surprised and worried, she questioned the duty nurse. The nurse shrugged, saying,

"They told me he'd been moved, that's all I know," Cathleen immediately went in search of Dr Colwell.

"Have you a personal interest in the patient, Sister?" the Doctor said, surprised at the amount of concern Cathleen showed.

"Yes, I suppose I have in a way Doctor. You remember I said he seemed familiar."

"Yes."

"Well his name is Henry Gough, he lives in the same street as my mother and he has two children."

"Oh well, that's a bit of luck. I thought we knew nothing about him. Is there a wife? Has she been notified?"

"That's the problem Doctor. She was one of the casualties in Saturday's air raid."

"Oh God! Can this fellow's luck get any worse? Yes, Saturday was a terrible day for this city."

"And his two children were evacuated on Monday. Until he can tell us if he has any other family I think someone should be looking out for him and his children."

"Ah, now, that presents a problem doesn't it?"

"No, not really Doctor. My mother is trying to find out where his children have been sent. If I know which ward he's in, I'll keep an eye on him. Then as soon as he's well enough to…"

"That's what I meant by a problem, Sister. He's been moved to another hospital. We believe he has a blood clot and we are not equipped to treat it. We've transferred him to a hospital more equipped to deal with his problem. I think his chances are very slim. Even if they manage to disperse the blood clot, there's always a risk of some brain damage. Either way I think he'll need a long convalescence. Goodness me, this chap has certainly had his share of bad luck, toes shot off, wife killed in the Blitz! But I suppose having you to worry about him is some consolation, especially as it's purely platonic." Doctor Colwell tilted his head to one side and gave a wry smile, saying, "It is purely platonic, isn't it, Miss Masters?"

"Of course," Cathleen said, turning slightly red.

"In that case, he's gone to London's Albert General, just off Albert Square. If you come to my office later today, I'll give you the phone number."

"Bloody hell! Not you again," Elsie Craven stood with her arms folded glaring down at Nell Masters from her doorstep. "That's twice in one year you've knocked my door. People will start to talk if we're not careful. What do you want now?" Nell tried to ignore Elsie's cold reception,

"You *do* know about Martia being in the Blue Anchor when it was hit?"

"The whole bleeding street knows about it, so what?" Stunned by Elsie's lack of compassion, Nell answered,

"Well, it was Janice and Billy I was concerned about. You said you were going to see them off on the morning train and I wondered if you could let me have the addresses they've been sent to?"

"No, I've got no idea," Elsie lied. "Matter of fact I got up late. When I called to take them to the station, they had already left. Far as I know, the girl went to some family in Liphook and the boy was going on to Haslemere. You could nip round to their school and ask their teachers. But I really wouldn't know."

"You don't really care very much either, do you?"

"What do you mean by that?"

"You were supposed to be her friend, you practically lived in her house, yet to listen to you now, it's as if you hardly knew her. You promised to look after her kids, You promised to see them on the train. And even knowing they've lost their mother, you couldn't be bothered to drag your tired arse out of bed to see them off. What kind of woman are you?"

"One that minds her own bloody business. So why not take a leaf out of my book and shove off." With that, Nell had the door slammed in her face.

Elsie Craven had barely reached her living room, when there was another knock at her door. Her anger mounted as she stormed back along her passage, ready to give Nell a blazing mouthful. She swung the front door open and was shaken to see, not Nell, but two different, yet familiar figures standing there.

"Oh…Mr Davage! I thought it was someone else."

"Yes, we just caught the end of it as we got out of the car. And it's Inspector Davage when I'm on official business. This is my assistant, Sergeant Nolan. I assume you don't get on too well with Nell Masters?"

"You could say that, do you know her then?"

"Yes from many years ago. She's a very nice lady. But that's not why I'm here. Can we come in? I'm sure you don't want the neighbours hearing our business."

Elsie led them into the front room where she made herself comfortable in an armchair. Davage chose one facing her, while Nolan stood in the doorway.

"OK fire away, what's it all about?" With regard to intellect, Elsie had a low opinion of Davage. She believed that in a battle of wits, she would win every time, hence, she in no way felt afraid or intimidated by him at that moment.

"Finger prints," Davage blurted, while looking for some reaction from Elsie, but there was none. She simply raised her eyebrows as if waiting for him to elaborate.

"Mrs Moody"?

"She wasn't married." Elsie said, without emotion.

"Not important. What is, is the fact that we have a problem over fingerprints and the chair that she presumably climbed on to, to do the deed." This did surprise Elsie, although she was careful not to show it. She remembered carefully wiping the chair from top to bottom and then, only touching it with a cloth when laying it on its side in the passage. Maybe, she'd not been quite careful enough.

"Well I was very friendly with the girl, I was always popping in for a cuppa you know. There's bound to be some of my fingerprints on things in there," Elsie said, scratching the back of her hand.

"Yes, that's what we thought, yet there was no prints found on that particular chair. Oh, we found other prints around the place but they didn't concern us, at least not at the time. It was just that chair I was interested in. Don't you see? It doesn't make sense; how could she have carried it without leaving prints? We couldn't find even one."

"Well, you're the detective," she answered derisively. Elsie was now picking at the little scabs on the back of her hand, and they had started to bleed. "What do you make of it?"

"What do I think, you ask!" said Davage pausing to comically peer over both of his shoulders as if someone might be listening. He then leaned forward, his expression serious and his face only inches from Elsie's, he said, "I think the poor girl was murdered."

For the first time, Elsie was frightened. She knew Davage suspected that she had something to do with Helen Moody's death and she knew that his intention was to frighten her into letting something slip, but she was determined to stay alert and on her guard. She saw him staring at her hand, which was now visibly bleeding.

"That's a nasty habit you've got, Elsie. You should put something on that! Anyway, do you want to hear why I think she was murdered?"

"Have I got a choice?" Elsie said, trying to appear calm and disinterested.

"As a matter of fact, yes. You could come clean and tell us what you know."

"Well as I know nothing, I'm sure your story will be much more interesting," Elsie said, brazenly keeping up the sarcasm.

"OK," said Davage, grinning at Nolan and rubbing his hands together as if enjoying himself.

"Well, I said that we found other fingerprints, but these were not on the chair. No, that had been wiped clean. Big mistake! That was the first thing that made me suspicious. But they were every where else, doors, tables even on door handles, where only Helen Moody's fingerprints should have been. Then there was the rope. Do you remember I mentioned engine-oil being on the rope? Now there's not too many cars owned by people in this street, is there sergeant?"

"Not a one sir." Nolan seemed pleased that he eventually had something to say.

"Yet," Davage continued, "when the people in this street were questioned, it's amazing how many mentioned a black Vauxhall that is always parked outside your door. We know who owns it, we know who drives it and both of them are on record. Now then, are you sure you don't want to come clean?" Elsie stared out of the window, and refused to speak. "OK. Well, it gets better," Savage went on. "We're pretty sure one, or both of these men murdered Helen Moody. We don't know why they did it, but we think they were working for you and we know that you started running your sordid little business even before your husband died. Maybe she owed you money or was holding out on you or something, I don't know. Anyway, having got this far I still wasn't sure we had you. Some clever barrister might have got you all off. But then guess what? Another body turns up. Where! I hear you cry? Under the rubble of a pub called the Blue Anchor, no less. Nothing surprising about that, you might say; quite a few died that day, but you'd be wrong."

Elsie stood up with this last remark saying. "Would you both like a drink? Oh no, you're on duty aren't you. Oh well I think I will." She went to a cabinet and poured herself a large whisky. Davage noticed how her hands were shaking as she sat back down.

"You know Elsie, I must admit," Davage went on. "If this was your idea, you would have done well in the Force. If it hadn't been for a stroke of bad luck you might have got away with it, but a newspaper printed all the names and photos of that Saturday's casualties. Any photos that they couldn't get from the bereaved families, they took at the morgue, and you'll not believe this." At this point, Davage gave a little giggle. "A sailor, who had seen the photo's in the newspaper, walks into his local police station with a copy of the paper and a couple of his own wedding photos, pictures taken hours after the Portsmouth air raid, after the Blue Anchor was flattened, taken miles away on a station platform and guess who's behind the happy couple looking out of the train window? Yes, you guessed it." Davage said joyfully. "Danny Clark and a ghost by the name of Martia Gough."

Lyons terrace once again thronged with kids and inquisitive turban-headed women.

They stood in little groups staring at the Riley Pathfinder slowly driving past them. Only one face registered with Elsie Craven as she stared forlornly out of the back window, It was the smiling face of Nell Masters.

At the Craven trial, as it become known, all four members of the gang were charged with the murder of Martia Gough. Three were found guilty of manslaughter and received various terms of imprisonment. Of these, Elsie, deemed the leader, received the harshest sentence of ten years as she was said to be the only one with murderous intent. However, it was generally believed that the tragic loss of her husband and son had a strong influence on the judge when passing sentence. Danny received seven years and Sandy, four. In real time, it could be argued that Bunny received the longest sentence, as he was sent to a high security psychiatric hospital for an indefinite period.

As Danny was taken down to the cells, he passed the grinning face of Inspector Davage. Danny grinned back at him.

"Don't look so bleeding smug, Davage. I can do a little stretch like this, standing on my head. I'll be out in no time."

"Oh I do hope so Danny," Davage said, widening his grin. "Because I've still got this other body of Helen Moody and the matter of an oily rope to sort out."

Nine months had passed since the trial and Nell was going through a depressing time. She had not seen, or heard a word from Alfie, and she was starting to wonder if his wife, Brenda, had talked him out of the divorce, or if he'd had second thoughts about renewing their relationship. She even wondered if it was because she had not shown enough enthusiasm on their last encounter. Cathleen hardly visited her lately, since she was spending so much of her spare time travelling to visit Henry who was still comatose. On one occasion, Cathleen came to visit and remarked how miserable Nell seemed.

"Get a phone put in mum," she said. "It isn't as though you can't afford one. Then we can at least have a chat when you're feeling a bit low."

It was now Sunday. Nell had always found Sundays to be her most depressing day of the week, however, today was especially so. It was her birthday and almost 3 o'clock. Nell was sure Cathy had forgotten her. Cathy had not even mentioned her birthday. Usually it was: I'm taking you out for a meal, mum, or, I've got tickets for a show, but this year, not even a card. No, she must have forgotten. She stood looking at the black shiny new object on her hall table. "A lot of bloody good you are," she voiced, giving the phone a quick flick with a duster. As she did, it rang. Startled, she picked it up and a voice said,

"Hello Mum? Look I'm ringing to ask you a favour."

"Where are you?"

"I'm at the hospital. I had to work this weekend. But I'll be home at my flat about four. I wondered if you could come round and give me a hand."

"To do what?"

"Put up some new curtains. I bought them yesterday. You know what I'm like with that sort of thing: hopeless. Could you come round about five? That'll give me a chance to get settled in."

"Yes…alright."

"Thanks mum."

Nell heard Cathleen's receiver click. "That's it! Nell thought, she's definitely forgotten, something she's never done before. But then that was before Henry came on the scene. It's the first time she's really had someone else to think about. Never mind, at least I'll have some company today."

Nell arrived at Cathleen's apartment two minutes early.

"Thanks for coming mum," Cathy said, kissing Nell on the cheek. "You know how useless I am when it comes to décor. Go on through mum, I'll show you the material I've chosen. Are you OK? You don't seem very happy." Nell entered Cathy's living room and let out a gasp. There, at a candle lit table, laden with food and gift-wrapped parcels, sat Alfie Button.

"Happy birthday Mum," Cathy hugged her mother while Alfie held out a bunch of flowers,

"Happy birthday Nell,"

Nell tried wiping her tears away with the back of her hand while at the same time laughing at her own embarrassment "Take no notice of me," she said. "It's just that I really am happy."

Nell's spirits were lifted that night, to a height they'd not reached for some time, and as the evening drew to a close Alfie pulled a final parcel from under the table.

"Oh, not another present Alfie, now you really are spoiling me."

"Well this one is really for both of us Nell," said Alfie, "and it poses a question." Nell looked puzzled, she looked at Cathleen, who failed to hide her amusement as she said,

"Go on, open it mum, I'm as excited as you are. He hasn't told me what it is either."

Nell pulled the ribbon and the brown paper partly unfolded. Nell had no need to open it further; she could see the word "Decree" at the top of the paper.

"You're divorced? Oh Alfie, I am pleased. So what was the question?" Nell said, glancing at Cathy's grinning face.

Alfie took hold of Nell's hand and said.

"Nell, will you marry me?"

Billy and George had rearranged their beds in the dormitory so they could be together.

One night, Billy whispered across to George a question that had been troubling him for some time.

"George...did it really happen, or was I dreaming?"

"Yes," George answered, needing no confirmation as to what Billy was referring.

"And you've not told anyone?"

"No. Have you?"

"No."

"Good, I don't want to wake one night with him looking at me. Do you remember what he did that night and how he warned us?"

"Yes," Billy whispered, recalling the last night he spent at George's house. George had been so frightened that night. He'd pleaded with him to leave his bed and go sleep with him next door. At first he'd refused, being afraid that his mother might discover him missing, not to mention his own fear of the men who were frightening George. But he couldn't sleep. He felt bad about refusing to help his friend. Billy opened his window again and threw a crayon at George's window. George had quietly let Billy in the front door, but neither of them could sleep through the noise going on downstairs. Billy remembered how they had crept out onto the landing and peered over the banister. That's when they first saw the monster, the great bull-necked man with a rope. The commotion downstairs had ceased and they watched the monster patiently untangle the rope. Needing somewhere to tie it, he suddenly looked up. George and Billy were watching him and could not move back fast enough. They'd been discovered, but the rope man just grinned at them. He put his fore finger to his lips signifying silence. It was almost like he was playing a game, until his expression changed. He then frowned at them and drew the same finger across his throat. The two boys were in no doubt as to his meaning. They had raced back to George's bed and pulled the covers over their heads. Later, when all sounds in the house had ceased, they made a pact never to tell what they had seen.

For the next three years, Billy lived and schooled at the catholic orphanage. He took heed of the older boys advice. In many respects he gained a better knowledge of the real world than if his misfortune had not placed him there. He learnt to evade the sexual deviants: men who masqueraded as God's messengers behind their black cassocks. He learnt to distinguish the difference between a priest's smile that said, I love you boy, as God intended, and one that emitted a hidden warning of: Billy, don't get caught alone with this man. To a large degree, it helped that Billy and George were practically inseparable; they learnt that there was safety in numbers. Unfortunately, the dark of night rendered them defenceless.

It was 1945 and the two boys were nine when, for some reason unknown to Billy, George became very distant and morose. He would shut himself away for hours, shunning Billy's company. This went on for some weeks. Then he suddenly announced to Billy that he was going to a foster home and within a few days George was gone, leaving Billy sad, lonely and somewhat confused.

"What's up with you kid?" Ernie said to Billy one day at the breakfast table. "Don't tell me, you're miffed cause George is gone, right?"

"Yes, and I don't know why he wanted to leave."

"I thought he would have told you."

"What do you mean? Told me what?"

"That's just the trouble, I don't know. But I bet it had something to do with that new maths teacher, Father Mead." Just as Ernie spoke his name, the priest walked behind him.

"What about me, Baxter. You were saying?"

"Oh, nothing sir. I was just saying that you seemed to like it here."

"Well less talking, just eat your breakfast." Ernie waited until the priest had moved on.

"Yes, it was something to do with him," said Ernie jabbing a thumb over his shoulder. "George was frightened of him, but he wouldn't say why. Thought he might have told you though?"

"No, but I know George never liked maths; he wasn't very good at it. Mead was always picking on him. You know, making him look silly."

"Yes, but it was more than that. He was definitely frightened of the bloke. I watched his face whenever Mead got near him. George never wanted to go to a foster home before Mead came here. He always played up when people came to see him, you know, to put them off taking him. No, something happened to make him want to leave, and I'm wondering if Mead is another pervie. If he is, he'd better not try it on with me."

"What would you do, Ernie?" Ernie leaned towards Billy, cupped a hand round Billy's ear and whispered. He then sat back saying;

"I promise you, he'd never try it again."

Billy made other friends in the home but Ernie was the closest, despite their age difference of three years. Ernie taught Billy to be not only street wise, but life-wise too. He'd take Billy out with him to the pictures or to Southsea's beach where, on warm days, he taught Billy to swim in the sea.

It was after a day's swimming that Billy had the dream, a dream that turned into a nightmare. In it, he and Ernie were swimming off Southsea beach. Billy had swum out to the limit of his safe depth when he saw something floating a few yards farther out. Curiosity triumphed over fear and he swam towards it. He could hear Ernie shouting to him to come back but he had to see what it was and it was only a few more feet away. Then the object of his curiosity was there, all around him, just a mass of floating seaweed. He laughed holding up a handful to show Ernie, but as he did he could feel the slimy vegetation closing in on him, touching his legs, wrapping itself around his arms. He tried to pull it off, but pulling it in one place only tightened it in another. It started to close in around his neck and shoulders. Then his arms wouldn't move. The slimy weed was wrapping itself around his face, covering his mouth so that he couldn't speak, or call out for help. He could see Ernie, frantically swimming toward him but he was too far away.

Suddenly Billy awoke with the substance of his dream taking on a different form. It was dark and his eyes were slow in adjusting. Billy guessed it was the middle of the night. He was being carried through corridors, dimly lit by night-lights. His abductor held him so that his arms could not move. He tried to protest but something covered his mouth. He struggled but his abductor ignored him. It was Father Mead. Billy now understood why his nightmare seemed so real. They were now at the bathroom door. Mead was a big man but he struggled to open the door while still holding Billy's arms. Now they were inside, Mead locked the door and stood Billy down on the cold stone floor. Steam came from the bath and Billy could see that it had been filled. Billy tried to pull the plaster from his mouth but Mead slapped him hard across the chest, sending Billy sprawling on the floor and hitting his head on the bath. Mead helped him to stand up. Billy wanted to cry out, his eyes were heavy with tears. His hand automatically went up again to pull the plaster off, this time Mead slapped his face.

"Listen, you little bastard," Mead said. "That's just a taste of what you'll get if you make a sound when I take that plaster off. Now I'm not going to hurt you as long as you behave yourself. We're just going to take a little bath together, now there's no harm in that is there? Your little friend George and I did it lots of times, but you mustn't tell anyone do you understand?" Billy nodded, while trying not to cry. "Right, now get the pyjamas off." Billy did as he was told while Mead tested the water temperature, but all the time Billy's mind was actively planning. Mead carefully pulled the plaster away from Billy's mouth, picked Billy up and stood him in the bath. Billy's eyes went to the door as the priest stepped out of his sandals. Then Mead did a strange thing, he pulled his cassock up above his knees and stepped into the bath facing his little captive. Mead looked down at Billy, smiled then pulled the black gown up over his head, for a moment his head and arms were enfolded within the garment.

This was Billy's moment. The one chance he was likely to get. Ernie's whispered words came back to him, "He'd never try it again." Billy's hand suddenly shot out grabbing Mead by the scrotum, Billy squeezed without mercy. The priest's screams carried through the corridors, waking both teachers and boys alike. Mead fell backwards out of the bath careering into the heavy slate covered shelf as he fell. The shelf supports broke away, bringing the shelf crashing down on top of him. The few sound sleepers that were not awoken by Mead's screams, were now awake. Billy jumped out of the bath and quickly gathered up his pyjamas and a towel. He could hear a commotion in the corridor and before Mead could recover, Billy had unlocked the door.

Several boys were stood outside in their pyjamas, when the staff started arriving. Some were rubbing the sleep from their eyes while others stood watching in bewilderment as the near-naked figure of Father Mead writhed in agony on the bathroom floor.

Father Crowley sat in his office. He stared across his desk, frowning at Mead as he waited for the maths teacher to be seated. Mead no longer wore the cassock but sat there in grey flannel trousers, sports coat and an open necked shirt. His eyes darted about the room, unable to look Father Crowley in the eye except for fleeting moments.

"You're an evil man Mr Mead," said Father Crowley. You betrayed my trust, you betrayed the boys in this orphanage and you betrayed the church." Mead shifted about in his chair and adjusted the sling on his arm, but said nothing. "However, if any good has come out of this matter, it is that you have taught me a lesson. I have been naïve; a home full of small boys to a predator like you, is like jam to a wasp. I also believe there are others of your kind here in the orphanage. In time I will root them out and like you, I will see to it that they never work around young children again. I have arranged any money's due to you, to be made up. Collect it from the secretary on your way out and do not go near the boys' dormitory."

Three weeks later Billy was called to Father Crowley's office. Billy walked in to see a plump and jolly-faced woman sitting beside his desk.

"Ah! Billy," said Father Crowley. "I'd like you to meet Mrs Cole."

A month later, near the village of Liphook, some twenty-five miles away, Delia Webster quickly dried her eyes as she heard the front door slam shut.

"Hello, darling I'm home."

Delia heard the kitchen door open and close, then the lounge door opened. "Ah, there you are. I thought you were out when you didn't answer." Steven Webster kissed his wife on the cheek. "You're usually in the kitchen when I come home. Smells good whatever it is you're cooking. Where are the girls?"

"Debbie stayed at school for netball practice and Jan's in her room."

"Oh, well I'll just go and wash up for…say, have you been crying?"

Delia knew there was no point trying to hide what was troubling her. "Oh Steven, I've got this awful feeling we're going to lose her."

"Who, Jan? Why, what do you mean?"

"I'm not sure but when I came home I found her sitting on her bed. She had that little box opened." Steven looked perplexed. "You know, that evacuation box she brought with her when she arrived."

"Yes, I remember."

"Well she had a few photos in it and she was just staring at them especially the one of her little brother. Steven, her face was wet with tears and I think she was on the verge of running away."

"Oh I'm sure you're over-reacting, don't worry, Dee, I'll have a word with her. I'm sure she's happy here."

"Yes I thought she was until today, but apparently a girl at her school had overheard her parents talking about some newspaper story. Apparently, there's been some abuse going on, at an orphanage in Portsmouth. She's worried about her brother."

Steven said nothing for some moments but appeared to be deep in thought. Then he said,

"I suppose this Billy would be about eight or nine now, wouldn't he."

"Yes," Delia said, in anticipation. She was remembering when Janice first arrived, when she suggested to Steven that they might foster Jan's brother. The discussion had ended in a terrible row and the subject had not been mentioned since.

"Well," said Steven with the corners of his mouth showing a hint of a smile. "Do you think you can handle a nine year old boy?"

Delia flung her arms around his neck and kissed him with a passion she'd not shown him for some time. She then ran to tell Janice the news.

Part Three
23
Three plus one make friends

The three children were charged with excitement, as was often the case when in each other's company.

The two boys, Barry: six and Luke, not yet five, pressed their noses against the heavy steel mesh that formed the side barriers of the railway footbridge, while Dorothy, Luke's nine-year-old sister, had climbed up to look over the bridge's side structure to get a clearer view of Fratton's freight yard.

The bridge was located at the end of a short alley, off Walmer Road, where the children lived. The bridge was not a public right of way, but was specifically built for railway workers to access the freight yard. But the children lived only yards away from the bridge, and it had become a special kind of meeting place for them.

July's weather, so far, was all one could have wished for; the afternoon sun smiled on the three war babies, and the day was just starting to lose the hot stickiness of an ongoing heat wave. There was Barry, conspicuous by his silvery blonde hair and empty left sleeve, and Luke, the youngest, always noticeable by his grubby white sun hat. Luke had not yet lost his infant puppy fat despite knowing hunger and being the youngest of a large and poor family.

The two boys were looking pensively down at the steam engine below them.

It stood motionless, hissing and puffing, to Barry's imagination, getting its breath back from pulling a heavy load of freight trucks.

Luke huddled close to Barry, his chubby face turned toward him watching his expression, for he knew it would tell him when the excitement was about to start.

Suddenly there came a loud clank from below and the man in the black cap started to walk toward the front of the engine.

Barry turned his head slowly toward Luke, whose smile grew wider, for he knew the routine so well. Then, for the third time that morning and in his best mystery voice, Barry whispered in Luke's ear.

"It's coming!"

"Doffy, it's coming!" Luke shouted, jumping to his feet while putting his own interpretation to his sister's name.

Dorothy unhooked her bare toes from the steel mesh, while her thin arms lowered her down onto the wooden floor of the bridge.

It was common to see Dorothy without shoes; Barry thought it was her choice, but then he had little knowledge of poverty. And unlike Dorothy and Luke, Barry had not known what it was like to go hungry. Only friends were important to him. The truth was, Dorothy had one pair of shoes and they had to be kept for school. Now and again on cold days, she could be seen wearing an old pair of button-up plimsolls. These were usually too large as they would always be hand-me-downs from an older sister, of which she had three. Luke was the younger of her two brothers, Spencer being twenty, the eldest.

It was the start of the summer holidays and the July sun had warmed the wooden floorboards of the bridge, so consequently wearing shoes, to Dorothy, were an unnecessary accessory.

Quickly she joined the others. Then she noticed the open safety pin attached to Barry's shirtsleeve, and the empty sleeve hanging loose.

She pulled him toward her.

"How many more times do I have to do this, you'll have to ask your mum for a new pin, Barry." Taking hold of the empty sleeve Dorothy started to pin it up high against his shoulder.

"Hurry up, it's coming," said Barry anxiously." Dorothy finished the task just in time to see the engine shunt slowly beneath them. Great billows of warm steam gushed upward through gaps in the oak boards and side grating, surrounding the three children with a warm and pleasant dampness. Excitedly, Luke ran to and fro, trying to catch handfuls of the magic mist before it disappeared, as sadly, it always did. Dorothy and Barry, meantime, ran to see the engine emerge on the other side of the bridge.

Strategically, Portsmouth had been an obvious target throughout the war, and it had been hit hard by German warplanes. Even the little footbridge on Walmer Road, carried the scars; evidence that the Fratton freight yard as well as the Naval Dockyard had been on Germany's hit list.

Luke ran his tiny hand over some rounded blisters that protruded on one of the bridge's steel uprights.

"What these is for, Barry?" Luke's vocabulary was not exactly incomprehensible, but sometimes got a little jumbled.

"Bullet holes!" his sister intervened, with an air of cockiness.

"That's silly," said Barry. "They're not holes, they're bumps!" Barry tried constantly to prove Dorothy wrong in all matters.

"Yes but they were made by bullets," she argued while using the said bumps as a foothold to climb back up to her resting place. "You can ask my dad. He say's the roof in the engine shed are full of bullet holes from the German planes, and he should know, because that's where he works" argued Dorothy and to Barry's further annoyance, finishing her sentence with "So there!"

Luke had lost interest, and not knowing what they were talking about anyway, he had gone to the far end of the bridge and was currently exercising his own form of exercise; this was to bend over with his hands on the floor and look through his legs at the world from an upside down view. He was currently looking at his sister and Barry through his chubby legs. The large patch in his ill-fitting short trousers was starting to come away and bare skin could now be seen; not that it bothered Luke. Just as he was deciding which way up his two playmates looked best, he saw a new face appear above the top step of the bridge. Standing upright and replacing his fallen hat, He viewed the intruder from a more familiar aspect. It was a young boy holding a small book and a pencil; the boy appeared not to notice the presence of the other children, but stopped a few yards from Barry and Dorothy who had not yet noticed him. They were preoccupied with their ongoing argument about bullets and German planes.

With pencil poised over his open book, the young boy peered out toward the maze of converging railway lines.

Luke skipped the length of the bridge past Dorothy and Barry to stop close to the newcomer. Shyness was not one of Luke's failings, so grinning up at the boy, he said,

"What you doing?"

"Collecting train numbers!" The boy answered, looking down at Luke's smiling face.

The sound of voices caught Barry and Dorothy's attention. Dorothy climbed down and the two of them sidled up to where Luke and the boy stood.

"What for?" Luke persisted, scuffing his sandal to and fro on the floor.

"Don't see the point of that," interrupted Dorothy in a mocking tone.

The boy shrugged his shoulders, refusing to be goaded by her manner.

"What are you called?" Luke said. The boy frowned at the infant while decoding this strange order of words.

"He means what's your name!" Barry explained. The boy hadn't time to answer before Dorothy broke in with,

"I know all about him! He's that new boy. He lives over the road from my house." Then to the boy, "you came from an orphanage didn't you? I even know your name, it's Billy!"
Barry and Luke stood gawking at the newcomer. The boy's clothes, together with his frail stature, showed the same degree of poverty as Dorothy and Luke's. An elasticised belt with an "s" shaped buckle held up baggy short trousers. His shirt appeared too large and was badly frayed about the collar and the buckles of his worn brown sandals had been sewn on with black thread.

However, to Barry, these details faded into insignificance as it occurred to him that this boy could be described as pretty and that wasn't right, only girls were meant to be pretty. Even his black eye, which looked quite swollen, could not detract from his good looks. His pale skin complemented curly black hair, and long dark lashes canopied his light blue eyes. As he studied him, a story sprang to Barry's mind and he imagined Billy holding out an empty bowl, while asking for more porridge.

"You live with Mrs Cole, don't you?" Dorothy's words were more of a statement than a question. "How old are you?"

"Nine!" The boy responded reluctantly for the first time to Dorothy's unfriendly barrage of questions.

"You're going to be in my class after the holiday! I saw Mrs Cole talking to my teacher before the holiday started. You live with Mrs Cole and I know you got that black eye from fighting with Ginger Griggs up the rec. (*recreation ground or park*) You *do* live with Mrs Cole don't you?" Dorothy pressed the question again, while Barry could not understand why she was being so sharp and unfriendly.

"I know Mrs Cole!" Barry said, wanting to alleviate the discomfort that he could see on Billy's face. "She lives just along from my house. Is she your Gran?"

"Well... not really." Billy said, looking sheepish.

Dorothy chased the subject. "You're a foster boy, aren't you? My mum say's Mrs Cole is always taking in foster kids; she only does it for the money."

Luke tugged at his sister's thin dress, "What's a foster boy Doffy," he asked. Barry looked at her with the same inquisitiveness, but glad that he didn't have to ask.

"They're kids that got no mum or dad, and the people that look after them are called foster," she said smugly.

"So why is Mrs Cole called Mrs Cole," said Barry, trying to take Dorothy down a peg for her know-it-all manner. This started another argument between the two of them until Barry noticed that Billy had returned to his train watching position and stood with his back to them.

"Is that true Billy? She says you got no mum," said Barry hoping Dorothy would at least be proved wrong about something. Billy didn't answer. Dorothy went over to him. Billy's head was bowed and his forehead rested against the grating.

"Are you deaf?" Dorothy snapped. Still, Billy did not answer, but turned away from her. Barry and Luke stood behind her. Then Dorothy took Billy by the shoulders and spun him round. Dorothy's tone immediately changed. "Are you crying?" she asked quietly. Billy sniffed back a tear without answering. "Was it me, because of what I said?"

Barry stood quietly looking up at him, his safety pin had come undone again and Luke stood twisting to and fro with outstretched arms, swatting Barry's empty sleeve.

"She's dead!" Billy said sniffing loudly.

Dorothy's ability to feel compassion, could only have been a legacy from some distant relative, for she had been shown precious little by the members of her own family. Spencer was the only one to show her any kindness. Her elder sisters used her to run errands, her mother used her as a nanny for Luke, and her father used her to alleviate his bad temper.

"I'm sorry Billy. My dad is always saying I can't hold my tongue. You can be our friend if you like."

Without Billy having to say anything, Barry knew that Dorothy had worked her magic and that Billy would now be okay.

"Guess what!" she said excitedly turning to Barry and relieving Billy of any further embarrassment. "Spencer said if I run some errands for him tomorrow and Saturday, he'll pay for me to go to pictures. I'll take you if your mum will let you go, Barry."

"She might. What film is it?"

"It's Charlie Chaplin, and it's at the Troxy. He's really funny. What about you, Billy, can you come?"

"I've seen it," he said, gazing down at a train that was about to pass below them. "But I wouldn't mind seeing it again."

"Will Mrs Cole give you the money to go?" Dorothy asked.

"She don't have to, I've got my own money and I can go wherever I like."

Barry and Dorothy looked at each other in surprise. Dorothy thought that Billy's statement was just one of bravado.

"It's one and thrupence, you know!" Dorothy said, like it was a small fortune.

"So! I got lots of money." Billy replied, with an air of cockiness.

"Yes, and I'm the Queen of England."

"Okay then," Billy said, pulling a folded envelope from his shirt pocket. "Bet you haven't seen one of these." Carefully, Billy unfolded the letter inside to reveal a white five-pound note.

Dorothy took a deep breath with her mouth open wide. "Is it real?" she said.

"Course its real," said Billy."

"What is it?" said Barry, who had never seen one."

"It's a five pound note." Billy said proudly. "My big sister sent it to me at the boys home. She said it's to buy some new clothes and a train ticket."

"Wow, said Barry is she rich?"

"No, but I think the people that she lives with, might be."

"Why do you need a train ticket, where are you going?" Barry said.

"I'm going to see her and to meet the people she lives with, and she wrote and said I've got to look smart."

"Well, in that case you can't spend it on pictures, can you? And should you be carrying it about in your shirt pocket?" Dorothy, sounded quite worried that Billy might spend, or lose the precious note.

"Well, it's safer than leaving it where old mother Cole can find it. Anyway, I've got a couple of shillings of my own saved up, so I won't have to spend it."

"How far is it, and when have you got to go?" said Barry.

"It's a place called Liphook and it's not this Sunday, or the next, but the next. So when are we going to the pictures?"

Dorothy was about to answer when Luke pulled at her dress again, pleading.

"And me? Doffy. And me?"

Dorothy crouched down and hugged him; saying, "No love, you're too little. They won't let you in." Luke's bottom lip started to protrude, and Barry expected him to cry, Luke's protruding bottom lip was usually the introduction to a bout of bawling. Dorothy read the sign and before the lip started to quiver,

"But I'll try to get you some of your favourite sweets instead, but only if you're good." This did the trick. The lip receded and the smile reappeared.

Railwaymen had started to cross the bridge, as the afternoon shift was about to start. The three oldest children went on chatting for some time about films they had seen, then Dorothy used the fore mentioned bumps in the steel uprights to climb up to the top girder again, and this brought back the argument about planes and bullets.

Meanwhile Luke saw the familiar shiny black cap of a railwayman appear between them at the end of the platform, then his father's face appeared above the top step. Luke immediately ran towards him.

Each day Jack Vine: Dorothy and Luke's father, would carry his heavy pushbike up the wooden steps of the bridge in order to ride to the engine sheds on the other side. He would often lift Luke onto the saddle and scoot him the length of the bridge, a treat that Luke never tired of.

Lowering the heavy cycle down from his shoulder, Jack Vine stood panting; he was a big man in his early forties. Some women might have considered him handsome. To young Barry, however, the darkness of his features was a symbol of his dark and evil temper, a trait that he'd often seen Dorothy fall foul of.

The three older children had not yet noticed his presence, and before Luke had reached him, Jack Vine's voice boomed out.

"Get down!" The four children looked up, startled.

Dorothy, in an effort to climb down quickly, hitched her thin cotton dress on a jagged piece of grating. The sound of the rip was loud and Barry was sure Dorothy's father had heard it, but either she hoped that he had not, or thought she could evade possible reprisals by distracting her father with a question. She ran toward him saying excitedly,

"Dad, didn't you say these bumps were made by German bullets?" She was still moving forwards when the resounding slap came, the sound echoed the length of the bridge as Dorothy fell backwards banging her head against the side grating, while clutching her burning face.

Barry was disturbed by this brutal act, but Billy had seen this kind of treatment before. He had often seen it used on his sister, and been on the receiving end himself more recently, since being parted from her. Yes, Billy was less distressed or surprised by the event.

After the initial shock of the blow, Dorothy looked at Billy and Barry and as the tears started to flood her large brown eyes; Barry could see the pain and embarrassment on her face. What he could not see was her total feeling of despair, Barry felt a strong impulse to somehow comfort her, put his arm around her, anything to ease her pain.

"I've told you about climbing up there," said her father. "Do you think I like working all hours, just for you to tear up the clothes I have to buy, well?" His eyes blazed as he bellowed the last word, waiting for an answer.

"I'm sorry daddy!" Dorothy sobbed.

Luke stood pounding his father's leg with his tiny clenched fist for making his sister cry.

"Now get indoors, and tell your mother why I've punished you."
With that, he jerked his leg forward viciously. Luke fell heavily on
his back, banging his head and displaying the increasing split in his
shorts. Ignoring Luke's loud wailing, his father added, "Has he torn
those pants since you've been out?"

"No Mr Vine. It's the stitches, they're coming undone" Barry
answered hurriedly, prompted by the vulnerable position of Luke
sitting at his father's feet.

Giving the two boys no more than a glancing glare, Jack Vine
pointed at Luke, saying,

"Get him indoors and tell your mother to fix his pants."

They all stood feeling relief as they watched Jack Vine reach the
far side of the bridge and disappear down the steps.

"We had better go Luke," said Dorothy, picking Luke's hat up
and making little hiccup noises as her sobbing subsided. "I expect
dinner will be ready."

Billy said nothing and Barry was at a loss for words, while
feeling sorry for Dorothy. He knew Dorothy's remark about dinner
was for Billy and his benefit; he had never seen her go into her
house during the day long enough to eat a dinner. On occasions,
he'd knock her front door and wait for her to come out. He would
often hear shouting from inside, and was always glad when Dorothy
appeared, and they could get away from her house. Sometimes she
would come to the door, tearful and embarrassed, saying she was
not allowed out, or she would appear eating a thin slice of jam-
covered bread.

Taking Luke by the hand, Dorothy led him down the oak steps.
Barry and Billy watched Dorothy and Luke until the wretched and
ragged pair turned the corner of the alley and were out of sight.

The two boys resumed their train watching, but it wasn't the
same, not for Barry. Dorothy was his closest friend, and the incident
with Jack Vine had spoilt what up until then had been a happy day.

Billy sat on the floor quietly thumbing through his train book
while Barry stood for a while studying the clanking and buffeting of
the freight trains. He was hoping to see his eldest brother, Claude,
who had just started work in the freight yard, however, Claude did
not appear. Barry became bored and just as he considered going
home, Billy said,

"What happened to your arm?"

Barry shrugged his shoulders "Don't know."

"That's silly, you must know. Everyone's got two arms!"

"Not me. But I will have, soon."

"How's that then? Are you going to grow one?"

"No, silly! They are going to make me one."

"Now who's being silly?"

"I didn't mean a real one. Doctors at the hospital are going to make it. They called it artificial." Then, wanting to change the subject, Barry asked, "Could I collect train numbers?"

"If you had one of these you could," said Billy, flicking the pages of his book. He opened the small paperback. "Look. See all these numbers?"

"Yes."

"Well, when you see a train, it will have one of these numbers on the front. All you have to do is find that number in the book and draw a line under it. That means you have spotted it."

A whistle sounded in the distance and Billy got up. "There's a steam train coming, they're better, because they've got names. And all the names are in this book. If you watch, I'll show you what to do." They watched and waited in silence. Slowly from a bend in the track, appeared the great engine. "Quick, we have to get on the far side of the bridge or we won't be able to see the name. As the train came closer, they counted fourteen coaches.

"Lancelot!" Billy shouted; I haven't got that one." The massive engine passed noisily beneath them. They watched it until the train was far in the distance. "Look, this is what you do." Billy sat down on the wooden decking again with his back to the grating. Barry huddled beside him filled with curiosity. The boy opened the book and ran his fingers down the pages. "There it is, see?" He said pointing to a word while waiting for Barry's response. Barry looked closely at the word. Silently mouthing the letters, he'd got as far as Sir L-a-n-, when Billy pulled the book away to mark it.

"You can't bloody read can you?"

"I can! But you never gave me enough time." Barry said, irritably. "And you shouldn't swear."

"Well it doesn't matter, you could still collect numbers," Billy said, ignoring Barry's rebuke.

"But I haven't got one of those," Barry said, poking a finger at Billy's book.

"Ask your mum to get you one. They're only sixpence."

"Okay, I will, but I've got to ask her for some picture money first."

"Don't expect you'll have much trouble there, your mum looks like she's got lots of money. Have you got any money on you now?"

Barry remembered the change in his pocket from the sweet money his mother had given him that morning. He pushed his hand deep into the pocket of his shorts bringing out two halfpennies. Holding them out for Billy to see, he said.

"Do you know my mum then?"

"I've seen her," said Billy looking at the two small coins in Barry's hand. "That's not enough for a train book," he said with a wry grin "But I know how to make those two halfpennies turn into pennies."

"How?" Barry was intrigued, and fascinated by anything to do with magic; his brother Ramon was always showing Barry card tricks, and making coins appear from behind his ear.

"Come with me," said Billy. Grabbing the two halfpenny coins out of Barry's hand, he jumped up and ran to the far steps of the bridge. On this side, the bridge took a ninety-degree turn before its steps descended to the edge of the track. Barry followed but became worried when they reached the big red notice warning against descending the steps on this side of the bridge.

"What you doing now?" Barry said as he watched Billy peering down the steps. Barry felt uneasy; he hoped he wouldn't be asked to go down those steps. If his brother saw him, he knew he would be in big trouble.

Where they stood was a sacred boundary, never to be crossed. He knew that at the bottom of those steps were the railway lines and all the dangers that went with them. He felt that Billy was about to do something bad and he was wishing Dorothy was there. She would know what to do.

Billy turned to Barry and whispered dramatically,

"We can't let anyone see us, this is against the law and very dangerous. I want you to stay here and keep watch. If anyone comes up the steps at the other end of the bridge, I want you to shout out bloody loud, okay?" Now Barry was worried but at the same time excited.

"Okay," he said, "but why do you keep swearing?"

"Cause I bloody well like it," said Billy, grinning." Then with another quick glance around the corner, Billy ran down the steps.

He had only been gone for a minute but to Barry it seemed an age. He thought about his mother and Dorothy and how they had warned him of the dangers at the bottom of these steps. A train could hit you, Dorothy had told him. Workmen have been electrocuted, said his mother. He peered round the steel upright and down the oak steps. He could see the railway lines but no Billy. He wished he would hurry up, but it was the most exciting time he could remember. He peered toward the street side of the bridge expecting any minute to see a black cap appear above the floor. Barry jumped as someone touched his shoulder, Billy had returned.

"Now we wait," said Billy, seating himself back down on the wooden boards. Barry sat beside him, their backs against the steel grating. Barry was happy that the episode was over, and that he'd made a new friend. He didn't know why Billy had gone down to the railway lines, or what had happened to the coins. But Billy had done what neither Dorothy nor he would have done, and that made Barry proud to be Billy's friend, even if he did swear.

As they sat, Billy took off a dirty grey plimsoll to shake out a stone, he wore no socks and Barry noticed how dirty his feet were, and that his legs were almost as thin as Dorothy's.

"Who's Ginger Griggs?" Barry asked, scrutinising Billy's black eye.

"Just some kid up the park, he fired a catapult and hit a little girl on a swing. I told him I was going to send the police to his house, then we had a fight." Changing the subject Billy then said, "That lady with the white hair is your mum. Her name's Lily, right?"

"Yes, but its not white, its blonde."

"Well it looks white to me!" Billy said as he scrutinised the top of Barry's head. "Ma Cole said your mum's hair came out of a bottle. Is she rich?"

"Don't think so!" Barry said, not daring to ask why anyone should want to keep hair in a bottle, and so settling for a safer question. "How much money does it take to be rich?" he asked, pulling out the safety pin that had come undone again. He then tried stretching his legs out to the same length as Billy's.

"Rich is when you got enough money to buy anything you want. Your mum looks rich." Barry thought for a moment. He had not seen Billy before that day and could not understand how he knew so much about him or his mother.

"You don't know my mum, so there," Barry said, using Dorothy's favourite ending.

"I know lots of things, you live in Walmer Road like me and you live in a house called Sunnyside, you've got two sisters and I know one is called Brenda and you got two big brothers."

Barry was astounded, thinking this boy to be truly magical, but not wanting Billy to have the last word said,

"Well you're wrong, because I've got three sisters, see?"

"Really?"

"Yes, the other one lives in London, her name is Eunice.

"Oh! Well, I didn't do bad though, did I?" After a spell of silence, Barry decided to break it with a question,

"What happened to *your* mum Billy?"

"She's dead!" Billy answered abruptly.

"Was she old then?"

"No."

"How come she's dead then?" Billy sighed as though tired of Barry's questions.

"She was in a place that got bombed," Billy said, never having learnt the truth of the matter. Barry let the horror of Billy's words filter through him for a minute, before asking,

"Haven't you got anyone else? You know, a dad or someone?"

"Only my sister, but she was evacuated to Liphook when my Dad disappeared. She said my dad got killed in the war, but I think the rope-man got him."

"Who's the rope-man?"

"He's an ugly monster that comes out at night and if he gets you, he hangs you up with his rope."

"That's silly. There's no such thing."

"Yes there is cause I've seen him."

"When?"

"I told you. When he took my dad, and another time when he got my friend's mum."

"How come he didn't get you then?"

"I don't know!" Billy snapped. "And I don't want to talk about him any more," Billy said, annoyed that Barry obviously didn't believe him. However, Barry loved stories, whether they were true or not.

"What else do you do, besides collect train numbers?"

"I used to like playing football when I was at the Boys' Home. What about you? What do you like doing?"

Barry had to think for a while. "I like music, I like listening to music on the wireless and singing."

"Can you sing then?" Billy asked.

"Yes. Well my mum likes me to sing. And my brother: Ray, can play the piano."

Billy was about to question Barry further when there came the sound of an engine passing beneath the bridge. As the steam enveloped them, Billy jumped up and dashed across to watch its trucks emerge on the other side. "Now then," Billy said. "When the engine pulls those trucks back on the other line, you keep watch again. OK?"

Barry nodded. They waited patiently for the last truck to clear the points and for the driver to pull the leaver that would send the trucks back on another line. "Get ready," Billy said excitedly.

Barry was not so hesitant this time, but excited that he had an important job to do. The routine was much the same but this time Billy returned more quickly. "Phew, that was close. That driver nearly saw me," Billy panted. "Hold out your hand." Barry did so while Billy held a grubby clenched fist over it and slowly opened his fingers. Barry could hardly believe his eyes. The two copper coins had grown to an enormous size although they did seem somewhat thinner, and one was bent.

"Wow! That is magic," exclaimed Barry.

With that, they looked up to see Dorothy skipping along the bridge toward them, closely followed by Luke, carrying a large red tin bus with passengers painted in its windows. The bus was badly dented and only had three wheels but it was Luke's favourite toy.

"Dorothy look!" Barry shouted, thrusting out his hand with the two flattened halfpennies in it. "Billy did it. He can do magic." Dorothy peered at the two flattened coins in Barry's hand, and showing complete indifference to Barry's monetary revelation, she turned to Billy and with a scowl said,

"Have you been down by those rails?"

"What if I have?" Billy said uncaringly, yet starting to colour up.

"How did you know?" said Barry.

"Oh don't be silly, Barry." Dorothy pointed at the coins in Barry's hand. "How do you think he did that? He put them on the rail for them to be run over by an engine. My Dad said they have caught kids doing that sort of thing before. I hope *you* didn't go down there. Did you!" she said frowning at Barry.

"Course he bloody didn't! I wouldn't let him go down there, what do you take me for?" said Billy.

"Well you best not."

"Yeh, best not!" Luke said, copying his sister's tone of voice, while giving his bus an almighty shove along the bridge.

"And *you* better not go down there again either, or my dad will be over to see Mrs Cole. Is that clear?" Dorothy waited for her words to sink in before saying, "I don't usually tell tales Billy, but this is serious; you could get killed. Don't you know that?"

Billy shrugged his shoulders and climbed up on the girder.

The following Saturday afternoon found Dorothy, Billy and Barry happily making their way along Penhale Rd, heading toward the Troxy cinema.

Billy had on a clean shirt and socks. Dorothy had sewn up the tear in her dress and was looking pretty in her clean white socks and best school shoes.

"I've just got to stop at Mr Banks, a few doors along here," said Dorothy.

"Who's he?" Billy asked.

"The horse-man," said Barry. "Everyone knows that."

"Well I didn't. Has he got four legs then, or does he look like a horse, or what?"

Barry started to laugh, "No silly, he takes people's money when they gamble on horse races."

"Oh! Well, you haven't got money to gamble with, have you?" Billy said to Dorothy.

"Don't be daft, it's for my dad. Anyway, I wouldn't even if I did have the money. My brother is always telling my dad it's a mug's game." They stopped and she knocked the door of a mid-terraced house. The door opened and Dorothy handed an envelope to a miserable long-faced man. The man grunted and closed the door.

"Well, I think I was right the first time." Billy remarked. "He did look like a horse!" This time, they all laughed.

Minutes later Billy stopped to pull some coins from his pocket. "How much are the tickets, Dor?" Billy had now taken to shortening Dorothy's name; something she was even less happy about than his swearing.

"One and thrupence. You *have* got enough I hope?" she said worriedly.

"Yep, and enough for an ice-cream in the interval."

"And me," chipped in Barry. "My mum gave me two shillings!" They continued walking.

"How about you Dor!" said Billy. "Have you got some ice-cream money?" Dorothy was slow answering. "Well! Have you?" Billy persisted.

"Yes, but I don't want one. And don't keep calling me Dor, my name's Dorothy!" she said irritably.

"I've got enough for two, Dorothy, so we can all have one!" Barry said, eagerly.

"I told you! I don't want one." Dorothy was sounding annoyed.

"Show us then," said Billy. "Go on, show us your money, if you say you've got enough." Dorothy stopped and from a little pocket in her dress, she pulled out a small bundle. She unwrapped a little grubby hanky to reveal a shilling piece, a sixpenny piece and thrupenny piece.

"So there," she said, poking her tongue out at Billy. They walked on in silence for some time; Dorothy only spoke to tell Barry off for dragging his empty sleeve along railings as they passed their own school. Dorothy did not appear to be in the best of moods.

"I don't know why your mum don't sew this up," Dorothy said irritably, as she pinned up Barry's shirtsleeve again. "When are you going to get this new arm that you keep on about?"

"I asked my mum that this morning. She said it would be a few weeks."

"Good! Because I'm getting fed up with pinning up this bloody sleeve"

"Wheee! Dor, you swore," said Billy, giggling.

"Oh shut up!"

They reached the end of Penhale Road and turned into the High Street. This was Fratton Road and the Troxy cinema stood on the opposite side of the main road. Before crossing Dorothy stopped at a confectionery shop and as she scanned the sweets in the window, Barry enquired,

"What you doing Dorothy, won't we be late for the film?"

"I thought I might buy some sweets instead of an ice-cream." she said with an air of cockiness.

"That's it!" Billy exclaimed in a loud mocking voice. "That's why you couldn't buy an ice-cream. I remember! You promised Luke some sweets. I'm right aren't I? Why didn't you say so? " Dorothy started to blush until Billy said,

"How many coupons have you got? Dorothy pulled a grubby page of Sweet Coupons from another pocket and before she could open up the crumpled page, Billy snatched it from her hand.

"Come on!" he said. Before they could do or say anything, Billy had disappeared into the shop. They followed him in. Billy was peering into the jars on the counter while the assistant waited for him to make his choice. He turned to Dorothy,

"What sweets does Luke like?" she looked surprised.

"Er, Black Jacks, he likes Black Jacks"

Billy bought the Black Jacks and several other varieties of sweets. Dorothy tried to stop him, saying: "Billy, you haven't got enough money. You won't be able to get into the Pictures." Billy ignored her until he'd spent all but sixpence of his money. Before they left the shop, he asked the lady behind the counter for three extra paper bags.

"Hold these out," said Billy when they were outside. Handing them each a bag, he then proceeded to fill them until he had shared all the sweets evenly, leaving only the bag of Black Jacks. "They're for Luke, you can look after them," said Billy, handing Dorothy the fourth bag. Barry and Dorothy looked at each other, hardly believing what Billy had just done.

"Didn't you want to come to the Pictures then, Billy?" said Barry, knowing that Billy only had sixpence left.

"Sure I did. Still do, that's why I saved my ice-cream money."

"But how…" Billy stopped Dorothy's question short with,

"It's easy! Look, you take Barry in. Get a seat down the front, over by the ladies toilet okay? As soon as the lights go down, you go out to the ladies toilet. In the left-hand toilet is a small window, if it's not open, open it. Then go back to your seat, I'll find you."

Dorothy stood open-mouthed looking at Billy "You mean you're going to bunk in! What if you get caught?" she said, sounding angry.

"I won't, but even if I do, I wouldn't tell them you helped. Don't worry, me and my sister did it all the time."

Reluctantly Dorothy carried out Billy's instructions. Returning from the ladies toilet, she edged past Barry to leave an empty seat on the end of the row. The cinema was in semi-darkness and there were very few patrons; most of these sat in the centre isles. Dorothy and Barry sat where Billy had instructed, on the left-hand side, three rows back from the front. The first film had started, but Dorothy could not forget about Billy and kept glancing toward the drapes that covered the toilet door. What she did not notice, was the man who had moved up behind them from three rows back. Gradually, she became engrossed in the "B" film, until she suddenly realised Billy was sitting next to Barry at the beginning of the row. She glanced back to the rear of the cinema, wondering if any staff had seen Billy enter. Images of policemen knocking at her door to tell her father that she had broken the law, were too unbearable to consider.

Fortunately, there were no usherettes to be seen and Dorothy started to relax.

It was not until after the interval and they had eaten their ice creams that Dorothy noticed that the three of them were not the only occupants of their row, and that a fat man was sitting farther along against the wall. Dorothy could not remember his presence when they came in and she was sure no one had edged past them. She thought that maybe he had arrived when she got up to get their ice creams.

The lights started to dim and Dorothy dismissed all distractions from her mind to enjoy the big film.

Laughter became contagious among the three children as they watched the antics of Charlie Chaplin, until Dorothy felt something brush against her leg. Looking to her left, she was disturbed to see that the fat man had moved up to the seat beside her, she was also aware of his sickly smell of perspiration. His raucous laughter was in accord with the rest of the audience making it first appear to Dorothy that his attention was focussed on the film. But she was far from being a stupid girl and from that moment on, Dorothy could not relax. For her, the film had suddenly lost its humour.

Minutes later she felt a hand on her knee. Without looking in the man's direction, she pushed it away. Charlie had just sat down to make a meal of one of his boots and Billy leaned forward to see if Dorothy, like Barry, was also crying with laughter.

Three times Dorothy pushed the man's hand away, only to feel it return moments later, each time resting higher on her thigh. Dorothy did not want to draw attention to her sickening situation, especially knowing that Billy had not bought a ticket, but she was becoming very frightened.

Roughly, she pushed the hand away for the fourth time, saying, "Would you please stop doing that?" Barry was totally absorbed in the film and unaware of anything going on beside him. The fat man leaned sideways towards Dorothy and whispered,

"I won't tell! I know you helped your little friend bunk in." Dorothy understood this as a threat, yet regardless of this she made up her mind that if the hand touched her again, she would grab it and sink her teeth in it, regardless of the consequences.

Minutes later the hand came to rest on her leg again, but before Dorothy could grab it, the fat mans face seemed to light up. She turned her head to become dazzled by the same source of light: two powerful torches.

Dorothy's eyes slowly adjusted to the light. The first object to materialise was the silver badge on the police officer's helmet, and once again, fear gripped her. Gradually the scene became clear. Holding the second torch was the cinema manager. Billy stood between the two of them pointing in her direction. The policeman's voice boomed out.

"Hello Gerald, up to your old tricks again? Come on lets go. You kids stay there, I'll be back to see you." As the fat man meekly followed his captors up the aisle, Billy pushed past Barry to sit beside Dorothy.

"He's for it now," he giggled in Dorothy's ear.

"What happened," said Barry, who was completely perplexed by the whole episode.

"He was being rude, wasn't he Dor, he was trying to…"

"Shut up Billy, I don't want you to talk about it." Dorothy was on the edge of tears.

"He was though, wasn't he, Dor? I saw him, that's why I went and told the manager."

"But why did that policeman take him away?" Barry persisted.

"Bloody hell Barry, I've just told you, He was a pervy."

"What's that?"

"Oh shut up, both of you!" Dorothy intervened loudly, but she was unable to hide the sob in her voice. Billy detected it.

"He didn't hurt you did he?"

"No, but my dad will, when he finds out, and the police are bound to tell him."

"But you've done nothing wrong. Why should he?"

"You don't know my dad. He'll say it was my fault," she said, while mopping away her tears with a tiny hanky. Billy turned in his seat to scan the cinema entrance, the policeman had not yet appeared. Turning back to her, Billy said,

"I do know your dad, I was on the bridge when you tore your dress, remember? Anyway, they can only tell him if they know where you live. Come on quick!" Billy hustled Dorothy and Barry out of their seats and into the aisle. He guided them quickly back through the toilet door where he had entered. Opening the end cubicle, he jumped up on the toilet seat and opened the small window. "Look I'll go through first, you shove Barry through and I'll catch him, in case he bounces on his bleeding head," said Billy with a giggle. "You should have no trouble squeezing through, Dor, not with your skinny arse."

Dorothy kept looking toward the door, expecting any moment for it to be opened by the large policeman, but Billy's proposition seemed a far better alternative than being at home waiting for the law to knock on the door.

Billy clambered through the window almost as fast as he could open it. Unfortunately, he didn't notice the five-pound note slip from his pocket and be swept along the draughty alleyway. Dorothy struggled to lift Barry up to the window. Having got his legs through she eventually heard Billy shout, "I've got him."

The last stage of the big escape was for Dorothy to climb on to the top of the cubicle, turn herself over and put her legs through the window first, then wriggle herself out backwards. Just as she was thinking that matters couldn't get any worse, one by one Luke's Blackjacks started to fall from her little pocket. She was almost out. Just her head and shoulders remained inside the window when she heard the inside door open and a man's voice, "The little sods have done a bunk!"

Seventy miles away, a silver-haired doctor Mason switched off his torch and raised the powerful magnifying device from his eyes.

"Well Henry," he said as he opened the blinds, "Your wife is going to have quite a shock the next time she comes in. Or should I say pleasant surprise. Lets face it, it can't be much fun for her to keep travelling here from Portsmouth just to watch someone lie in bed and dribble."

"No! Doc, tell me it's not true, I didn't, did I?" Henry said. "God, I hate the thought of anyone seeing me like that."

"Mind you," Mason continued with a wry grin. "You didn't smell so bad, once she bathed you and got the beard shaved off." Henry groaned at the thought. "Never seemed to bother your wife though, the way she's fussed around you. Up until a month ago, we were beginning to think you would never recover. That's what makes this job so interesting. Of course, not every patient goes from frog to prince over night, but getting one now and again makes it all worthwhile. You know, the brain is so amazing, fragile, yet in some cases robust in its ability to self heal. And what's more, your memory seems to be getting better by the minute."

"Yes," said Henry. "Little details from different times. Does that make sense?"

"Yes I think I know what you mean, and I also think, eventually it will all come back to you. At least everything that's important. Your wife will help, I'm sure."

"Well I know I've got two great kids I can remember that much. I hope she brings them, but I'm a little scared. How much will they have changed and will they feel the same towards me? I mean it has been a long time and kids grow up so fast."

"Well your wife can tell you all about them when she gets here. She should have got my letter by now. I think she will be here this weekend. I'd like to think my wife would be as dedicated. You're a lucky man."

"Yes, and yet its strange. I can picture my kids, yet I can't picture her!"

24
Cats out

Cathleen Masters turned back two pages. She was trying to find the last passage that she'd actually absorbed before her mind had drifted from the story she was reading. It was hopeless. She couldn't concentrate. Putting the book down on the seat beside her, she gazed out at the countryside. The clickety-clack of the train wheels would normally have put her to sleep as it had many times before since she'd been visiting Henry. Once, she made the journey in her little Austin Ruby, but the London traffic made her nervous, especially after just finishing a night shift at the Royal. This time she knew she wouldn't sleep, this time it was different. She'd been summoned to see Dr Mason. She liked him; he was not at all like the doctors at the Royal, they were so formal and business like, while Dr Mason was always bubbly, joking and full of life. Even when things were not going too well, he was always focussed on the positive.

What was it he wanted to see her about she wondered? Had he somehow discovered that she was not Henry's wife? Surely, even if he had, it would not concern him. Maybe there's been a change in Henry's condition. Has he taken a turn for the worse? No, she didn't want to think about that, but the questions and possible answers pestered her all the way to Waterloo station and again on the underground, until she found herself knocking on Dr Jules Mason's office door.

"Mrs Gough! Nice to see you again."

From day one, Dr Mason assumed that Cathy was Henry's wife. She intended to tell him the truth, but after spending her first visit washing and tending Henry in a wifely manner, she could not bring herself to end the lie.

"Come in and take a seat," he said. "How's life in Pompey, getting back to normal? I remember them having had a pretty bad time of it, down south."

"Yes it was quite frightening," Cathy said nervously. She sat pensively facing him across his desk.

"Don't look so worried, Mrs Gough, I've got good news for you. Henry's out of it!" Cathy just stared at him open mouthed. Mason could see she'd not taken that in. "The coma," he said, grinning widely, "The big sleep. Sleep perchance to dream." Then, still aware of her confusion he leaned across his desk towards her "Mrs Gough, Henry's awake."

Cathy put her hands up to her face, "Oh! My God," was all she could say.

"Yes, God may have had something to do with it," he said jovially. "Although I'd like to believe that my brilliance also had a hand in it. Anyway, apart from wanting to give you the good news myself, I thought it best that you didn't walk into his room and faint."

Tears were now flooding Cathy's eyes, while her hands still covered her face. "Anyway," he went on, ignoring her emotional display. "As remarkable as his recovery is, he still has some gaps in his memory, but even they seem to be closing fast. We want to keep an eye on him for a few weeks. Build up his muscles and suchlike; he's been on his back a very long time. And then you can take him home." This time he waited for her to speak but her,

"Thank you doctor" came out as a squeak, making them both laugh.

To get to Henry's room from Dr Mason's office meant crossing a courtyard and passing the hospital main gate. It was at this point that Cathleen seriously considered walking out of Henry's life and never seeing him again. However, the urge to see him awake after all this time was too much.

She reached his room and looked through the window. He sat in the chair beside his bed reading a newspaper. Dr Mason would have told him his wife was coming, she thought. Henry would be expecting Martia. What would his reaction be if *she* walked in instead? Would she be able to stomach seeing the disappointment on his face? No, it was no good she could not bear the awful rejection. She would die if she saw disappointment on his face. She turned and made her way back along the corridor. Just as she reached the swing doors that led back into the courtyard, they burst open almost knocking her over as Dr Mason came through them.

"Ah! Glad I caught you Mrs Gough, I've got…." He paused, frowning. "Forgotten what room it is? Come on I'll show you." Taking her by the arm, he practically marched her back to Henry's room. Henry looked up as they came through the door.

"Cathleen!" Henry's shock and surprise quickly turned to smiles, melting Cathy's doubt and fear in seconds.

"Hell!" Dr Mason said. "I wish people looked that elated when I walked into a room." turning to Cathy, he said, "Well he certainly remembered you."

Henry started to speak, "But I thought…." Cathy's heart skipped a beat, thinking that Henry was about to let the cat out of the bag.

"What! That she wasn't coming?" interrupted Mason. "I told you she'd be here. Anyway, before I leave you two to get acquainted again, I must tell you why I came over here. The front desk has just taken this telephone message from a woman and its left me totally confused. It was obviously meant for you Mrs Gough because she said it was for the lady presently visiting Henry, but she called you Cathy Masters."

"Ah yes my mother, you know how old ladies get confused sometimes," Cathy said smiling sweetly, at the two of them. "She still thinks I'm single." This seemed to satisfy Dr Mason, although Henry was now looking very confused.

"Oh I see. Yes, the brain can play some nasty tricks on the aged. Anyway, her message was, that a man called. He was looking for Henry and that he was working for Mrs Gough. Now if this lady here is your wife, Henry, then this other one must be either be your mother or your sister."

"I haven't got a sister," said Henry.

"Then it must be your mother. I'll leave you to sort it out, there's a phone in the sisters office. I'll see you later."

The swing doors closed behind Dr Mason, leaving an awkward silence. Henry looked at Cathy with a frown. Then he patted the bed.

"You'd better come and sit down. I think you have some explaining to do, *Mrs Gough*," Henry said wryly. "And I think you'd better start at the beginning."

"I'm afraid most of what I have to tell, is going to upset you," said Cathy looking almost afraid.

Henry sat bolt upright. "My kids are alright?"

"Yes, at least I think so, but it's not about Janice and Billy." He watched Cathleen delve into her handbag. "Maybe you should read this first. The police found this in Elsie Craven's house." Cathy turned her face away as Henry unfolded the letter. After he'd read it, he turned his head away from her. Cathy knew his tears embarrassed him. She wanted to give him some privacy but didn't quite know how to offer it. As if on cue, Henry said:

"Cathy, there's a kitchen along the corridor, would you ask them if we could get some tea?"

Cathleen came back with the tea, and was pleased that Henry seemed more composed.

"Do you know what the letter was about Cathy?"

"I didn't read it but the police said it was bad news about your father. I'm guessing that he died."

"Yes, but look at the post mark. It's over three years ago that my mother sent this. All this time! God, she must be thinking I'm dead. What other surprises have you got for me?"

Cathy told Henry everything she knew, from the time she recognised him in the Royal Hospital, taking hold of his hand when telling him about the death of Martia and the Craven trial. She told him the story the papers had revealed of Elsie Craven's revenge for the death of her husband and son. Henry listened emotionless, until Cathy had finished. Henry was silent for a while. He lay staring out the window. Apart from looking a little glassy eyed, Cathleen was surprised how little Henry appeared to be affected by the news of his wife's death.

"Then that phone call must have been my Mother," he said. "I must get in touch with her. What about the kids Cathy? Do you know where they are? Do they know where I am?" Cathy was amazed that he had nothing to say on the subject of Martia. Reading the look of disbelief on her face, he asked, "What?"

"I can't believe it! I tell you that your wife's been murdered and you…"

"Cathleen, any feelings I had for Martia died long before she did. Furthermore, although I disliked Elsie Craven, I can't hate her for what she did. I was there, on the station platform. I witnessed it. Martia stood on that railway platform and watched Elsie's husband jump with their little boy in front of an express train. I have re-lived that scene so many times and I believe now, that Martia sensed what he was about to do and did nothing to stop him."

Henry gave Cathy time to dwell on his words and then he said, "It's strange, Dr Mason has been telling me what a wonderful devoted wife I had. How she sat with me for hours, nursing me like a professional even though I was practically brain dead. What he was telling me didn't make sense; it just wasn't Martia's way. Maybe that's why I couldn't remember her." Cathy sat on the bed smiling at him. Henry lifted his hand to brush back the lock of hair she'd arranged so carefully over her birthmark. Instinctively Cathy's hand went up to stop him, but something in his manner eased her embarrassment. His hand cradled her neck, pulling her down toward him. Softly, he kissed the offending birth mark and then her tear-strewn face. "Now tell me what you know about Janice and Billy."

A few weeks later at around 6pm, Steven and Delia Webster sat listening to the radio. Deborah sat sewing her school emblem on her new blazer while Janice sat writing a letter.

"I really don't think its necessary to write another letter to your brother Jan," said Delia.

"I phoned the orphanage this morning as you asked, they assured me that your letter had arrived and that Billy took it with him to his foster home."

"Yes, but what if someone gets hold of it. They could easily steal the money."

"Good gracious!" said Steven. "What a mistrustful girl you are. One would have thought after all this time here, you'd have learnt to have more faith in humanity."

"You mean like my mother trusted that Craven woman? I don't think so."

"Well, I think that going through life with such a cynical outlook will turn you into a miserable old dried up witch," said Steven, making Deborah giggle.

"Oh Steven," said Delia. "How could anyone as pretty as Janice turn into a witch, dried up or otherwise?"

"Thank you Delia," said Janice, flippantly "That was much appreciated." They all still laughing when there came the sound of car tyres on the gravel drive. Deborah dropped her sewing and dashed to the window.

"Dad, It's a Rolls Royce, and guess what? It's newer than yours."

"No! Don't you just hate people like that," said Steven, grinning?" He got up to answer the front door. He closed the lounge door behind him and Delia and the two girls soon heard the sound of muffled voices.

"Must be one of daddy's golfing crowd," said Deborah. I don't know anyone else around here with a Rolls." Suddenly the voices stopped and Steven opened the door again. He looked pale and worried as he said,

"Janice love. Prepare yourself for a shock." Then he moved aside and Henry Gough stood in the doorway.

"Daddy!" Janice ran to throw herself at Henry. They kissed and hugged each other for some time before Jan noticed that two more people had entered the room.

"Jan, you remember Cathleen Masters," said Henry.

"Hello Cathy how's Aunt Nell?" Jan said hugging Cathleen.

"Mum's fine, love."

"And Janice, this lady is my mother, your Grandmother, Janice smiled and hugged the old lady kissing her cheek while their tears mingled.

Delia Webster was starting to become emotional, fearing that her family's own lives were about to be upended. Steven put his arm around his wife, while young Deborah looked on the scene in total confusion. Henry looked at the Websters and read the look of apprehension and confusion on all of their faces.

"I think you wonderful people are due an explanation. And as I am still a little confused myself, Cathy here, will explain."

Cathleen explained to the Websters that Henry had been in a coma and that they were sure his injuries were linked to the Craven gang. She explained the reason she had not told them that Henry was still alive was because no one was sure he would ever regain consciousness, it was decided that it was best in both Janice and their interest. She told them that some while ago, she had taken it on herself to drive to the girls school in Liphook. How she sat in her car outside Janice's school to see if Janice was being cared for and if she seemed happy. She smiled at Deborah and said she had never seen Janice looking happier or better cared for.

In the time Janice had spent with the Websters, they had come to think her as their own and though Steven and Delia were aware that a relative might someday turn up, their daughter Deborah had no such notion. To her, Janice had become a sister.

"She can't leave!" Deborah shouted hysterically, "Daddy, tell them she belongs here. Steven hugged her saying,

"It's not the end of the world, love. Janice can come for holidays. Cant she Mr Gough?"

"She certainly can." Henry smiled at his mother. "And how about it Mum, have you got room for three holiday makers in Scotland?"

"Well, it's only a small castle but I think we could squeeze three more in," said Jane. Laughter filled the room. Even Deborah found herself giggling between sniffs.

25
The Setback

Billy had not been seen for three days and Dorothy and Barry were missing him. It was early and the park was almost empty. Dorothy sat on the outer bar of the kiddies' roundabout and lazily kept it turning with the push of her foot. Barry sat in the centre, having experienced the physics of centrifugal force, and remembering how he once lost his grip when an over-enthusiastic teenager had tried to make the thing take off.

"What did Mrs Cole say when you knocked her door yesterday?"

"All she said was, Billy wasn't well and wouldn't be coming out," Barry said, flicking through the pages of a new train-spotting book his mother had bought him. The weather had taken a turn and although it had not yet rained, the sky was a threatening grey, adding to their melancholy mood. They had not known Billy very long but already his absence was sadly felt. While Barry was keen to show him his new train-spotting book, Dorothy wanted to know if he had been to buy his new clothes for the trip to see his sister.

"Didn't she say what was wrong with him?" said Dorothy.

"She just said he had a chesty cough, that's all."

"That was yesterday he might be alright now. Why don't you go and knock his door?"

"How come its always me. Why don't you go?" Barry said indignantly.

"Because I don't think old mother Cole likes me. And I don't like her very much either. Besides, that man always peers at me from her window whenever I knock her door."

"That's Tom Cole, he's Mrs Cole's brother. He won't hurt you. My mum says he's a hero. She said he lost his legs in the war saving his friend. That's why he sits in that wheelchair, looking out the window. Billy said Tom tells him some great stories about the war." Just then they heard footsteps on the gravel. It was Billy. Their mood brightened immediately as they greeted him.

"Are you alright now Billy? What was wrong with you?" asked Dorothy, but before Billy could answer, Barry shoved his new book under his nose,

"Look Billy it's the same as yours!" Billy let out a loud barking cough. "Yeah, that's great, Barry," he said pushing his hand away."

Barry sensed Billy's lack of enthusiasm. Billy, in return, saw his disappointment and immediately added, "We'll be able to collect our numbers together now." It was enough to put a smile back on Barry's face.

"When are you going to buy your new clothes? And can we come?" Dorothy said eagerly.

"I don't know if I'll be getting any new clothes now," said Billy glumly.

Dorothy noticed how Billy's eyes appeared to suddenly fill with tears.

"Why not.?" said Barry thinking a shopping trip with his two friends might be another adventure.

"I lost the money."

"What!" yelled Dorothy "Oh no! Where?"

"I'm not sure, maybe old mother Cole took it."

"Billy! That's a wicked thing to say," said Dorothy

"I know, but you don't know what she's like, I don't trust her. That's why I never left the money home. Tom said he'd give me the five pounds to make up for it, but she wouldn't let him."

"So, what are you going to do? How will you get to Liphook now?"

"I'm not sure yet. I know a way to make some money, but I don't know how much I'll need. I came to see if you two would walk to Fratton station with me. I've got to get Tom some tobacco on the way and I'm going to find out how much the train fare is to Liphook. Then I thought we'd walk back along Fratton Road to the Co-op."

"What for, groceries?" said Barry.

"No, the outfitters, I've got one good shirt but I need some trousers. I can't wear these to meet my sister and I need to find out how much money I need."

Barry and Dorothy looked critically at Billy's short trousers and the way the waist splayed out above his frayed elastic belt.

"I think you need some braces, too, if you can afford them," said Dorothy "You're a bit skinny to wear a belt." Barry giggled.

"Oh!" remarked Billy. "Look who's talking, Miss slack drawers!" With that, Barry howled with laughter, and was still laughing for most of the trek to Fratton Station.

"Right, well that's not too bad," said Billy as they left the station ticket office. "Reckon I can make that much money without too much trouble. Now to find out how much my clothes are going to cost."

"Come on then!" Dorothy said, with renewed enthusiasm.

The three set off to visit the Co-op outfitters in Fratton Road and as they walked, Dorothy was reminded of something Billy said.

"Billy what did you mean when you said you might be able to get enough money; how are you going to get it, can we help?"

"Larking!" Billy said. Barry and Dorothy stared blankly at each other, and Billy saw their ignorance. "You know! Mud larking. On a good day you can make a lot of money."

"I've heard of it, but my dad says it's begging."

"Yeah, I know, but my sister Jan and me used to do it just to buy food when we were really hungry. Jan used to say, if you're entertaining people, then you're not begging, mud larking's no different than buskin'." Billy could see Dorothy was not convinced and Barry's silence told him the boy had no idea what he was talking about.

"You don't have to come Dor, if you don't want to."

"I will!" Barry chimed in. Billy put his arm around him and hugged him.

They reached their destination and did a tour of the multi-floored Co-operative store. That is, until the store manager decided that Dorothy and Billy's shabby appearance did nothing to embellish the stores décor, or promote his goods. He promptly evicted them, albeit to an array of Billy's colourful language, showing his two comrades that "bloody" could be used many more times in a sentence than they thought possible.

But their exercise was complete and Billy had his financial goal. As they made their way back to Walmer Road Dorothy said,

"Five pounds, how are you going to get that much?" as if Billy might as well be asking for the moon. "I don't know if I can, but I'm going to have a bloody good try."

"You could run errands for people!" Barry said, eagerly trying to help.

"By the time I've run enough errands to make half that amount, I'd be too bloody old to run," Billy quipped. This brought more laughter and lightened the sombre mood of being faced with what seemed an impossible task. "No, the only way I'm gonna do it, is by mud larking. I've done it before!"

"I'd like to help you Billy," said Dorothy, "but I'm scared my Dad will find out."

"Well never mind, Dor. I reckon Barry and me could do this on our own, but I'd like you to come, even if you only watch. It will have to be this Saturday. I'll ask Tom Cole to check the tide times in the paper. We have to get there at low tide."

"Why Saturday?"

"Because that's when it's busy and you can make the most money."

"I don't mind coming," said Dorothy. "If I get up early and get my chores done, that is. But I might have to take Luke." Dorothy read concern on Billy's face. "What's wrong? Can't Luke come then?"

"Well it's a long walk, and we would have to keep an eye on him when we get there. It can be dangerous." Billy said, with an air of mystery.

"What about me, do you think I could mud lark?" said Barry eagerly.

"Yes, course you can. I bet you'd make more than anyone."

For the next few days, the children planned their trip. Billy kept Barry and Dorothy in the dark as to what exactly was expected of one, to be a good mud larker, but they were keen to see Billy achieve his financial goal and they trusted him without question. Dorothy, having done all her chores, had told her mother they were going on a picnic, hence her excuse to take sandwiches. Barry did likewise. It was all part of their plan.

26
The Trek

Saturday came and Dorothy looked at the clock as she tied the laces on Luke's plimsolls.

"Is it beach are we going, Doffy?" Luke loved the beach. The promise of a candyfloss was enough to keep him happy for hours.

"I don't know love, Billy's taking us somewhere and I'm not sure where, but I've made you your favourite posh sandwiches just how you like them, with fish paste, and with the crusts cut off."

"Can I take my bus?"

"No, It's too big to carry, but if you hurry up you can take one of your little toys. And don't forget your hat, I think its going to be another hot day."

Luke ran off in search of his toy box and came back carrying a Dinky toy version of a bread van. Grabbing their sandwiches that she'd prepared the night before, Dorothy led Luke out the front door. Billy was waiting, sat on the forecourt wall of Barry's house. When he saw Dorothy and Luke, he jumped down and walked up to Barry's front door.

"Have you knocked for Barry yet?" Dorothy asked him.

"No, I was waiting for you first," he said as he rang the bell of 155 with its shiny brass plaque with the words, Sunny Side. Barry came to the door.

"My mum is just making my sandwiches but I have to run up Bert's shop to get a loaf first." Seeing the look of frustration on Billy's face, Barry quickly added: "I won't be long. If you don't walk too fast I can catch you up." Dorothy knew that if they waited around in the street, one of her family was bound to make her run errands, so they agreed to walk on.

Barry waited impatiently for his mother to find her purse, while he imagined his friends disappearing over the horizon. He ran as fast as his legs would carry him to Bert's the local grocers. There, he became more frustrated. An old woman customer insisted finishing her story to Bert about her husband's ulcer, which ran into fine detail. Eventually, Barry got his loaf and raced back at an even faster pace. As he reached the last few yards, he froze as he saw the familiar shape of a Riley Pathfinder, the car used by the Portsmouth Police Force. Barry watched it stop outside Billy's house. Barry hid his face behind the loaf of bread and slipped into his front porch as a uniformed policeman knocked Billy's door. Barry waited. "How could they have found us?" he thought. "None of us gave our address that day in the cinema." He peered round the wall, hoping the car would soon leave. He heard Billy's front door close and saw the policeman come out of the gate, but to Barry's horror, he didn't get back in the car, but crossed the road. Quickly, Barry turned the key in his door and hurried inside. He entered the front room with the loaf still under his arm to peer through the curtain. He saw the policeman now looking up at Dorothy's door. "He's bound to come here next." Barry thought. He suddenly wanted to curl up in a corner, close his eyes tight and shut the world out.

"Barry! Is that you? Have you got that loaf?" his mother called. "Your sandwiches are on the kitchen table." He took the bread into the kitchen and grabbed his sandwiches. He waited, expecting to hear a knock at the front door at any moment. The knock never came; Barry opened the front door and to his great relief the policeman and the car were gone.

He ran toward Fratton road, thinking his friends would be so far away by now, and he had such important but worrying news for them. He reached Penhale Road and was pleased to see they had waited for him. The three of them were sitting on a wall, opposite his school.

"Billy, there was a policeman at your house!" Barry said, reaching them breathlessly.

Billy and Dorothy looked at each other and Billy smiled.

"Yeah, nice one Barry. You had me going there for a minute."

"It's true, he went to your house too Dorothy." The two looked at Barry and realised that it wasn't a joke.

"Do you know what the police wanted?" asked Billy. Barry shook his head.

"My dad will kill me." said Dorothy, her eyes glassy with tears. Billy put his arm round her shoulders, while Luke pushed out his bottom lip and hugged her round the legs.

"Hey, don't get yourself in a stew," said Billy. "It may have nothing to do with the Troxy. I mean how could they have found us. We never told them anything. It's probably got nothing to do with that."

"That's right Dorothy," said Barry. "He never came to my house, and I was at the Troxy as well." Dorothy dried her eyes. The boys' words were a comfort but she still had doubts.

"Well, whatever it's about, there's not much we can do about it now, so we might as well keep going," she said.

The four set off, on what promised to be a fine day. After crossing a busy Fratton Road, they turned the corner to start the long stretch along Arundel Street. German bombers had hit a great deal of this road and much of it had already been cleared, as much for safety reasons as for redevelopment.

One bombed site that had not been cleared was at the corner of Commercial Road and Arundel Street. It was on this site that the Landport Drapery Bazaar had previously stood, one of Portsmouth's largest stores: This had taken a direct hit. The massive bomb had left a gigantic crater. Weeds and other vegetation had already covered much of its waste ground. When the four reached it, they saw several children sliding down the slopes of the crater on a length of corrugated steel, once part of an Anderson shelter.

Dorothy's group stood at the edge of the pit watching three boys preparing to take the plunge and slide down. They placed the steel slide so that it teetered on the edge of the pit, then carefully they started to seat themselves behind each other on the sled, the two boys at the back, each with his legs around the boy in front him. The boys had seen the newcomers and knew they were being watched. They seemed happy to have attracted an audience.

"OK, let her go!" shouted the boy at the back. All three leaned forward causing the sled to be front heavy. The sled started to rise at the back, but just wouldn't start to slide.

"Give us a push mate!" The boy that spoke was looking at Billy.

"Come on," Billy said, earnestly. "They might let us have a go."

Dorothy and Barry stood either side of the sled and pushed the boy at the back while Billy lifted the rear of the sled to a steeper angle. Suddenly the sled took off with the three lads shouting their delight, all the way to the bottom of the crater.

On their ascent, they offered the corrugated sled to the four children saying they had to go.

The four spent a fun hour on the slope, almost forgetting the reason they had come. Then, on the last ascent they looked up to see two policemen staring down at them.

"What do you lot think you're doing," the larger of the two officers said. Dorothy nervously tried to hide her face, as she saw the three stripes on the big man's arm and recognised the same booming voice that had caused her several sleepless nights.

"We weren't doing no harm Mr," Billy said. "We were only playing."

"Oh yes, and what's your father going to say when you get home with no arse in your trousers?" Then raising an eyebrow he said, "Don't I know you?"

"No. I don't think so." Billy replied, without hesitation.

"Yes I do, Troxy wasn't it?"

"No I expect that was George."

"Who's George?"

"My twin brother. He's always at the pictures."

"Well I want to see him. What's the address?"

There was a slight pause before Billy answered "Number 49 Clive Road."

The Sergeant took out a notebook and scribbled in it. "OK. Well I want you kids off this site. It's dangerous. Do you hear me?" The children nodded, and the two policemen sauntered off.

"Phew! That was close," said Billy, when the policemen were out of sight.

"Yes, but how come he didn't say anything to me?" Dorothy said.

"Well it was dark in the Troxy, and he only saw you with a torch, but it was daylight in the foyer, that's why he recognised me."

As the four continued their journey, Dorothy suddenly asked, "Who's George?"

Billy grinned. "I've got no idea." Barry laughed while Dorothy bit her bottom lip indicating her concern at Billy's daring.

"And I suppose you've got no idea who lives at 49 Clive Road?"

"Yes I do,"

"Who?"

"The kid who blacked my eye: Ginger Griggs."

They were still laughing five minutes later as they reached Edinburgh Road.

Barry noticed that every now and then, Billy would pick up a cigarette end and put it in a little tin that he carried in his pocket.

"What do you want them for Billy?" asked Barry. "Are you going to smoke them?"

"No silly, I pick them up for Tom; He keeps running out of tobacco. Old mother Cole is always saying she forgot to get it. I think it's because she's too mean. So, I got this idea, when I see a clean cigarette end, I save it, then when I get home I take the tobacco out. He doesn't even know that I top his tin up."

They turned into Edinburgh Road and Luke was getting irritable; having to run to keep pace with the others. He started complaining, so Dorothy and Billy took turns in giving him piggyback rides until they became tired. Barry even tried carrying him a short distance.

They passed Edinburgh Road and were now outside the Royal Naval Barracks and the beginning of Queen Street. Uniformed sailors were everywhere. Billy suddenly spotted two uniforms that were different.

"Bloody Hell, the Yanks are in! Do you know what that means?" Dorothy and Barry looked at him, waiting for an answer. "It means we're going to make that five pounds in no time."

"Why for they got funny hats Doffy?" Luke remarked, as the two American sailors came towards them. The two young seamen appeared to be arguing. They stopped as they reached the children, and one confronted Dorothy.

"Hey kid, how much is this funny-money worth?" He said, peeling a brown note from the wad in his hand.

"Wow!" exclaimed Billy, looking at the large amount of money the young seaman held. "That's a ten shilling note. And those are one-pound notes. That one's a five-pound note. Blimey! Do all Yanks have that much money?"

"Only if they're good at poker, kid," the young sailor said, grinning at his friend." Billy looked about him before emphasising his next words,

"You didn't ought to flash it around mister; not round here." Ignoring Billy's words, the second sailor pulled out a handful of change.

"And what about these?"

"Those are half-crowns," said Dorothy. She then went on to explain, "Four of those make one of those brown notes." She continued until she had explained all the currency in the sailor's hands and even went on to explain the spending value down to a pint of beer.

"You're a clever kid," one said, smiling at Dorothy. "Thanks a heap." Billy thought it might be a good time to try his luck,

"Have you got any bubble gum mister?" The sailors looked inquiringly at each other. "No, sorry kid." They started to walk on. The four children continued in the opposite direction. They hadn't gone but a few yards when they heard, "HEY KIDS!" The four turned to see the first sailor hurrying back toward them.

"There you go. Get yourselves some gum." The young sailor pressed a pound note into Dorothy's hand then ran back to catch up with his friend.

"There you go Billy," said Dorothy, grinning and copying the sailor's phrase. "Only four to go."

The four pressed on. Luke now had his legs wrapped around Dorothy's waist, his head resting on her shoulder almost asleep.

"Couldn't we have a rest?" Barry had tried not to complain, wanting only to be as tough as his two friends, but his shoes were rubbing his heels and one had started to bleed.

Billy could see the corner of Lyons Terrace only a few yards away.

"Look, my Aunty Nell lives in the next street. You wait on the corner. I'll see if she'll get us a drink of water." They reached the corner of the narrow street. The terraced houses were shabby looking, and the characters that hung around them eyed the four children inquisitively. Barry returned their stares with curiosity, his mind conjuring up pictures of Fagin's pickpockets. Queen Street held a different fascination for Dorothy. She was a girl who had learnt to listen to parents and grownups and only ask questions when it was prudent to do so. She knew Queen Street to be famous for its prostitutes, but she had no knowledge of them being any threat to children, and therefore had no fear of them.

As if Dorothy's thoughts were a cue, suddenly a door opened to emit a loud stream of abuse, and a sailor fell drunkenly out of it, knocking Barry over. The two tumbled into the road.

The children stood staring in amazement, as a young woman in high heeled shoes, stood over the sailor, angrily swearing at him. The sailor tried picking himself up while slurring some kind of apology to Barry.

"Billy, we don't have to stop, you know," said Dorothy. "You said the place wasn't very far now. We won't mind if you want to carry on instead of stopping at your Auntie's."

"Look! Just wait here a minute."

Billy left them and hurried along Lyons Terrace to Nell Masters house that he remembered so well. He knocked the door and as he stood staring across the street at number 12, memories came flooding back to him, especially of Jan and the happy times they had, seldom, though they were.

"There's nobody home, love!" The voice broke his melancholy thoughts and he looked up to see a familiar face peering out of the next porch to Nell's. Billy recognised Mrs Emily Rogers, Nell's next-door neighbour, who spent hours in the summer, as she was now, sitting on a chair just inside her open front door, a nice lady as Billy remembered.

"Nell's not there love, what did you... Here! I know you...Billy, Billy Gough. Well I never, you've grown. A bit skinnier, but still a handsome little sod though." Emily read the disappointment on Billy's face at learning of Nell's absence. "Yes, I don't know what all the excitements been about, cars and people been coming and going from Nell's house all morning. Was it something important you wanted to see her about, love?"

"No, it's just that we've walked a long way and I was going to ask Nell if we could get a drink of water."

"Who's we?" Billy pointed to the corner of the street where his three friends sat on the kerb. "How far have you walked?"

"From Walmer Road."

"What, with that little boy? You must be mad. Go and get your friends, I'll get you all a drink."

Emily Rogers made them all a lemon drink and as they rested, Emily fell in love with Luke and jokingly asked Dorothy if she could leave him behind.

"I suppose you're going down to the flats are you Billy. I wouldn't leave it too late, I heard one of the kids say low tide was about midday and it's nearly that now. Have you not got a bucket?"

"No I forgot to bring one."

Emily disappeared along her passage and came back carrying an old galvanized pail. There you go. You can keep that one. Keep an eye on this little angel though," she said, cuddling Luke. "And Blondie here." She pulled Barry to her and fixed his safety pin that had come undone. To his amazement, she never even asked what had happened to his arm.

27
A Shilling Too Far

The children thanked Emily Rogers and commenced their journey.

"How much farther is it Billy?" Dorothy said. "And what did that lady mean when she said I suppose you're going down the flats?"

"You'll see, its not far now." Gradually the smell of the sea became stronger and the sound of seagulls brought back sweet memories to Billy; thoughts of Janice, cinemas and hot loaves. The four finally reached the end of Queen Street.

"Look! The sea, shouted Luke." They were now looking at the harbour. To their right, was the Portsmouth Dockyard's main gate. To the left, the causeway that led across the mud flats to the Harbour Station and the Isle of Wight ferry. The harbour wall stood directly across the road in front of them. The whole area was bustling with sailors and commuters.

"God, I've never seen it this crowded," said Billy excitedly. "I reckon Pompey must have a big football match on or something. Come on. Lets see if the tides out."

They held hands and crossed the busy road. Barry climbed up to look over the sea wall.

"Phew. It stinks!" He said, emphasising his comment by holding his nose with two fingers.

"It always smells like that when the tide's out," said Billy. "Larkers don't worry about that."

Billy could still see a look of doubt on Dorothy's face. "You don't have to come Dor, but I've only got a week to get this money, and after coming all this way, I'm not going home until I've made some dough."

"Nor me. I'm not scared," said Barry. Billy put his arm round Barry's shoulders and hugged him.

"What do we have to do Billy?" Dorothy still sounded unsure as visions of her father's leather belt, sliding from around his waist, became vivid in her mind.

"I'll show you," Billy said, tossing the bucket over the sea wall and climbing over after it. The tide was low and had not reached the wall for some time. The three started to undress on a dry pebbled beach area. Except for Luke, they took off their shoes and stripped to their underclothes.

"Aren't you going to take your vest off?" Barry said to Dorothy.

"No I'm not!" She said coyly, looking at Billy. Dorothy was aware that her breasts were just becoming apparent, and Barry's question had embarrassed her.

"Well, you might be sorry you didn't," said Billy, not understanding the reason for her flushed look.

Dorothy had trouble in persuading Luke to stay on the shore.

"Why not me can go?" he said, pushing out his bottom lip again.

"Because you're too small, it's dangerous and we need you to mind our clothes." Eventually, a fish-paste sandwich shoved in his hand, and a promise of some sweets on the way home produced the goods and Luke agreed to stay put.

"OK," Billy said, grabbing the bucket. "Just follow me, and make sure you stay right behind me, the mud can get deep in places."

They started to make their way across the mud flats. The smelly black ooze sucked at their feet tugging them backwards with every awkward stride. Foul crab-crawling seaweed became tangled around their feet, impeding their progress. By the time they had reached the area below the pier where Billy had guided them, all three at some point had fallen over at least once and were already covered with thick black slime.

"What's my dad going to say when he sees me like this?" Dorothy said, looking as if she was about to cry. Her arms and one whole side of her body were covered in thick mud.

"Don't worry," said Billy, trying not to laugh at Dorothy's pitiful appearance. "We can wash it off when the tide comes in. I did warn you about the vest though, didn't I?"

Standing below the great steel supports of the causeway that led to the Station and Ferry terminus, they could hear the bustle of people above them.

Billy placed the bucket near one of the steel uprights, then, turning to his two friends, he said, "Now watch this." Wiping the mud from his hands in the small area of his underpants that was not already covered with mud, he put two fingers in his mouth and let out the most piercing whistle in the direction of the bustling crowd above. After two or three attempts at this, a face appeared over the safety rail.

Billy cupped his hands and called, "Chuck us a coin Mr!" The man obviously knew the routine. Almost immediately, a silver coin flashed in the sunlight as a shilling left the stranger's hand. Even before it had plopped into the mud a few feet from the children, there were a half dozen more faces peering over the railings.

"Now for the entertainment." Billy said, grinning at his friends. To Barry and Dorothy's amazement, the nine year old put the palms of his hands together and in comical pose reminiscent of a Charlie Chaplin stunt, he dived head first in the mud where the coin had entered. This had the desired effect on the now, large collection of spectators above. Their laughter reached the children.

Billy emerged from the mud holding up the coin to delighted applause from the onlookers above.

Looking like a black and white minstrel with the whites of his eyes and teeth gleaming through the mud, Billy grinned at his two friends. "And now you know what that's for," he said tossing the coin into the bucket.

Dorothy and Barry soon caught on to the routine that was expected of them. As the coins rained down, they each found their individual ways of making the crowd laugh. Occasionally Dorothy would journey back to the sea wall to check on Luke and to feed him with more food and promises.

Two hours later Cathleen Masters was slowly driving along Commercial Road, while Nell sat beside her. In the back seat, sat Janice, Billy's sister. All three were scanning the many shoppers and pedestrians searching for four children.

"Their father said the little boy is four and will be wearing a white sun hat. And his sister has dark hair," said Cathleen

"Yes I heard! A little blond boy with one arm, hell, I was listening Cathy," said Nell, tersely.

"Okay Mum, what's gotten into you, we're all upset you know. Don't worry, we'll find them."

"Yes, sorry love, I was just thinking about that horrible man back there, His two children are missing and all he could think about was punishing his little girl when she got home. Can you imagine what it must be like having a father like that?"

Janice sat quietly listening and wondering if it could be any worse than having a mother like it? "Yes," Nell said. "and what's the family thinking about, letting a four year old out of their sight for hours on end. God! The girl's only nine."

"I know mum," said Cathy, "but all we can do is help to find them. The girls mother said her daughter had made sandwiches and that they might have gone on a picnic."

"Yes," said Nell. "Now where would kids go for a picnic in this bombed site of a city? Maybe your father and Grandmother are having more luck, Janice."

"We've been along this road twice, Cathy," said Nell. "You'd better drive to my place and I'll phone the police again. They may have some news."

It had taken Dorothy and Billy many trips back to the shore to check on Luke and all kinds of persuasive bribes to keep him from complaining. Their main aim was to keep him from venturing across the mud flats in an attempt to reach them. Once, when Luke was making just such an effort he had managed to get half way between the shore and the children before Barry spotted him. That particular time Billy took him back to the shore and used some of their spoils to buy him a treat. He took him to a nearby sweet shop and bought him a toffee apple but he made it clear to Luke that he could only have the treat if he promised to stay firmly on the shore until they came back to collect him. Up to a point this had solved the problem and Luke, comforted with his apple on a stick, agreed to stay put. Billy then found him an old kiddies sand castle type bucket, showed him how to fill it and start making sand castles. Content with the thought that the infant would now keep himself amused for a while Billy left Luke and trudged back to his two friends. Luke sat on the shore until he'd quietly devoured his apple. The bucket and sand had worked for a while, until Luke lost interest. He then ambled down to the waters edge and managed to amuse himself for some time by poking a rather angry crab with his now bare, toffee apple stick.

"I don't think he likes that very much." Startled by the deep voice, Luke looked up into the face of an elderly man towering over him. The man carried a sack on his shoulder. He wore a ragged jumper and grime-shiny trousers tucked into sea-boots that were turned down to half their length. His sun-bleached white hair, long beard and laughing blue eyes, instantly reminded Luke of a picture in one of Dorothy's books. She told him it was Santa Clause. "How would you like it, if someone kept poking you with a stick?" the man said, frowning at the infant.

"I not was hurt him." said Luke, defensively.

"Well thinks I, hurt him you was." The man said grinning at his own attempt to speak Luke's language. The old man glanced about him "Where's your mother and who left you here on your own?" The man's question never registered, Luke was looking at his sack, thinking it might be full of toys, "Come on I think we'd better find her." The man took Luke's hand and started to pull him away from the waters edge. The man's grip was quite painful and Luke's regard for what he first thought was a kindly old man, suddenly changed and his sack became a more sinister accessory.

Cathleen pulled up in Lyons Terrace and before she or Nell could get out of the car Emily Rogers was tapping on the window.

"You've had a visitor Nell, guess who? Do you remember little Billy Gough? He and his little friends have gone down to the mud flats."

"Stay with Jan, and phone the police, Cathy. I'm going down there on foot."

Dorothy and Barry were excited and delighted with the way the day had gone. Barry loved the sound that came from the bucket with each coin that was tossed in it, not the hollow clank that it made with Billy's first shilling. Now it made a merry chink as it became heavier.

To Dorothy and Barry, time had lost all significance, until Billy suddenly said,

"OK kids, let's go!"

"What for?" protested Dorothy, who was now fully into the swing of things.

"Look at your feet," Billy said. Dorothy looked down to see the hollows where she stood were filling with water. "Now look behind you." Dorothy was horrified to see that not only was the tide coming in, but because they were standing on a mud bank the water had moved in behind them, threatening to cut them off from the shore.

"Oh God! Quick Barry. We've got to hurry," she said, grabbing Barry's arm.

"It's okay," Billy said, tugging at the handle of the bucket. "We can still get back, but we wouldn't if we had left it much longer." The bucket had sunk deeply in the mud due to its weight. "Just help me pull this bloody bucket out."

The three started to trudge their way back to the shore. The going was much harder. Water had started to soften the mud again, causing their feet to sink even deeper into it. The tide was leaving peaks and troughs in the surface of the mud and as the incoming tide filled the troughs the children tried following the peaks where the sun had partly dried the mud. This meant leaping from one mud peak to the next. Billy led the way while Dorothy and Barry followed carrying the bucket between them The three meandered their way across the little islets of mud, sometimes having to backtrack because a trough was too deep or too wide to cross. They had almost completed the watery maze and were almost to the shore when Billy stopped.

"Where's Luke?" he shouted. They scanned the shoreline, but Luke was nowhere to be seen. Only the pile of clothes he had been detailed to watch lay where Luke had been sitting when Dorothy last checked on him.

Dorothy ignored the tide and ran splashing straight for the shore leaving the others to follow. She ran up the beach, oblivious to the pain as sharp stones and seashells cut into her feet. She peered over the low sea wall; her view of the road was at knee height. She scanned the pavements either side of the road peering between pedestrians' legs as they passed. Luke was nowhere in sight. Unaware of the comical sight that her mud-caked face made, she looked desperately up into the faces of passers-by, mentally pleading with them to tell her that Luke was safe and that one of them had just seen him.

She ran back toward the shoreline looking even more comical as her tears created white tracks down her mud-covered face. She saw that Billy had reached the shore and was making his way up the beach, Billy reached the wall, his eyes scanning the road beyond it.

"Who are you looking for, son." Billy looked at the old man who sat close by, filling his pipe.

"I'm looking for a little boy in a white hat."

"Funny you should say that. I was pondering that myself, he was here a little while ago. I thought he was lost. I was going to take him to the police but he pulled away from me and ran back down to the shore. That was about ten minutes ago, I thought his mother must have come for him."

Barry had stopped by the waters edge and was looking back across the mudflats, his gaze seemed fixed in the direction of a small dinghy tied to its mooring some distance out. Dorothy ran towards him.

"Barry, is it Luke, can you see him?"

"I don't know, but I think I heard something. It came from that little boat out there."

Dorothy cupped her hands to shield her eyes from the, now, low-lying sun. The little dinghy was still resting on its side but the incoming tide was just deep enough to give it movement. As the two children stared at it, the little rowboat seemed to move more erratically than was normal, considering the gentler movement of the waves. Dorothy started to panic. She imagined Luke being on the far side of the little boat, holding desperately to its mooring rope while slowly sinking into the mud. She ran splashing into the water toward the little boat until the water became too deep. She then started to wade out in its direction shouting Luke's name.

"Don't Dorothy, don't go back, it's too late." Dorothy ignored Barry's warnings. With her arms held out wide like a tightrope walker, she tried to keep her balance. The black ooze beneath the water seemed to wrestle against her every step, sucking at her legs as if pleading with her to stay put, but the thought of Luke being out there forced her onward.

Billy, at that moment, knew nothing of Dorothy's actions. He had climbed up onto the sea wall to scan the crowd, thinking that someone must have taken Luke. He started to ask passers by if they'd seen a little boy in a sun hat. Then he heard Dorothy calling for Luke. He turned and was horrified to see Dorothy heading out again toward the small boat. The water was up to her waist, and Billy knew she was in an area of dangerously deep mud. Her arms were flailing about but she did not appear to be moving. Billy jumped off the wall and ran back down the beach.

"Dorothy, don't struggle!" he shouted. "You'll sink deeper." Pedestrians heard the shouting and started to congregate at the sea wall. People up on the causeway who had stopped to watch a Naval frigate cross the harbour entrance, now turned their attention to the commotion in the harbour below them. From their high vantage point, they could see what could not be seen from the shore and some were pointing towards the dinghy. Dorothy started to cry for help. A young sailor heard her and jumped the sea wall. He started to run down the beach and in his desperation to reach her, his running changed to hopping while pulling his shoes off.

"Don't struggle love, I'm coming to get you," he shouted.

People were leaning over the causeway railings now, shouting encouragement to the sailor.

Both Billy and Barry were crying as they watched helpless.

"Please save them mister!" Billy shouted as the sailor dashed past him. "The mud's really deep out there."

"Get up to the road quick," the sailor yelled back at him. "Ask someone to call the Fire Brigade. Hurry!"

Billy ran back toward the sea wall and started pleading with the crowd to call the Fire Brigade. Meanwhile, Barry watched horrified, as the drama unfolded out in the harbour.

The water was now past Dorothy's waist, but she stayed motionless, as the sailor had instructed. She stared at the dinghy as it now floated upright. She called Luke's name repeatedly, convinced that he was on the far side of it. Slowly, the little dinghy floated in a circular motion. The sailor was now only yards from Dorothy, but his legs were becoming heavier with each forward stride as the mud sucked at his feet. He heard Dorothy let out a stifled cry as she saw Luke come into view. He clung with one hand to the side of the boat, while desperately trying to reach up with the other. Fear on the infant's face told Dorothy he could not hold on much longer.

"Don't let go Luke!" Dorothy shouted at him. "A man's coming to get you, please don't let go." The water was now up to her shoulders and the sailor was just feet away from Dorothy when the wake from the frigate reached them. The motion of the waves was just too much for the strength left in Luke's tiny fingers and Dorothy screamed as she watched him slip beneath the water.

Thirty minutes later, hundreds of people lined the beach and the railings of the causeway. They were eager for news that the rescue attempt had been successful and that they had at least saved one of the children. They had watched while with the aid of two longboats, men hoisted both Dorothy and Luke from the water. They now waited patiently while the ambulance team did their job.

A lone sailor sat on the shore, hands covering his face as he tried to hide his tears. A policeman crouched beside him,

"Don't take it so hard, son, you did your best, and you did it without a thought for your own safety." The young sailor sniffed back his tears, saying,

"But I was almost there! If only she hadn't made a grab for that stupid hat? Why did she do it, she could see I was almost there. I could have got her into the boat, I could have at least saved her." The policeman looked thoughtful for a moment, then put a hand on the young sailor's shoulder, and pointed toward Billy and Barry who'd been watching and praying as the ambulance team had tried in vain to resuscitate the two siblings.

"You see those two little boys over there?" The sailor looked up. "Well, I've been talking to them. They told me that the little girl you tried to save, never went anywhere without her little brother. Seems to me she was like a mother to him. They also told me she was frightened of her father, and that they've seen him beat her. So, it makes you wonder if she really wanted to be saved. We can only imagine what her life would have been worth, had you saved her. I'd like to think, maybe she and her little brother are still together."

The faint sound of crying guided Nell Masters through the crowd. At the water's edge she found a police constable standing with two little boys Billy had his arm around a little blond boy. Their mud coated faces kept moistened by their tears. They were unaware of Nell's presence as they watched the back doors of the ambulance close on the bodies of their two friends. Nell put her hand on Billy's shoulder,

"Billy!" He turned and as he recognised her, he clasped his arms around her, and cried bitterly until he was able to speak.

"It was all my fault, Aunt Nell, Dorothy only did it for me. They would still be here if it wasn't for me."

"Don't blame yourself, Billy. It's not your fault," said Nell cradling both him and Barry to her as a stiffening wind chilled her own tears. "But remember, nothing else can hurt them now." The constable, having questioned Billy, gave Nell an account of what happened.

"It seems that these two and the little girl were out there mud larking. They tried to get her little brother to stay on the shore, but I'm guessing he tried to reach his sister. With the tide coming in, he may have been forced in the wrong direction and ended up in the deep mud."

"But surely," said Nell, "with all these people about, someone must have seen him!"

"That's what I thought, but once he got among the moored up boats I suppose he was out of sight."

Billy and Barry sat alone on a wooden bench seat. They were in a cold bare room of a police station, still filthy with mud. Their crying had subsided to an occasional bout of sobbing.

"What will they do to us Billy?"

"They won't do anything to you; it wasn't your idea to go down there. Nell said the police will take you home, and she said I would feel better after someone has been to see me, but I won't. I'll never feel better. Nothing will bring Dorothy and Luke back and I don't think anything can make up for that. I hope Nell comes back though, She's been gone a long time, where do you suppose that policeman took her?"

Five minutes later, the door opened. Billy instantly recognised Jan who was followed by Nell and Cathy. Billy ran to Jan, burying his face against her, and again, could not hold back the tears.

"It was all my fault Jan," he sobbed "They're gone because of me. All because I lost the money you sent. I had to make enough for the train fare, so they came to help me. God will really punish me now, Jan." Jan cradled Billy's head but looked to Nell, afraid she'd not find the right words to comfort her brother. Nell sat down next to Barry and pulled Billy to her.

"Listen Billy, God don't punish little boys just for wanting to be with their family. Maybe God decided to take Dorothy and Luke for a reason. Like I told you, no one can hurt them any more. They will never be hungry or frightened again. God works in mysterious ways Billy, and I'm guessing that the only people that God will punish are those who mistreated them."

Nell's words took Billy's mind back to the little railway bridge the first day that he met Dorothy and Luke. He remembered the resounding slap that Dorothy received for accidentally tearing her dress, the vicious way Luke was kicked to the floor. Nell's words suddenly made sense, and Billy hugged her and kissed her cheek. Cathy then crouched in front of Billy and took his hands in hers and said,

"Billy, do you remember your Dad?"

"Course I do. He's dead."

"No Billy, he isn't. He's here in Portsmouth. He's come back to get you and Jan."

"That's a lie, God will punish you." The room went silent, Jan had to cover her mouth to stop herself giggling. Nell and Cathy then saw the funny side of Billy's comment as the door opened and Billy looked up to see Henry standing in the doorway.

28
Tears of a sweeter taste

A week later when Barry knocked on Mrs Cole's door, she told him Billy was gone, and that he didn't live there any more. Barry thought he'd seen the last of Billy and for a while he became unhappy and depressed. Then a few days later as he sat on the kerbside outside his house, a chauffeur driven Rolls Royce pulled up outside Mrs Cole's house. The chauffeur got out and opened the rear door. To Barry's surprise Billy emerged from the car looking smart as a new pin and disappeared into Mrs Cole's house.

Barry sauntered up to the car where he stood staring at the chauffeur. Ten minutes later Billy came out.

"Hi ya Barry, how do you like my Grandmother's car? And this is Gordon. Don't you think he's bloody smart?" Gordon nodded solemnly to Barry. "Gran said he could bring me to say goodbye to you and Tom. We're going to live in a castle! What do you think about that then?"

"Wow."

"I haven't got much to give you as a going away present but I have got something. This is from the three of us," said Billy thrusting a brown paper bag into Barry's hand. Then he hugged him tight, kissed his cheek, and in seconds was back in the car and gone.

Barry sat back down on the kerb. He tried to fathom Billy's last words as he put his hand in the bag and pulled out Billy's train spotting book, a folded piece of paper and a bag, full of coins. He unfolded the note and read:

Dear Barry. Not all the money is here. Bought Tom some fags. Love Dorothy Luke and Billy.

Barry unwrapped the bundle to find a white five-pound note and some coins. It was only when he saw the coins were covered in dry mud that he realised that it wasn't a bag but something he would treasure for a very long time; Luke's white sun hat,

29
New lives

Cathleen hugged and kissed Nell while trying to control her own tears.

"Hey come on now," said Nell. "This should be the happiest day of your life. You've got the man of your dreams and a ready made family."

"Yes but you won't be there mum."

"I know but it's not the end of the world, only the end of the country. We'll still see each other. Besides I've got someone else to look after now and he'll keep me warm at night," Nell said grinning.

"Oh, I hope everything works out for you mum."

"Why shouldn't it?"

"Well, you said Alfie is letting his wife and daughter keep their house, so I was wondering how he will feel about living in Lyons Terrace."

"Hopefully, he won't have to. Not for long anyway. We've seen a place that's up for sale and we've discussed it and decided that if I sell a few properties and Alfie sells his business, we'll be able to afford it."

"A few properties! My god, how big is this place?"

"You should know. Don't you remember? It's called Clearview."

Eight years later

"Come along son. End of the line," Barry suddenly awoke to find the conductor pulling at his shoulder.

"Where are we?"

"Harbour Station son. The train don't go any farther unless we want to end up in the drink," he said, smiling. "Did you miss your stop?"

"Yes I fell asleep. I wanted to get off at Fratton."

"Never mind, you can catch a bus outside the Dockyard gates, it'll take you to Fratton Road."

"Okay, thanks." Barry reached up and dragged his case from the luggage rack.

"Here for the Pompey match are you, son?"

"No. I've been away for six weeks in Roehampton Hospital. Its where they teach you to use artificial limbs."

"I know all about Roehampton," said the conductor. He bent down and rapped the side of his leg, which produced a hollow sound. "I'd only been in France a week when some blighter shot this off. But I know you're not old enough to have lost your arm like that. What are you, sixteen?"

"Fifteen. No, I was born like it. I've just been to Roehampton for training. This is the new one they gave me."

"Of course, the glove gives it away."

"Yes but its better than a safety pin holding up your sleeve."

"Your right, well best of luck son. You'll do okay."

Barry left the station and the smell of the sea immediately stirred memories. He was halfway across the causeway when, like a voice from the past, he heard,

"Oi, mate, chuck us a coin!" Barry looked over the railings to see a young boy standing up to his thighs in mud. Barry dropped his case and searched his pockets. He brought out a two-shilling piece and a half crown. Knowing his bus fare was only a few pence he dropped the smallest coin back in his pocket and leaned over the rails again. Three or four others were now looking over the railing.

"Are you ready?" he shouted to the boy.

"Yeah, ready."

Barry flicked the coin and watched the boy make a perfect dive, retrieving it almost before it could sink. Holding the half crown aloft the boy shouted,

"Cor! Thanks mate." Others started to throw coins, and as Barry watched the boy's antics, his thoughts were suddenly of the little railway bridge in Walmer Road. He could almost smell the sooty steam billowing through the gaps in the wooden floor, and little Luke running excitedly through it, grabbing handfuls of the disappearing mist. Through the white swirling cloud, he saw Dorothy's thin arms and legs as she perched with her toes through the grating. As the steam faded, so did the vision of Luke and Dorothy, leaving the very last vision he remembered on the bridge before it was demolished: Jack Vine's old bicycle. A fortnight after the death of Dorothy and Luke, Jack Vine left the house one morning and never came home. Barry discovered the bike. He'd gone up on the bridge to use Billy's train-spotting book. Immediately, he ran back and told Dorothy's brother, Spencer.

It's believed that Jack Vine caught the early morning express, or to be more precise, it caught him. His body was never found, although many years later; a human skull was found wedged in the steel girders under Fratton Bridge, but its identity was never discovered.

Barry picked up his case, took one last look over the railings and called out,

"Got to go now kid, keep an eye on the tide."

"I will mate. Thanks."